Praise for Lexi Blake and Masters and Mercenaries...

"I can always trust Lexi Blake's Dominants to leave me breathless...and in love. If you want sensual, exciting BDSM wrapped in an awesome love story, then look for a Lexi Blake book."

~Cherise Sinclair USA Today Bestselling author

"Lexi Blake's MASTERS AND MERCENARIES series is beautifully written and deliciously hot. She's got a real way with both action and sex. I also love the way Blake writes her gorgeous Dom heroes--they make me want to do bad, bad things. Her heroines are intelligent and gutsy ladies whose taste for submission definitely does not make them dish rags. Can't wait for the next book!"

~Angela Knight, New York Times Bestselling author

"A Dom is Forever is action packed, both in the bedroom and out. Expect agents, spies, guns, killing and lots of kink as Liam goes after the mysterious Mr. Black and finds his past and his future... The action and espionage keep this story moving along quickly while the sex and kink provides a totally different type of interest. Everything is very well balanced and flows together wonderfully."

~A Night Owl "Top Pick", Terri, Night Owl Erotica

"A Dom Is Forever is everything that is good in erotic romance. The story was fast-paced and suspenseful, the characters were flawed but made me root for them every step of the way, and the hotness factor was off the charts mostly due to a bad boy Dom with a penchant for dirty talk."

~Rho, The Romance Reviews

"A good read that kept me on my toes, guessing until the big reveal, and thinking survival skills should be a must for all men."

~Chris, Night Owl Reviews

No Time to Lie

Other Books by Lexi Blake

ROMANTIC SUSPENSE

Masters and Mercenaries
The Dom Who Loved Me
The Men With The Golden Cuffs
A Dom is Forever
On Her Master's Secret Service
Sanctum: A Masters and Mercenaries Novella
Love and Let Die
Unconditional: A Masters and Mercenaries Novella
Dungeon Royale
Dungeon Games: A Masters and Mercenaries Novella
A View to a Thrill
Cherished: A Masters and Mercenaries Novella
You Only Love Twice
Luscious: Masters and Mercenaries~Topped
Adored: A Masters and Mercenaries Novella
Master No
Just One Taste: Masters and Mercenaries~Topped 2
From Sanctum with Love
Devoted: A Masters and Mercenaries Novella
Dominance Never Dies
Submission is Not Enough
Master Bits and Mercenary Bites~The Secret Recipes of Topped
Perfectly Paired: Masters and Mercenaries~Topped 3
For His Eyes Only
Arranged: A Masters and Mercenaries Novella
Love Another Day
At Your Service: Masters and Mercenaries~Topped 4
Master Bits and Mercenary Bites~Girls Night
Nobody Does It Better
Close Cover
Protected: A Masters and Mercenaries Novella
Enchanted: A Masters and Mercenaries Novella
Charmed: A Masters and Mercenaries Novella
Taggart Family Values
Treasured: A Masters and Mercenaries Novella
Delighted: A Masters and Mercenaries Novella

The Perfect Gentlemen (by Shayla Black and Lexi Blake)
Scandal Never Sleeps
Seduction in Session
Big Easy Temptation
Smoke and Sin
At the Pleasure of the President

URBAN FANTASY

Thieves
Steal the Light
Steal the Day
Steal the Moon
Steal the Sun
Steal the Night
Ripper
Addict
Sleeper
Outcast
Stealing Summer
The Rebel Queen
The Rebel Guardian, Coming October 11, 2022

LEXI BLAKE WRITING AS SOPHIE OAK

Texas Sirens
Small Town Siren
Siren in the City
Siren Enslaved
Siren Beloved
Siren in Waiting
Siren in Bloom
Siren Unleashed
Siren Reborn

Nights in Bliss, Colorado
Three to Ride
Two to Love
One to Keep
Lost in Bliss

Found in Bliss
Pure Bliss
Chasing Bliss
Once Upon a Time in Bliss
Back in Bliss
Sirens in Bliss
Happily Ever After in Bliss
Far from Bliss
Unexpected Bliss, Coming 2022

A Faery Story
Bound
Beast
Beauty

Standalone
Away From Me
Snowed In

No Time to Lie

Masters and Mercenaries: Reloaded, Book 4

Lexi Blake

No Time to Lie
Masters and Mercenaries: Reloaded, Book 4
Lexi Blake

Published by DLZ Entertainment LLC
Copyright 2022 DLZ Entertainment LLC
Edited by Chloe Vale
ISBN: 978-1-942297-72-7

This is a work of fiction. Names, places, characters and incidents are the product of the author's imagination and are fictitious. Any resemblance to actual persons, living or dead, events or establishments is solely coincidental.

Sign up for Lexi Blake's newsletter
and be entered to win a $25 gift certificate
to the bookseller of your choice.

Join us for news, fun, and exclusive content
including free Thieves short stories.

There's a new contest every month!

Go to www.LexiBlake.net to subscribe.

Acknowledgments

I had to write this book shortly after I was diagnosed with breast cancer. To say throwing myself into this book during such a chaotic time was hard would be an understatement. Anyone who gets a cancer diagnosis understands the anxiety and horror of facing one's own mortality in a visceral way. No Time to Lie was written between getting the original diagnosis and my surgery, so there is likely a lot I worked through in this book. Sometimes I don't see it until much later. Or perhaps this was merely a place I ran to in order to escape my problems. Either way, what I've learned is that sometimes plans change and we have to adapt. And sometimes we need to take a problem and look at it from all sides to see if there is something good we can find in what seems like endless darkness. As I write this, I'm in radiation therapy. I started exactly four years to the day I lost my mother to cancer. At first that sent me into a depression, but weeks later I think maybe it was the universe telling me she's here with me, leading me through this.

This book is dedicated to the doctors and nurses who saw me through. From my gynecologist who cried on the phone with me when she gave me the diagnosis. To everyone who works at Solis Mammography who guided me through each test. To my nurse navigator who basically held my hand and talked me through every process. To my kind-hearted surgeon and her NP. To my plastic surgeon who is absolutely a genius and will end up in a book one day. To my radiation oncologist who took the time to really see me.

By the time this book is published, I'll be through radiation and then we hope I move into survivorship, but whatever happens, I'll be glad that they were with me.

To everyone out there still fighting – I am with you.

Part One

Romania

Eighteen Months Before

Chapter One

Snow beat against the windshield of the sedan, the stark white nearly blinding him.

Drake Radcliffe felt the burning pain in his side and prayed he could make it to the safe house. When he'd taken the hit, it hadn't felt too bad. He'd had far worse, but now it ached like a mother, and he was pretty sure he'd reopened the damn wound when he'd swerved on the highway. Was that blood he felt? There was a lot of it. He had to force his hands to stay steady on the wheel, his eyes on the…was it a road?

The events of the day slammed into him once again, and he could see his operative lying on the cobblestone street, blood just starting to stain the stones. Whoever had been behind that bullet had used a suppressor because Drake had barely heard the sound before he saw the hole in his operative's chest open up and then felt the pain in his own side.

Where the hell was the cabin? It was a cabin, right? He was on the side of a fucking mountain, so he was pretty sure there was a cabin and not an apartment building.

Guilt swamped him. He should have known something was wrong, that they'd been found out. His operative…what was his name…he didn't like to use names because it was easier to move around chess pieces than people. That was what he did. He played chess with people's lives, and he'd lost a pawn and he couldn't even remember the pawn's name because he was a piece of shit.

Come with me, brother. Think about what we could do with that kind of power. We could take over the group and then we would rule the world. Just like we always knew we would.

That had been a joke between him and his sister. They were smart. They were kind of assholes who joked about being smarter than everyone else around them and so the world should simply do what they said.

Except one of them had been serious…

Where was the cabin? He was so fucking tired. He'd driven for hours and hours. Almost eight hours with a hole in his side he'd basically stuck a bandage on. He needed stitches and antibiotics, but there was no way he was going to a hospital at this point. The safe house couldn't be too far away. He thought he might remember some of the markers but everything was fucking trees, and the road that was barely more than a trail was covered in snow.

How much blood had he lost? His head felt fuzzy, and now he was worried he'd made the wrong choice and should have tried to find a hospital.

But the nature of his business was…delicate, to say the least. If anyone found out he was in a hospital and vulnerable…

He had the drive his operative had delivered, and if it fell into the wrong hands then all his work would have been for nothing. His death would mean nothing. He had to get to the safe house and call in. There was a safe there.

A safe in the safe house. Safety. Safe. Safe. Safe. Safe.

Such a funny word when he thought about it. Was anyone safe? He said it out loud. It sounded weird to him.

Safe.

His dad had stepped down from his dangerous job, and he was supposed to be safe. Safe from lies. But Julia built her whole world on lies. Julia didn't believe in safety, and it had cost their family everything.

The world was starting to blur and his brain was as soft as the snow and he wasn't home. Snow didn't look like this in Virginia. Snow was a soft thing there, something they complained about and watched through windows and encouraged on Christmas. He would sit and watch the snow with his mom and his…

The very thought of his sister forced his mind back to his task.

Julia was dead and he'd had a hand in it, and if his mother ever found out he wouldn't have a mother anymore, and the snow kept falling. The wipers couldn't keep up. The hits just kept coming.

Julia was dead, and Kyle had left and he wasn't coming back. He was with his uncle now, and the whole found family thing was bullshit. Kyle had been his friend, one of the only friends he'd ever truly gotten close to, but Kyle had to kill Julia because she'd…

His cell phone rang through the connection on the sedan, the sound waking him up again. He glanced at the screen. Safety. Command.

The car he was driving was Agency approved. It had all kinds of security gadgets on it a person couldn't buy at a big box store. But he still had to be careful.

"This is Gray." He went by Gray for now. He'd gone by all the names. Black. White. Green. Brown.

Not Magenta. That had been Taggart, and he was an asshole. It was funny that all these years later he still remembered that meeting with Taggart in Paris when his daughters had watched through the railing of the banister and he'd wondered what it would be like to be Taggart—a man who'd gotten out and had a life and family and kids.

He'd thought he was moving toward that. Not in a traditional way. But he'd been building his little spy family with his sister and Kyle Hawthorne and he was going to be the weird uncle, and then Julia had turned out to be everything he hated. Everything he'd ever feared he could be himself.

He could still remember everything she'd said to him that terrible day.

This is who you are, little brother. Don't look at me like I'm a monster. You're nothing but a reflection of me. You're fooling yourself if you think anything else.

His dad pretended like he'd never worked for the Agency at all. Since he'd retired, he wouldn't even talk about work with Drake. How was his sister dead and now it was him and a father who barely acknowledged him and his mom and he could lose her, too, if she ever found out? He would be alone.

Of course the way he felt right now he might be dead soon, so maybe he should worry about that.

Was his family cursed?

"Gray? Gray, are you there?"

Did the guy on the other end of the line even know his real name? Or was he this guy's pawn? That was how the Agency worked. Lives were interchangeable. There was always some new idiot willing to risk his or her life for their country. For America.

That was a funny word, too.

"Gray?"

Reality was starting to become fuzzy, and he had to hold on. His operative was dead, and the mission was his now. The mission was all that mattered. The mission was everything. "I'm here. Is this line secure?"

"As secure as a pig in mud."

For a moment his brain didn't connect the odd reply. Codes. Little things that let an agent know it was okay to talk. He'd asked if the line was secure. It was Thursday. Pigs were Thursday this week.

Such a low-tech protocol for a high-tech job.

He had the intel in his pocket. All that information on a tiny drive. He would call in and someone would show up, and if he didn't die in the meantime, the op would be successful.

That was all that mattered. The op.

How much blood had he lost? "I have the data. I'm on my way to 124."

"124?" the voice over the line asked. "Why are you in Romania? Drake, there was a safe house in Kraków. Why wouldn't you go there?"

The sound of his name woke him up a bit. He slowed down, the twin beams of the headlights illuminating the powder white snow in front of him. He was fairly certain he didn't want to look off to the right because it was dark and likely a long way down.

"They knew about it." It was one of the last things that fucker who'd shot him had said right before Drake had taken him out. He'd rolled to the side of the alley behind a trash bin and the Russian agent had told Drake there was nowhere to run. There wasn't a hospital they wouldn't be looking for him at, and they knew about the townhouse in Ludwinów.

So he'd killed the man, gotten into the sedan, and headed for the safe house known as 124. It was a level three safe house, meaning it was only known to high-level operatives and only used in emergencies. No one would know about the small cabin just across the border in the Romanian Carpathian Mountains. It had an old hard line that connected to the US Embassy in Bucharest. He could download the intel safely once he was there and then...

Well, then he might die because that wound he'd taken seemed to have opened up. He'd thought it was a glancing blow, but he was weakening now.

"According to the map, I'm almost to 124." He hoped. The roads were winding, and he wasn't exactly in a proper car for this kind of driving. It was supposed to be early spring, but this freak blizzard had popped up and he could drive right off the edge of a mountain. "I have the intel. I will download asap."

"I'll alert our agent in the embassy. But you...not...she's..."

Static broke up the call. He made another turn and noticed that it wasn't so dark now. The pitch black of night was giving way to a deep, velvety blue. Almost sunrise. "Say again."

Up ahead he could see the start of warm lights glowing in the distance. The cabin. The porch light was on. So close.

"124...careful..."

He was losing the signal, and the wound in his side was aching again.

"Important asset..."

"What about the asset?" Drake looked down to see where the phone had gone.

That was the moment the road seemed to slide out from under him and he spun, the world tilting, and he heard someone scream.

Then the world seemed white and so cold. So fucking cold.

His gut churned and there was a pain that seemed to take over his entire body.

Was this death? It felt empty because there wasn't some wonderful flash of his life, not even a bunch of regrets of the roads he hadn't taken. There was only failure because he wouldn't complete his mission.

Shouldn't there have been something more?

The light faded and questions no longer mattered as the cold took him under.

* * * *

Taylor Cline woke to the sound of a crash. It hadn't been loud, but it was so quiet on the mountain that sometimes she could hear the crunch of animals walking in the snow at night. She sat straight up in bed, reaching for her Glock with the ease of long practice. She'd been sleeping with a gun close since she was seven when her father had decided to come back into her life and the world had changed. She'd missed her mom—missed her so deeply in those first days, but her big bear of a father had stormed in and made sure she wasn't alone.

Unfortunately, he'd brought all of his problems with him. Hence the gun.

She took a deep breath and assessed the situation.

The green light on the wall told her the cabin hadn't been breached. The security system was functioning.

Everything was quiet again but something was wrong. She could feel it deep down. That sound hadn't been a bear or deer. And it had stopped.

Was her father back? Had he been followed? Was he outside?

She slipped into a pair of sweatpants and tugged on a sweater before moving through the cabin to the small room that held all the tech, including the monitor for the twenty security cameras placed around the property and the paths that led here.

When the CIA built a safe house, they kept tabs on the sucker.

She began with the cameras that were closest to the cabin and worked her way out. Dawn was beginning to break, and there was a small rat-like creature on the front porch. Likely trying to hide from the feral cat who hung around because she kept feeding the sad-looking thing.

It was almost sunrise, that weird time between utter darkness and the sky becoming a flaming variety of sherbet colors. Dawn here reminded her of the ice creams her dad used to buy her. No matter where they went her dad would find someplace that served lime and strawberry and pineapple frozen treats. Ice cream. Gelato. Frozen ice. She liked it all, and those colors reminded her of her dad.

Who wasn't on the monitors. She touched the keyboard to move to the perimeter cameras. Every now and then she would catch sight of a brown bear or one of the lynxes that prowled across these mountains, and she would stop and stare because they were so rare now. But today there was nothing.

The phone rang. Not her cell. That didn't work so high up on the mountain. She had to go down at least a hundred and fifty meters to get a signal. The phone that rang was an old-school rotary from at least 1955.

Sometimes the best security was low tech. She picked up the earpiece. "This is Delta."

It was her designation with the Agency. Her father was known as Alpha. They'd tried to stick her with Beta, but she'd refused.

"Delta, we have a situation that might need taking care of," the deep voice on the other end of the line said.

"I'm standing by." It looked like this cushy assignment was about to turn interesting.

"We're not sure what happened but one of our higher-level agents was supposed to pick up valuable intel from an asset last night in Kraków. Something went wrong and he's coming to 124," the agent explained. "I was talking to him a few moments ago when the call dropped. Has he shown up?"

If he was coming from Kraków, he'd driven a long way. It must have been important for him to get out of Poland. She flipped through the screens and then stopped, her breath catching.

Right outside the final curve, a BMW was smashed against a large tree. Smashed was hyperbole. It was more like slightly crushed, like the driver had been doing five miles an hour and taken his eyes off the road for a moment and lightly tapped the poor tree. "He's had an accident."

"Is he alive?"

"Unsure." Though if he was dead, it wouldn't be from that accident. She would bet the car was still running. She stood. She couldn't tell anything from here. She would need to go to the site. "Is there a possibility he was followed?"

"Satellite tracking shows you're alone. He wasn't followed. Damn. Is that a car? Why isn't he getting out? He should be fine," the man breathed, losing his smooth tones. "Delta, the intel he has is important but so is he. He's the son of a US senator who doesn't know her baby boy is a spy. If he dies…"

She sighed and grabbed her boots. "Yeah, don't let the rich kid die. Got it. I'll report back when I'm done." She hung up the line and shoved her feet into the boots. "Come to Romania, they said. It'll be quiet, and you can get work done while you wait for your dad to come in."

What the hell had that agent been doing trying to get up the mountain in a sedan?

She stomped out of the cabin. Had the guy fallen asleep? No one had mentioned prior injuries, and the Agency was pretty good about knowing what was going on with their field operatives. Especially the important ones. She'd learned that the CIA was like pretty much everywhere else. There were people who mattered and there were goats they led to slaughter without a second thought.

Why couldn't her dad have been like a history professor? Or a trash guy. Yeah. Sanitation services professionals did important work, and for the most part none of them had to run for their lives on a daily basis. If they were lucky, they got tips at Christmas time. No one ever gave a spy a tip. Not the monetary kind. Honestly, as careers went, spying was low on the pay to danger ratio.

She worked her way across the big yard, her boots crunching in the snow. No one should be driving up the mountain in the middle of a late-spring blizzard, much less in a luxury sedan more suited for the Autobahn than this treacherous part of the Carpathians. She had a Land Rover and she wouldn't drive in these conditions.

"Hello." She called out to him because if she could get him out of the vehicle on his own, that would be optimal.

Nothing but the sound of the wind. Snow swirled around her, and she picked up the pace. Just because base hadn't told her this dude was hurt didn't mean he wasn't. Some operatives liked to play down injuries. Once her dad had taken two bullets to his shoulder and told his handler he had a couple of scratches.

She jogged across the snow, her feet already threatening to go numb. The headlights from the car made twin beams in the predawn, lighting her way to the site. The snow reached her ankles, but she was able to jog. If he'd been here three weeks ago, she would have had to find snowshoes. Now she worried she wouldn't be able to carry him back to the house if he was unconscious.

She made it to the car, and the driver was slumped over the steering wheel. Taylor reached for the driver's side door and pulled the handle. Locked.

She had to wake him up or knock out one of the windows. If it was an Agency car, that would be hard to do. The windows would be reinforced against bullets, so her trying to kick it in wouldn't do a lot. She slapped a hand against the window. "Hey. Hey, buddy, I'm going to need you to wake up."

Please wake up. She didn't want this guy to die on her. She could see the shallow movement of his back, signaling he was still breathing.

If she wanted him to stay that way, she needed to get him inside.

She knocked again, shaking the car. "Hey! Wake up!"

His head shifted slightly, coming off the wheel and slowly moving up as though every centimeter caused him pain.

The good news was she had pain meds. There was a fully stocked, more than first aid kit back in the cabin for just such an occasion, but she had to get him there. "Hey, I'm Taylor. I'm going to help you today. I've been in touch with base. We need to get you to the cabin."

His whole body shuddered, and his head hit the wheel again.

She knocked, pulling on the door handle with her other hand. The motion seemed to rouse him before. "Hey, stay with me. I need you to open the door."

Nothing.

She kicked the door, making the whole car shake. Movement seemed to disturb him. He might have a concussion, and that meant keeping him awake. There was no blood on his skin, though he was pale as the snow that kept coming down around them.

His head tilted, moving around so she could see his eyes were open slightly. Storm gray eyes stared back at her, dark hair tumbling over his forehead. She would bet he slicked back that hair a lot of the time. "Hey."

Good. He could talk. "Hey. I need you to open the door so I can get you out of there."

"I had a car accident. It was bad. I'm not sure I can move."

She looked to the car. It was fairly pristine, with the singular exception of the tiny dent where he'd hit the tree. What else was going on? "I can help you. We need to get to the cabin. I can call for help from there."

He nodded and then his hand came out, and she heard the door lock pop.

Taylor breathed a sigh of relief. She opened the door, and that was when she realized he had a gun on her.

Damn it. She held her hands up. "Easy there. I'm Agency."

He groaned and sat up. Now she could see the blood on his shirt. It stained his left side. "I need to get to the hard line."

He was obviously serious about the mission. Now she wished she'd gotten his name from base. "Okay, it's inside, but you need some help."

Another deep groan and he was twisting his body to get out of the car. "Step back. If you're here for the package, you should know I already killed the other agent."

He was a wounded predator, and she had to treat him like it. Dangerous. Any wrong move could set him off. "I'm Agency. I'm stationed here at 124 for a week or so. I do analysis work and serve as backup for my father, Lev Sokolov."

Normally she wouldn't mention her dad at all, but he was a legend, and if invoking his name meant she didn't get shot, she would do it.

He stood. Damn he was tall. At least six four, with a lanky but strong frame. He towered over her five-foot-three-inch self.

"No one's supposed to be at 124. It's remote. The only reason we still have it is the hard line," he said, his voice deep and husky.

Someone a long time ago had taken the time to bury an actual line between 124 and Bucharest, 450 km away. It was considered the most secure way to get important information where it needed to go, but it was hard to keep up which was why there weren't hard lines across the globe. The Agency had put them in decades before when the world was initially being wired for the Internet. Those old cables had been replaced by satellites and wireless networks, but some of them remained. He'd come all that way injured to use that secure line, and that told her his op was a serious one.

Which made him even more dangerous.

"Yes, the hard line is why I'm here, too. I can't explain my mission. I don't know your clearance, but I assure you I'm not working for anyone but the Agency." She kept her tone as calm as possible. "You look like you took some fire. Can I help you with that? I'm a trained medic. Is it a gunshot wound?"

He looked down to his side as though he'd forgotten it was there and frowned. "I...I was in Kraków and I..." His head shook, and he refocused on her. "Give me the gun."

Oh, she wasn't giving up her gun. He was in trouble, and it was obvious he needed help. Like a lot of men, he didn't know how to ask for it, and also like his brethren, he'd been trained to avoid help if possible. "Your hands are shaking. What can I do to make you comfortable with me? Besides disarming, because I'm not sure you won't shoot me. You've been through something traumatic."

He huffed. "You think this is traumatic? You think I can't hand..." He tried to steady himself but he stumbled. "Back away or I'll shoot."

And she was done with him. He was off kilter and way past dangerous, and it was time to handle things.

She kicked out, easily sending his semiautomatic into the snow. He started to react, but she reached for his wrist, twisting it up and back, taking control. "Calm down. I told you I'm here to help you, but I can't let you shoot me. I've got a mission, too."

He struggled, trying to pull his arm away. If he was running at full capacity he probably would have given her hell, but he immediately went to his knees, obviously overwhelmed with the pain. Blood stained the snow around him.

She sighed and let go. "Can we please go inside and take a look at your side?"

He seemed to find some energy and brought his head back. If he'd had some speed he might have caught her on the chin and sent her to the ground.

But he didn't, so she simply brought her arm forward and knocked him back down.

Stubborn man.

With a low groan he managed to turn over, gray eyes staring up at her. "Are you really Agency?"

She sighed. "If I wasn't, wouldn't I have killed you by now?"

"You want the drive. I won't tell you where it is."

"The drive is hanging out of your pocket, buddy." She reached down and grabbed it, dangling it in front of him. "Now we have two choices. I can help you inside and patch you up and let you get this to base, or I can leave you here and I'll go and send this in. I'm going to warn you, if you choose the second path, there are a couple of bears out here and one lynx. If you want to go out being a meal for an endangered species, this is the way to do it."

He frowned and put a hand to his side. "Okay, now I believe you're Agency. Fucking sarcastic assholes every single one. Can I have the drive back?"

"If it will make you feel better." After all, she could always take it back when he died.

She put it in his outstretched hand. He caught her, holding her palm against his, the drive there between them. "This is important. Promise me if I don't make it, you'll get this to command."

He wasn't some pampered prick whose daddy had gotten him a cushy job. He was aching and still trying to fight to complete his mission. She dropped to one knee. "I promise. I'll do everything I can to save you and to get this where it needs to go. I'm with you… What's your name? Don't give me Black or White. We're about to get real cozy because even if you survive, that storm is going to keep us together for a while. Make up a name if you're still worried about me, but no Agency crap."

She wasn't sure if what he did next was about the fact that he was beyond weary or that he needed comfort. He pulled her hand down with his, laying it over his chest and letting her feel his heartbeat.

"It's Drake. I'm Drake. Like the duck."

It made her grin. "Well, Drake like the duck, I'm Taylor. I'm going to save you and your mission."

His lips curled up in the sweetest smile, and she could see how gorgeous this man was when he wasn't passing out from possible blood loss. "Taylor. My hero."

And then he passed out.

Fuck. Was he going to die on her? She didn't want him to die. She shoved the drive in her pocket and felt for a pulse. If she needed to, she would start CPR out here.

His pulse was strong.

His breathing was steady.

She pulled back the corner of his dress shirt, revealing the wound he'd taken. He'd been shot in the side and needed a stitch up, but it should have been easily handled in any ER or back at the Kraków safe house. Hell, he likely could have done it himself with a needle and thread.

"Stubborn boy." She sighed as she stood again. Beautiful boy. He was quite stunning, and she was going to have to find a way to get him all the way back to the cabin because he'd passed out from blood loss. Luckily there was a mini clinic inside, and she was well versed in stitching up stubborn men. After all, she'd learned at a young age.

"Stitch him up, wait out the storm, send him on his way." She said the words out loud so she could make it happen.

Because she was already attracted to him and he was half dead and had tried to halfheartedly kill her.

She was not going there. Nope. No way.

She hopped in the car, praying it still worked. It would be easier to drive him the last hundred yards than carry him, and infinitely better on him than dragging him through the snow.

The car was still purring, the expensive engine not at all damaged by its bump with the big beech tree. She put it in reverse and eased it back onto the actual road before parking it again and getting out to open up the back seat door.

Maybe he wasn't as pretty as she'd thought. Maybe it was a trick of the light. It was soft, but dawn was here with its yellows and pinks and purples and blues, and it would reveal him to be another normal, run-of-the-mill dude who would not be worth the effort.

Although she'd learned he could be hot as hell and not worth the effort while guys who weren't gorgeous could be worth everything.

She stared down at Drake like the duck and sure enough, he was still lovely. Lovely and so much trouble.

"All right, buddy. Let's hope you weigh less than you look." She grabbed his ankles and pulled.

Nope. He was all muscle, and it showed. Still, she wasn't exactly a lightweight herself. She got him in and started for the cabin.

Get him healed. Finish his mission and then ignore him for a couple of days and then he would be gone and she wouldn't see him again.

Easy peasy. Lemon squeezy.

She parked the car in front of the cabin and got to work.

Chapter Two

Don't be ridiculous. You can't think that the world really works that way. Drake, you've been around politics all your life. You can't be this naïve.

The words echoed through his brain, bouncing around and infecting his dreams.

He was dreaming, right? It was all a dream, and his sister hadn't pulled a fucking gun on him and he hadn't watched her die.

No. He didn't want to be there. He was in control. He was in charge. He wanted to be somewhere else.

The dream shifted from the delicate, warm Southeast Asian landscape to some place infinitely colder. Colder, but he was still out of control.

Damn, Taggart was right. It was better to be in control. He'd enjoyed playing games, had learned he could play a lot of games, but he was different now. Now he needed to be the top.

He wanted to top her. He could top her. He could tie her up and play with her, and maybe he would forget what had happened months before. Maybe he could forget that his family had fractured beyond repair and would never be the same again.

Maybe he could forget that he was alone.

But he couldn't top her because he was weak, and the world was spinning and then she was there.

There had been a beautiful woman and she'd challenged him, and then she'd put soft hands on him and he'd felt safe for a moment.

It was the safe part that let him know he was dreaming.

It was the flash of pain in his side that let him know it was time to wake up.

Long practice made him stay still. He didn't wake up like most people. He remained still, allowed his senses· to slowly bring him data.

He wasn't in his own bed, and he wasn't alone.

"I don't know," a soft voice was saying. "I didn't look at anything. I sent it to base and that's it."

The world went quiet again, the only sound her feet shuffling across the floor. Was she pacing?

"No, I'm not curious because in a few weeks I'm out," she said quietly. "They told me to take care of him so I am. I'm doing this job and then I'm done."

The night before flashed through him.

His asset was dead, killed by whoever didn't want the intel he'd brought to fall into Agency hands. He had proof that Russia was planning a coordinated attack on three separate Western embassies in Eastern Europe. Russia's intelligence agency had been hard at work trying to shake the walls of Western democracy, and this operation would leave the blame placed firmly on a group inside a country looking to join NATO.

He'd had to get that intel to the Agency, and the fact that he'd been shot couldn't stop him. He'd taken a bullet to the gut. Oh, at first he'd been sure it was nothing more than a flesh wound, but the hours he'd spent on the road to Romania had proven he'd been wrong. No flesh wound could hurt as much as that fucker. He'd been woozy at the end.

The car accident flashed through him. A blinding white and then the world had upended and he'd felt the crash of the car. How had he survived?

"How about you worry about you and I'll handle DC boy."

There was a pause and then a sigh. "He fought hard. I don't think he's your typical trust fund kid. But he's heavy as hell, and my back hurts from getting him inside."

Was he a prisoner? He couldn't remember anything after the horrific car accident.

Wait. He could see a flash of blonde hair and hands reaching for him.

Where was he? He'd been heading to a safe house. How had she found him? He'd been so sure he wasn't being followed.

The sound of her voice wasn't close, and it was moving. She was in another room, likely pacing as she spoke. Cautiously, he opened his eyes. He was staring at a ceiling, big logs crossing smaller ones. Cabin.

Deep breath. Move slowly. He was in a bed, and daylight streamed through the place where the curtains didn't meet. He took stock of his body. The pain was there, but it was manageable.

He needed to ease out of bed and find a weapon. He wasn't about to underestimate his opponent. The fact that she was a woman meant nothing. Some of the deadliest people he knew were women.

He shoved thoughts of his sister out of his head.

Kyle would never let him live it down if he got shot and taken out because he crashed a car. It wouldn't matter that the accident had been something most people wouldn't survive.

Not that Kyle would know. Kyle was happy. Kyle was surrounded by family members who would never choose their careers over him or evil, for that matter. Julia had chosen literal evil over him.

Was he using the word *literal* right? His mom complained about the overuse of that word by his generation.

What the hell was he doing?

"Be safe. *Ya tebya lyublyu.*"

Russian. She was speaking Russian. *I love you.* She'd told someone she loved them in Russian, and her accent had been perfect. He could often tell a native speaker from the accent.

He was in serious trouble. His heart rate ticked up, adrenaline starting to flow through his veins.

He heard the slight clatter of the phone being hung up. Was she using a landline?

Maybe he should question what century he'd landed in.

He slipped out of the bed. He still had pants on, but his shirt was gone and so were his shoes. There was gauze wrapped around his waist holding a big bandage to his side. Whoever had taken him obviously wanted him alive. Where was the drive? Had it been lost in the crash? Surely a crash that bad had caused enough damage that the drive might have been ruined.

Drake stood, the pain still there but a minor thing in the face of what he needed to do. The door to the small, utilitarian room was slightly open. He needed to get the upper hand and quickly. She could be walking in here any moment. He arranged the pillows under the thick blanket he'd slept beneath. It wouldn't fool her for long, but he only needed a moment.

A creak let him know she was coming his way. He moved to the door, stepping to the side where she would have trouble seeing him until she turned.

He didn't intend to let her turn.

This was going to hurt.

The door came open and she walked in, gingerly moving toward the bed as though trying not to disturb him. He had a glimpse of blonde hair in a ponytail and a feminine figure in a sweater and leggings. She was roughly a foot shorter than he was, but that didn't mean a damn thing if she was well trained.

She stopped, and that was the moment he pounced.

Drake moved in, wrapping an arm around her neck and the other around her waist, dragging her back and close so she wouldn't have room to fight. "Hold still or I'll might hurt you, and I don't want to do that."

Her whole chest moved with the force of her sigh. "I'm not going to move because if I do, I'll reopen that wound I spent so much time fixing. I'm fairly certain it wasn't all bullet. Did you tear it at some point?"

She was calm. He would give her that. "I had a fight with one of your agents before I managed to kill him. He got a couple of good hits in."

"One of my agents?"

"Na kovo vy rabotayete?" His Russian was excellent. As was his Mandarin and Cantonese. His father had started to teach him when he was barely old enough to speak English.

Don't ever let anyone know how fluent you are in Russian. They'll forgive you the Chinese, but question the Russian. It could hurt your mother's career, but it will help yours. You'll see one day. I know I push you, son, but one day you'll appreciate it.

"You heard me speaking Russian and now you're convinced I'm a Russian agent. It might be a good time to point out you seem to speak it well." She was completely relaxed. "Drake, I'm with the Agency. My name is Taylor Cline. I'm here at 124 waiting on my father. You would know him as Alpha."

Lev Sokolov.

He was a legend. He'd left his job as a Russian operative nearly twenty years before and had become one of the Agency's most dangerous operatives. He was a deep-cover guy and out in the field most of the time.

He was also one of the operatives every other intelligence agency in the world would like to kill.

"I serve as my dad's handler. He's the only operative I work with, and for obvious reasons I do it from remote locations like this one," she explained in a steady tone. "You're at a safe house in Romania. I received a call at five forty-two this morning that you had an accident roughly one kilometer away. I found you in your vehicle and got you back here. After I stitched you up and gave you pain meds, I called back to base and updated them. I then took the drive and uploaded it. You're free to use the landline to call base and verify everything I've told you."

As stories went, it was a pretty good one.

Lev Sokolov had a daughter. He'd met her years and years ago. Back when his father still worked for the Agency, when he'd been training his children to do the same, though they hadn't understood it at the time.

"If you're Taylor, tell me what we talked about that day."

Now she stiffened, her body going on alert. "That day?"

He had an excellent way to test her. "If you're Lev Sokolov's daughter, then we've met. I was fourteen and my mother was on a tour of the embassy in Warsaw. She was meeting with the leaders of Eastern European states to bolster democracy. My father was meeting with yours because he had valuable intel."

"Ujazdów Park. They left us on the playground and told us not to leave," she said in hushed tones. "We talked about anime. You tried to convince me that *Fullmetal Alchemist* is the greatest anime of all time, but I was all about *Sailor Moon*."

He breathed a deep sigh of relief and stepped back, releasing her. She couldn't possibly know that unless she'd been there. Even his father didn't know what he'd talked to the younger girl about in that park in Poland. "I'm sorry. I heard you speaking Russian, and the last asshole who tried to murder me spoke Russian, too."

She turned and damn, but she'd grown up well. Warm brown eyes and honey-colored hair, with full lips that turned up in a wry half smile. Yes, there was the woman from his dreams. "I didn't remember your name."

He shrugged. "I didn't remember yours, but I remember your dad. Big, scary guy."

"He's not scary." She shrugged. "I mean not to me he isn't. Of course I've seen him in a tiara, so my point of view might be skewed. How are you feeling?"

Weird now that he knew she wasn't some foreign operative who'd kidnapped him. He knew her. Had known her. She represented one of the best afternoons of his life. One of the last times he'd felt kind of free. "Uhm, a little foggy."

"That's the pain meds," she replied. "I'm sorry. I know that was a sucky thing to do to a fellow agent, but you were already out of it. You wouldn't stay still for me to fix the damage, and I was worried about blood loss. You have some color back now. I think you're going to be okay, which is a good thing because getting you to a hospital wasn't in the cards. We're snowed in. It was a freak storm. It's not usually this bad this time of year, but the weather is ever changing on us now."

He didn't want to think about that problem. He had plenty of his own. "You found the drive?"

She nodded. "Yes. You were insistent that the data get downloaded as soon as possible. Even after I got you inside, you insisted I download it before I fixed you up. You were bleeding pretty freely by then. I think the seatbelt cut into you when you hit the tree."

He was surprised he hadn't broken his nose when the airbags deployed. His chest didn't feel as sore as it should, but that could be the meds. "How did you get me to swallow meds?"

She stared at him for a moment, that look in another person's eyes that told a man he should know that answer.

"Please tell me you didn't use a tranq gun. Is that why my butt hurts?"

Those glorious lips curled up. "You were hyper focused on completing the op, and it didn't matter that you were bleeding all over the place. When you got your second wind, you were very strong."

Vague memories of the night before came back. The accident, and then he'd been cold, trying to walk up the steps. She'd been there, lending him her strength.

And then yelling at him. A lot.

"Sorry about that. I'm surprised I survived that car accident." He was definitely surprised he hadn't broken a bone or five. "I seem to have come out of it all right."

"Yeah, you really…" She bit her bottom lip, humor in her eyes. "I was going to say dodged a bullet, but you definitely didn't do that. As for the accident, well, it wasn't as bad as it seemed. Are you hungry at all? Eating could help clear the drugs from your system. I made sure we're well stocked. I could make us some lunch while you call in."

It was good that she was encouraging him. If she'd expected him to believe her, had acted hurt he might not, he would be on edge. She was doing and saying all the right things.

But he would still make that call.

"Thank you. I would enjoy that, and I would like to make the call if you'll show me to the comms room." Every safe house had one, and knowing he had access would make him trust her more.

"Of course." She led him out of the room. "We're pretty tight in here. There are only two bedrooms, and we share a bathroom. The kitchen's up front along with a nice-sized great room, but no

37

satellite hookup in there. Believe it or not there's an old-school DVD player connected to the TV. That's all we have. Hope you like romcoms and eighties action movies. And here is the door to the pantry." She opened it and allowed him in. "The landline is here, but the truly secure line is in the basement. Feel under the middle shelf and you'll find the switch that pulls it back. The stairs lead you to the comms room and all the toys."

Toys. He could use some toys on her.

Damn it. He wasn't thinking that way. He wasn't some asshole who saw a woman and immediately started thinking about getting her in bed. He wasn't a player, but she was…

Off limits. A coworker. Someone he probably wouldn't work with again but might.

A paid killer's daughter. That's what her dad was. Sure he killed people to protect the good old US of A, but Drake bet Sokolov could make a side project of him if he wanted to.

"I'll be here when you're done." She slipped out of the pantry and away.

He watched her go. He'd been through too fucking much in the last twenty-four hours to possibly have his mind on sex. Yet here he was. He was held together with baling wire and duct tape, and he was wondering if she had a boyfriend.

He was a creeping creeper, and he should do his job.

He made his way down the stairs to the comms room, which looked pretty much like the comms room in every safe house he'd ever been in. He quickly found the computer, and Taylor had laid the drive next to where she would have uploaded the data. The drive had been crushed in the same fashion he would have used had he been the one to upload it. He would have waited to ensure it uploaded properly and then he would have destroyed the drive.

All in all, she definitely knew Agency protocol.

He sat down and quickly dialed into the network, the signal pinging around the globe until it made its way to one specific number back in Virginia.

He glanced at the clock and estimated the time difference. It should be early morning on the East Coast, but someone would answer. Drake dialed the number and someone immediately answered.

"Drake?"

It was kind of nice that someone was worried enough about him to come in early. "Hey, Brad."

Brad Perry had been with the Agency for a few years longer than Drake had, but they were both considered wunderkind. Brad had been in his early twenties when he'd joined the Agency, while Drake's father had brought him in in his teens. They'd worked several ops in which youth was a necessary part of the cover.

He'd been called *21 Jump Street* more than once.

A long sigh came over the line. "Man, I'm glad to hear your voice. What the hell happened? You should know the entire team stayed until dawn trying to figure out if you were alive or dead. Thank god Delta was at the safe house or we'd still be in the dark. After what happened with…well, we weren't sure how to handle it."

With his sister. Julia's death had created a mess for the Agency on several levels. Drake had been the one to sit down and craft a fiction about his sister's disappearance that didn't tell his mom she'd A) been working for the Agency, and B) died a traitor to everything they'd been raised to believe in.

"I'm fine. I'll write up a report. Did Delta send the intel?" He used her call sign. She probably shouldn't have given her real name, but they knew each other. Still, he wasn't going to let Brad know that Taylor was the girl in the park he'd talked about a couple of times.

He certainly wasn't going to let him know that she'd turned into a gorgeous woman who'd apparently managed to drag him out of a wrecked car, give him medical care, and complete his op for him.

Her competency was every bit as sexy as those pouty lips of hers.

"Yes, the data was received and counterintelligence is already working on it." A pause came over the line. "I'm sorry about Borys. He did some good work for us."

Borys. Damn, that was his name. Borys had fed them excellent intel over the years he'd been embedded in Eastern Europe. "Yeah. We need to figure out who killed him. I'm sending you a couple of pictures of the guy. He had a thick accent. Russian, I think. If you could get me an ID, I would appreciate it. Whoever he was working for knew about the meet, and I was pretty sure only Borys and I knew the exact spot. I'd like to know if we have a leak somewhere."

"You know that could be anything. It doesn't have to be a leak. Borys could have said something to the wrong person. He could have been identified as a probable asset and followed." Brad offered a number of reasonable explanations.

Drake wasn't sure. "Or my sister could still be causing trouble even after she's dead. I wasn't careful enough around her. She could have given valuable information on assets to any number of foreign agencies."

"That's not what she was doing," Brad pointed out. "She was working for a cabal, and all that group cares about is money and power. If anything, they would want the world stable. Most of these corporations moved out of Russia. They don't have interests there."

But there was still money to be made. "I want to know if there's any connection at all. If Julia was recruited by The Consortium, then it's a good bet she's not the only one. We need to figure out who else is a double."

"Okay. I'll get on it. Hey, I'm going to bring Lydia on the line. She's got a few things she needs you to know."

Lydia was the tech he worked with when he needed support. She was often the voice in his ear.

"Hey, Drake. Are you okay? I followed your car on the satellite, but they wouldn't let me talk to you," Lydia said, her worry obvious in the tremulous sound of her voice. "You should have gone to a hospital."

"I had to get the data to a secure line," he countered. "And I'm fine, thanks to Delta. It was a lucky thing she was here."

A suspicious pause came over the line.

"Lydia?" When he was in the field, she often had access to information he didn't. "Is there something I should know?"

She was silent for a moment.

"I've heard some rumors about Delta, and more importantly, about Alpha." Her voice had gone low.

Brad sighed over the line. "She's not wrong. There are some worries about people Alpha's been meeting with."

Lev Sokolov had been with the Agency for years and proven himself time and time again.

But then so had Julia.

"What kind of people? You know he meets with people from his old SVR unit from time to time to get intel we need." Lev often handled the bribery elements of getting intel from his former home. Corruption in government meant opportunity for spies.

"He's evaded his handler a couple of times now. It's why they put his daughter in charge, but we know she lied about his whereabouts on two occasions. Be careful around her," Lydia said. "I'm looking at weather reports for 124 and it looks like you're going to be stuck there for at least a week."

He glanced back, but the door was firmly closed. "She sent the intel on the hardline. Do we know if she used any other comms device in the last twelve hours?"

"She used the landline to talk to her father, but there was nothing suspicious about the conversation. That was the only other time she called out," Brad said.

"But she did leave the cabin. There's no cameras inside, but we keep CCTV cams outside," Lydia explained. "She was out of range of the cameras for twenty minutes earlier today. There's no cellular on that mountain, but…"

A smart spy could work around that.

"You might want to keep an eye on her." Brad sounded resigned. "I'm sure they'll ask you to get her talking once they realize you're stuck with her. I'll let them know you're already on the job."

"You said it's going to take a week to get out of here?" He had some time before his mother would start looking for him. She was busy looking for Julia. Looking for a daughter who was never coming home because the man who'd loved her had been forced to kill her.

"At the very least a couple of days," Lydia promised. "I'll keep up with the weather and send you an evac if we need to. And Brad's right. I've been told by the big boss he wouldn't mind you spending time with Delta and giving him your thoughts when you get back."

He wasn't a fool. He knew exactly what that meant. They

41

wanted him to get close to her, see if she gave anything up. If her father was turning on them, it was a big fucking deal. Lev Sokolov knew where a lot of bodies were buried, and it wasn't like he hadn't turned on his country before.

"All right. I'll report back. If my mother…"

"I'll let her know you're out of pocket and you'll call her as soon as you can," Lydia assured him. Lydia often played the role of his assistant when it came to his mother. The same way his father's support staff had done when he'd worked for his import/export facilitation business. It was a good cover because he traveled so much and because almost no one understood what it meant.

"Thanks."

"All right," Brad said. "Stay warm, and I'll start working on things from this end."

Brad's line went quiet, but Lydia's was still open.

"Be careful around her." Lydia's voice went quiet again. "If her dad shows up, be very careful. If he wants to turn, bringing in someone like you would potentially get him anything he could want."

Because he had the highest level of classification. Because his mother was a United States senator.

"Will do." He hung up and checked the door again. Still safe and secure.

But he wasn't anymore.

He couldn't view Taylor as a sweet memory of his childhood because she might be the enemy.

* * * *

Taylor still couldn't believe Drake Radcliffe was the skinny kid she'd met that day in the park. She looked across the table, trying to find some connection between the kid who'd argued anime with her and the gorgeous, deeply serious man in front of her. "Is it okay?"

He'd come out of the comms room and gone to clean himself up. He'd showered and found a set of sweats that mostly fit him. When she'd told him lunch was ready, he'd joined her, but there was a grimness about him that made her worry something had gone wrong with the call.

He looked up from the pasta she'd made. "It's good. I appreciate it very much. I worried I would be on MREs."

"Oh, I made sure to stock up before I came." There were plenty of bland, ready-to-eat meals, but she preferred to cook.

"How long have you been here?" Drake asked.

"A couple of days." She wasn't going to talk about her father's mission. If Drake knew, he knew. If he didn't, then he wasn't supposed to know. She hadn't gone through the data he'd wanted uploaded. She'd simply done it for him and destroyed the drive when base had asked her to. She was a soldier, and she knew how to follow orders.

Well, most of the time.

"Are you meeting your father here?" Drake asked.

"No. I'm meeting him in Bucharest." She could be honest about her travel plans. If he was worried her dad might show up in the middle of the night and mistake him for a punching bag, she could put those fears to rest. "The good news is there's enough room for us to not bump into each other too much while you're stuck here. There's a desk in my bedroom. I can work in there or here in the kitchen and you can take the comms room."

She worried his grimness was a reaction to getting stuck here with some woman he didn't know. As a class of male, the Agency operative didn't tend to rank high on the small-talk scale.

"Why would you do that?" Drake asked.

"So we both have some privacy. I understand that you didn't expect anyone to be here," she replied. "I didn't either. I have some research I need to do and some reports to analyze. I'm going to respect your space, and I hope you can respect mine."

"I have clearance on anything you're working on." There was the arrogance she'd expected from him. "I know I'm young, but I'm a senior operative and I work at the highest levels. You don't have to hide from me. If there's research you need to do, I can help. If you're worried about my access to sensitive materials, we can walk downstairs and get the director on the line."

"You just plop that big dick right on the table, don't you?" She wasn't going to play around with him. If he wanted to be an asshole, she could give it out, too. "I was trying to tell you I would respect your privacy, trying to make you comfortable. If you don't want to be comfortable, we can make it as awkward as you like."

He frowned. "I wasn't trying to... I guess I went there. Huh. I'm sorry. I was being a dick. Your work is your work. I thought you were trying to tell me you didn't want to have anything to do with me. Which you should be able to do without some man pushing back. I'm the intruder here. Can I hide behind the whole got shot and then nearly died in a horrible accident?"

"Horrible accident?"

"The car wreck. Do we need to do something about the car, by the way?" It was likely sitting in the road. "We'll have to clear it at some point. No one else will be able to get to the cabin unless there's another road that comes up the other side of the mountain."

"No." He was under some mistaken impressions. "The car is in the garage, along with my Land Rover. When the snow breaks, I think you should still let me drive you down. That sedan is not going to do well on the roads when they're muddy."

He stared at her for a moment as though trying to figure out if she was joking. "How did you get it in the garage? I thought you were alone here."

"I drove it into the garage." She took a sip of her water. She'd briefly been excited at the prospect of having someone to talk to, especially someone she remembered with fondness. Her childhood hadn't been filled with great memories, but that day in the park with him was one that stood out. She should have realized the boy was gone and the man was an operative. They didn't make the best of friends.

And she wasn't looking for anything more. No matter how hot he was.

The chair he was sitting in dragged across the wooden floor as he pushed himself back and set his napkin down. He stood and walked to the front door without a word. She heard it open and close.

So he was going to be fun to hang around with. Luckily, she had wine and did not mind watching old DVDs. She had a date with *Legally Blonde* and Pinot Noir tonight, and Mr. Fussy could do whatever he wanted as long as he left her alone.

I thought you were trying to tell me you didn't want to have anything to do with me.

She could understand the sting of rejection, but he'd basically told her he was the boss of her, and she wasn't about to let him walk all over her.

And now you've let him know he won't take over your research, so what's the harm? How long has it been? He's hot. You're horny. You're literally snowed in. It's practically a romance novel.

And the romance novel part was the trouble. Even her horny hormonal inner voice still thought in terms of romance. If she could have sex with a guy and not get involved, it would be one thing. But she knew herself well enough. If she wound up in bed with a guy she would develop feelings—one way or another.

She was sure a therapist would tell her it was left over from a chaotic childhood. She kept trying to make connections, to set down roots when it wasn't smart to.

So Pinot and Elle Woods it was.

The door came open again and Drake moved back inside, his whole body shaking because he'd walked into the snow without a coat.

He pointed toward the garage. "I had a terrible car accident. I remember it. I was going to die and probably go over the side of the mountain."

He was awfully cute when he was indignant. "You hit a tree. Well, I mean I think you rolled into a tree. The tree is fine, if you were wondering."

He stood there for a moment, shivers going through his body, and she wondered which way he was going to go. Would he be utterly insufferable or go the quiet, forget about it route?

He suddenly doubled over, and a deep laugh boomed through the cabin. He straightened and the smile on his face damn near lit up the room.

Oh, that boy's smile did something to her.

"I...I was so sure..." He could barely talk through his laughter. It was that amusement that came from the gut and couldn't be denied. "There's a tiny dent. I thought..." Tears leaked out of his eyes. "In my head it was this big 'Jesus take the wheel' moment."

She couldn't help but smile back. "Well, maybe he did and that's why you only tapped that tree. I mean when you think about it, you could have gone off the side of the mountain."

"It's so…ridiculous." He doubled over again and then winced as he straightened up, putting a hand to his side.

She pushed her chair back crossing to him. "Hey, you'd been shot and drove eight hours to finish your mission. You were in shock."

He let her help him back to the chair. "I remember my life flashed before me and I was sure I was about to die, and I was sure the car was spinning out."

There wasn't room on that road to spin out, but she was sure it had felt that way. It had been his head that had done the spinning. He'd been at the end of his physical limits, and he'd still almost made it. She could respect that. "How about when they ask I say it was a miracle you survived?"

He took a deep breath, his lips tugging up as he relaxed back. "I think that was you, not a miracle."

She snorted. It wasn't a pretty sound, but it came out of her way more often than she would like. She moved back to her chair. "I think you would have found your way."

His head shook. "I was out. I would have frozen to death."

He seemed to enjoy the drama of the situation. "I doubt that. I think if I hadn't been here, base would have figured out what had happened and sent someone to save you. I was under strict orders to not let you die."

He sobered. "Ah, they called you."

In this she had some good news for him. "Oh, I heard the crash. It's just things are so quiet here that any noise can wake you up. You'll find that out. It's eerily quiet. But seriously, what you did was brave and heroic. The fact that you managed to not tear up that car is icing on the cake."

His eyes lit with amusement. "Wait. There's cake? No one told me there would be cake. I would have gotten here way sooner if I'd known there was cake."

He was way easier to ignore when he wasn't being charming.

And she'd found him pretty hard to ignore then. "There is absolutely no cake. But I do have the ingredients to make one. What can I say? I have a sweet tooth."

"And I am excellent at doing dishes," he replied with a wry smile.

"Really?"

He shrugged. "I've seen them done before. I think I can manage." He was quiet for a moment. "It's good to see you again, Sailor Moon. I'm sorry I was an asshole. That afternoon meant a lot to me, and I'm not good at being myself. I would like very much to be myself around you."

"Do you know who yourself is? I sometimes wonder." This was why they'd fit together so beautifully that day. They understood each other's lives. "Sometimes I think I've spent so much time hiding who I am that I don't know me."

"Well, that got serious fast. I was just asking for some cake, but if you want to do a deep dive, I'm ready." He was staring at her with the sexiest smirk on his face that made her think that deep dive he was talking about wouldn't be into her psyche.

She sighed and rolled her eyes to cover for the fact that she found him ridiculously adorable.

She wasn't going there. No way. No how. He would be gone in a couple of days and then she could go on with her life. "You're going to be obnoxious, aren't you?"

"That's what I'm saying, Taylor. I'm going to be the best roommate ever. I'm putting away my worries and I'm going to relax for once. And all that work you talked about me doing... Yeah, I'm injured and taking some time to recover," he vowed. "Did I thank you for stitching me together again?"

"No, actually you pretty much cursed me until I knocked you out."

"Thank you." He got back to his lunch. "And this is delicious. You saved me and fed me and didn't even make fun of me for thinking I wrecked the car. I'm going to have to find a way to pay you back."

She could think of a few ways.

But she wasn't going to. Horny Taylor was going to get shoved down deep. Horny Taylor wasn't going to boink the Agency's golden boy and get herself in trouble.

She had a job to do and didn't need distractions.

But a distraction could be fun. And it's not like you're going to see him again. He works in an entirely different world than you. Besides, you're getting out soon. A couple of nights with a spy would be a good way to go out, sister.

Nope. She was going to college after this job was done. Her father promised her some normalcy when he finished this one last job.

She got the feeling sex with Drake Radcliffe wouldn't be normal.

"I think doing the dishes will suffice. And I get to pick the movies." She was having her romcom night.

It would remind her that spies didn't do happily ever afters.

"Done," he promised.

Just a couple more days and she would be free.

Chapter Three

Four days later and the snow was still coming down. "How is this happening? It's April."

Drake looked up from the book he was reading. "In the Carpathian Mountains. I would bet it's not sticking down in the valley. Give it another day or two and it'll all melt. Are you getting cabin fever? You want to take a hike?"

She was getting fever, but not the cabin kind. Four days in and she should find him obnoxious. She should be bored with him.

He was kind of awesome.

"No." She sank down on the couch across from him. "I just thought…"

A brow rose over his eyes. "You just thought? What? I would be gone by now?"

Yes. And to say it would be rude. "I thought I would be able to go into town by now."

"Liar," he said quietly, but there was a hint of a smile on his face. He set the book down and leaned her way. "Taylor, what's wrong?"

What was wrong was that he was nearly perfect. After the rough start, he'd proven to be a pleasant companion. He let her work when she needed to work and relaxed with her when she wanted to relax. He complimented her cooking and did the dishes. If he got up first, there was a pot of coffee waiting for her even though he didn't drink coffee.

She'd relented a bit after talking to base and confirming Drake's status. He was going over some of the communications she was monitoring concerning Russian separatists in old Eastern bloc countries. The Kremlin was always trying to foment trouble in that part of the world, and the mafia had made a massive resurgence lately. Her father believed the mafia was beginning to work with a group of corporations, taking a cut of profits for doing the dirty work they needed done while the CEOs kept their hands clean.

Drake had been interested in her father's project.

She had to make sure no one found out about her father's other project. They were due in Havana in three weeks, and she would have to find a plausible reason to be in the Caribbean.

Of course it had to stop snowing or she might be stuck here with Drake forever.

Would that be so bad?

"Maybe I do have cabin fever." She stood. "I'll go and chop some wood. That'll clear my head."

He reached out, catching her wrist and gently drawing her toward him. "It's almost dark and there's a brown bear in the area. We have plenty of firewood. Come on. Tell me what's going on in that head of yours. Did you find something today?"

She found herself falling deeper and deeper into this guy's web, and that was a terrible idea that seemed less terrible every day she spent with him.

Once her father was done with his business in Havana, he wouldn't need her to cover for him and she could go to a crappy community college because her high school diploma was a GED. But from there she could get the grades she needed for a four-year school. She would be the oldest freshman there, but she didn't care.

"No, but I'm sure I'll find the connection," she insisted.

"Did you hear from your dad today?" He didn't let go of her hand, and she didn't pull it away. "I'm sorry. I should call him your operative. Is it weird?"

She gave up and sat down beside him, breaking their contact. If he kept touching her, she might end up on his lap. "So weird. But you know how it is. You worked with your dad."

"I was trained by my dad. I never actually worked with him. He retired before I went active, which was good because I probably would have murdered him." He sobered and then stood, crossing to the small bar and grabbing the good whiskey. It was Irish and deliciously loamy He popped it open, the cork sounding through the room. "Of course I didn't know he was retiring. I thought he would be there for me, but he kind of walked away and didn't look back."

It was there on the tip of her tongue to talk to him about her dad. About how close she'd come to losing him.

But she could still lose him, and he could lose everything if she talked.

"It was a real punch in the gut. It was like my dad had done his job in preparing me and then I was totally on my own. You know he kept the secret from my mom," Drake said, pouring himself a healthy glass of the whiskey and looking her way.

She nodded. It was a whiskey kind of night.

Yes, and if you drink enough we might get over our puritanical senses and fall in bed with the hot guy.

Her inner voice was super horny tonight.

That was wrong. Horny she could deal with. Horny could be handled with a couple of fingers in the shower or the "massager" she carried in her suitcase. This was beyond horny because it was no longer about how hot he was. It was about how they connected. It was in the weird sense of peace she had when he was around.

Safe. He felt safe.

She could ignore dangerous attraction. Safety? Oh, that word had a pull she couldn't deny.

She had to remind herself that he was involved in a world she was leaving and soon. It would be a good time to tell him she was tired and to go to bed. They'd had dinner and it was time to separate.

"How did he keep it from your mom but not you? I got the feeling you knew back then." She couldn't do it. She couldn't walk away. She wanted to know his story.

"Oh, I knew. My dad told me when I was ten, and he started

training me then. My sister was twelve, and he told her too. I think he meant it to bond us."

"I didn't know you had a sister."

He stopped, staring at her like he was deciding how to proceed. "Her name was Julia. Technically she was my half sister. We share a mom, but her dad wasn't in her life, so she called my dad her dad. He was the one she knew."

"What does she do?"

He stiffened again, holding both glasses.

She knew when she'd tread too far. "You do not have to answer that."

He moved toward her, but his shoulders were still up. "I'm wondering if you know what happened and you're pretending you don't."

She could understand that. They worked in an industry of secrets and manipulations. "I didn't even know you were with the Agency until you showed up here. You didn't mention a sister when we met in Poland. I don't know. I keep my eyes on my father's missions. I'm not trying to move up, Drake. I'm planning on getting out, so you should assume that I know nothing."

"Getting out?"

"I want to go to college and have a life that has nothing to do with state's secrets. I kind of want to teach. I don't know. I want to explore my options, but I can't do that until I finish this op."

"I'm struggling to understand how you get out."

"What do you mean?"

"You know too much. How do they let you out?"

"I don't know too much. I know very little outside of my father's work. You know I wasn't always with him, right? I was born in America. My mom was a tourist my dad hooked up with. They weren't some great love story or anything. He knew I existed, but he didn't have anything to do with me until I was seven and my mom died. I didn't have any other family, and I went into the foster care system. Then one night my dad showed up and he took me away." She could still remember him standing in the doorway of her foster mom's ramshackle house. There had been three other kids there, and every day had felt like torment. He'd shown up, and she should have been terrified of the massive, scarred man, but he'd gotten to one knee and looked her in the eyes and explained that he was her father and he would take care of her now.

"That would have been around the time he defected, right?"

She shook her head. "He'd been in the States for a year at that point. I've been told he'd planned to contact my mom after he settled in. I didn't realize he'd sent her money the whole time."

"Did he defect for you?" Drake asked.

"My father rabidly hated the Kremlin. Not in the beginning, of course. He was a soldier who became one of SVR's top spies, but he saw the corruption and how it hurt people. He had a friend who was an analyst. He tried to call out some corrupt officials and they wiped out his family. That was when he left."

Drake nodded as though the story didn't surprise him at all. "Why didn't he contact you before?"

"He was settling in. You know they didn't trust him for the longest time. They kept eyes on him for years. Even after he came and got me, I remember handlers being around. Sometimes they babysat me while he was on an op."

"My father didn't do the same kinds of ops as yours," Drake replied. "He wasn't a James Bond type. He mostly traveled with my mother and met with people the Agency wanted information from. These were all people who worked for highly placed politicians. Mom would be working some diplomatic angle with the president of the country while my dad was getting dirt on the same politician from the man's assistant or his private chef. My mom worked in the State Department for many years before she ran for office."

"I know there are a lot of spies who work for embassies. That is definitely not what my dad does. The crazier, more death-defying the mission, the happier he is," she explained. It was nice to talk to someone who understood what it was like to be raised by a spy. "So your mom still doesn't know?"

He shook his head. "Nope. I don't know if she ever even suspected. My mother is focused on her job. I'm not saying she wasn't a good mom. She was, but she was very much a child of her upbringing. She had a nanny most of the time. She divorced her first husband because he cheated on her. I think one of the things she liked about my father was how willing he was to travel with her, to put her career first. She didn't question it. She reveled in it. She liked that he was willing to take me and my sister with him, and he was our primary caretaker. She liked that he took control of those parts of our family life so much that she didn't question it when he replaced the nanny she'd hired with an Agency employee who worked as his assistant for years."

They had such weird lives. "So you were ten when you found out. You said he started your training then? How do you train a ten-year-old?"

"I suppose the first training was simply in how to keep secrets. I started to learn how to unearth secrets a few years later when I was placed in an elite private boarding school," Drake began, easing back into his seat. "It was filled with the sons of politicians and CEOs and the wealthiest of the wealthy."

"Let me guess." There were a lot of elite schools, but one was particularly popular among the political set. "Creighton Academy."

He nodded and leaned back against the sofa. "That's the one. Anyway, I was in seventh grade when he asked me casually what was going on with some of my friends. I knew a lot of helpful information, including the fact that one of the sons of the leader of a country we were having some problems with talked about the fact that his mother and father fought constantly. However they couldn't divorce because it wasn't allowed in their country. The father was a serial cheater, and the mother didn't take kindly to it."

"So your father was able to turn her into an asset?" She knew the plays the Agency could make. They looked for a weakness, anything that might allow an operative in.

"Yes, and then he explained to me how I could help the country and that my older sister was already doing her part, and I had to keep it from my mother because she could lose her job if she knew the truth."

"That's a lot to put on a kid."

"You would know."

"Not in that way. My dad kept me out of things as much as he could," she explained. "I didn't start working with him until a couple of years ago, though I did learn a lot of first aid during those years. Did your sister go into the service?"

"My sister is classified," he said tightly before taking a long sip. "She passed away during an op I cannot talk about."

It was obvious she'd stepped on a land mine, and now she had to mitigate the damage. "So what do you want to watch tonight? Or shall we play a game? If you want to read, I've got some movies stored on my laptop. I know it's been a lot of togetherness."

"I like the togetherness, Taylor."

The room seemed to get a little hotter, a little cozier at the deep tones of his voice. "So that's yes to the movie?"

"It's yes to anything you want." He sat up, and his attention was suddenly completely focused on her. "I think I want to be honest and upfront with you. I'm attracted to you, and I think you feel the same."

She felt a jolt of heat power through her. "Even if I was, I don't think it's a good idea."

"Can I ask why?"

She didn't sense any threat from him. With any man who hit on her, she had to assess the potential of him taking rejection poorly. She didn't think Drake was one of those guys. The last couple of days had made her comfortable with him. "I don't think it's smart to get involved with someone I work with."

"You don't work with me. From what you've said, you won't be with the Agency for much longer."

"Yes, and you will be," she pointed out.

A thoughtful expression came over his face. "That's kind of what makes it workable in my mind. I can't tell anyone what I do. That makes for difficult relationships. You already know, and it won't surprise you that I don't talk about my work. You won't get upset if I have to be gone for a couple of weeks without notice. I have a hard time making connections to people, but it was easy with you. Even if you're not interested in me in a physical way, I hope we can be...friends." He said the word like it didn't quite make sense to him. Like it was a foreign word on his tongue.

How close had he been to his sister? How hard had it been to lose her?

She didn't know many people who had family working for the

Agency, but she knew they existed.

He'd been in service since he was a kid. How had he ever connected with anyone? He'd had to lie to his own mother, was still lying. He carried a lot around, and she felt deeply for him.

And there was no way for her to deny the electricity between them. She wasn't sure she even wanted to. That inner voice kept getting stronger.

What would be the harm in seeing if it could work? You might get an orgasm or two out of it. He's not saying he's going to walk at the end. He's actually saying he wants to see you outside this cabin. Why not try?

She was a careful woman. She'd learned that lesson from watching her father throw himself into deadly situations again and again.

But what was she risking? He was right. It was hard for her to connect. She'd had a couple of boyfriends over the years, and she had to hold back so much of herself to even have a chance at making the relationship work. She couldn't talk about what her father did, couldn't mention her own work. Wouldn't it be refreshing to have no secrets between them?

Well, maybe one, but hopefully that would be resolved soon.

"Did I make you uncomfortable?" Drake asked. "Because we can pretend like I didn't say anything. This snow is going to stop soon, and I should be out of here in a couple of days."

She reached for his hand. "You didn't make me uncomfortable. I'm glad you were honest with me. The last couple of days have been...nice."

A slow smile spread across his face, and he threaded his fingers through hers. "Nice? Awful sexual tension is nice to you?"

"I wouldn't say awful. Anticipation can be fun." It was good to know she hadn't been the only one who felt the heat between them. "Besides, we've run through most of the good movies. I think we're down to *Dude, Where's My Car*."

"Are you saying yes?" Drake asked.

Did she want to let him walk out of here and never know what it felt like to be in his arms? They'd been thrown together for a reason. It couldn't be some random thing that they'd met again. She would hate herself if she didn't give it a shot.

In a couple of months she would be out of this life and might be able to find some kind of normalcy. Maybe it was time to take a chance.

"Yes," she said.

"Then come here and let me kiss you and tell you how the night's going to go," he said in a commanding tone.

Her whole body responded. She moved, standing and twisting so she sat on his lap. "How is my night going to go, Drake?"

One big hand cupped the nape of her neck while his other arm wound around her waist. "Let's find out."

* * * *

This was a huge mistake, and he couldn't quite stop himself from making it.

Days of being close to her had made him soft. It didn't matter that he'd been warned to be careful around her. All that mattered was the fact that she was sitting on his lap, and nothing in his world had ever felt as right as being here with Taylor Cline. A couple of days with her had erased years of being taught how to be alone.

He didn't feel alone with her—even when she was quiet. Even when she was ignoring him because she was so involved in work she'd barely looked up from it all afternoon.

She was a distraction to a man who was considered so focused nothing fazed him.

She fazed him. She made his brain go fuzzy and his dick go hard.

And she'd told him yes.

He tightened his hold on her, drawing her in and bringing their lips together for the first time. Soft. She was so fucking soft, and his world had been hard lately. This was what he'd needed forever.

He'd needed her.

He brushed his lips over hers, ignoring the urge to brand her as quickly as possible. He might never have had a long-term relationship with a woman, but he knew how to do this, knew how to slow the world down and drown his partner in sensuality.

Her hands found his shoulders and she leaned in, opening her mouth slightly.

It was an invitation he wasn't about to refuse.

Somewhere deep down an alarm bell was going off, but he ignored it. It was so much nicer to focus on her.

She was perfect. She was getting out of the Agency, but she knew what his work meant. He wouldn't have to hide from her.

His body went hot as their tongues brushed together, and he took control of the kiss.

He let his fingers find her hair, sinking into the soft silk and gently tilting her so he had more access to her mouth. He stroked her tongue with his, felt her tightening around him.

She pulled back slightly, her breath ragged. "Drake, I should make myself clear. I don't want to just have sex. I like you. If you aren't interested in anything but sex, I'm going to ask you to tell me so I can take the night and decide what I'm willing to give."

He wanted everything she had to give. "I'm interested in pursuing this thing between us, Taylor. No matter where it leads. You live in DC, right?"

"I have an apartment there," she acknowledged. "I was planning on going to school there. Technically I've lived there for most of my life, but I barely know the city."

Because she'd traveled the world with her father. She wanted roots, wanted some normalcy. He wanted that, too. She could give him a place to be himself. She could be the one person in the world who knew both sides of him. "I know it well. When you get back, I'll take you on a proper date. One where you don't have to cook, and then we'll find a bar and drink and talk and stay so long they'll have to kick us out."

"It's a date," she said with a slow smile.

He had to be careful with her. He knew what it meant to feel vulnerable, and he didn't want to put her in that position. She should know he would take care of her. He took a deep breath and kissed her one more time, this one a soft touch of his lips to hers. "It's a date. And if you want to wait until then, I can do that. You're worth the wait. We can turn on those bad movies and simply enjoy each other's company."

"Or…" Her eyes had widened, and she made no attempt to move from his lap. "You could kiss me again and see where it goes."

"I know where it will go."

"Tell me."

"This ends with you in bed with me. If we make it to the bed. I need you to understand that." He let his hand move along her hip, tracing her curves. She was wearing pajama bottoms, a sweatshirt, and thick socks. The cold wasn't conducive to tank tops, but he'd gotten glimpses of how gorgeous she was. He wanted her naked, but he had to make a few things clear first. "Taylor, I'm going to be in control of this."

"In control?" Her lips quirked up. "Like tie me up in control."

"If that's what you like."

"I've never tried it. I would be open to experimenting. Despite all the glamor of traveling the world with my spy dad, you should understand that I have way more experience hacking the CCTV cameras in a public area than I do with sex," she admitted. "I've had a couple of boyfriends, but we move around a lot, and one-night stands never held much appeal."

He'd had his share of them, but he was far more interested in having an actual relationship than he cared to admit. She made him feel vulnerable. She scared the fuck out of him, but he couldn't quite make himself walk away. Not when he was so close. His hand slipped under the heavy sweatshirt, and he felt soft, warm skin. "A lot of my experience came from a woman who is still a friend of mine. I met her when I was in my early twenties and while I wasn't a virgin at the time, I also hadn't had real sex until I met her."

"Real sex?"

He shouldn't be talking about this. "I thought sex was quick and that women were like men and got off fast. No one had complained. She complained. A lot. And then offered to teach me. When I think about it, I had a sex tutor, and she was older than my mom and she was hot. She was also into BDSM."

Taylor gasped, but her eyes lit with mirth. "She wanted you to spank her?"

He liked how comfortable he was with her. Comfortable enough to really talk. "Not exactly."

"Drake," she began, that smile widening. "Did she spank you?"

It made it way easier for him to be open with her. "Yes. And she tied me up and basically taught me everything I know about pleasure. I loved her. I wasn't in love with her. I figured out the difference. We were friends and she helped me through some rough times. What I'm trying to explain is that I know who I am when it comes to sex now. I know I prefer to top a woman. I'd like the chance to top you, Taylor."

A single brow arched. "What would this entail? Because I was planning on falling in bed with you and then like walking away the next morning and going back to my harem of men."

There would be none of that, but he liked that she teased him. Too many people in his life put him in a box where he didn't have a single emotion, no needs past getting his job done.

He wanted more.

He stood, hoisting her up without a problem. He liked the weight of her in his arms, liked how her eyes widened and her arms tightened around him. "First it means that harem of men has to go. Any harem you happen to have. I know people who don't mind sharing their subs, but you'll find I'm a possessive top. And when we get back to the States, I'm going to properly court you."

"That sounds very old fashioned."

"What I'm about to do to you isn't. Or maybe it is. I've got an old mentor who claims people have always been perverts and we should accept it." He walked through the hallway to his bedroom where he'd spent every night since he'd gotten here thinking about her. "But I promise when we get back home, I'll show you around DC. We won't just be about sex. If you like, we can go to a club and explore the lifestyle further."

"For now, how about you kiss me again," she said, looking up at him.

That he could do. He set her on her feet inside his bedroom, and his mouth was on hers before she could speak again.

He couldn't wait to get her back to his place.

She didn't know it, but he already had plans. He would give her a couple of months, but if this worked out, he wanted her safely installed in his condo where she would be waiting for him. She could go to college, have her life, but at night she would be all his. He would keep her safe from his world. Safe and close.

She would be his reward for everything he'd had to get through, payment for a job well done.

He dragged the sweatshirt up and over her head. She wasn't wearing a bra, and yes, those breasts were every bit as perfect as he'd imagined them. Beautifully formed, with tight nipples that he would get in his mouth soon enough. He let his hand cup one while he kissed her again, his tongue greedy for the taste of her.

Her hands found the bottom of his shirt, and he allowed her to pull it off him. This wasn't going to be a long, slow D/s scene. They were both too hungry, but the way the snow was going, they would have plenty of time for that. This first time was about slaking a thirst.

Her hands roamed over his skin, and he looked down to find her staring at his chest. She traced some of his scars, but there was a fascination in her eyes that let him know she wasn't deterred by them. But then she'd been around scars all her life. She was in his world but not ruined by it like he feared he'd been.

He found himself reaching up, holding her hand to his chest as though he couldn't stand the thought of her not touching him.

And he couldn't. He could get seriously addicted to being with her.

He lowered his head again, brushing his lips over her and letting himself go for the first time in forever. If he'd met her anywhere else, he wouldn't have let her in. Being stuck here with her had forced him to watch her, to get to know her in a way he hadn't with any other woman in his life.

He palmed one breast and released her hand so he could draw her in closer. Her skin was soft as any silk, and he loved the way her nipple peaked against his hand. He kissed her while he played with that nipple, twisting lightly and making her squirm against his cock.

Her hand traced a path down his chest toward the waistband of his pants.

If she touched him, he might go off like a rocket, and he wasn't about to let that happen. He needed to take care of her first. He moved away, twisting her around so her backside was nestled against his cock. He let his fingers slip inside her pants, moving under her panties to ease toward her clitoris. "Move with me. Show me what you need."

Her arm came back around, hand cupping the nape of his neck as she pressed her hips up and his fingers slipped over her clitoris.

She gasped, and her head dropped back against his shoulder.

"Tell me how that feels." He wanted to hear her voice. She was already so wet. His fingers slipped easily between her labia and back to her clit.

"It feels so good." Her hips rolled again.

He brought his free hand up to cup her breast again as he allowed his mouth to play along her neck. He nipped at her ear and she whimpered, a sexy sound. "Was that too much?"

Her head shook. "I want more."

He was ready to give it to her.

Chapter Four

Taylor hadn't known she could get this hot for a man. Up until this moment sex had been pleasant, fun, even, but this was beyond anything she'd experienced before.

Her body felt like it was on fire in the absolute best way. Electric. That was how she felt. Like she was a live wire waiting to go off.

He surrounded her, his arms the sweetest of cages. He had the most beautiful chest. The scars she'd found there only enhanced how lovely he was, even the latest one that was still healing. Over the last couple of days she'd figured out he wasn't some desk jockey who made decisions without ever having been in the field. He was a serious operative, and he'd obviously risked his life more than once.

The fact that he was now focusing all that energy her way was not lost on her.

"I want you to come for me and then I'm going to make you come again," he said against her ear. "We're not playing tonight, but we will. Tonight is about pleasure. Tomorrow morning, we'll talk and see if we can come to terms."

"Terms?"

"About a relationship." That finger of his didn't let up. It stroked and swirled around her clitoris. It sank lightly into the folds of her pussy. "I'd like to talk about what I want out of it, and I want you to tell me what you want. How you want us to relate to each other."

"I was going to go with the flow."

"How has that worked out for you so far?" He whispered the question. "Because it hasn't worked for me, and I don't want this to fade away. I'd like to try with you. I'd like to go into this with a seriousness of purpose. If I was going with the flow, I would already have you on your back and I would be finished. My instinct tells me to take you as hard and fast as I can. I'm fighting that instinct because I want this to be good for you. Trust me. It's not my instinct to talk about relationships, but I've learned if I want a good one, I have to try."

Going with the flow hadn't worked for her. Not in sex and not in relationships. If he was willing to try, then so was she. She knew a bit about the lifestyle he was talking about. Who didn't know a bit? She wasn't afraid. If they could ease into it, it might be fun to focus on sex for once, to figure out what truly worked for her and what didn't.

If he was willing to be serious about a relationship, how serious would he be about pleasure?

"Yes."

He dragged his tongue over the shell of her ear before nipping it and sending a thrill of arousal zinging through her like lightning. "Yes to what?"

"Everything." She wasn't about to say no to the man who was playing her body like an instrument. And he was a maestro.

"Excellent, because I want everything from you. Starting now." He pressed gently against her clit and rotated again and again until she couldn't hold back. A rush of pleasure took her over, and she moaned and gasped in his arms. She could feel her pussy soaking her undies and his hand, but in that moment she couldn't make herself care.

Every muscle of her body suddenly felt loose and relaxed. She wasn't what she would call a relaxed person. She'd grown up knowing how hard the world could be, that every moment could potentially bring disaster. It made her calm in the face of danger, but not relaxed.

She was not the kind of woman who slumped in a guy's arms and expected him to keep her from falling, and yet that was exactly what Drake did. Instead of hitting the floor, she found herself wrapped up in his arms, and he turned toward the bed. It wasn't a big bed. They didn't do big beds in tiny European cabins, but she got the feeling it would be nice to cuddle with him.

After he had his turn.

He laid her down on the bed, but not the way she thought he would. Not with her head on the pillow, but rather across. He brought one foot up and dragged the sock off. She should be cold without her shirt, and likely would have been had her body not been hot with arousal. Even now that she was coming down from the first orgasm, she was already heating up again. It was bound to be disappointing since she'd never actually orgasmed from penetration, but she didn't care. He'd taken time to ensure she'd had some pleasure, and now she would wrap herself around him while he had his.

He ran his teeth over the arch of her foot, and a shudder went through her. He lightly dragged the edge over her delicate skin and up her calf. The sensation was stimulating in a jangly, worrying way. Would he bite down or simply make her skin tingle?

If it had been anyone else, she would have moved away, but she was fascinated with him, with the way he was both predatory and tender at the same time. He moved to her other foot, giving it the same attention, pushing up the leg of her pajama bottoms when he kissed and nibbled on her calf, making her skin sing with sensation. "I told you I would make a meal out of you."

She shook her head. "No, you didn't. There was talk about contracts and ending up in bed, but no meals."

The sexiest smirk hit his lips, and he gripped her pajama bottoms and dragged them off her with a single sweep of his hands. "Then let me warn you. I'm hungry, Taylor, and you smell fucking delicious. Look at that. That's all for me."

He was staring at her underwear. Her soaking wet underwear. He'd pulled her down the bed along with her pants, and now he stood between her legs, his eyes on her pussy, which he could plainly see because she was wearing white cotton undies and they'd soaked through. A wet T-shirt on her privates.

A flash of embarrassment started to spark through her, and she tried to push back, her heels on the side of the bed.

He caught her ankles, holding her there. "Don't move. I like you where you are. And I definitely like this."

He drew his hand up, skimming over one leg to reach her core. He touched her briefly before gripping the waistband of her panties and tugging them down. He moved back so he could get them off her, leaving her naked on the bed.

"Keep your legs apart. Heels on the edge of the bed."

There was something in the commanding way he said the words that had her moving before she could think better of it. The position he'd gotten her in to was an intimate one. A vulnerable one. She was completely naked and open to him and he was still wearing jeans, though she could see the line of his erection clearly against the denim.

She wanted to see him naked. Wanted to see that cock in all its glory. She'd never really wanted to see a cock before, but she wanted to look at his. Like he was looking at her. Like she was some artform he wanted to study.

With his gaze on her, she didn't feel so awkward.

"Yes, just like that. Fuck, you're gorgeous." His hair hung over one side of his face, shadowing him and making him look the tiniest bit dangerous. He dropped to his knees. "And you're going to taste like heaven. Don't move or we'll talk about discipline."

Discipline? What was that supposed to...

All thoughts fled as he put his mouth on her pussy and dragged his tongue up. A low growl rumbled over her sensitive flesh.

He breathed her in, and she looked down her body to see her arousal glistening on his lips. He pointedly ran his tongue over them. "Just what I thought. Heaven. Now be a good girl and stay still while I have my fill of you."

"Drake, I want you," she began. Only a moment ago she'd thought penetration would be something she'd accept because she'd already had an orgasm. Now her whole body was on fire again, and she wanted more. She wanted his cock, and she wanted it now.

His head shook. "No. Be still. You'll have me, but only after

I'm satisfied that this pussy has received my thorough attention." He pressed a finger inside, rotating it and making her lie back while she fought to breathe. That finger wasn't enough, but she wanted it. "I was serious about discipline, love. We're going to talk about it in the morning. I can't wait to get you over my lap, that pretty ass of yours in the air."

Somehow she couldn't either. She'd never given the idea of spanking much thought, but she did now. She thought about all the delicious things his obviously creative mind could come up with. All the things they could do together.

Then she couldn't think at all. All she could do was feel his tongue piercing her. He didn't hold back. He dove in, licking and sucking and fucking her with his mouth. Over and over his tongue plunged deep, showing her what he was going to do with his cock. Her back bowed with pleasure but she kept her hips still, allowing him full access to her most private flesh.

Her hands fisted the quilt beneath her as she came again.

Then he was on his feet, his hands at the waist of his jeans, working the fly.

Taylor laid back, ready to give that man anything he wanted.

* * * *

His cock was dying. She was the single sexiest woman he'd ever seen, ever stood over and known he was going to have.

He wanted her in a way that scared him, but his cock overruled any fear his head might have.

Nothing was going to stop him from getting inside Taylor Cline. He toed off his socks and then shoved his jeans and boxer briefs to the floor. He didn't feel the cold. There was no cold when she was naked and waiting for him.

She sat up suddenly, her eyes wide. "I want to touch you."

Fuck. She was going to kill him. He couldn't say *no, baby, there's no time to touch.* She'd been patient with him, given him all the access to her gorgeous body that he'd wanted, and they hadn't set up rules beforehand. A mistake on his part, but one he rather thought he would make again and again with this woman.

He forced his hands to his sides because he wasn't fooling himself that she wanted to touch his chest again. The light in her eyes as she moved to the edge of the bed made his frustration worth it. She was gorgeous, with her blonde hair cascading around her shoulders, the tips brushing her nipples. She stared at him for a moment and then her hand came out, a light brush of her fingertips over his dick.

He had to grit his teeth as his cock responded, force himself to not come then and there.

"I think you're beautiful, Drake," she said, touching his cock, tracing the lines of it.

"Baby, I know you want to give back to me," he began. "But if you put that mouth on me, I'm going to come, and I would like to know what it feels like to be inside you. I promise I'll get my cock in that gorgeous mouth of yours, but not this time."

Her lips curled up. "Promise."

Fuck, she was going to lead him around by his cock. That might have been a problem if they worked together. Luckily, she would be outside that part of his life. She would be the good part, the part that made everything else worth it. "I promise. Now put this thing on me so I can fuck you."

He reached for the condom that had been left in the nightstand next to his bed. The Agency believed in being prepared. Or the last dude who'd been here had at least. He appreciated it because it wasn't like he'd packed before he'd fled Kraków, and he wasn't the guy who kept one in his wallet at all times.

So good on whoever had stocked the place because the idea of not being able to fuck Taylor was unimaginable. Right now, his whole world felt like it revolved around fucking Taylor.

He wasn't sure he would survive fucking Taylor.

She opened the condom and pulled it out, slipping it over his cock with a completely inexpert hand that threatened to cause him to not need the damn thing.

He took over and quickly rolled it on his aching cock. "I'm going to teach you how to do that."

She grinned up at him, blonde hair caressing her cheeks. "I didn't learn how to in school. I had an eclectic education, but none of it covered how to put a condom on a guy."

He was going to teach her so many dirty, filthy, gorgeous things. And he suspected he would learn from her, too. Learn to relax. Learn to have a life outside of work.

Learn to trust again.

The fact that her father was under investigation played around in the back of his head, but he shoved the thought aside. She wasn't her father, and the truth was everyone was pretty much always being watched. She was getting out, and it wouldn't be a problem. He could deal with her and her father separately. Everyone would be in their boxes, and he would be happy when he was with her.

He moved in, pressing her back against the bed. She wound her legs around him. This was what he'd wanted pretty much from the moment he'd seen her, pulled her back against his body when he'd thought she might be an enemy. Even then something deep inside him had reacted to her. He'd connected to her despite everything in between them.

And what was about to happen felt utterly inevitable. Standing over her, his cock nestled to her pussy, felt like fate.

It was far too easy to slide into her body. Like she'd been built for him. He stood there, looking down at her. With her hair like a halo around her and her body laid out for him, he thrust inside her welcoming pussy.

Her eyes widened, bottom lip disappearing behind her teeth as she shifted, adjusting to him. He held himself still though all he wanted to do was pound inside her. She felt so good wrapped around his dick. Hot and perfect. When her hips tilted up in invitation, he took it.

Drake pressed himself against her, the pleasure coursing through him.

This was what it felt like to truly be connected to a woman. He dragged his cock back out and thrust in again, watching how his cock disappeared inside her. Over and over, watching them connect.

She pushed back against him. "More. Drake, I need more."

He could give her more. He fucked her hard, driving inside, his hips moving in time with hers. He held her hips, forcing his cock deeper and deeper. Every inch was pure pleasure. Every stroke one step closer to what he wanted.

Pure connection. With her.

Her head tilted back, a low moan coming from her throat, and then he felt her tighten around him. Fire lit up his spine, and he couldn't hold back. He wanted to stay in this moment with her, but her orgasm forced his own. A rush of pleasure coasted through him, and he thrust and thrust until he had nothing more to give.

He stared down at her, her whole body flushed a rosy pink. "Taylor, I…"

She nodded as though she knew what he was feeling. "Me, too."

He was crazy about her, could plan his whole life around her if she let him. He could fall for her…probably was already falling for her.

He was about to tell her everything in his heart. He was surprised at that. He'd kind of thought he didn't have a functional heart. Oh, he loved his family, but a part of that had died when Julia had proven so very evil.

Taylor was bringing it back to life.

Maybe it was time to think about retiring from the field, staying in Langley and doing analysis work. He could spend more time with her, have a real life.

He was about to tell her all those things.

The entire cabin shook with the force of the pounding on the door.

It was a shock to his system, and he found himself pulling away, breaking the connection they had long before he wanted to.

But adrenaline was pumping through his body now, and not the happy kind. "I'll go see who it is."

Taylor wasn't some shrinking violet. Before he could start rolling the condom off and reaching for his pants, she'd gotten off the bed. "You stay here. I'm supposed to be here. You're not. It might be my father. We were supposed to meet in Bucharest, but it wouldn't be the first time his plans changed."

She was stiff, all that relaxation she'd had gone with this new arrival.

Shit. All of his relaxation was gone. He was about to meet his girlfriend's dad. Fuck. He'd never met a girlfriend's dad before. Not one he actually cared about. He'd met the parents of targets he was investigating, usually sometime before he had all of them arrested because the family was usually in on it.

He was kind of a bastard.

But that was about to change because he wouldn't seduce anyone for intel again. He cared about Taylor, and he was going to put her first. "I'll get dressed, but don't lie to him about us. I'm not some random operative who needed a place to hide."

She tugged her shirt over her head, her pajama bottoms already on. She'd left off the soaked undies. "Uh, that's kind of exactly how we met."

He tossed the condom in the bathroom trash and reached for his pants. "But it's not what we are now. Don't lie to him." There was another loud banging. "Maybe you should wait for me."

She waved him off. "I'm fine. No one knows we're here except my dad and both of our bosses. I don't think the bears would knock. The good news is if they made it here, we can probably get down the mountain."

She strode away and he kind of stumbled, trying to get his pants on. His muscles weren't working properly yet. They were going to have a long talk about when she needed to obey him for safety's sake. Of course at this point she was Agency, too, but when she wasn't, he was going to make sure she didn't ever put herself in the line of fire. Even with her father.

He finally managed to get his damn pants on and found his SIG. He better walk out and find her armed no matter how sure she was about who was at the door.

Then he was moving into the living area—the same one where they'd begun this incredibly important moment in their lives—and his heart dropped.

Brad stood there, a grim look on his face and a file in his hands. "Hey, Drake. We need to talk."

What the hell was Brad doing here? He wasn't a field agent. He rarely left Langley. That was the moment he realized something was wrong. And that something was missing. Something important.

"Where's Taylor?" The door was closed, and he heard the sound of tires crunching on the snow. He moved to the door, flinging it open. A cold wind hit his chest, sending a chill where once he'd been warm.

A big SUV was driving away.

"She's been taken into custody. Drake, what's happened with her… It's going to be classified at a level you won't be able to deal with. I don't even know what exactly has happened," Brad admitted. "Though I know it's bad, and we probably won't see her again. I think the higher-ups have figured out why her father's been making regular trips to Cuba and covering it up."

His stomach took a deep dive. This couldn't be happening again. "Cuba?"

Lev Sokolov was a former Russian operative. Had he been a double all this time? Cuba would be a good place to meet with his Russian handlers.

Brad nodded. "Yes. Over the last couple of months, he's taken several trips to Havana. He lied about where he was. That's what Lydia managed to discover. Beyond that, not even her sources inside the support staff are talking about."

His logistics and communications tech was excellent at ferreting out gossip among her coworkers and bringing it back to him. Even inside the Agency, intel was valuable. If Lydia couldn't find it out, it was bad. Very bad. Classified beyond his rank bad.

"Taylor wasn't involved." He said the words but even as they came out of his mouth his brain was already working overtime.

That was what you thought about Julia when Kyle came to you. Your sister couldn't be involved. Your sister was…she was your sister and you didn't know who she was. Why the fuck would you think you know who a chick you fucked once is?

Because it hadn't been fucking. It had been something more. It had felt like something more.

"I don't know." Brad tapped the folder in his hand. "But I'll check into it. Uhm, is there something I should know, man? I wasn't close to her when they took her out, but she was saying something about needing to talk to you. And she wasn't…well, she seemed as quickly dressed as you do. Did something happen?"

Drake felt his heart harden. How could this have happened twice in such a short amount of time? Julia had tricked him and now

Taylor. She'd likely thought he could help her when the Agency found out what her father had been doing.

Or she'd thought she could use him to better her father's position with his Russian homeland. So when they went back, they could go in glory, and he would be the idiot spy who gave up all his country's secrets to a woman who led him around by his cock.

She could have cost him his whole career, could have cost his family everything. His mother would lose her legacy if anyone found out about Julia. He'd been careful to cover it up and then he'd nearly fucked it all up by falling for a damn Russian asset.

He forced himself to go cold as he turned to the man he considered a friend. "I was working her. You told me to figure out what was going on. You could have given me a heads-up that I didn't need to fuck her to get the intel. If you'd been an hour quicker, you might have spared me the experience."

He hated every word that came out of his mouth, but he needed them because he might not survive if anyone ever figured out how close he'd come to giving that woman his soul.

"I'm sorry." Brad frowned. "The bosses didn't want to give her a heads-up. I'm so sorry. I didn't mean for you to sleep with her. But I can make up for it. I've got a lead you're going to want. I think I know who killed Borys."

He stared for a moment, though the SUV that had taken her away was long gone.

He still had a job to do, and it looked like he'd barely missed taking yet another bullet for a woman he'd loved.

Love. What a fucking word.

He hadn't loved Taylor. He'd been vulnerable, and she'd been a good memory. A memory from a time when the world hadn't seemed so complex. She couldn't have known he would end up here, but she'd been excellent at using him once he was.

Or maybe she'd had something to do with it. He couldn't count that out.

He shoved it aside and closed the door before turning to Brad. "Tell me."

It was time to get back to work.

Part Two

Wyoming

Present Day

Chapter Five

"Are you sure you're ready for this?" a familiar voice asked.

The floor beneath Taylor's feet rocked with the rowdy sounds of the bar below. The Cowgirl's Choice was hopping on a Friday night. She wished she could walk down there, take a seat at the bar, and wait for some big, gorgeous cowboy to sit beside her and offer to buy her a drink.

Not that she would let him, but it would be nice to have the option. Instead she was stuck upstairs with an Agency handler. Well, one former operative who happened to be the only person Taylor Cline would listen to, the only one her father had believed in. "Ready? I've been training for this for over a year. These people killed my father. I'm ready to take them down and then get on with my life."

If she had a life when she was done with The Consortium. The truth of the matter was she knew this could end up being a mission she didn't come back from, and she didn't honestly care.

Even if she could go downstairs and join the party, she wouldn't. She would sit up here and go over dossiers and mission briefs. She hadn't had sex since…

She wasn't thinking about that fucker tonight. Liar. That was Drake Radcliffe to a *T*. He'd lied to her so he could figure out what her father was doing, if her father was a double. After that awful day when the Agency had shown up at the safe house in Romania, she'd never heard from him again. He'd stayed behind and let her walk into an ambush and probably never thought of her again.

She'd been hauled away from the cabin by a CIA agent she'd never met before who informed her that her father had been killed. She could still remember how vulnerable she'd felt. How she'd wished Drake had been there to hold her.

That was when the interrogations about why her father had been in Havana had started.

Since Mr. Gray wasn't able to get the information from you in a nicer way, I'm going to have to ask outright, the agent had explained.

Drake had used her, and she wouldn't allow herself to ever be used again.

She'd agreed to this mission for one reason and one reason only—revenge.

If she survived this mission, she would be out and she would never have to worry about running into that fucker. She would leave Virginia and start her life all over.

Alone.

"I meant are you ready to meet the Agency manager for this op?" Kimberly Solomon Kent was a gorgeous blonde who'd been an operative for years before she'd gone on the run. She'd been burned by another operative, and it had taken years to get her life back.

She understood the woman who'd formerly been known as Solo. It was precisely why she'd been willing to let Solo advise her. "I thought Brad Perry was working this one. He's the agent who's signed off on what I've done up to this point."

"Up to this point, the whole op has mostly been on paper, but apparently there's a more senior agent coming in now that you're getting in deep," Kim explained. "You're still working for Brad, but from what I understand your op is bumping up against something that happened recently, so you'll have to deal with two chefs in the kitchen. It's not ideal and I wasn't informed who's coming in, so I'm working in the dark. All I know is Brad is going to be here and he'll explain how the two missions coincide. I do know one of the guys who's working the other side is already here."

"The brooding hottie who hates washing dishes?" Taylor sighed and sank down to the couch. "I think I'd rather take Sandra in with me. She did some work for the Agency, right?"

"No, she worked for McKay-Taggart and MT worked for the Agency. In as much as Big Tag ever works for the Agency." Kim sat down across from her. "You got the dossier on him, right? Because he's going to be here tomorrow for the overall debrief. The hottie is his nephew. When you go to Europe to meet with the target, you'll be using Tag's team as backup. Brad is worried there's a leak at the Agency. I'm worried about it, too. What happened to your father wasn't an accident, and that's why I think you should consider what you're about to do."

"I've read the dossier on Taggart, and my father liked him very much. He also trusted Tennessee Smith, who works for him, too. I don't know if he worked with Damon Knight, but if Smith and Taggart work with him, I can as well." She'd had to consider every single step she'd taken since that day she'd learned her father was dead. "But I'm not sure about his nephew. He's a hot mess."

And she did mean hot. Kyle Hawthorne was gorgeous, not that she allowed herself to be swayed by a nice set of abs and a killer jawline anymore.

"I've been told there's a good reason he's assigned to this case," Kim explained. "He was involved with the target at one point. He and the agent working the case with Brad. There have been a few events that have taken place recently that forced the Agency to up the timeline on the other guy's op and bring in extra handlers for you, but he's going to have to explain. I don't have clearance for this anymore. I'm strictly supposed to make sure you're comfortable and to get you here without incident."

Kim had agreed to leave her husband and son so she could make sure Taylor got where she needed to go. "I appreciate it. You can't know how much."

"Well, I owe your dad. He saved my ass several times over the years. He would be proud of you. This is one of the more brilliant plays I've ever seen. I'm interested to see how this works out," Kim said with a hint of a smile on her face. "Besides, there are a couple of guys I can't wait to see again. Since you want to keep the amount of Agency assets used to a minimum, we're bringing in some Taggart-approved guys."

Taylor knew about that, too. "Yes. One of the people I'm supposed to steal data from in order to prove myself is married to an ex-Taggart employee, so I thought bringing in his old friends would make Owen Shaw feel more comfortable. And his wife, Rebecca, of course. She's been thoroughly briefed about the fact that I'll have to run an op around her research."

Rebecca Shaw was a neurologist working on therapies for degenerative brain diseases that some in big pharma wanted suppressed. The operative known as "Constance Tyne" had already "stolen" some data from Rebecca's studies that hadn't been released to the public. Rebecca herself had forged the data, but it had been impressive enough to get them a real meeting with The Consortium.

A meeting Taylor meant to keep because she was taking this whole thing down.

She needed a backup team, and that meant bringing in people Owen and Rebecca would be comfortable with.

"They're excited to get to work a job again," Kim said, a light in her eyes that told Taylor she was happy to be working again, too. "You got the reports on them, right?"

Jax Lee was a nature guide who specialized in mountain camping and white-water rafting. Timothy Seeger—who apparently went by Tucker—was a general practitioner right here in Wyoming. She'd been told Sandra Croft was his mother-in-law.

Both men had been out of action for years. She hoped she knew what she was doing. "Yes. I'm looking forward to meeting them in person. We've got two weeks before I'm due in London. I hope to get everyone up to speed by then. And I hope Kyle is a little more sane at that point. Are you sure we have to take him? I could always make someone else up. After all, it worked with Constance."

Kim grinned. "Oh, I bet you could. After this you should think about writing fiction. But I think we're stuck with Kyle. I was told he's the subject matter expert on this."

"Well, I was told he killed this chick the first time around and now she's back, so he can't be too much of an expert. I think we can do better." Julia Ennis's CIA file was classified, and she'd been told she wouldn't get to read it until the op was given the final go-ahead, and that would be up to the big wig they were sending to meet her tonight.

She'd spent a year and a half working on finding a way to get into The Consortium so she could identify their operatives, the companies they worked for, and the governments who continued to fund them. She'd bounced against a couple of walls inside the Agency, but she could guess why. Julia Ennis had been an agent and she'd turned. It was a tale as old as time to a spy. Hawthorne had been her partner, and he'd been forced to take her out or she would have taken him down.

Honestly, Taylor didn't get why she wasn't allowed to see that file. It could have given her important intel, but she'd played the game.

Now it was time to move the game along, and she would be getting in on the action. She wasn't about to let a salty ex-agent give her hell.

"Give him a chance." Kim seemed to be all team Hawthorne. "You've read his records."

"The ones that don't involve Julia Ennis," Taylor countered.

"Well, once the Agency handler is in place, I suspect Kyle will open up a bit more," Kim allowed. "But he's been burned before. You have to know he's going to be suspicious of you. He's likely heard the rumors about your dad."

She had some classified files of her own. "He can fuck himself."

"Not the attitude you should take," Kim said with a sigh. "You have to get along with these guys. I know you've been on your own, but this is going to be different."

She'd been working on her own for a year and a half, moving around the globe so it looked like Constance was moving, faking jobs, doing a couple, making slight mistakes so she didn't come off as far too good. She'd played a tightrope game, and now she was about to reel in the big fish. She was going to take down the group that had ordered her father's assassination.

She was ready. "I can handle whoever the Agency sends. I know Kyle Hawthorne is a trained field operative, but the new guy will be pure Agency bureaucrat. He'll be obnoxious and pretentious, and I'll handle him like I used to handle the men who thought they knew better than my father."

Kim sighed and leaned back. "Yeah, I remember the type. You know you won't get that with Jax and Tucker. They understand where you are, and they'll back you up. I work with Jax, you know. I guide tours from time to time when Beck and I aren't working on a case."

Kim and her husband, Beckett Kent, worked with law enforcement to find missing persons across the globe, though they rarely left the Colorado town where they were raising their son. They worked remotely for the most part and were excellent at their jobs.

If they'd been the ones looking into her father, they would have figured out what he'd been doing in Havana and the Agency wouldn't have needed to send in someone to try to fuck the information out of her.

So why hadn't he asked? There was a voice inside her that always wondered.

Because he didn't have time, moron. There was a much louder voice that answered. *Because your father died, and the Agency moved up the timetable. He probably would have gotten you in bed another dozen times before he got down to business. He was slick, and you were naïve and desperate for attention.*

None of this was helping. She shoved the thoughts aside and got back to reality and the job in front of her.

"Good, then it will be at least three against two, though I would bet hottie dishwasher isn't good with authority figures, either." When she'd been introduced to Kyle, he'd looked her up and down and the only words he'd said to her were good luck before he'd gone back to complaining about how hard it was to get caked cheese off plastic.

"So if you need someone to run interference for you with the handler, Jax and Tucker will be your boys," Kim promised. "They know how to distract a boss. As for Kyle, I'm worried he's going to cause chaos. He won't mean to, but from what I can tell, he's too close to this job. Reading between the lines of what I've been told, I think he was involved romantically with his partner."

She wouldn't be surprised. From what she'd heard Hawthorne had been paired with Julia Ennis on several ops over the course of his time with the Agency. He'd started as her military backup and moved into an operative role at some point, usually working with her. They would have spent a lot of time together, thrown into situations that were stressful.

But it wasn't stress that got you flat on your back for Drake Radcliffe.

Nope. It had been a carefully planned-out manipulation that had tricked her into his bed. He'd said all the right things. All lies.

"That's an excellent reason for him to not be involved." Why was she thinking about Drake after all this time? Probably because she was close to the finish line now, and when this was done she would either move on or she would be dead. "If he's emotional about the situation, he can't be trusted."

"I don't think you're going to be able to get rid of him." Kim checked her cell phone and her lips curled up. "Big Tag won't support the op if his nephew isn't involved. There's also the bait factor. The Agency thinks they can use Kyle as bait."

"I thought Kyle was supposed to be dead." That was the impression she'd received, though Kyle hadn't wanted to talk. She'd gotten some information from Sandra—who did not care what the Agency thought. Sandra was doing this as a favor to the Taggart family and nothing more. "That's why we're here in the wilds of Wyoming instead of back in Virginia. Because no one wants to give up the fact that Hawthorne's alive."

"I think there's more to it," Kim allowed. She was obviously distracted by whatever was on her phone. "Kyle should explain it to you."

"If you have something else to do, you should do it." She didn't say it in a testy way. Kim was doing her a favor. "I know you left your family. If you need to call them or something, it's okay. I can hang here on my own for a couple of hours."

Kim's blonde hair shook. "Sorry. Beck is sending me Bliss gossip. He's at the town hall meeting, and those always go sideways where I'm from. He and Roman bought popcorn and they're watching the show. You should come sometime. I wish you'd been able to stay at my place for a couple of days."

Kim liked to talk about the tiny town she and her husband lived in. It sounded like a lot of fun, but Taylor couldn't even conceive of living in one place. Having roots. Her apartment in Virginia had been rented fully furnished, and it was bland, with none of her own personality in it.

She wasn't sure she had much personality at this point. All of her hopes and dreams had been shattered that day a year and a half ago. Sometimes she looked in the mirror and didn't recognize the face that stared back.

It was funny how having a family—even one person in the world—tethered a person to reality. Since her father had died, the days all seemed the same, each meshing into the next.

What would it be like to be free of this need for vengeance? Would she ask Kim to show her the way to Bliss and spend a couple of weeks hanging with the only person who was kind of a friend?

Or would she be alone without even a mission? Would she go back to the Agency because it was the only thing she'd known?

Would she drift forever in this numb, gray reality?

There was a knock on the door and it opened, Brad Perry walking through. He looked out of place in his tailored suit and polished loafers.

The perfect bureaucrat.

Taylor turned, absolutely ready to stop thinking about her impending existential crisis and get back to the job. The good news was if she died, she didn't have to worry about what to do with the rest of her lonely life.

"Hello, Taylor." Brad nodded Kim's way. "Hey, Solo. Thanks so much for getting our girl here. I was overseas, and I just got in a couple of hours ago. How long was the drive?"

"She flew in by a private jet to Bliss. Lucky for her we've got a couple of rich people who like to fly, hence the private runway," Kim explained. "It's about eight hours from there, but it's gorgeous country so I didn't mind. It kept her under the radar."

Kim's words reminded her that she'd had a ridiculously long day. She'd flown by private jet to Oklahoma City, and then in an even smaller private plane to Bliss. All so no one could track her. She'd started the day at the awful hour of four a.m. eastern time. It was a little over three hours to Oklahoma, and then another three plus to Bliss, and all that driving.

She was exhausted, and there were still talks to be had. But the bed looked so inviting at this point.

If she put her head down, she could close her eyes and hopefully forget for a little while.

Of course she could also dream. Dream of him and have to wake up and remember who he'd turned out to be.

"Well, I'm sorry you have to turn around and do it all again, Solo," Brad said. "But I promise you I can take it from here. I need to have a talk with Taylor before the big boss gets here in a few hours."

Kim chuckled. "Nah. I think I'm staying for the time being. I'm on retainer, Brad. Gotta earn those big bucks."

"I thought Kim was staying until we were ready to go to London." She didn't like the thought of being all alone with the Agency. Which was sad since they were her employers, and she didn't trust them.

"I am," Kim assured her.

"There's no need." Brad sighed, a long-suffering sound. "I understand that Taggart wants some of his people in place, but I would like to keep this team tight."

"Good," Kim countered. "Then you can pick who stays from you and whoever the Agency sent. We don't need two handlers."

Taylor yawned, going to the window and looking outside while Kim started arguing with Brad. She didn't care. She wanted to get through it and be done and see what the hell was on the other side of this.

God, she missed her dad.

Though there was a part of her that was glad her dad hadn't ever had to know how stupid she'd been.

"Why does Taggart want you here? He's going to be here himself tomorrow afternoon," Brad argued.

"Good. Then it will be super easy for you to ask him yourself," Kim countered.

Her dad wouldn't blame her for being dumb enough to fall for Drake Radcliffe. He would wrap his arms around her and kiss her forehead like he did when she was a child and tell her that her heart was far too big and open for this world, and she couldn't help but try to give pieces of it away.

Then he would have quietly killed Drake Radcliffe, taken his body apart, and buried it on different continents.

She really, really missed her dad.

"I don't understand. It's not like Drake hasn't worked with Big Tag before," Brad returned with an exasperated tone.

"Again, something you should ask Big Tag." Kim wasn't backing down.

Maybe she could sneak away. She could slip down the stairs and out into the Wyoming wilderness. She knew a lot of survival skills. Half of surviving was simply being aware of what was around you. Listening.

Listening. Hearing danger before it came her way.

What?

"Drake?" She turned from the window.

Brad's jaw went tight. "Yes. I didn't tell you because I wasn't sure you would work with him given your prior relationship."

Kim's eyes had gone wide. "Relationship? With the kid?"

The "kid" was a whole-ass grown man who had to be pushing thirty at this point. Maybe past. "Why would you bring up Drake Radcliffe's name?"

Brad's expression turned grim. "Because he's taking the co-lead on this. He's going to have to explain to you why, but this case is personal to him, too. I hope you can understand that. He's coming up to talk to you in a minute, and I wanted to warn you."

"Warn her?" Kim had her hands on her hips, staring Brad down. "You don't warn a person two minutes before a bomb goes off. You wanted to ambush her so she didn't have anywhere to go and no way out. And now we know why Big Tag wants me here. I don't know what's going on, but no woman goes that pale over a man who treated her well, and I won't be a part of this. Fuck you. Fuck the Agency. Pack up, Taylor. We're going back to Bliss. We'll reassess from the road."

At least someone was on her side.

How could they have done this to her? When she agreed to take this job, to put her life on the line, she'd had one deal breaker. She wouldn't work with Drake Radcliffe.

Now a year and a half into the op and they slipped him in without giving her the option of saying no.

Only one person could have set this up.

The liar himself. "I'll go. But I think I'll say hi first."

She knew exactly the language to use.

* * * *

Drake couldn't believe how different Kyle Hawthorne looked. And how familiar.

In the weeks since he'd faked his death and come here to Wyoming to lay low until they were ready, Kyle had gone from looking like one of the happiest fuckers in the world to a dark and bitter bastard who likely killed people. Like he'd looked after he'd been forced to kill his fiancée.

Kyle had walked away from the Agency, left Drake all by himself to deal with Julia's treachery. He'd gone to work for McKay-Taggart in some meathead bodyguard job that didn't touch his true talents and he'd met a girl who'd slowly brought him back to life.

MaeBe Vaughn. How fucking bitter Drake had been when he'd realized Kyle had fallen in love with McKay-Taggart's resident hacker/gamer girl and she'd loved him back. MaeBe had pink hair, goth clothes, and a genuinely good soul.

When Drake had "fallen" it had been for one more traitor.

His life was full of them.

And he hadn't been able to stop thinking about the last one. He'd been angry and bitter about Taylor Cline for long enough. It was time to do something about her.

After he finished this one last op.

He didn't actually have a life outside of work since Taylor. Now he didn't even consider trying to have a relationship because no one compared to her. He'd briefly romanced a scientist, but it had never even gotten to a kiss. Still, being around Maddie Hill had made him miss…not Taylor. The idea of Taylor. Who Taylor was in his head.

It no longer mattered. He'd made his decision about Taylor, and he was going to go through with it. He'd never been able to move on, and now she was going to get what she'd wanted all those months before. She was going to take him down, and he would be the one who blew it all to hell for her.

"Are you still with me, man?" Kyle was staring at him with dark eyes.

Drake tried to shake off the past. Julia was alive, and Taylor had been so much a part of his life right after Julia had been dead. It seemed all his ghosts were haunting him again.

Or he could stop fooling himself and accept that there hadn't been a day that had gone by that he didn't think about her, didn't worry about where she was and what was happening to her and how he could find her and make her pay for what she'd done to him.

"Of course." He took a long breath and forced himself to try to relax. "You said Constance was upstairs? I'd like to meet her and get this thing going. We're due in London soon, and I want to be sure she's ready for the op. It's dangerous, and I don't want to send her in unprepared."

He was fairly certain the mysterious Constance Tyne would be irritated with him, but he'd never met her before and while she'd passed all of the Agency's yearly tests for the past five years, there was no video of her, no way for him to feel comfortable going in with her.

He had two weeks to decide if this op was happening.

Yeah, Constance would be irritated with that, too, but she was going to have to deal with it. This was his op now, and she was his asset. Up until now she'd been overseen by Brad, who let her run pretty wild, but that was about to change. She was the gun he would point and shoot and hopefully kill his sister with.

Then he would deal with Taylor. He had been looking for months now with no luck, but he was going to start rattling cages until he figured out exactly where they were holding her. He'd eliminated the usual suspects. The Agency had to have her in one of their smaller prisons.

"She's not what I expected." Kyle wore a dark T-shirt and jeans and sneakers. He slid the thick white apron he'd worn over his head and laid it on the table to his left. The kitchen at Cowgirl's Choice smelled like fried food and bleach, proving Sandra believed in giving her customers what they wanted and in proper cleaning techniques.

"How so?" He trusted Kyle's instincts. They'd been close once, but Julia's death had broken their friendship.

Was it terrible to think that her rebirth could mend it?

Kyle seemed to think for a moment, leaning against the stainless steel countertop. "She looks more fragile than I expected. When I read her records, I was kind of expecting She Hulk to walk through the door. I know there are plenty of petite badasses, but she doesn't come off that way. She reminds me the tiniest bit of MaeBe. Like I would peg her as a computer jockey."

"Everything reminds you of MaeBe." Constance wasn't the only one he needed to test to ensure she was ready for the op. "Are you still keeping tabs on her through that game?"

One big shoulder shrugged. "I like to think of it as keeping her company."

A few days ago he'd figured out that Kyle was playing some massive multiplayer game under an alias, and he'd befriended the woman who was supposed to think he'd died in California.

"You know she doesn't think you're dead according to Big Tag."

Another shrug. "I needed a big gesture. It's the only thing Julia understands. I was hoping Mae would believe it so she could move on, but it doesn't matter as long as she stays away from me. I need them all to stay away from me. You know Julia and you know her rules of engagement. I had to do something to prove to her I'm not going to bring my family into this."

"She already did." He was worried that was how Kyle was seeing things. "Since we figured out she survived both you shooting her and you blowing up the building you left her body in, I've done a deep dive into what's been going on with your family in the last half a year or so."

Kyle's jaw squared. "Are you still mad at me about this? I'm sorry. I know she was your sister and you loved her, but there was no other way."

Drake took a long breath, trying to banish the difficult swirl of emotions that happened whenever he thought about Julia and that particular time. It was all combined with her betrayal and his parents' grief, losing his closest friend and everything that had gone on with Taylor. In a lot of ways he'd shut down completely after he'd learned the truth about Taylor, and it had been bliss. Not having to feel anything, going through the motions with his soul tuned out had been exactly what he needed. When Kyle had been pulled into his investigation of Maddie Hill's boss—that was when it had all started to fall apart.

And then Maddie's boss had been involved with a Consortium operative who'd turned out to be none other than his supposed-to-be-dead traitorous sister, and his fucking world had turned upside down again.

Hence him being here in the wilds of Wyoming listening to country music and getting ready to deal with the most sarcastic asshole he'd ever met. And it wasn't Kyle Hawthorne.

"I know you did what you had to do." He wasn't going to take this out on Kyle. Kyle had been as hurt as he'd been, and now he had to give up a good woman to protect her from his bad choice. He had to remember that. He hadn't chosen to be Julia's younger brother. Kyle had picked her. He had to live with that every day. "And I know you think you understand her, but I think the fact that she betrayed us all means we know nothing and should move forward with that understanding."

"I'm doing the best I can," Kyle argued. "And in this I do know Julia. She's been fucking with me for months, and I didn't see it."

"Because you thought she was dead." He felt the need to point that out. It was a bit of self-preservation. He'd thought many times over the last few weeks that he should have fucking known.

Kyle's expression shuttered. "There were too many coincidences. My stepfather's had a bunch of bad luck lately. If I'm right, she's been screwing with his businesses, and she's sabotaged my siblings. Hell, I'm suspicious of everything at this point. My credit rating got fucked up. Pretty sure she did that. I'd like to know if she's the reason Carys got outed, and Luke's accident was sketchy. My uncle is going to update us when he gets here. He's probably going to kick my ass, too."

"Because of what you put your parents through? Yes. He likely will."

Kyle's eyes rolled. "No. My mom and stepdad know I'm alive. I would never do that to my family. Luke and Carys know, too. I wouldn't put my siblings through this. The funeral was complete bullshit where I'm sure my family and friends threw darts at my picture and complained bitterly about what a dumbass I am. Hell, I'm almost certain Julia knows. This was never about fooling Julia. It was about keeping this war between the two of us. The people closest to me know."

"MaeBe's not close to you?" Not that she didn't know, but Drake got the feeling no one in the family would confirm her deeply held belief.

"Not anymore." Kyle's shoulders squared, and he turned toward a door that led out of the kitchen.

"And if we manage to do the job properly this time?" He couldn't force himself to say the right words.

If they managed to kill his sister. If they stopped her and wiped her from the face of the earth. If he put a bullet in her heart and buried his only sibling in the ground.

I'm not going to let anything bad happen to you, Drake. You and me. We're in this together. Pinkie promise, little brother.

His stomach turned.

"Then I return to the Agency and I get back to work. I'm not…" Kyle stopped for a moment. "It's not like Julia's the only one out there who could come after me. You were right when you told me this isn't the kind of job you walk away from. Once you're in, you're in for life."

He'd been trying to talk Kyle out of quitting. He hadn't wanted to lose the only person in the world he could talk to. His father didn't have clearance anymore, and his mother didn't even know Julia had been a spy. Kyle had been the only one he could talk to, and he'd walked away like Drake had been as tainted as Julia. And he was forgetting a few things. "Talk to your uncle about how it worked for him. Or Tennessee Smith. Or Damon Knight. Kayla Summers looked real happy with how her life played out after the CIA."

They'd seen the ex-operative, and the only reason she'd been unhappy was letting the Agency back into her life briefly. They'd caused a whole bunch of problems for the former deep undercover agent that she'd had to deal with. Julia had laid a trap, and they'd foolishly fallen right into it.

"Somehow I don't think my uncle was as deep in as I was," Kyle replied.

Drake managed to not roll his eyes. Barely. "I'm going to let Ian handle that misconception. I want to get this op started. You understand why we're not using Agency resources beyond the bare minimum, right?"

"Because we don't trust anyone." Kyle proved he understood.

Drake nodded. He was keeping his circle on this to a minimum. His normal tech didn't even know the truth of where he was and what he was doing. She thought he was on vacation. Only Brad knew he was here, and only because Brad had been overseeing Constance and the small team that was so classified even he had no idea who had been working on it. Brad had explained that it was an employee who had been around for a long time and was above reproach.

No one was above reproach, but he couldn't exactly fire Brad and Constance. He had to deal with them, and part of mitigating the risk was working with Kyle instead of Agency backup. He would get through this and then…

He wasn't even thinking about the future. The future was a never-ending series of days that led to other days and never quite became anything vaguely resembling a life. Which was awful because before he'd met Taylor he'd rather thought his life was perfect. He had good work, was respected, had a family he felt comfortable in. He'd had a friend and enjoyed what he did.

Julia had fucked over most of that, but he blamed Taylor for the sense of dissatisfaction with his potential future. He'd seen what he might have had, and nothing else came close.

At some point in the last few weeks he'd decided to break her out of whatever prison they'd put her in. She'd had enough time to think about her actions and to see what she would get if she betrayed him a second time. He would break her out and then go on the run. He knew how to hide, knew where enough skeletons were buried that the Agency could be handled if they needed to be. He had enough money to take care of them.

This time they would have an ironclad contract in place. Big Tag was right. It was the only way to have a relationship. There would be a contract that detailed every aspect of their relationship, and it would also lay out all the punishments if she stepped even an inch out of line.

He had everything in place and he was going to walk away from everything and everyone he knew for a woman who'd used him.

He was a dumbass, but there was nothing else he could do.

He would deal with Julia and then blow up his whole life for a woman who'd lied to him, who'd betrayed her country.

Who was the only woman who'd ever moved his soul.

"So we're going up?" Kyle stared at him like he'd been waiting for a while. "Because if you're not, then I'm going to my room because my shift is over and if I hustle I can make the raid we're supposed to go on tonight at midnight Texas time. I told MaeBe I had to work, but if I can be there I will. She's hanging with Erin right now and doesn't get online until after the kids go to bed."

Yeah, Kyle was really walking away from that relationship fast.

"Is Brad here?" He needed to get started.

Every second he wasted, she was in a prison.

"He got in a couple of hours before Solo and the Constance chick, though she goes by something else." Kyle slid a key card out of his pocket and touched it to the security pad before pushing through the door.

The Cowgirl's Choice was set back from the highway, and it looked like Sandra had built a whole compound on her land. He'd noticed several buildings behind the bar. It was dark, but the building that held the bar was at least three stories. He wasn't sure what she used all those for.

Drake strode through. The door led to a stairwell, and to his right he could see another doorway. This one had to lead from the back parking lot, but it didn't look like an employee entrance. This part of the building was different from the rustic chic of the bar. There was plush red carpet beneath his feet and a big desk at the door that looked like an expensively done security station. The door was made of dark wood and stained glass.

"Does Sandra live here?"

Kyle stopped on the first step, turning his way. "No, she and Angie have a house on property, but we'll be staying on the third floor. She's got a couple of suites up there. The women have two of the singles, I have one, and you and Brad will be sharing the big suite. Don't worry. It's got two beds, and only one of them is rigged for suspension play."

And then he knew what the other part of The Cowgirl's Choice served as. "Am I in another BDSM club?"

Kyle snorted. "Where did you think you were going? Didn't you and Sandra used to…"

Drake held up a hand. "We worked together for a couple of jobs."

"Yeah, I heard there was more to it."

Drake felt his eyes narrow. "You know how it is. You partner with a sexy woman and things happen. At least mine didn't turn out to be a psychotic killer."

Kyle's jaw dropped. "Fuck you. She was your sister."

"Half sister." The distinction suddenly seemed important. "And I enjoyed my time with Sandra. I know she's way older than me, but she was excellent in bed and she taught me a lot. And I only had to worry about her trying to talk me into trying exotic lubes and bottoming for her in crazy fucked-up ways."

"And leaving you for a woman." Kyle's lips had turned up, his eyes lighting.

It was worth it to see him not look so grim. "She was always bi. I knew that. And we weren't ever exclusive. She was a friend and she showed me some things. So there. I'm happy she's married now and probably using those crazy lubes on someone else."

Kyle's head fell back, and a booming laugh broke through the space. "I love that you had a relationship with Sandra. I love that you bottomed for her for a while."

"I was experimenting. You know I had a lot of fun." But when he'd really looked at it, really thought about what he enjoyed, he wasn't much of a switch. He could play at it from time to time, but the most connection he'd ever felt was from topping a woman who genuinely needed to submit. That time with Sandra had taught him so damn much about himself. It had gotten him ready for what he wanted.

Taylor.

Fuck. He wanted Taylor. He missed her like an actual hole in his fucking soul, and nothing was ever going to fill it.

"You okay?" Kyle had a hand on his chest as though he was taking a long breath after a laugh he'd needed desperately.

"I think I'm going to leave the Agency after this is done and I'm going to commit a whole bunch of crimes and go into hiding for the rest of my life." It felt kind of good to say it out loud.

"Are you serious?" Kyle looked around, obviously trying to make sure they hadn't been heard.

He was going to have to tell someone. He would need backup if he was going to break Taylor out, and there was no one who enjoyed fucking over the Agency more than the Taggarts. "Do you remember Lev Sokolov?"

"The Russian double who died?"

Drake nodded. It was stupid to talk about this right now, but he couldn't help it. He'd spent a couple of days with Kyle weeks ago, and it had taken everything Drake had not to confess to him. "I think his daughter and I have unfinished business, and I have to find her. She'll be held in a facility somewhere. Probably a prison outside the States."

Kyle moved back down the steps to stand in front of him. "What's going on, man?"

"I can't talk about it now, but she's important to me." After the initial meeting with Constance, he would sit down at the bar with Kyle and go over everything. Everything that happened with Taylor, and maybe Kyle could talk him out of throwing his life away for a woman who'd lied to him.

Or maybe Kyle would understand.

Kyle put a hand on his shoulder. "All right. If she's important, then we'll figure out what to do."

For the first time in forever, he felt like he could breathe. From the moment he'd stood in that cabin to now, something tight had a stranglehold on him. Now it eased a bit as if merely acknowledging the potential solution allowed him to relax.

"Hey, you're here." Brad was suddenly coming down the stairs, looking more worried than usual. Brad was almost always polished and poised. "Man, I have to tell you something and you're not going to like it one bit. I thought you would be the one I had trouble with, but she's pissed. Like beyond pissed."

"Constance?" He wasn't sure how a woman he'd never met could be so angry with him. "What did I do to her?"

"It doesn't matter what you did. All that matters is I'm not giving you a chance to do it again."

Drake felt his jaw drop because Taylor was standing at the top of the stairs. Oh, she didn't look like the sweet blonde she'd been before. She'd cut her hair into a short bob that barely reached her jawline, and it was a rich mahogany red. She'd lost weight, or maybe not since muscle weighed more. Her arms were proof of how much time she'd spent in a gym. She looked harder.

Even sexier than she'd been before.

Way, way more angry.

Drake stared for a moment and realized the world had turned once again, and he had landed on his ass.

Chapter Six

He looked exactly the same. Same Superman-type jawline. Same floppy well-cut hair. Same piercing eyes. She was sure if he took off the well-tailored suit she would see the same ridiculously cut abs that had once led her down the stupidest path she'd ever been on.

Luckily she wasn't the same dumbass girl she'd been when she'd met him. That woman had been different. She'd had a dad who loved her, a future she was looking forward to.

Now she had vengeance.

Yeah, it wasn't a fun version of herself.

And there was still a bit of the stupid girl inside because she couldn't help but think about how good he looked.

"Taylor. I…" His eyes were wide and his jaw slightly open as though he couldn't quite believe what he was seeing. Like he'd seen a ghost. He turned his gaze to Brad. "You told me she was in custody."

Brad had a hand to his head and had to take a long breath before he replied. There was a defensiveness to his stance that couldn't be denied. "No. I never said that. I told you her whereabouts were classified. I know you're not going to believe me, but I only figured out she was Taylor Cline a few days ago. Due to the nature of this op, keeping her face from being seen by anyone at the Agency who she might come in contact with was paramount. I worked with her remotely. She had a call sign, and that was what we used to communicate with. When I got her actual records I knew we would have to have a talk, but this is more than I expected, too. I didn't get the whole story from you, did I?"

Whole story? She got the feeling she was the one who didn't know it. Taylor felt Kim move in behind her, and it was good to know she wasn't alone here. Drake and Kyle looked comfy, and a couple of things fell into place.

Drake was the one Kyle had worked with. Drake had been the agent who'd overseen Julia Ennis and Kyle Hawthorne's missions. Julia Ennis had been turned by The Consortium. Taylor's mission was all about taking down that group, hence it made sense he would be the one to take over.

Unfortunately for him, sense didn't mean a thing to her. She wasn't working with the man who'd fucked her over.

"I didn't get the whole story either." There was a whole lot of accusation in Drake's tone. "I was led to assume that her being in custody meant that she was in some kind of prison. I'd like to know where she was held and when she was let out. I want an entire report on what she's been doing the last year and a half."

Oh, was he not happy to see her? "There's no need for you to get my files. I won't be working with you."

Drake's expression softened, a sure sign he still thought he could get to her. "Taylor, I want to talk to you. I need to talk to you, but I have to sort this out with Brad first. This mission is important or I promise you I would drop everything for the chance to talk to you again. Can we meet in an hour? Have you had dinner?"

"Dude, she is not going to talk to you alone," Kyle whispered loud enough that she could hear. "That woman is pissed, and she's going to take your balls if she gets a chance."

At least one of them had good instincts. She might keep Kyle when she dumped Drake—who seemed to be under the mistaken impression that he was the one who wasn't expendable. He seemed to think the op could go on without her, and that made her wonder exactly what he'd been told.

"She has zero reason to be angry with me," Drake replied. "But I am confused about a whole lot of things. However, the mission comes first. Taylor, are you working tech on this? I was told the crew was small. I didn't realize Constance had a tech."

"He doesn't know." Kim's voice was far lower than Kyle's, proving she actually didn't want to be heard. "He has no idea. How do you know him?"

"It doesn't matter," Taylor whispered before turning Drake's way. "Constance doesn't have a tech."

"Then why are you here? Did you come looking for me?" Drake asked, one side of his mouth curling up slightly in an arrogant smile.

Of course he thought that. He thought she'd been pining for him, had begged for the assignment so she could get close to him again. He thought she was some pathetic thing who would actually long for the man who'd tricked her into bed. He'd probably done it a thousand times. "I barely remember your name. If I'd known you were the one they were sending, I would have explained to Brad that I won't be working with you."

His lips flattened out. "Okay, I'm not sure what that attitude is about, but we're going to talk about it after I deal with Brad and Constance."

"Drake," Brad began.

Oh, she wasn't about to let Brad take this moment from her. "I am Constance."

The room seemed to freeze for a moment, and then Kyle chuckled. "I was about to say I'm pretty sure she's Constance. So how did he screw you over? Was it on an op or did it involve his dick?"

"Oh, as mad as she is it was definitely his dick," Kim replied. "It might have been on an op, but his dick was involved."

What had truly been involved was her naivety. "It doesn't matter. Brad, I'm not going to work with Mr. Radcliffe. He goes or the op is off."

"How are you Constance?" Drake was shaking his head. "Constance has been with the Agency for twelve years. She's one of our deadliest operatives."

"Constance is exactly who I say she is." She'd come up with the idea to create an operative. The classified nature of the Agency and intelligence operations around the world meant she could get away with a lot. With the help of a couple of people who didn't know exactly what they were doing—and one who did—she'd managed to hack into some of the most secure data bases in the world in order to support the fiction she'd created.

"I don't understand." Drake took a step toward her, those expensive loafers climbing on the stairs.

She could explain the last eighteen months of her life to him, could point out all the ways she'd been brilliant and had fooled the entire intelligence world. But she didn't care. "You don't have to. You can leave or I will. I'm not working with you."

"Taylor, I'm not sure what mistaken impression you've been given, but we can fix this," he vowed, still moving toward her. "Let's grab a beer and talk this out. I know it's going to surprise you, but I've been thinking a lot about you lately. I have a confession to make. I'm glad you're here because I was planning on breaking you out of wherever the Agency was holding you, baby. This saves me potential jail time."

She had to laugh at the thought, though she wasn't feeling amused. He honestly thought she was a moron. "I've been gone for a year and a half, and I suspect you could have found out where I was at any point in time."

"No, he couldn't have." Brad didn't look amused either, but then he should know she was going to fire him, too. "I didn't know where you were half the time. Only the director and his deputy knew precisely where you were, and I didn't know your real name until very recently or I would have dealt with this situation. Taylor, I know he went about trying to get information about your father in a way that seems distasteful..."

"Distasteful?" Outrage sparked through her.

"I wasn't trying to..." Drake stopped two steps down from her, his hands fisting at his sides. "Taylor, I did not sleep with you to get information on your father."

"You asshole." Kim moved out from behind her.

Drake's hand came up as though he was trying to fend off the oncoming attack. "Now, Solo, you know how these things go. It was mentioned to me that she and her father were lying about his whereabouts. I knew he was taking side trips to Moscow-friendly countries. So yes, I know her father was a double, but I don't blame her. Of course she helped him. He was her father. She might not have known what was happening."

Despite the fact that she'd known what the Agency suspected, hearing it from Drake's lips made her flush with anger all over again. Did everyone think her father was a traitor? Had the Agency used those rumors to bolster their position in the world? Did everyone who knew her before think she was in prison because she'd betrayed her country?

"So you slept with her to find out," Kim accused.

"No. I slept with her because she's gorgeous and I cared about her. I slept with her because I wanted to sleep with her," Drake argued.

Well, of course he did now that there was an op involved. It wasn't like the man had come looking for her. He said he'd been "planning" to find her, but he'd likely known where she was all along.

"But you knew the Agency was investigating Lev," Kim countered.

"He knew because I told him." Brad jumped into the fray.

"He told me, but I never once asked her a question." Drake stared Kim down. "I didn't use my position with her for anything but to get close on a personal level. She was leaving. She was getting out. I made plans with her for after she left."

He'd made lots of plans. All of them lies.

"Look, I told him what I knew because he was there and he needed all the information I could give him," Brad explained. "I certainly didn't tell him to sleep with her. I told him to be careful."

He had been. He'd carefully maneuvered her into a position where she would have told him anything. Those questions had been coming. Drake would never have been so overt as to simply ask her. Not in the beginning. He'd set himself up to be in her life for a little while. He would have taken that time to make her comfortable. When she'd slept, he might have slipped out of bed and looked through her laptop. Probably downloaded it for later inspection. If they'd had more time, he would have casually gotten her to talk about her father.

Her father's death had fucked with Drake's plans. How sad for him.

Drake held up both hands. "We're not getting anywhere with this. I need to know what happened that day. I need to know where they took Taylor and where her father is. I'm done being kept in the dark. Where's the conference room? We're going to sit down and hash this out after I've spoken to Taylor privately."

She wasn't going to be alone with him. "You can do whatever you like. I'm going to call the director and explain that I'm not going to work with you."

"And he'll explain that there is no op without me," Drake returned with a savage edge. "You have no idea how close I am to this. This doesn't happen without me or Kyle."

"Then find yourself another operative." She wasn't actually going to walk away. She'd worked too hard for this, but she wasn't letting Drake have the upper hand. She turned and started up the stairs. "Kim, if you're okay with it, we can head back to Bliss."

She'd made it to the big landing when she felt a hand on her elbow. She turned and Drake was right there, his handsome face flushed with emotion.

"You're not going anywhere. I know there's been some kind of apocalyptic misunderstanding here, but if you're involved in this op then you're involved with me."

She pulled her arm away. "I assure you, no one is more involved than me, and I don't care if you were the one who was asleep at the wheel when Julia Ennis turned. Your guilt means nothing to me. I'm sure you're feeling like your ego got trashed because a female agent outwitted you, but I don't care. Julia Ennis set in motion the plan that ended up killing my father. At least that's what we thought at the time. Now we know she's been alive all this time, so she might have been the one to actually pull the trigger. That's why he's dead. You didn't stop her. Hell, she was probably pretty and you were too busy trying to fuck her to see she was working you over."

"Don't."

That shouted command hadn't come from Drake. It had come from Kyle Hawthorne. Drake had gone from a red flush to his face a pasty white, and he'd taken a step back.

Kyle, on the other hand, was the perfect vision of rage. "Don't talk to him like that. I don't know what he did to you, and right now I couldn't care less. He's not the one who fucked Julia. That was me. I was the one who couldn't see the snake in my bed. Don't talk to him like that because he lost more than anyone. She was his sister. She was his only sibling in the world, and she betrayed him utterly. So back the fuck off because he's not going anywhere."

Sister?

"She was…" Drake took a moment. "Sorry. I've thought she was dead for long enough that I have to remind myself to use the present. Julia is my half sister. We share a mother but not a father. I didn't talk about her much then because she'd recently died. Well, she'd been injured and managed to go underground until a few weeks ago. We won't be dismissed from this op because no one knows her better than Kyle and me. Though apparently I don't know everything since I had no idea she'd killed your father. Was he working with her?"

"Fuck you, Drake." She turned again. He'd slammed her with that information, but he was still the same man. He still thought her father was a traitor, and he'd used her to try to prove it. The fact that his sister had been involved made it all the more suspect that he would want to prove her dad was a bad guy.

"You're one to talk. Your father was a literal double agent," he shot back. "Don't look at me like I'm tainted, Taylor. I would think you would have some sympathy for me. At least I didn't help Julia. I might have been a moron when it came to my sister, but you facilitated your father's crimes. You helped him cover up the fact that he was meeting his Kremlin handlers in Havana."

It was more than she could take, and she rounded on him. "He was meeting doctors in Havana."

That seemed to stop him cold. The self-righteous look on his face faltered. "Doctors? Why would he need Cuban doctors? He could have had American doctors."

Ah, Americans couldn't admit anyone knew more than they did.

She was an American and even she saw this flaw in her homeland. No one could possibly know more than an American. "American doctors don't have access to CIMAvax. It's too tainted, you know. Might get socialism from it. Or you might cure lung cancer. My father didn't turn. He got sick and he refused to die because the government won't let doctors use the one drug that might have cured him."

Her father hadn't been the only America citizen in those clinics. Wealthy Americans worked around the rules all the time.

He'd wanted to live because he'd been all she had, because he'd had more work to do, because he should have been able to.

Her heart ached, and then she was weary all over again.

Kim put a hand on her shoulder. "Come on. Let's give the guys some time to cool off. We can talk about how to proceed."

At least someone was the voice of reason. It seemed like the Agency's twisty-turny rules of who knew what and when had fucked them both over, but it didn't change what Drake had done. It only made it worse, leaving her feeling vulnerable in a way she hadn't for months. Not since she'd woken up in a CIA black ops site and realized the world had shifted and she'd been left alone.

"Taylor," he called out as she started up the stairs.

She didn't turn around. There wasn't anything left to say.

* * * *

Drake stared at her, feeling more helpless than he had in forever.

He wasn't the guy who felt helpless. He was the guy who controlled everything, the one who shifted the players around on the board because he was the mastermind. It was what his father had trained him to be since he was a little kid. He would be the puppet master, a benevolent god who took care of the world and all those innocent people in it.

Except it had all been a lie because he didn't control shit.

Sometimes he wondered if it had been his father who'd sold him on a lie or if he'd simply not been up to the task set for him.

"Hey, man, are you okay?"

He knew something had to be seriously wrong for Kyle to

sound like he gave a shit. "I am confused and angry, and I know who I'm mad at and it isn't her."

Nope. If Taylor had been lied to, then he was sure he looked like the bad guy. Of course, he knew who the real bad guy was.

Brad must have seen the rage in his eyes because he took a step back. "I know you're not going to believe me, but I didn't know it was her until recently. I'm telling you they've kept this op as classified as possible. No one knew about it until they were ready to go. She's been working directly with the deputy director, and she hasn't been talking. I thought she was gone, too. I just got the records on what's been happening."

"And why didn't I get them?"

Brad's eyes narrowed. "Because I'm supposed to make the call as to whether you even work on this, Drake. I'm supposed to bring the two of you out here and assess whether or not you're capable of working this. I know you think you're in charge, but you're not. I am until such time as I sign off and let you take over. She's nonnegotiable. She is the op. You're being allowed in because of your prior knowledge to the target and because…"

"Because I'm my father's son."

"Something like that, yes," Brad allowed, and his defensive posture seemed to melt. "Drake, we've been friends for years. Come on. Let's sit down and have a drink and I'll tell you what I know and we'll figure this thing out. Hawthorne, you have to know where the good stuff is."

Kyle sighed as though he wanted to argue but had decided against it. "Yeah. Come on. There's a bar in the dungeon."

"Dungeon?" Brad asked.

At least one thing had gone right. He got to watch his uptight coworker deal with the fact that he was in a sex club. "Yeah, it's a BDSM club. You should get used to it if you're going to kick me out and work the op yourself."

How had Taylor taken the news? Had she been shocked?

If the world hadn't intervened, she would be used to clubs by now because they would be regulars. She would be wearing his collar, and he would be used to taking care of her.

The world? It hadn't been the world. It had been the CIA.

Where was her room? He needed to explain some things to her.

Kyle had started up the stairs and put a hand on his shoulder. "Don't follow her. You'll only make things worse. I can assure you Solo won't let her leave until she understands what's going on. My uncle is coming in tomorrow. She'll want to talk to him. You need a plan in place if you want to stay on this op and have any chance of talking to her again. You go after her tonight and Solo changes her mind. I can promise you that."

"She's already texted me." Brad held his phone up. "Solo says she's talking to Taylor now, and if you leave her be they'll hang around for the meeting with Taggart."

"She can't expect me not to talk to her." It was obvious they'd both been played. Surely she could see that.

"You need a plan, and not one where you expect anything from her," Kyle said with a shake of his head. "Like I said. That woman would rather carve your balls off with a rusty spoon than talk to you, and I do the dishes around here. She can find one. You need a strategic retreat and to replan this whole op or you're going to be the one on the other side of the fence, and I need you, man. I cannot have whatever went down between you and Constan...Taylor...whatever her name is endanger this mission. Julia is out there, and while I might have bought us some time with the whole blowing myself up thing, she's going to come after me eventually. So you can come with me and strategize or I can walk up there and tell Taylor I'm all in with her and call my uncle and cut you out."

Bitterness washed over him. "Of course you would."

Kyle sighed. "I know you're not going to like this, but it's tough love. I don't have the time or patience right now to do what I should do and handle you with kid gloves. Something went down between the two of you and it's rattled you. So let's find out what Brad knows and then figure out where to go from there. And let's do it over some excellent whiskey that Sandra owes me because she pays shit."

"The kid is right," Brad said. "We need to talk this out. I'll tell you everything I know."

"The kid is over thirty and has more blood on his hands than you'll ever know," Kyle said with an arrogant smirk as he strode by Brad. "So fuck off and know I'm watching you."

Brad frowned Drake's way. "What is that supposed to mean?"

Drake began to follow. Kyle was probably right. The instinct to go after Taylor would likely get him in trouble, and he did need to figure out what Brad knew. His whole night was fucked, and he could use a drink.

He didn't pay attention to where he was going, simply followed Kyle down the long hallway. Out of the corner of his eye he caught sight of what looked like a playroom. There was a St. Andrew's Cross on the wall and several spanking benches. He was sure if he walked in there would be familiar objects.

Yep. He'd walked back into Taggart world, and this was proof. Kyle turned left and walked through a set of French doors into what looked like an oddly elegant Wild West saloon. There was a big bar and seating that overlooked another part of the dungeon, this one seemingly constructed for suspension play. There were three stages across the big ballroom, and it would be easy to watch what was going on from the luxurious bar. In addition to the bar proper, there was a seating area with loungers and big fluffy pillows for sweet subs to sit on while their Masters and Mistresses took the sturdy chairs. He eyed a long poker table to the side.

Sandra had finally built her version of heaven, and he was happy for her.

Unfortunately, her version of heaven looked like it would be his own personal Waterloo.

Kyle moved around the bar and grabbed a bottle from the cabinet underneath. "Brad, you should start talking."

Brad had followed them, and he stood at the doorway. "What is this place?"

Well, it was good to know he wasn't the only one whose night hadn't gone the way he'd thought it would. Drake sank down to one of the chairs around a table in the center of the area. "It's a dungeon. Get used to it. When are play nights?"

Kyle set the bottle on the table along with three glasses. "The usual. Thursday through Saturday nights. The entrance is in the back so the club and the bar stay separate, but you'll find it's a little different than Dallas. This is the West, gentlemen, and not a lot has changed in the last hundred years. People mind their business. When they say no gossip here, they mean it."

So no one would be talking about the strangers walking around. That was probably why Taggart had hidden his nephew here. Sandra would have made sure her employees didn't talk, and the rest wouldn't care about the stranger as long as he kept to himself and didn't cause trouble.

They had no idea what kind of trouble Kyle could cause.

Brad stood there, looking at the room like it was some ring of hell he wouldn't be able to get out of if he walked in. "I've never been in a club like this."

"You've never worked with my uncle." Kyle poured out two fingers into all three glasses. "No one's going to force you to fuck, Brad. The good news is you've reached the planet of consent. You're way safer here then you are in one of your bro bars."

Brad walked over to the table. "Is this where you spend your time?"

"Here? No. I've never been here," Drake replied.

Brad huffed, a frustrated sound. "No. I mean in DC. You never come out with us, but I'm pretty sure I've heard you talking about going to a club."

"It's called The Court, and yes, I'm a member." He wasn't ashamed of his proclivities. He enjoyed the lifestyle and the honesty it offered. He'd watched powerful men get their asses kicked out of The Court by the Domme who ran it. "I'm a member of several clubs."

"Not Sanctum," Kyle said, passing him a glass.

"You're not at Sanctum, either, buddy." He wasn't sure why Kyle was pushing him, but he could push back. "We're both at The Club. Tell me something. Is MaeBe a member of The Club or Sanctum?"

"I thought Sanctum was the club," Brad said, sinking to his seat. "Wait. Did Julia go to a club?"

"No," they both said at the same time.

Kyle picked up one of the glasses and shot it back. "But she knows about me. Part of her play with Nolan Byrne was to tell him she'd had a Dom. I was never her top. Not once. I didn't get involved in the lifestyle until my uncle basically shoved me at Julian Lodge and told him to fix me. Which is rude."

"Did he?" Drake knew how those things went. Sex wouldn't have been the only thing on the menu. Therapy would have been a big part of getting into The Club, and Big Tag would have been sneaky about it. There would have been sessions to see if the applicant was a good fit that would have led to the applicant talking about shit he hadn't meant to and oops, he suddenly felt better and...

He suddenly wanted to talk to The Court's resident therapist. Damn it. It had worked on him, too. Fucking lifestylists needed everyone to be healthy and shit.

"Did he make me feel better that the woman I thought I cared about turned bad and I had to kill her?" Kyle asked, pouring out another drink. "Yes. Until she came back from the dead. Now I'm questioning things again."

Drake was pretty much questioning everything. In this case at least a couple of his questions could be answered by the man sitting across the table from him. "Start talking."

Brad frowned down at the glass in front of him. "Shouldn't this have like some soda in it? Or ice?"

Kyle snorted. If there was one thing Kyle could be pretentious about it was liquor. He had surprisingly elevated tastes when it came to liquor and wine. And food. Or maybe not surprisingly since his mom and stepdad ran a restaurant empire, and Top didn't serve fast food. Kyle reached for Brad's glass, taking it away from him. "You don't cut this perfection with freaking soda. This was aged in oak barrels for fifteen years. When you smell it you can smell the peat and loam of the Highlands of Scotland. There is history in this glass. You don't deserve it. Go make yourself a white wine spritzer or something."

"Oh, that sounds..." Brad shook his head. "I'm fine. Working. No need to drink, and also I get the feeling I'll have to sleep with one eye open, and that's not really fair."

"Talk or you'll sleep way longer than you want," Drake threatened.

A long sigh went through Brad, and he sat back. "The day I

showed up in Romania to get you all I'd been told was that Lev Sokolov's handlers were done playing around and were ready to bring his daughter in for questioning. I assumed that meant they'd decided the likelihood of him being a true double agent was too much of a risk to leave him in the field, and they were going to use Taylor to get him to talk."

"And you were okay with that?" He could only imagine how they would use Taylor. Most of the people he knew had a conscience and would never hurt a prisoner, but those weren't the people who usually were left with prisoners. He knew sometimes it was important to get a person to talk—especially when other lives were at risk—but he couldn't stand the thought of Taylor being left at the mercy of the Agency's best interrogators.

"It wasn't my place to be okay with anything, Drake." Brad took on a professional tone. "I was working another mission, and you were involved in it. As far as I knew, you had done exactly what you'd told me you'd done. You had slept with her to get intel, and you didn't care what happened to her. You pivoted quickly. We were in Budapest eight hours later, and you never mentioned her name again."

"That feels cold." Kyle took another drink, sipping this time. "And maybe meant as a distraction. Drake's not good at acknowledging his feelings."

Drake sent Kyle a pointed stare. "And you are?"

A big shoulder shrugged. "Takes one to know one. How did you end up meeting her? I ask because I've been your friend for years and never heard her name, yet there seems to be a connection."

"She was after."

Kyle nodded. "Understood."

After the world had blown up. After Kyle had walked away.

"I met her at a safe house. We were both there at the same time. I was into her but then the Agency came and hauled her away and I had to rethink. Until now I worried maybe her being there wasn't such a coincidence," Drake admitted. "I know that sounds paranoid, but I'd been caught in a bad place, and we were worried about a potential leak. She was in the area. I wasn't sure if she'd meant for me to need the safe house or if that was merely an effect of what she'd done. We figured out a few months later that she had nothing to do with my asset being killed, but by then the damage was done and she was still under investigation for aiding her father's betrayal. Which turns out to not be a betrayal at all."

"What's the deal with Cuban medicine?" Kyle asked. "She said her dad could only get..."

"CIMAvax," Brad replied. "Years ago the Cubans created a vaccine against lung cancer. It works as a treatment as well. Because of trade embargoes and sanctions against the Cuban government, these medications aren't available to Americans unless they sneak into the country. I believe the drugs are available in Peru as well. There are similar drugs now making their way through the FDA, but it could still be a while before they're routine."

"And they work?" Kyle asked.

Drake nodded, his gut in a knot. Taylor had been trying to save her father's life, not helping him betray his country. It was illegal, what he'd done, but Drake could understand it. How could someone simply accept death when there was a drug out there that could prolong their life or cure them? Wouldn't anyone with the resources have done what Taylor did? "All indications are yes. We'll have them on the American market at some point, but that doesn't help the people who are dying here now. Is Lev Sokolov actually dead?"

"As far as I know. In our world is anyone really dead?" Brad asked. "Isn't that why we're in the position we're in now?"

"Julia seemed pretty fucking dead to me." Kyle poured himself another drink. "I left her body in a burning building. Next time I'll make sure to take it with me so I can kill her again if she wakes up."

"As for Lev, all our intel shows he died on a mission. On a mission that included The Consortium operative we now believe was actually Julia," Brad explained. "Now that we understand who we're looking for, we believe Julia spent a couple of weeks recovering from the damage she took in Singapore. After that, she began working full time for The Consortium. The security cameras were grainy, but we believe it was her. Killing Lev was one of her first acts, perhaps the one that solidified her place with the group."

"How did she know about Lev?" His treacherous sister had killed Taylor's dad. She would never forgive him. While he'd been seducing her, his sister had been taking out her father. "Why target him?"

"Because he was working on The Consortium," Kyle said, sitting back, glass still in hand. "I even remember talking to him in a bar one night. Not while Julia was around. I worked with him a couple of times, though I never met Taylor."

"He kept her out of sight as much as he could," Brad explained. "It was important to Lev that Taylor not show up on anyone's radar. She was insistent about running her father's tech. She'd done it since she was a kid. Very strange education, that one."

"I can only imagine." She'd talked a lot about how she'd moved across the globe with her father, trained in ways most preteens didn't. She'd basically grown up in the Agency. Like he had. Another way they connected, though he'd had a prep school education. Of course that education had been as much about gathering intel for his father as it had getting into an Ivy League. He'd basically been undercover since he'd understood what it meant to be.

Except with her. He'd been himself with her. Or some version of himself he'd actually liked.

"Lev was working on identifying the group that had taken up the work of The Collective, and that included recruiting operatives from intelligence agencies across the globe," Brad explained. "It's in the report, and I'll be going over everything with Taggart's group tomorrow afternoon. If he's still coming. Do we still have an op? I'm not sure she'll want to work with me. You do understand that there's no op without Constance Tyne, and Constance Tyne doesn't exist without Taylor. That day she was taken into custody and once everything was sorted out, she was offered this mission. From what I can tell, she's the one who came up with the idea of creating a superagent for The Consortium to recruit. She's not going anywhere."

Yeah, his brain was already working on that one, but he might have to shelve that plan. "She's not getting rid of me, and I'm not allowing her to walk away."

It was the one thing he couldn't do. Now that he'd seen her again, he knew he'd been a stupid bastard to have not gone after her.

It had been shitty timing. Had it happened today, he would have gone after her. Had it happened before Julia's death, he would have gone after her. But he'd been caught between mourning his sister and hating her, believing his every instinct was wrong, and how could something as good as Taylor be real?

Brad stood. "All right, then. I'm going to go and talk to Solo and make sure they don't slip away in the night. You know where you're going? We've got a room on the third floor. Now that I know where I am, I have questions about the room."

Drake shook his head. "Ask Sandra."

Brad ambled out, seemingly happy to be getting back to business.

"So you're in love with Taylor." Kyle didn't make it a question.

"You've hung around your family far too long." Drake took his first drink. Kyle was right. The whiskey tasted of peat and smoke and spice. It was delicious. It was probably going to get the job done if he drank enough of it. Maybe if he drank the bottle he could forget the look on Taylor's face when she'd seen him.

"Okay. We're not ready to use the *L* word yet," Kyle allowed. "Are you telling me you're going to be able to keep your emotions out of this and simply do the job?"

"Nope." Well, he wasn't going to lie to the man.

"So we need a plan because I assure you she's making one right now," Kyle pointed out. "If you're not careful, you're going to get kicked off the op, and I need you."

He sighed. She wouldn't like what he was about to do. What he was about to do would make him seem like the entitled asshole she thought he was. Still, he had to make sure she didn't kick him off the op. He pulled his cell phone out and hit number four on his speed dial. Despite the lateness of the hour, it picked up immediately.

"Hey, did you get in okay?" Lydia sounded like she'd been sitting there waiting for him to call. "How is the vacation going? I'm going to need you to send me proof that you're actually relaxing."

He would have to handle this carefully. "It's great. I checked into the hotel and it's as nice as you promised. Everything is going well but something crept up, and I have one last thing I need to take care of."

Lydia groaned over the line. "I knew this was about work. Why not just tell me? I can be out there in the morning. What's the op?"

There was a reason he'd left Lydia out of this. "It's a loose end I need to clean up but a big one. After this I'm hopping on a yacht for a couple of days, and I promise I'll send you some pics to prove I'm relaxing." Lydia had been his tech for years, but he wasn't her only operative. She didn't have clearance for this, and he would rather keep the circle tight. Still, she'd taken a liking to him a long time ago, probably because she was a smart girl and knew he would carry her with him as he made his way through the ranks. And he had. "I need you to call some of your contacts and have the big guy call me in the morning."

"The director? I can get him on the line tonight," Lydia promised.

"Not the director. The really big guy," Drake corrected.

There was a pause on the line. "All right. I can get him on the line, too. I've heard he's a night owl. Are you sure you're okay?"

He tried to sound as positive as possible. "I'm fine. Just one problem I need to cut off at the pass and then I can relax."

"All right, give me a minute. You know I would only ever do this for you." She hung up, and Drake sat back.

"Who's bigger than the director?" Kyle's brow had risen.

"No one, according to him."

If Kyle cared that he hadn't answered his question, he didn't show it. "Well, the big guy in my life should be here in roughly twelve hours, and you better be able to explain why the op has already gone south."

"It hasn't."

"If we lose Taylor it has."

"She won't be going anywhere." Now that he thought about it, he could call her bluff. He simply needed an ironclad place in this operation and she would fold. She'd loved her father. She wanted revenge. She would have to decide if her need for revenge was greater than her need to fuck him over. He was betting his career on the outcome of that small but significant battle.

And then the bigger battle could begin because this op was

more important than ever. He'd thought this op was about cleaning up the past.

Now he knew it was about securing his future with her.

"How do you know that?" Kyle asked.

His cell trilled and he picked it up, a feminine voice coming over the line and asking him to hold. Which he did. Then a deep voice.

"Radcliffe?"

"Hello, Mr. President. Thank you for taking my call."

Kyle's eyes rolled. "Show off."

He started his call and accepted that the battle had begun.

Chapter Seven

"What do you mean he's untouchable?" Taylor stared at Kim over coffee in the private dining room. Not that they had a chef or anything. She'd been told this room served as an informal meeting space for members of Sandra Croft's club.

When she'd heard she was going to be staying in a BDSM club, she'd kind of been excited. She'd studied up, and the one thing she'd allowed herself to do in the last year and a half was go to clubs in the areas she'd been in. She'd claimed she needed them because many of the high-powered CEOs who might be in The Consortium also attended the clubs. It would be good, she'd explained, to have a practical knowledge of clubs. But she'd been lying. She'd wanted to escape.

You wanted to see if it would be the same with someone else. Except then you refused to sleep with someone else because someone else wasn't Drake.

She took a long sip of coffee, banishing that damn voice in her head. She'd shut it up the night before, too, when it had told her to go find him and have the fight they'd needed for almost two years.

They didn't need anything because there was no *they*. There was her and him, and never shall they meet again.

Except they were going to because if what Kim had told her was true, Drake wasn't going anywhere.

"Beck called me early this morning." Kim looked gorgeous with her long blonde hair framing her face. "My husband still has some serious connections. Apparently someone got the president up in the middle of the night, and suddenly I'm getting a call from the deputy director who explains that I need to get you on board because Drake Radcliffe isn't going anywhere. I can put two and two together. He's gone around you and made sure you can't dismiss him."

That overly privileged asshole. Well, he could force himself into the situation, but he couldn't force her to stay. "Then he can have the whole op. Let's see him deal with it."

"You're going to let him get his way?" Sandra walked over from the buffet she'd put together. "You know he almost always does. It would do the kid some good to get set on his ass for once."

Sandra was a lovely woman. Her file claimed she was in her seventies, but she looked far younger. There was a vibrancy about the woman. And a certain level of authority. She would bet Sandra wore the leathers in her relationship. Her wife was a bit younger and far softer than Sandra.

"I don't think I can call up the leader of the free world and make him change his mind." Frustration had a stranglehold on her this morning. Morning? It had been choking her since the moment she'd realized Drake was in the house.

Sandra sank onto the chair beside her. "So you're going to give up an op you've been working for months. I don't know a lot about it, but I've heard you've been brilliant. Most people would want to see it through. What did the kid do to you?"

Kim leaned over. "I think he seduced her for info on her dad."

Seduced was such a soft word. Fucked over was much more descriptive.

"I seduced her because I wanted to sleep with her, but I can't make her see that." Drake stepped into the room. His hair wasn't slicked back like normal, and he was wearing flannel pajama bottoms and a V-neck T-shirt. He looked like he'd recently woken up and wasn't happy about it. He glanced Sandra's way. "Hey, I drank your whiskey last night. Sorry. It was a rough night, and that whiskey was too tempting to pass up since I couldn't have what I truly wanted. I'll replace it."

Sandra chuckled. "That was Angie's. She's the whiskey drinker, and she'll appreciate the fact that you didn't call it Scotch. I prefer tequila myself. There's coffee over there. Is Kyle as hung over as you are?"

"Kyle barely looked like he drank anything, but he had half that bottle. I don't know where he puts it. His liver must be gold plated or something." He put a hand to his back, looking adorably rumpled. "I think I slept on a spanking bench."

Sandra chuckled. "If you're in the big privacy room and you weren't smart enough to know there's a Murphy bed in the wall, then you probably did. Didn't want to cuddle with the Agency suit?"

As far as she could tell Drake *was* the Agency suit.

That wasn't fair. She knew about his record, knew the missions he'd been on, but he was obviously in management now and had been for a while.

Had he known his sister was going after her father? Had he been sent to Romania to distract her?

There was a leak somewhere in the Agency, and it just might be Drake Radcliffe.

She hadn't thought about it. She'd been so dragged down by her own misery and shame that she hadn't thought about the fact that he could be the leak. It made sense. He'd been there. He'd been the reason she'd been distracted that week.

She needed to go back over every minute of that time they'd spent together. He'd been so injured. So injured that the bullet hadn't hit any vital organs, and he'd managed to drive himself all the way up a mountain only to have an accident that hadn't exactly been dangerous.

What if it had all been for show? What if there had been no mission he'd gotten hurt on?

What if she'd always been the mission?

"I'm kind of mad at him," Drake was saying. "Not kind of. I'm extremely mad at him. And I don't cuddle with people I'm mad at."

"No. You only do that with the ones you need information

from."

She had not meant to say that out loud. She'd intended to ignore the man completely until she figured out how to get around the whole he knew the president thing. She wasn't giving up on getting rid of him.

He turned her way. "We didn't get to cuddle. Brad interrupted our cuddle time, and I'm pissed about that, too. I'm an excellent cuddler, and if you knew that maybe we wouldn't have wasted a year and a half."

So that was his play. He was going to be charming again. Well, it had worked once, so it wasn't a bad plan. It wouldn't work again, but he probably had a low opinion of her IQ and instincts.

"I don't consider it wasted. I spent that time on an important mission that now I have to walk away from because your ego can't handle stepping aside and letting me do my job." She stood, sick to death at what she might have to do. "Kim, I know you agreed to work another couple of days, but I think I'm done here."

Kim's eyes had gone wide. "I think you should at least wait until Big Tag gets here. If you're walking away, you have to bring everyone up to speed on the op. We can't do anything if you're unwilling to even talk to the team you're handing this off to."

"I will answer any questions Mr. Taggart has." Didn't she get some time to think? Obviously not. Drake was here and all of her power was gone. She was supposed to be the head of this op, but naturally some man had walked in and decided he knew more than she did, had more of a stake than she did.

Was she willing to walk away?

"Why don't we take a walk and talk about this?" Kim offered.

It was an excellent idea. Kim was the voice of reason, but she didn't want reason right now. She'd worked herself up to start this mission, and now it was falling apart around her.

"Or she could sit down with me and we could talk this out." Drake poured himself a cup of coffee. "If we're going to work together, we should probably talk like adults."

She didn't like the accusation that she hadn't been an adult up to this point, but perhaps it was time to talk to him. "Fine. You should talk fast."

She strode out of the dining room and into the hall, Drake hard on her heels.

"I did not come here to step on your toes, Taylor. And I'm truly sorry about your father. I was going off what Brad told me at the time. We seem to have both misunderstood the situation."

"Yes, I can see this is my fault, too." Asshole.

"I didn't mean it like that." He moved quickly to get in front of her, stopping her before she made it to the stairs. "I meant you're under the assumption that our relationship was about gathering intel, and nothing could be further from the truth."

"Did you know my father was under investigation? When you went into the comms room the day after you got to the safe house, did anyone mention my father?" She was sure they had since her initial interrogators had told her they hadn't gotten any real information out of Drake. She'd heard them talking. But she suspected Drake wouldn't tell her the truth.

He went silent for a moment, and his head hung slightly, a weary expression. He glanced down the hallway and then gently gripped her elbow, guiding her into the room to her left. He opened the door and ushered her inside. "Yeah. They mentioned it. My tech always has her ear to the ground, and she gives me every piece of information she can. It's what makes her valuable. But that doesn't mean I act on every rumor or bit of intelligence she gives me."

The lights sputtered on, a soft blue coating the room. He'd found one of the playrooms, of course. This one was done in greens and blues, with soft surfaces all around and a gilded cage in the center that would likely hold several naughty subs. They could be held there for various infractions or held there before they were "auctioned" off for the night. All in all, it looked like a fun place to play.

Drake didn't look around. All of his attention was on her. "After you told me you were planning on getting out, I didn't consider you as any kind of threat."

It was nice to know he could be honest about some things. "And my father?"

"You are not your father," he said quietly. "You weren't then and you aren't now."

"No, I'm not, but I assure you I am every inch his daughter." She'd been planning on proving it to everyone.

"Do you honestly think he would want you involved in something this dangerous?" Drake asked, his tone going gentle. "Do you think he would want to put you in this position?"

Her father had taught her how to work tech for him when she was twelve. "I think he prepared me for the world he lived in. Are you going to tell me I'm incompetent now?"

The blue from the lights above shaded his expression. What would he look like walking through this space in leathers?

"Absolutely not," Drake replied. "From what I can tell, you're perfectly competent when it comes to crafting a mission. I've looked through some of the Constance Tyne records and I would never be able to tell they're not more than a year old. You're brilliant when it comes to that, but my sister is the target, and being excellent at forging records and building urban legends around an agent who doesn't exist won't save you from her."

She'd sat up a good portion of the night before thinking about his family situation, but it didn't matter in the end if she decided to walk away.

Of course if she walked away, wasn't she also walking away from a chance to get to scratch under his surface and see what lay beneath? Wasn't there a chance she was handing over her carefully laid out investigation to the very man who needed to be investigated? How much of a coincidence was it that Julia Ennis resurfaced just as Taylor was finally breaking into The Consortium's inner circle?

Was he the trap Julia had laid out for her? The bait to get her to walk in so they could take her out?

She wouldn't ever know if she walked away.

"I can handle myself."

"We're going to find out." Drake stood up taller, obviously going into professional mode. "If you're going into the field under my watch, I'm going to make sure you're ready for anything that might come your way, and that means you'll be in training for the next two weeks, and I'm going to test you. I don't know many techs who make the transition from behind the computer to in the field."

He likely didn't know many techs who'd been raised by paranoid operative fathers, but him underestimating her was in her favor. "If I go."

Drake shrugged. "That's your call, Taylor. If you want to back out, I'll still make this work. Like I said, this mission is important to me, and I'll make sure it succeeds. Either way, I would like a chance to talk to you. I'm not trying to run you off this mission."

She hated how reasonable he sounded. "But you're doing a thorough job of it nonetheless. You called in the big guns."

"Yes, and that should show you how serious I am about this op. My family is in danger."

She huffed out a laugh, though she was deeply unamused by anything about this situation. "The target is your family. The target killed my only family, so I think I have the bigger claim to this op, not to mention the fact that I've been working on it nonstop for a year and half. You've known about the op for what? A day?"

The arrogance of him. He'd walked in like he was the expert.

"I've been prepping for this since the moment we realized Julia was alive. You know that's the piece of the puzzle that clicked into place and made this op a go, right? You wouldn't be here if we hadn't figured that out."

"All that did was ramp up my timeline and potentially make things more dangerous." She'd known why the trigger had been pulled earlier than she'd expected.

"Kyle was also the one who first identified The Consortium," Drake pointed out.

"My father was working on it six months before Kyle ever made that report," she countered. "He just didn't have a desperate need for credit. Also, it was good for you to ID the very group your sister was working for. You should be commended."

"Damn, that's colder than I expected you to be."

"Well, your sister killed my dad, so there's that."

"And she would kill the rest of my family if she had to." Drake's expression turned grave. "I'm sorry I didn't see who Julia had become but I did grow up with her, so I do know her. My blinders are off now, and there's no one in the world who wants to bring her to justice more than me, except maybe Kyle. I owe Kyle most of all. You have no idea what he's given up to be here, and there's a woman out there who's still in danger. She's a woman Kyle loves, and he'll be devastated if Julia hurts her again."

"Again?" She was interested in Kyle. She should know more about the man she would be going into battle with.

"Yes, she was caught in the crossfire on the last op we were on. She works tech for McKay-Taggart. She wasn't ever supposed to get out from behind her computer, but Julia brought her into the middle of the fight. Julia is obsessed with Kyle."

"Yes, that's been made clear." He was being awfully open with her. If he was telling her the truth.

"Then you have to know this is hard on him. And not because he's in love with her."

"Because he feels betrayed. He can't love her because he never truly knew her. He's very likely questioning his every instinct. She made it hard for him to believe in himself, and her being alive and back in his life is the hardest thing he's ever gone through." Yes, she could relate to Kyle. She'd been through betrayal, too.

Drake stared at her for a moment. "It's not the same."

"I'm not sure how it's not."

A look of pure frustration crossed his face. "Because I wasn't lying to you about my feelings. Because I was right there with you, and I'm sorry I listened to a person I've trusted for a long time. I'm sorry I let my bitterness over my sister's betrayal cloud my judgment when they came for you that day. I listened to them. I believed them, and I shouldn't have. I think in some ways they wanted to separate us."

"There was no *us*." She forced herself to say the words because he was getting to her, and she couldn't let that happen. He couldn't sneak under her defenses. This time she'd built them so high and strong no one ever would again.

Was that how she wanted to live?

"Wasn't there? It felt like it to me. I know the thought of you betraying me sent me right back into an awful spiral I'd just started coming out of. Like I told you last night, I was getting ready to come looking for you, Taylor, and I didn't care where you were. I had identified a couple of places to start. I was going to find you and make sure you never got in trouble again."

"I wasn't in trouble in the first place." She couldn't believe that he'd actually thought she'd been in custody all this time.

"Well, I didn't know that." He took a cautious step toward her like he wanted to see if she would move away. "I was working under the assumption that you were in a prison. That should tell you something. I was going to break you out, and if I had to, go on the run with you."

She stood her ground. "Oh, that sounds like fun, but I think I'll have to pass."

"Not until you hear what I would have done with you." His voice had gone deeper, a sound that had haunted her every dream. That voice of his was silky and could caress her every bit as much as his big hands. "You should understand the depths of my plans when it came to you. I was going to make you my submissive, train you so that you could never betray me again."

Every word seemed to brush against her skin, making the room feel warmer than it had been before. She wasn't falling for this again. "So you were going to break me out of the Agency's prison to put me in your prison? You want to break me, Radcliffe? I'm sure you have your torture methods."

"Oh, I do," he assured her. "Mostly they involve my mouth on your pussy."

A blast of heat flashed through her along with the memory of exactly what he'd wanted her to envision. That night had been a landmark—one of those events she knew had marked her forever. He'd shown her how good sex could be and then she'd been tossed into the trash before she could even process what she'd felt. Hadn't she always wondered if that night had been a mirage? It couldn't possibly have been as good as she'd remembered. "So you were going to force yourself on me."

"Ah, but in this scenario I was the hero," he corrected. "I was the man who got you out of a terrible situation and offered you a better life than you deserved. I was the man who shut everything down so you got out, and that made you willing to show me your appreciation."

"Well, then we should be glad that scenario didn't prove to be true." Because she would never sub for him. He'd promised her they would play but that had been...not a lie, precisely. She was sure if they'd had more time, he would have shown her a thing or two. Would it have changed anything if she'd been his submissive? Why was she even thinking of this?

"Should we? It could be fun. I assure you there was no torture outside of giving you so much pleasure and taking such good care of you that you couldn't ever consider betraying me again. I was going to make sure you didn't have the energy to plot behind my back. You were going to be my sweet submissive. Did you look up what that meant? We talked about it that day, but we never got around to playing."

"We wouldn't have. I wasn't interested. I was horny, but you're making way too much of this, Drake." She was the one who was lying now. "I would never have bottomed for you."

A brow rose over his handsome face. "For a person who wasn't interested in the lifestyle, you seem to know the terminology. And don't make promises you can't keep. Did you know we're standing in a club right now?"

"Yes, I got the tour last night, and even if I hadn't the fact that the bed I'm sleeping in has a spreader bar built into the footboard would have given it away." The way she kept giving herself away.

"So you know what a spreader bar is and you know to use the word bottoming rather than submitting, but you weren't interested in the lifestyle."

She could still turn this around. "Fine. Maybe I did look into it. Maybe I was interested, but I won't bottom for you. I'll probably walk into this dungeon when it opens tonight because I need a session given the amount of stress I'm dealing with and maybe I'll pick out some hot cowboy top to help with my stress relief, but it won't be you."

"And what do I win if it is?"

"You'll win my dead body because that's what it would take."

"I like a challenge, Taylor."

"I'm not a challenge, Drake." But she could already feel the heat building between them. They'd had this insane chemistry from the moment they'd met.

125

What if he's telling the truth? What if he didn't know?

And what if he did? How would she ever know if she walked away? How would she find the truth if she took herself out of play? Perhaps she was going about this all wrong.

Perhaps in order to take down the man who'd betrayed her she needed to bring him in instead of pushing him away.

After all, wasn't that what she was doing with The Consortium?

He'd fucked her for intel. Why shouldn't she do the same?

"I know." His voice had lost the seductive quality, and there was a wealth of affection in it now. "I'm so sorry. I should have come after you no matter what I thought. Like I said, I was still bruised and battered from what happened with Julia. I was still…am still processing. I don't think I'll ever be done. She was my sister. It should be easy to hate her, but I remember playing with her, her being my friend. It's hard because she's the only person in the world who knows what it was like to grow up with our parents. Her dad was out of her life. She saw him some during the summers, but my dad took care of her most of the time."

Taylor needed time to think, and listening to his sad stories wouldn't help her make a decision. Still, she found herself wondering what it would be like to have a sibling and then to have him or her taken away, to feel the sting of betrayal from someone so close.

Would she have looked at the data the Agency would almost certainly have given him and judged herself, too?

"Hey, I was trying to find… Oh, hi, Taylor." Kyle Hawthorne stood in the doorway looking like he'd fared far better than Drake after their drinking the night before. "I'm sorry to interrupt but my uncle's on his way in. He took an earlier flight."

In other words, it was almost time for the curtain to go up, and she would be center stage.

Unless she walked away.

Drake's hand came out, fingers brushing up her arm and making her skin tingle like it was coming awake after a long sleep. "Don't be worried about Taggart. His bark is way worse than his bite, and he's quite a softie when it comes to women."

Kyle snorted. "Sure he is. That man answers to one person in the world, and my Aunt Charlotte isn't here, so good luck with that. I'm going to go find Brad and warn him. I hope there's more whiskey here. My uncle can be a bear. And I need to find someone who's good with lemons."

She had no idea what he needed with lemons, but it was a good cue to leave before she made a fool of herself.

"Hey, I was serious about talking more," Drake said as she moved by him. "It really is good to see you."

She ignored the urge to look back and see him again, too.

She walked back to her room, her mind more confused than ever.

* * * *

"No, I don't know how to make lemon bars." Drake sent Kyle a frown. "You know you're acting like the queen of England is coming to tea and you're some British debutante. He's your uncle not a celebrity you have a crush on."

"I don't have crushes on celebrities." Kyle's face settled in a fierce frown. "He's my only connection to my family. He's the only one who takes me seriously. I can't contact my mom or my brother."

"Why don't you catfish them online like you do your girlfriend?" Drake shot back. He was irritated with the way the morning had gone, and it wasn't all about the nasty hangover he had.

It was about the fact that he'd thought he had her for a moment. When he'd opened up about Julia to her, she'd been affected by his words. He'd watched her, and those shoulders had come down, her eyes had softened. If Kyle hadn't walked in she might have offered him a hug, and if he could get under her skin he might be able to salvage this thing.

Suddenly salvaging his relationship with Taylor seemed like the most important thing in the world.

"Could you two be serious for a minute?" Brad's gaze went back and forth between the two of them. He was all business this morning. He'd set up in the conference room, and he'd barely looked up from his computer. "If Taggart isn't satisfied with this plan of Taylor's, we're going to have to find another team to work with, and given the fact that we're running out of time, I suggest we make the best presentation we can."

"Like Tag's going to say no. He's not, so we can all stop treating this like a royal visit." The last thing he needed was Taggart walking in like he owned the place. He didn't. At least he was pretty sure he didn't. Big Tag could make investments in people he liked, and Sandra fit that bill.

Shit. He probably did own part of this place. But that didn't mean the man got to run his op. He was a contractor on this op, and not even a close one as the men who were working with them were former employees.

It was all complex and shitty, and what he really wanted to do was track down Taylor and talk to her some more. If he talked to her he could soften her up, tell the truth about how he'd felt back then and how he was feeling now. She'd soaked that up.

Turned out honesty and vulnerability did work. At least they'd seemed to be working.

Then she'd retreated, and he hadn't seen her for a couple of hours now. She was likely talking to Solo about ditching the op altogether and finding all kinds of new and dangerous ways to get revenge for her father's death. Drake had been astonished at the truth about Lev Sokolov. He'd known Lev had no longer been working for the Agency, and he'd believed the rumors about the man. The truth had only been in Sokolov's records and those were classified above Drake's paygrade. If he hadn't been attached to this op, he would never have known Taylor's father hadn't been a double. "We're sure Lev is dead?"

"We went over this. As sure as we can be. He looked dead, and they did an autopsy and everything," Brad replied. "But then there's an autopsy record on this guy here, and he's looking pretty lively."

Kyle sent Brad his middle finger and went back to staring out the window at the long drive that led from the highway to the bar's parking lot. The Cowgirl's Choice was set back from the highway, though there was no way to miss the big neon sign that lit up the night. It was a pink and blue and green monstrosity of a cowgirl riding a bull. Mastering a bull was more like it.

Sandra did enjoy a heavy metaphor.

"From everything I understand Lev loved his daughter. He wouldn't have faked his death and left her to the wolves," Kyle said, not looking up. "And don't say that's what I did to MaeBe. I was getting the wolf off her back, and I left her with people who will protect her. She's doing okay."

He knew because he was talking to her online. Oh, he used a voice modifier to do it, but the asshole was literally catfishing the woman he'd tried to convince he was dead. That was not going to go well for him. "Do you talk to her about you?"

Kyle turned slightly, a brow rising as though he didn't like the accusation. "We talk about her life, and she's going through a healing process."

"Wait, so you blew up a house that you were supposed to be in, left this woman you care about, and now you're pretending to be someone else so you can talk her through her breakup. Her breakup with you?" Brad seemed to grasp the situation, though it was obvious he was confused. "And you did all of this because Julia hates her?"

"Julia doesn't hate her. That's where everyone gets it wrong. Julia doesn't feel much of anything. She's a sociopath who's excellent at pretending to be a real girl," Kyle explained. "By taking myself out of MaeBe's life, she won't have a reason to go after her."

"Or you left her without protection and Julia will use her as bait to get to you," Drake pointed out. He knew how his sister worked. She would consider MaeBe a pawn and wouldn't mind sacrificing her to get to the king she wanted. Julia had decided Kyle was the man for her, and she would get what she wanted or burn the world down.

That was what he hadn't understood before. He'd known Julia could be obsessive and a bit selfish, but she could also be fierce when it came to the people she loved. Except it wasn't love. It was ownership. It was possession. Julia would never sacrifice for someone she "loved." It simply wouldn't occur to her.

Malignant narcissist. It was a good label for his sister.

How had he thought for a single second that Taylor could have anything in common with his sister?

"I left Mae with my family. I assure you they will close ranks around her," Kyle said in a superior tone. "They did exactly what I knew they would. MaeBe hasn't been allowed to go back to her apartment alone. She's staying with friends. Friends who know how to protect her."

Drake frowned Kyle's way. "How long do you plan to keep her a prisoner?"

Kyle sighed, a long-suffering sound. "She's not a prisoner."

"I bet she feels like one." He knew he shouldn't get into this with Kyle, but he couldn't help himself. He had few people he'd ever truly connected to in this world, and Kyle had been one of them. "I know MaeBe. She's lived by herself for years. She's comfortable being alone and independent, and you're taking that from her."

Kyle's jaw went tight. "For a brief time so she can be alive when I take care of Julia. I don't know what you're trying to do, Drake. I get you fucked up with your girl, but that doesn't mean you get to tell me how to take care of mine."

"So you admit she's your girl." At least that was a good starting point. If he could get Kyle and MaeBe through this, there might be hope for him and Taylor.

When had he become this mushy, messy guy? He was supposed to be the ruthless bastard who lived for the game.

The game was getting harder and harder to play with no one beside him, with no one knowing who he really was.

"I admit I care about her," Kyle allowed. "But we both know I'm not good for her. You should think about that when you're pursuing Taylor. Julia's not happy with you either, but you're her brother and she'll want to talk at some point. There's a reason she resurfaced now. She wanted us to figure out she's alive, and she's out there right now planning her next move. She might use Taylor to get you to do what she wants you to."

Kyle wasn't telling him anything he didn't already know. "Well, I don't seem to have any influence at all over Taylor. Also, she's actively going after Julia. I think I have to stay close to her if I want to protect her. If she goes rogue, she could blow up the whole op and get herself hurt in the process. I can't have that. I know she's angry with me now, but I need time to make her see reason."

"I don't think there was much reason with her." Brad seemed fascinated by the conversation. "She's mad. Super mad. So mad I called in last night to explain the situation to my boss, but you had already called the president and I couldn't remove you. Not that I wanted to, but she's literally the heart of this op. I don't know who else we could get to work on this."

He already had a plan, but he wanted a few days before he sprung it. He had zero intentions of allowing Taylor to walk into an op where his sister could spring a trap and kill her. But if he dismissed her now, he likely wouldn't see her again.

He was an ass, but he was an ass who cared about her.

"I think that's my uncle." Kyle gestured to the window. "He likes a big-ass SUV. I hope the lemon meringue on the menu is up to snuff. I should have talked to Angie. She runs the kitchen. Is there someone in that car with him?"

He wouldn't be surprised if Big Tag showed up with Alex McKay or Liam O'Donnell just to fuck with them. *Them* being the Agency, who'd only given Taggart himself clearance at this point. Drake understood. If he'd had an Alex or a Liam, he would want someone watching his back, too. No matter how old and crotchety they were.

Drake looked out the window, and sure enough there was a big black SUV coming up the drive and…

Oh, Big Tag wasn't fucking with him. He was fucking with Kyle. "Is that your stepdad?"

Kyle's jaw dropped. "Fuck."

The SUV stopped and sure enough, Sean Taggart slid out of the passenger side of the vehicle and then did something far worse than merely being there. He opened the back door and held a hand up.

Meanwhile, Ian Taggart had gotten out of the car and yawned, looking like a lion who could use a nap. Or a nice meaty lunch.

"That's my mom. He brought my mom. My mom is here." Kyle had gone a pasty white.

"Oh, she does not have clearance." Brad stood, his hands going to his hips. "Nor does Sean Taggart. Did Mr. Taggart not understand?"

Brad was the one who didn't understand. "This isn't going to be a normal op. It ceased being normal the minute Taggart agreed to help. We're in his world now. The good news is the man usually gets things done. The bad news is how he does it. Should we hide you from your mom, Kyle?"

The operative who'd legit stared down death on numerous occasions suddenly looked like a kid who'd gotten caught with his hands in the cookie jar. "I think she would find me."

He got a good look at the expression on Grace Taggart's face as she glanced up at the building. That was a serious mom face. "Oh, she'll find you."

"Damn it. I thought they understood. It's not like I told Ian he couldn't let them know I was alive. I would never have done that to them." Kyle stalked toward the hallway.

He was glad his mom didn't know what he did.

"Well, this is going to take way more than a lemon pie," Kyle said as he turned and walked out.

Brad frowned, watching the door close behind Kyle. "I did not expect to have to deal with an operative's angry mother. I've never had to do that before."

Likely because for the most part the Agency tended to recruit people without strong family ties. It was precisely why they did it. So they didn't have a bunch of Graces running in trying to protect their baby boys.

Would his mom do the same? Or would she see what he'd done and turn her back on him?

Would she blame him for what happened to Julia?

"Like seriously, Drake, I don't know what I'm supposed to do." Brad huffed as he sat back down. "This is a classified operation, and now there's a Taggart family reunion? Am I supposed to call this in? You're having trouble with the most important piece of this op. It feels like it's going to blow up in my face, but I don't even know who I would call since I can't get you fired because of the president thing."

Poor Brad. He liked things to run smooth and easy, and this mission would be neither of those things. "You go back to DC and let me handle it. Brad, you don't have to be here. I can make this whole thing go away for you."

He felt a little guilty. It was Brad's career on the line, too. Though he wouldn't be out in the field, it could be his life on the line since Julia was so tricky.

"I'm not going to leave you on your own. I know what this means to you," Brad said and then frowned and sat down, his gaze going back to his screen. "And don't try to get me kicked out. I have friends, too."

He wasn't sure he would call the current president of the United States a friend, but the dude did owe him a couple of favors.

"What is going on?" Taylor stood in the doorway. "Is something happening? Kyle looked like the world is ending."

She was so fucking pretty. Blonde hair. Red hair. Long. Short. She looked good no matter what.

Or maybe his eyes saw her differently. Maybe when it came to her he saw with something else. His heart.

Shit. His stomach churned.

"Now you look like the world is ending." Her arms crossed over her chest. "What is happening, Drake? I have the right to know."

Well, Taylor, I just had the sappiest, most romantic thought I never thought I would have, and while I consider myself a relatively modern man, I'm wondering if I shouldn't hand in my man card and maybe check my balls to see if they're still properly functioning.

Yeah, he wasn't going to be that honest with her. But at least he had a great distraction. He waved her over. "Come here. This is going to be good. You remember how I told you Kyle faked his death and shit?"

Her lips started to curl up. "Yes. Is he going to do it again?"

"No, but he might wish he'd actually gone through with it. His mom is here."

Her eyes widened, and she hustled right over to the window. "Are you serious? I thought his uncle was supposed to be protecting him."

"Oh, Big Tag is a total asshole."

Taylor gasped. "Is that... That is the Sarge. I've seen him on the *Food Network*. Why is there a celebrity chef here? And that's his wife, Grace. She's even prettier in person. I'm confused."

"Grace Taggart used to be Grace Hawthorne."

Kyle strode out of the bar, jogging down the steps, and his mother flew across the yard, wrapping her arms around him.

"Oh, that's so sweet." Taylor put a hand to her heart as though she could feel Grace's relief.

Taylor didn't have a family. Taylor was all alone in the world. There was no mom out there worried about her. No father to protect her anymore.

He'd left her alone when he should have protected her. Even if he'd freaking thought she might have been guilty, he should have protected her, should have made sure.

He shoved that thought aside. She wasn't ready to hear him apologize yet.

Grace moved out of her son's arms, and her expression changed. She pointed a finger her son's way and started to let him have it.

Big bad Kyle took a step back.

"Oh, shit." Taylor's hand came up, covering her mouth as though she could hold in her laugh. "That's one mad mama."

Kyle's hands came up, and while Drake couldn't hear what was being said, he could imagine it. *"Sorry, Mom. My CIA job that you didn't know about went south, and I had to blow myself up."*

Taylor chuckled and started to play along. *"You know that's how all CIA jobs go. Someone's fake dying and coming back. Hope you kept my room clean."*

Oh, she was so mean, and he was here for it. He went into a bad Grace impersonation. *"Bad, Kyle. I would give you a spanking but we both know that would be weird because we're both into the lifestyle."*

Taylor's head tilted up, those gorgeous eyes filled with curiosity. "Seriously? The Soldier Chef spanks his wife?"

He was not about to let her imagination go wild. "He is happily married and way too old for you."

"That man is not too old for anyone." She looked back. "Wait. Does Kyle go to the same club as his mom?"

"Absolutely not." Out in the parking lot it looked like Sean was also having a word with Kyle. "There are several clubs in the Dallas area. Taggart owns one, but Kyle and his brother David go to a club owned by a man named Julian Lodge. Kyle says it's to avoid accidently seeing his mother's boobs. I can understand that. Not his mother's boobs. Those seem lovely, but I would not want to see my mother's boobs."

"Don't your mother's boobs belong to the Senate?" She was back to laughing and then a little gasp as Kyle threw his hands up. "What was that about?"

It was good to know he could get to her through gossip. She liked gossip? He could give it to her. Especially about Kyle. "I don't think being an elected official means her boobs belong to anyone, though my dad would probably disagree, and I would bet they just got on the subject of MaeBe."

"Maybe?"

"She's a woman not an adverb. Mae Beatrice Vaughn."

Taylor nodded. "Ah, the woman he's stalking online. She's going to find out about that. Is she going to be surprised he's alive?"

"Nah, but she will be surprised she's been flirting with him online. I mean he says they're only friends and he's helping her get over him, but his online name is Kraven, so we should not believe him."

Taylor made a vomiting sound. "That's such a gamer bro thing to call himself. Have you thought about joining his guild, working your way up and fucking with him?"

There was a project they could work on together. "I'm not a big gamer but that could be fun."

She turned, their bodies close together. "Seriously? You're a gaming noob?"

"I'm not sure what that means." This was the kind of honesty she needed right now. The kind that only sort of made him look ridiculous.

They were so close, and he could feel the heat between them. There was an electricity he felt the minute she walked in the room, and he'd forgotten how it brought him to life in a way he hadn't been before. There had been a reason he'd never stopped thinking about her. There was a reason he'd been ready to blow up his world to be near her again.

Her hair curled slightly at the tips, framing her jaw and giving her a mischievous look. "It means you're a newbie, and given your particular generation, the fact that you're not an expert gamer means you're a bit of a nerd."

He could deal with that. Gaming and online life were the foundations of their generation. "But I was too busy spying."

It was the truth. He'd spent the majority of his upbringing gathering intel and treating his peers like fountains of information to feed to his father. He hadn't done a lot of killing virtual aliens or raiding weird cyberpunk dungeons, and now that seemed like a mistake.

The slight smile on her face faded, and she stepped back, breaking that fragile connection. "Yeah. I should remember that." She moved away, looking to Brad. "When are we having the conference with Mr. Taggart?"

Brad's grim expression let him know he'd watched the entire scene. "As soon as Mr. Lee and Mr. Seeger join us. You should know I've also been informed by our host that we won't have access to the second level of the building tonight. Apparently there's some kind of…how to put this…"

"It's called play night." Taylor seemed to have dropped the whole "I don't know anything about BDSM" line. "And you might not have access, but some of us do. Text me when we're ready to go."

"Then you're staying on?" Brad sounded hopeful.

She wasn't going anywhere. Not yet. Not if he could help it.

"For now," she said and walked out without looking back.

"Damn, man. That was a lot. Like a lot." Brad had turned his head, watching her go. Drake couldn't exactly resent him for that. She looked so good, and it wasn't like she had a thing for Brad.

She still had a thing for him. She simply wasn't willing to admit it yet.

"It was a start," he allowed. She'd responded to him. For a moment she'd forgotten how angry she was with him and they'd slipped into the friendship they'd begun all those months before.

Outside he could hear Grace giving her son hell, but it wasn't as much fun to watch as it had been when Taylor had been with him.

"The start of what? World War III with sexual tension?" Brad asked with a long sigh. "This is not how an op is supposed to go. I've got two of you who probably should just throw down and get it out of your systems, one with parental issues, and now I have to hide in my room because apparently the entire headquarters is going to turn into a weird sex club. Also, why is there so much lube in our bathroom?"

"If you wanted a normal op, you shouldn't have called in Taggart," Drake pointed out, watching another vehicle start up the long trail. Likely Tucker and Jax.

"I didn't. Taylor did. You did," Brad shot back. "I assure you I wanted proper backup. She's the one who wanted to go this way. You backed her up by bringing Kyle back."

He'd gotten used to the idea of nonformal ops where no one gave a damn about anything but succeeding, where the players on the field were expendable. No one was expendable to Taggart, except maybe the guy who mistakenly ate the last piece of pie.

When had he started caring about something more than winning?

When you met Taylor. When she became more important than winning. When you realized you weren't some machine who had to give his whole soul to the cause.

When she proved to you that you had a soul.

The truck pulled up beside the SUV, and Tucker proved he could bring the chaos, too. In addition to Jax hauling his big body out of the truck, Tucker opened the door to the back of the cab and three kids jumped out. Two girls and a boy who immediately started running for the front doors.

Brad's head was going to explode.

But he rather thought Taylor would appreciate the humor in Tucker not finding a babysitter.

His day had just gotten more interesting.

Chapter Eight

"I'm so sorry. My wife got called in on an emergency. Susie Plack went into labor early, and Roni is way better with obstetrics than I am." Tucker Seeger slipped into his seat at the conference table.

She was the only woman in the entire room. Kim wouldn't be coming with her to Europe, so she wasn't allowed to be in this classified conference. Neither was Sandra Croft. The last time Taylor had seen her she'd been pulling her youngest grandchild off a sex swing because the tiny girl had toddled into the dungeon. The older girl had been in the kitchen happily helping with baking cookies with her Grandma Angie, and the boy, she'd been assured, wouldn't wander too far.

Most women her age would likely call out Tucker's parenting techniques, but she'd been raised by a spy dad who'd once left her in a hotel in Tokyo with five ramen packs and instructions on how to use the electric kettle to boil water. She'd also learned how to stitch a knife wound at the age of thirteen, so a toddler swinging on what she'd been assured was a thoroughly sanitized swing that also happened to be used for some rough sex didn't bother her.

"Yeah, Tucker couldn't find a babysitter." Jax Lee was a stunning man in his late thirties with a killer smile who seemed amused by the world around him. "What's your excuse, Kyle?"

Drake snorted, and she didn't want to think about how nice it was to see him smile.

Kyle, however, was neither smiling nor amused. "They're my parents. Not my kids. I did not have the option of whether or not they came. Someone couldn't keep his mouth shut about this meeting."

The big, gorgeous guy at the end of the table shrugged. "I could have kept my mouth shut, but where's the fun in that?"

"Well, sir, the fun is in keeping classified operations classified." Brad had been a fussy asshole all morning, but she could sympathize a bit. The Taggarts had brought some chaos, and he had not expected Tucker to bring three kiddos with him.

Big Tag sniffed the air. "What is that I smell?"

Kyle leaned back. "Sure as fuck not lemon tarts now. You can eat the oatmeal raisin cookies Sandra insists on putting on the menu."

Big Tag shook his head. "Nah. Sean's working on something for dinner. It was payment for selling your ass out. It's the faintest whiff of douche. The Agency suit is definitely here."

Drake chuckled. "Yeah, it's a combo of drug store body spray and desperation."

Brad shook his head. "You know I know what a douche is, and that's offensive. Also, when you think about it, it's nice because I'm a heterosexual male, and I like being in vaginas. And I bought this body spray at a department store, thank you, and the women in my office assure me it smells good. So fuck all of you, and I'm serious about classified shit."

The big guy's lips curled up slightly. He obviously didn't mind being called out. "Sean's not going to talk. Neither will Grace. They needed to see Kyle. I promise you won't have any leaks on that end, Body Spray."

"I do not need a nickname," Brad said with a frown.

"And yet the universe provides," Big Tag assured him and then sat up. "So where's Julia Ennis and how soon can we kill her? This whole op thing can be avoided. Give me a location and I'll send my sniper out and the problem is gone. His name is Boomer, and we need to work fast because he's got a girl now and when she finds out I pay him in tacos, she's going to insist on actual cash, so his price will be going up."

"That's going to be pricey because Boomer can eat a lot of tacos," Jax explained.

"I would like to do a study on that man's cholesterol," Tucker mused. "You would think it's super high, but it's not. I watched him eat a whole buffet once. The owner of the restaurant cried. Grown man, just sat in his lobby and cried. Then Boomer cried. Sensitive guy."

"We can't let Boomer snipe her until we know more about her organization." Drake seemed to get serious again. He was sitting next to her. Not her choice. She'd sat down first, and Drake had come in later. When she'd thought he would take the seat at the head of the table, he'd slipped in beside her, and by that time it would have looked bad for her to change seats.

But she'd wanted to because she hadn't wanted to.

He was turning her upside down, and it wasn't a place she needed to be. She needed to be in charge.

That obviously meant impressing the big dude. Taggart hadn't had a problem taking a place at the head of the table. He occupied that chair like a king on his throne.

Taggart reminded her of her dad. There was a deeply engrained authority about him but also a warmth that could likely go cold when he wanted. She intended to not see that side of the man.

"I wish it was so simple, Mr. Taggart," she said. "But I've built this op around the idea that if we can get an agent on the inside, we'll have a far easier time of mapping out the organization. An agent who is working for us, not against us. It appears we already have a couple of crossovers, but none that have worked to our advantage. I understand your group took down the first iteration of The Consortium."

"Yup. The fuckers called themselves The Collective back then," Taggart replied. "It's good to know they have a thesaurus and not a creative bone in their bodies. Next time they should go for something cooler. I would take them way more seriously if they called themselves The Killer Piranhas or Bloody Wild Cats or something."

She'd heard lots of stories about this man from her father. It looked like he was as sarcastic as she'd been told, but he was selling himself short. "I think you took them very seriously. You put the group out of commission for years. I'd like to do the same. I'm not naïve. There have been groups like this since business was invented. But the new world of hypercapitalism and politicians for sale has made these groups more dangerous than ever. I'd like to deal a blow that forces them back into their star chambers for a couple of decades."

Taggart looked at her seriously for the first time. "Good for you. I'm sure that's what your father would have wanted, and he would be proud of you."

"Or he would want you safe," Drake argued.

Taggart's gaze went lightning focused. "Seriously?"

One of Drake's shoulders shrugged. "You always told me it would happen."

Taggart groaned, and his head dropped and hit the table. "Fuck me."

She wasn't sure what was happening. "Is there a problem?"

Taggart's head came back up. "There's always a problem when the puppies start thinking with their penises. Has he tried to pee on you? I know that feels like an insult, but it's a sign of affection."

Kyle started laughing, and Drake sent him a nasty look.

She wasn't playing this game. It was obvious Drake had a relationship with the man who held the strings to important parts of this op, and she needed to make herself plain. But in a way that didn't make her the bitch. She'd heard Taggart liked being the protective older brother in every group he was in. She could use a protective older brother. She wouldn't mention that he could be her dad. Though only technically. The big guy was barely in his fifties and still wretchedly hot. "He did try to pee on me but only after he screwed me under false pretenses and then let the Agency take me away for questioning. I wasn't even given the chance to get dressed. I was held in an Eastern European jail for two weeks before they decided I wasn't a double agent. Did I ever thank you for helping my father? For helping me?"

There were things Drake didn't know either, and some of them could fuck him over. There was a reason she was so amenable to working with the Taggarts.

She'd never met the man personally, but she knew what he and his friends had done for her and her father.

"That was mostly Markovic." Taggart's gaze had softened. The man was definitely a top, but she would bet he was a wickedly indulgent one. His wife likely got whatever she wanted.

"Nick Markovic?" Tucker asked. "From the London office?"

She nodded. "He and my father came up through the ranks together in SVR, though my dad was older. He viewed Nicky as something of a younger brother. He was happy when Nicky made the move to get out and ended up with the London office. When we needed help getting into and out of Havana, the London office and its agents came to our aid. Undercover, of course. That was how we stayed off the radar."

"I don't normally condone smuggling anything but cigars and rum out of Cuba, but lifesaving cancer drugs seem like a good bet," Taggart replied. "I was so sorry to hear about his passing. Your father was a good man. He should be with us, and Drake is a fucking douchebag. Stay away from him."

"I thought I was a helpless puppy." Drake seemed upset at the turn of events.

Taggart pointed a finger his way. "Puppies can bite, and it looks like you did. Taylor, please continue. I'd like to know how you're going to get Tucker and Jax here killed. You should know that I'm full up on kids. You kill these two, you get all five of the little fuckers, and all the dogs, too."

She didn't take that as an insult. It was Taggart being Taggart.

"I think our wives would have something to say about that," Jax argued.

Tucker shook his head. "Nope. If I die Roni is shipping all three of them straight to the Agency. I've been warned."

She needed to get control again now that she was sure she'd made her point. "So let's get to the mission. If you read the packets Brad's placed in front of you, you'll get a detailed outline of what the parameters of my part of this mission have been so far. I began working on this a year ago. After the Agency figured out my father wasn't a double and I hadn't sold out my country, they laid out what had happened to him."

"Your father was investigating The Consortium at the same time as Kyle?" Taggart opened the folder.

"We were coming at it from two different angles. Neither Drake nor I realized anyone else was looking into the group." Kyle went into a professional tone. "From what I've read of Sokolov's notes, he identified a company in southeast Asia that was responsible for the deaths of at least ten people from polluted water, one of whom was an informant of Sokolov's. He worked for an underground group. Sokolov was curious."

"He was upset," she corrected. "My father took his assets seriously. He liked Niran. He followed the court case that happened and thought there was corruption involved. He was right, of course, but he realized he'd only scratched the surface, that the company was connected to other companies and there was further abuse and even what some would call terrorism. He identified the structure and several of the corporations. He had a theory that The Consortium was working with a couple of intelligence agencies and might actually have recruited some operatives of ours."

"He was ahead of us." Drake had gone grave as well. "We knew there was some kind of link between world corporations that had risen from the dust of The Collective, but we hadn't identified any intelligence operatives."

"Julia was working on that," Kyle pointed out. "Oddly, she didn't ID herself."

"She wasn't on my father's radar. But he did theorize that The Consortium was actively recruiting women in intelligence and government. He'd spent a year working his cover as a mercenary. He managed to get hired by a woman with The Consortium as part of a group. They were paid to create some chaos in order to send a non-Consortium company's stock plummeting. He managed to listen in on a conversation she had with her handler, and they talked about the other women in the group."

"My question is why would they only recruit women?" Brad was shuffling through papers.

"It's what I would do," Taggart said. "I want to fly under the radar, I bring in women. This isn't the Army. They aren't looking for big guys with big guns. They're looking for negotiators who can make everyone comfortable and also kill the people who step out of line. And it doesn't matter what you tell them, most men do not see women as physical threats."

"But a woman can shoot someone," Brad pointed out.

"But they tend not to." Taylor understood exactly why The Consortium's strong arm was exclusively women. There were some men who were brought in as muscle, but the women were the power brokers. "Women are always viewed as less threatening. What The Consortium is trying to do is use soft power. This is not an autocracy. There might be a CEO of the whole thing, but he's there because the board elected him, and he has to prove himself. Women know how to manipulate rather than dictate. We're taught from birth that we have to please others. And the agents of The Consortium are far more than assassins. They negotiate between members, bring member companies back in line, handle situations that could get out of hand."

"I think men can do those things, too. It seems very discriminatory," Brad said under his breath.

"When we take The Consortium down, I'll be sure to ask them what they have against men. No one ever thinks of the men." She wasn't getting into this but couldn't quite hold back her sarcasm.

Taggart chuckled. "Okay, I like her. Hey, Sokolova, when you're done with this, I can always use a good female operative, especially if she doesn't come with a whiny, jealous man-child attached to her breast. Because most of mine are married, and even though they're willing to flirt, their significant others get all pissy about it."

"Her last name is Cline." Drake sent Taggart a pointed look.

But she'd kind of liked the fact that Taggart had used her dad's last name. They'd never changed it because of his status as an operative. "I always wanted to hyphenate it so I would have my dad's last name, too. He always called me Sokolova." The memories of her father washed over her and again she was surprised at the meshing of sweetness and grief that seemed to sneak up on her at the most inopportune times.

She also liked that Taggart understood how Russian surnames worked, that he could honor that part of her heritage. Her father had been so angry at the Russian government but he'd shown her some of the beauty of the culture, and he'd always hoped his people would rise up and take back their country. She'd heard the Taggarts still kept up their Russian.

"Just a thought," Taggart offered.

"She has a job," Drake countered.

"For now." She was fairly certain she would get out of the Agency if she was alive at the end of this. She might need a place to land, and her Uncle Nicky spoke highly of Taggart. He wasn't her biological uncle, but he'd been close to her dad. "So does everyone understand what I did?"

Taggart's lips curled up. "You built a legend. Do you want to know how good all of this is? When I read the reports on Constance Tyne—the ones you can hack—I could have sworn I'd worked with her."

"That's because I used a name that's close to several actual Agency operatives over the years," she admitted. "I also used a computer-generated younger version of Constance so she has grounded records."

"But all the rumors are she's had extensive plastic surgery," Brad offered. "So she could look like anyone."

"Except the basic body type is Taylor's." Drake sounded disgruntled. "She didn't change that."

"Well, it's much harder to change height and basic body type than it is facial features, though you should know the computer-generated pictures of the younger Constance started out with my own facial measurements." She didn't want him to think he could shove her to the side and bring in someone else. She wasn't sure what game Drake was playing but she wouldn't allow him to shut her out.

This was her op, and no one was going to take it away from her. Especially someone she didn't trust. She would take the whole thing to Taggart and hire him before she would give it up to Drake or Brad or any Agency suit.

Lexi Blake

"I'm impressed with this whole setup." Taggart closed the file in front of him. "This is some next-level bullshit, and I mean that in the best way. Who made contact with you?"

"I don't know her name, but I was offered an enormous amount of money for what was a fairly easy job," she replied. "And before you ask, yes, I've tried to track down the woman. She first contacted me through a group of mercenaries Constance had worked with before."

Jax held up a hand. "That would be me. This whole thing has been fun. I spend all my time with tourists now, so it was fun to pretend to be a badass mercenary again. Brad got me some killer cutting-edge software that lets me ping signals all over the place. Though Taylor handled most of it. She just needed a male voice when the woman wanted to talk."

"Even if you hide behind a VPN, a good hacker can figure out where you are." Drake seemed determined to argue with every aspect of the setup.

"That's why I worked with a Russian mob group to make it look like the communication was coming from there part of the time," Taylor explained. "I coordinated with my father's second cousin. The mob ties are what sold it. Constance was rumored to work with them from time to time and maybe take a little on the side. Never much, but I needed her to be a good-looking target."

"So you brought the Russian mob in? You know as a group to work with goes, they're known for being easy. They tend to go with the highest bidder," Drake replied.

"So where do we go from here?" Taggart ignored Drake completely. "You did the job The Consortium asked. An audition, so to say. This was getting the data from Rebecca Walsh's lab?"

"Yes, when I realized who they were asking me about, I contacted Uncl...Nick Markovic and he coordinated with me," she replied. "Thank you for allowing him to aid me."

"He spoke highly of your dad, and I understand the importance of the op," Taggart said. "Especially since it's now on my doorstep."

"I'm trying to keep it off your doorstep," Kyle said, his voice tight. "I did everything I could, but you went soft on me and brought my parents right back in."

"That's the funny thing about parents. They don't tend to let the kiddos fuck up all alone," Taggart shot back. "They tend to want to be there to help out."

"They are not helping," Kyle said under his breath. "They are making themselves targets."

It was time to help Taggart out. He'd been so nice to her thus far. "Do you think Julia is watching us right now?"

Kyle's green eyes rolled. "No. Obviously."

"Then it was nice for your parents to get to see you alive and whole," Taylor pointed out.

"I would think you would want to keep this ship as tight as possible," Brad remarked.

"I want to go into the field with a support staff that isn't so worried about their families that they can't think straight," she shot back. "I know Kyle is irritated right now, but at some point the fact that he's been able to see and talk to his mom is going to settle something inside him. I know I wish I could talk to my dad."

"I wish I could talk to my mom," Drake said quietly.

"You can pick up the phone and talk to her." Brad seemed confused.

"She doesn't know." She wished he would stop saying things that made her feel for him, but she rather thought that was his point. "His mom doesn't know what he does, so he can't talk to her about this."

"Oh, we talk about it. I lie about it. I tell my mother lies about her dead daughter." Drake's shoulders had slumped as though he felt the weight of that secret. "Well, we thought she was dead. Now she doesn't know her daughter is a murdering sociopath who she likely wouldn't recognize because of all the plastic surgery she's had to fool the facial recognition software we use."

She'd seen the before and after pictures, though the after pics were caught by some grainy security cameras and a detailed sketch. Julia Ennis had a lot of work done. She was still lovely but there was something cold about her beauty even before she'd turned.

How hard was it to have a sister become the enemy?

If she was his enemy.

She forced herself to think the words because she was softening toward him, and she couldn't afford to do that. Not with Drake Radcliffe. She had to remember exactly what he was capable of.

Making you scream out his name. Doing that thing with his tongue that you still can't stop thinking about. Topping you in a way no one has before and making you understand how good it can be to submit.

Yep. That horny inner voice was precisely why she had to remember he wasn't above suspicion.

"I need you to understand that identifying Julia Ennis isn't my primary mission." Taylor felt like she needed to make that plain. "Getting a good feel for the organization of the group is."

Drake sat up taller, his brows coming together in obvious consternation. "How long do you intend to be on the inside?"

She shrugged. "As long as it takes."

Drake closed the folder. "Do you understand how dangerous this is? I know that your face is not well known at the Agency, but people have seen you."

"I'm willing to take that risk. Drake, you need to understand that if you try to kick me out, I'll run the op on my own. I get that you're the big man at the Agency and you have contacts I can't dream of, but I have some of my own. If I have to I'll send Nick all my data and let McKay-Taggart and Knight decide how and when the Agency gets it."

Drake's jaw went tight. "And I need you to understand that I won't…"

Big Tag stood abruptly. "Say another word. You won't say anything else that might upset this op." He turned to Taylor. "Could I have a moment to talk to my nephew and Drake? I think I might be able to clear some things up. I have every confidence that this op has been set up with care and competency, and I'm going to allow Tucker and Jax to participate and the London office to give you all the support you need."

She breathed a sigh of relief. "Thank you, sir. And, of course. I've got some work I need to do on the logistics side."

"If it's all right I'd like to see some of your physical skills," Taggart announced. "I know your father trained you, but I want to make sure…"

She had zero problem proving she could handle herself. "Of course. Sandra has a gym in her home, and I'll take any weapons test you would like."

Taggart nodded. "Excellent. Then you should know that dinner is at eight tonight and then I've been told the dungeon will open at ten. Sandra is offering club rights to everyone, though I'll be in the bar. My wife is home with seven kids. Probably more because Kala's friend Lou spends as much time at our house now as she does her own. Boomer tricked me into that one."

She kind of wanted to see the club when it was open, but she likely would spend that time in her room. "Thanks."

"Hey, we should talk later." Drake had stood beside her.

Not if she could avoid it. She simply turned and walked away.

She knew when to retreat.

* * * *

The minute the door closed, Drake rounded on Ian. "What the hell was that about? Are you trying to make me look like I can't handle myself?"

"I think he's pointing out the fact that you're fucking up when it comes to her." Tucker leaned back as though getting comfortable. "I missed this part. Everyone's stoic in my hometown. There's not a ton of drama."

"You should come to Bliss," Jax added. "Kim and Beck and I hang out in town square and let the kids play in the park and wait for the explosion. There's always an explosion. And when Ian's in town, there're many. You should see he and Marie go at it."

"That old woman has it in for me." But Tag's lips had curled up. "I like her. And you have to like any town where they regularly shoot tranq darts into people."

"Only Max Harper and Mel." Jax waved that off. "Mel gets weird about alien things, and I swear, Max appreciates the nap. He goads Doc into tranqing him from time to time. At first he would let Max sleep it off in his waiting room, but Max pissed him off so the last time he parked Max's drugged body on a park bench and left a couple of sharpies lying next to him. It did not go well for Max."

Drake was never going to that weird town. He needed to get everyone back on the subject at hand. "I'm pulling her from the op. She's not a deep-cover agent. She has no training in this. She's always been support."

"For one of the best undercover operatives in the world," Tag countered.

"I don't think she's going to let you get rid of her." Brad looked honestly confused. "Also, the op doesn't work without her."

"I can make it work." He could find someone else to take over. Someone who he wouldn't worry about every second of the day. "You can't tell me there isn't another operative out there who could handle this."

"You would need at least two," Tucker mused. "Because I don't know a lot of operatives who have her technical skills. That's the perfect thing about her. This is an extremely technical job. She can think on her feet. She doesn't need a voice in her ear telling her what to do."

Oh, but she did. Once she was actually out in the field, she would need support to help her, to watch and listen and give her the best advice they could. "She cannot do this alone. I'm not sending an untested operative into a high-risk situation."

"Then she'll do it alone without your backup." Ian frowned his way. "I don't think you understand how serious she is. You want to tell me how you know her and why she thinks you're an asshole? I mean I know why. She's obviously met you, but circumstances matter."

He was such a dick, but he could use the man's advice. Ever since Tag walked in the door, he'd been thinking about how to broach the subject with him. Tag had a dad vibe to him, an "I'm an asshole but also know what I'm talking about and I'm willing to discuss shit" dad vibe. His dad did not have that vibe. His dad had twelve-foot fences around him most of the time. "Can we do this without an audience?"

Tucker sighed and pushed back from the table. "Fine. You're no fun. Come on, Jax. We can go and make sure my kids aren't turning the dungeon into a pillow fort."

Jax chuckled. "But that sounds like fun. Now I wish I'd brought the boys."

Brad gathered his folders. "How about we go over a few of the protocols we're going to be using? I understand that you guys do things differently, but the CIA is still in charge of this."

Jax groaned and followed Tucker out the door.

Brad stood and closed his briefcase. "And you and I should talk, too. Unless you intend to try to get me thrown out. You know I've been working with her. She's our best shot at this. There's more at stake than what you want, Drake. Also, it feels totally wrong for a group of all men to be deciding how to deal with a woman operative. Like the optics on this are not good."

He turned and walked out the door.

He was making everyone happy today. He stared pointedly at Kyle.

Kyle merely shook his head. "Nah, I'm going to stay since this somehow involves me, too."

"I don't see how."

Kyle's gaze sharpened. "Because I gave up everything to be here, Drake. Because if this op doesn't get me close enough to Julia to take her out, I'll never be able to go home. So yes, it affects me."

"I thought you weren't planning on going home at all," Ian said, dropping back down to his seat.

Kyle sighed, a heavy sound. "Of course I am. I always intended to see my family again."

"Tell me you're not rejoining the Agency," Ian said.

"I can't tell you that. You know I can't. It might be the best place for me because it's the only way I'll ever be able to stay away from MaeBe," Kyle replied. "If I come home to stay, if I come back to McKay-Taggart, it'll be mere months before I'm trying to work my way into her life again, and that's not fair to her."

"I think she would disagree," Tag countered.

Drake knew she would. It was precisely why Kyle had done what he'd done. She would want to fight beside him, and Julia would try to hurt her, to kill her. He'd helped Kyle because he understood what he'd been trying to do.

Kyle's head shook. "No. I'm not bringing her into this life. And that's what Drake's trying to avoid. Taylor isn't an operative like

MaeBe isn't. She's not trained to do this any more than Mae would be."

"Yeah, you might not recognize MaeBe anymore," Taggart argued. "She's gotten excellent at kicking a man's balls back into his body cavity."

"Why the hell would she do that?" Kyle's brow had furrowed.

Tag shrugged. "Because I taught her. She's been an excellent student, and it was my balls on the line. Someone had to teach her how to defend herself."

"You're supposed to protect her," Kyle insisted.

"No," Tag countered. "I'm supposed to teach her how to live independently. She's not some shrinking violet who wants to spend the rest of her life in an ivory tower waiting for her prince to return."

Kyle's expression went mulish. "Good, because I'm not."

"You shouldn't, buddy, because I can tell you what she'll do to your balls will make mine look like a training session. Which it was. Also, if you're worried I spent too much time on balls, Erin taught her how to punch a tit in just the right way," Taggart reassured his nephew. "Apparently there's a secret, and she won't teach me. The women have mysterious ways."

Kyle huffed. "I didn't leave her in your care so you could turn her into…what? What are you trying to do to her?"

"I'm trying to make her strong enough and competent enough that if Julia shows up on her doorstep, she can handle herself," Tag explained. "And don't tell me she's supposed to hide for the rest of her life."

"No, only until we take care of the situation," Kyle replied. "And in this, I'm with Drake. We need to shut this op down the minute she finds Julia. Then we take over and handle it."

"Or we can use the work Taylor's done and send in an operative who knows what she's doing." It was good to know Kyle was on his side, but he would go further. "Taylor can handle tech if she wants. I can keep an eye on her that way."

"I don't think that's going to work out for you." Taggart's brow had risen over his icy eyes. "Any more than this bullshit he's pulling on Mae is going to work out for him. You're fucking up with her. The same way Kyle already fucked up the best relationship of his life."

Kyle's hands came out, shoving his chair back from the table. "Yes, I did it the minute I gave in to the attraction I had to that woman. I should have known I couldn't come back from a mistake like that. I ruined my future a long time ago."

He turned and walked away.

"That is one dramatic motherfucker," Taggart said with a groan.

It was true. Kyle seemed to think because he'd screwed up once he didn't deserve another chance. Drake couldn't let himself think that way. "My sister can mess with a guy's head. But I need to know what you think he should have done. He's right. Julia would have come after her. She won't allow anyone to take what she thinks belongs to her. She's been possessive since she was a child."

"She'll still come after MaeBe. Not today or tomorrow, but soon enough. And if Kyle had his way, she wouldn't be ready. I'm not the kind of man who thinks our women should hide every time danger comes near. That's not a practical solution for every situation they could be faced with. Charlie was already a badass when I met her. If I told her not to watch my back, I would have to watch my back, if you know what I mean."

There was one problem with Tag's scenario. "MaeBe isn't Charlotte. Neither is Taylor."

"She can be. I'm not saying every woman in the world has to learn how to assassinate a man, although I'm also not not saying it," Taggart said with a grin. "But I am saying if you love someone you help them have the best life they can possibly have, and that means ensuring they're not walking around scared all the time. Fear is not the place I want to be making a choice from, and I certainly don't want that for my daughters any more than I would my sons. My girls are every bit as competent and strong as my boys. They might not genetically have their physical strength but there are ways around it, and part of that is training. MaeBe isn't Charlie, but she's also not the fainting sweetheart that Kyle's made her out to be. He's got her on a pedestal, and that's a hard place to fall from."

"I think he just wants her protected."

"And there is no better way to protect her than to give her the knowledge and training to make her confident enough to fight for

Lexi Blake

herself. Also to know when to retreat and how to safely do it. I've taught her that, too," Tag assured him. "Everyone should know it. That doesn't mean she won't always have backup if I'm around, but I can't be there every second of the day. She's already done with the whole twenty-four/seven protection thing. She's going to want her independence, and I understand that. You are in a completely different situation."

"Yes, I am since I actually have a relationship with Taylor. At least I did. We had sex. I didn't do that pearl clutching, I'm not good enough for her thing. I knew damn well I wasn't, and I still slept with her." He didn't want to do this. Big Tag had been a weird sort of mentor to him at important times in his life. But Tag was also easily irritated and didn't always have the best opinion of him. This was a conversation he should have with his father. Except his father no longer wanted to talk about Agency business. After he'd retired, he'd closed down all talk about Drake's job.

Damn, he hadn't realized how alone he felt.

Tag considered him for a moment. "So you and Sokolov's daughter? You should be happy he's no longer with us or you would get your ass kicked."

"If he were still alive, I wouldn't have fucked up the way I did. She wouldn't have gotten taken away from me," he said, hearing the wistfulness in his tone. What the hell was happening? "Is it wrong that I kind of want to punch my own face for sounding so whiny?"

Taggart's head dropped, his laughter booming through the room. He was smiling when he looked back at Drake. "I should have known you would be the self-aware one."

He sank back into his seat. "I fucked her over. Not personally, but I let them take her."

Taggart sobered. "You couldn't have stopped them from questioning her."

"I could have been there with her. I could have stood by her." He could have had some faith in her.

"Why didn't you?" Tag asked.

"Because I didn't trust her. I didn't trust anyone." He'd had a hole in his soul, and he hadn't realized how she'd filled it until he'd seen her again.

"So this happened right around the time you figured out your sister had been tricking you for years. I can understand that. But I can tell you that if someone had shown up to take my Charlie, no matter how pissed I was at her, I would have gone after her."

"I had a plan. I've been trying to figure out exactly where she was being held, and I was going to break her out. I've been thinking about it for months, and then my sister showed up again. Taylor's never going to believe me." He wouldn't believe him. She couldn't know how much he'd missed her.

"Not at first." Tag sat back. "You would have to regain her trust, but you're not going to do that by taking away her job."

Why couldn't he understand? Julia had already hurt people. "This is dangerous."

"And how would you feel if she tried to get you fired?"

"Oh, I'm sure she would have." He'd seen it on her face the night before. She'd been ready to do anything she had to in order to not work with him. It was precisely why he'd made that call. "I already cut her off at that pass. If I want to get her off this project, I can."

Tag sighed and nodded. "And then you will lose her. I will be right there to swoop in and give her a job because I really do need smart women agents. I can convince her. She'll come with me and long before I'm ready for it one of my dumbass single guys will figure out she's hot and smart and a good catch, and they will fumble their way into her life and you won't have another chance."

He wanted to argue, but he'd seen it happen way too many times. "And if I asked you not to hire her?"

Tag's head shook. "I would say you owe me way more favors than I owe you, and I would never not offer to help Lev Sokolov's daughter. If only for Nick's sake. So you have two choices. You can be an asshole and protect the little woman from herself or you can see if you work as a couple. You know there's more to it than sex, right?"

He rolled his eyes. "I wouldn't be making an idiot of myself if this was merely about sex."

"All right. Then what's it about?"

How did he put this into words that didn't sound dumb? Maybe it would always sound dumb. Maybe part of being in love with someone was a willingness to make of fool of oneself. "When I'm with her, I feel...peaceful. Like something is whole in me that wasn't before."

A long sigh came from Tag's chest. "Fuck."

It was good that he understood. "Yes. We did that. I think our real problem was timing."

"Don't be so literal. I was saying a universal fuck, as in we're all fucked because this doesn't sound like you're just trying to get into her pants. I was going to find other pants you could get into," Taggart explained.

"I don't want other pants. I want to get into her pants." Honestly, he would prefer she wasn't wearing pants at all. This was a weird conversation to have, but there was something comforting about it. This was something like what he'd had with Kyle for a while. When they'd worked together, they'd found a friendship that didn't have to be all about work. Being friends with Kyle had made him understand he hadn't really had friends before. He'd had coworkers and classmates, and he'd been taught to be ready to turn on any of them if he needed to use them to gain valuable intel.

That was what his father had taught him, and then when he was done with his work he'd expected Drake to pretend like it didn't exist.

He'd been brought up to believe he wasn't worth much beyond the information he could bring his father, and if he had no intel, then he wasn't worth anything to his dad at all. He had to face facts. "I have serious issues."

Tag pointed a finger his way. "Oh, yeah, you do. You look fine on the outside. Like you're perfectly normal and shit, but you have lied for so long about every aspect of your life that you sometimes don't know how to tell the truth."

He nodded because he knew truth when he heard it. That was the funny part. He could be honest when he wanted to. It just wasn't normal to him. He'd opened up to Taylor and then he'd regretted it because he hadn't trusted her.

Hadn't trusted his own emotions, his instincts.

"So I should tell her how I feel."

"Do you know how you feel?" Tag asked the question with a tone that let Drake know he didn't think the answer should be yes.

He knew what he felt. Didn't he? Normally he sat on decisions for long periods of time, but that hadn't worked with Taylor. His indecision had cost her. "I feel like I care about her more than I care about anyone else. I feel like she's the one, and she should let me take care of her. I feel like I should handle this and she and I should explore this relationship when the op is through."

"Okay. We're going to do a little improv, and I'm going to tell you how I think that conversation is going to go." Tag settled his big chin on his right fist and gave Drake big eyes. "Drake, I feel like shoving my designer shoe straight up your ass and giving it a hard wiggle while you cry."

Of course the willingness to help him talk through a situation also came with sarcasm. "She's not going to say that."

Taggart sat back. "She is absolutely going to say it if you give her the whole, *oh, baby, I love you so much I'm going to take away a job you deserve and keep it for myself because you're too sweet and pretty to be in danger, and also you have boobs so you can't possibly do a man's job.*"

"I definitely didn't fucking say that." Maybe there was a good reason he didn't talk through his feelings.

"That is what she will hear, and deep down in your dick brain, it's there."

Oh, he shouldn't pursue this but he couldn't help himself. "Dick brain?"

"Yeah, it's like a lizard brain," Tag began. "You know everyone has a lizard brain that thinks only of base instincts. Men also have dick brain. Sometimes it's good to listen to dick brain. Sometimes dick brain can save us. This is not one of those times. Dick brain is ignoring a couple thousand years of evolution and an entire movement that freed women from the whole 'my dick likes you so I own you' thing. It's why I invented BDSM. So I could feed my dick brain so my wife kills neither my actual dick nor my actual brain."

He was such an ass, and also stupidly charming when he wanted to be. Drake couldn't help but smile. "You invented BDSM?"

Taggart's lips curled up, but his expression went thoughtful.

"Don't we reinvent the things we do every day? I can tell you the D/s I practice with my Charlie isn't the one I thought I would practice. I was hard core in my younger days. I viewed a submissive as someone I was supposed to take care of and who filled my needs in return. Charlie changed that. I love her so I have to view her as more than a sub. She's half of my soul and so complex I'll never figure her out completely. She's a glorious puzzle who amuses and challenges and frustrates me in the best possible way. So I couldn't put her in the same pretty cage I'd put other subs in. She couldn't be a pet I protected and fed, who made me feel like a man. She had to be my partner, and while you protect your partner you have to be careful not to squash her soul. To never make her feel like she's less than she is. Do you honestly know Taylor isn't up to this job or is your dick brain telling you—girl pretty, dick must protect?"

He sighed because deep down Tag was probably right. "The work she's done on this so far is superlative, but she's never been tested in the field."

"Hasn't she? She supported her father for years. Would you have put yourself in the field when you were eighteen?"

He'd been in the field for years by that time. He'd been spying on his classmates and their families the whole time he was in school. Because school hadn't mattered. All that had mattered was pleasing his father. "I was in the… It's not the same."

"It is. Your father taught you," Tag said with surety. "He taught you way too young. He taught you how to spy before he taught you why you were spying. He taught a child who thought it was a game and who learned he needed to win in order to be worthy."

"That's not true." But wasn't it? He didn't think his father meant to twist his childhood the way he had.

"It is. I'm trying so hard to keep my girls out of the business," Tag said with a weary look. "I've got to give them enough to make them feel like they understand but not so much it hurts them. Your father might love you, but he did you harm. It doesn't take away your love for him, but you should recognize it so you can handle your damage. She's damaged, too. I understand what Lev was doing, what your dad was doing. They didn't understand how to have a relationship with their kids without bringing them into the world they lived in."

"You live in that world."

Tag's head shook. "Nope. I work in that world. I have a job, a career even, but my life is about my wife and kids and friends. It's about the family I built. It's about all those knuckleheads who somehow worked their way into my stupid heart and taking care of them. I didn't bring Sean and Grace here so he would feed me. I brought him here because Kyle needed to see his mother. Kyle needs to remember he has something to come home to. He can't get lost again because someone will always come and find him."

The words made his chest feel too tight.

Who would come find him? If he died, his mother would look. She would ache but she would be given any number of stories about how he was missing, and then they might be able to come up with a lie to explain away his death. If he was taken somewhere, they would give him a star on the wall at Langley and move on.

No one would be there.

"I wanted to be with her because I thought I could find a place where I wasn't… How do I put this? A place where I didn't have to be me."

"Yes, I remember that well," Tag admitted. "I remember compartmentalizing huge portions of my life when I worked for the Agency. I'd been in the lifestyle for a while, but I got serious about D/s when I started working as an operative. It was a way to put the agent in a box and be the Dom for a while. And then there was my family, who had their own box because they didn't know. That was the hardest part. Turns out that was the part I couldn't handle. After Charlie died, I needed my family, and I'm not talking about blood. I did need Sean, but I needed Alex and Eve and Li and Jake. And having Adam around to punch was very necessary."

"I remember how perfect she seemed for me because she was planning on getting out." Drake could remember every second he spent with her. Well, after the initial sad car accident thing. Even then he'd been doing exactly what Tag was accusing him of. "She was going to go to college, and I was already thinking about how I could buy her an apartment and I could stay with her when I was in town. She was perfect because she knew about the Agency but she wasn't going to be in the Agency."

"And that is why you need to take a big step back," Tag said, a grim look on his face. "How many days did you spend with her?"

"A week." It had been the best week of his life. He'd let himself be that week. She thought he'd been investigating her, but all he'd done was watch her, pray that he had more time with her.

"And then you didn't see her for a long time," Tag pointed out. "You don't know her."

That man was forgetting his own history. "How long did it take you to fall for Charlotte?"

Tag's expression softened as though the mention of her name did something to his soul. "I knew within a day. I married her within a month. I mourned her every minute we were apart, and despite what she will tell you, I fought her very little when she came back. She was gone for five years, three months, and twenty-two days. I felt every one of them."

"And there have been one year, six months, and twenty-nine days since they took her from me."

Ian's head shook. "Try again."

Damn it. He had to be honest or nothing would work. "Since I let them take her."

Ian pointed his way. "There you go. You didn't go after her. So that is your sin. You have to atone for that. You have to decide to never do that again. Ever. I believe you, Drake. And I believe that you're a dumbass who wasn't taught how to process the feelings you had. So what do we do about it?"

"I don't know." His chest felt way too tight. "I think I'm fucking this up and it will be the worst mistake of my life, but I also don't want her out there. I don't want her in danger. Shouldn't I want her safe more than I want her to love me?"

"That is a good question, but one you should turn around. Should she accept who you are?"

"Of course."

"Why should she expect less from you? Accept who she is. Accept that she is not a safe woman. Accept that she will run into the burning building, that she will place herself in danger to save others. Be grateful that you found someone who is so fucking worthy of being loved by you. This isn't a game, Drake. You don't get to weigh the pros and cons and treat her like a piece on the board that you can move around. If you want a real relationship, she's your partner. You make decisions together. Sometimes that means you sit down and decide only one of you is going to risk. Sometimes that person who is risking won't be you, and that is far more frightening than putting yourself out there. It's always easier to be the one who goes than the one who's left behind, the one who has to wait. Don't be a selfish prick when it comes to your partner's life. She gets to have one, too."

But he'd always looked at the people around him exactly the way Tag said. The man was right about everything, and now that Drake considered his life clearly he could see he was going the same way his father had gone. With a half life, with lies instead of a truth shared with the person he loved.

Did he want that? Did he want to keep a huge part of himself closed off?

"So what do I do to convince her I care about her? We got close so fast. It felt right, like nothing I ever experienced before, and I know she felt it, too."

"You have to make her feel it again," Tag said with a shrug. "You're not going to do that if you're irritating her by saying the shit you said today. You want to prove to her you care? Care about all of her. Care about the part of her that needs this mission. Care about the part of her that wants to prove herself, that wants to prove her father didn't die in vain. You want to take out your sister to assuage the guilt you have for not seeing who she was. She wants to make her father's death meaningful. You can achieve both, but you have to respect what she's trying to do."

He wasn't sure he could manage what Tag was advising, but he had to try. "All right. If I want her back, I need to be respectful and professional. We do this job and hopefully somewhere along the way she starts to trust me."

Tag grimaced. "You are so bad at this. Like epic bad, man. No. I mean do that, but you also have to get her in bed and give her a mega shit ton of orgasms."

"I'm confused." Drake wasn't sure where he'd gone wrong.

"Yeah, I get that. You have to do both, and that means you might have to convince her to compartmentalize a bit."

"I thought that was a bad thing."

"She's the one doing it, not you," Tag explained. "You are going to be the sneaky bastard who convinces her that the two of you can enjoy each other, get each other out of your systems. Maybe even say it couldn't possibly have been as good as you thought it was. Challenge her a little. She then thinks she can get some revenge on you. She can do to you what you did to her. She might even think she can get some information out of you."

"Information?" He wasn't sure he liked where this was going.

"If I were Taylor and I realized your sister killed my father, I would have some questions."

"You think she thinks I was involved?"

"It's not a terrible question, nor is it one a person who doesn't know you would be foolish to ask."

His gut tightened. "She thinks I'm as bad as my sister."

Tag's head shook. "I didn't say that, and I don't think that. But if I were her, I would have questions, especially since she thinks you were there to get information about her father, information that could have led your sister to him. You can't think it's not suspicious to the outsider. I might know who you are, but all she knows at this point is that you charmed her and got her in bed and she was arrested and you didn't show up again until yesterday when she discovered your sister is the very person who had her father killed, and you tried to take over her op. You should be happy she hasn't shoved your balls so far back into your body you can taste them yourself."

When he put it that way, it suddenly seemed overwhelming. "I do see that. I can understand it, too. What I don't see is how I can prove it to her. I was there with her when her father died. I was there because an op went wrong and it was the closest place to safely transfer the intel I had, but she can't be certain of that. If I look at it from her point of view, I'm the bad guy."

"So show her you're the good guy." Taggart stood, gathering his things. "Show her she can count on you. Be vulnerable to her but not so much she truly understands what a whiny man baby you can be. I've learned it's best to keep that inside until you've got a ring on her finger and you've put a couple of babies up in her. Then she's trapped and you can let your man baby out from time to time." He stepped close to Drake, putting a hand on his shoulder. "You can be charming, and you're excellent at manipulation. Use your powers for good this time. I heard her talking to Sandra about play night tonight. Maybe you should be there. You can point out the fact that it would be safer to play with someone on the team. You have to be careful about bringing anyone in. Give her the option of getting close to you. She's willing to do a lot to bring the people who killed her father to justice. Once she's sleeping with you, show her you couldn't have done it, would never have done it. Teach her that she can trust you."

"Do you think I can do that?" He could hear the wistful tone in his own voice. Yep. Whiny man baby was in there somewhere.

"I think you'll always regret it if you don't take the chance. The question is always going to be is she worth it. And are you worth it? Is she worth the pain you could go through if she walks away? If she's not, then you have your answer. If she is, then you should make sure you've got leathers because Sandra is strict about dress code." Tag's hand tapped against his shoulder, a brotherly show of affection. "Now I'm going to go and call my wife and make sure my girls haven't taken over the world yet. Good luck, Drake."

Drake watched the man go, the door closing behind him.

Luck. He was going to need it.

Chapter Nine

Taylor thought seriously about going to her room and going to bed. She had a good excuse. She'd been traveling for days, and she was dealing with stress of the upcoming op. No one would miss her since all anyone could talk about was the fact that Sean Taggart had been in the kitchens all afternoon braising something.

She wasn't sure what that meant, but it smelled delicious.

"I'll take a gin martini up with a twist." Kim stood beside her at the private bar where everyone was gathered waiting for dinner.

Everyone except Drake, who had still been in the conference room when she'd left.

"Are you not drinking because you're going to play later?" Kim asked. "You know you would be okay with a couple of glasses of wine given the fact that we're about to eat a huge meal. I've heard Sean is pulling out all the stops with this one. He brought his own meat."

Taylor glanced up at the bartender and nodded. "I'll take the same." She turned her attention back to Kim. "I don't think I'll play. I can use the sleep."

Of course, if she went to bed, she would probably lie there staring at the ceiling thinking about Drake Radcliffe. She would think about how much she hated him, how much he'd screwed her over.

She would think about how once he'd touched her like she was something precious.

Nope. She definitely didn't want to go to bed.

She glanced over at the clock and it was only three hours until the club would be open. The bartender handed her and Kim two martinis, the clear liquor making the yellow of the lemon twist look vibrant.

Everything seemed more vibrant here. Louder. More alive.

Had she spent so much time in the shadows that the light was too much for her now?

"I'm excited about dinner." Kim led her away from the bar toward the big bay windows that overlooked the back of Sandra's property. "I love Bliss, but it's not exactly a gourmet food destination. Oh, Stella's cook will tell you he's a celebrity chef, but he came in third on a local cable show's cooking competition. He's a wizard when it comes to diner food, but I question his special of the day choices. He's also surprisingly good with beets."

Taylor doubted there would be diner food on the menu tonight, but she was also worried she wasn't the target audience. "I grew up on ramen noodles and instant mac and cheese. I am not a foodie. I mostly eat protein bars now. I don't see the need to make a big deal out of a meal."

Kim took a sip of her drink. "Have you considered the fact that you might still be grieving?"

She wasn't sure how Kim had made that turn. "Of course I am. I'll always grieve for my father."

"Have you considered the fact that you might still be grieving Drake?"

Taylor snorted at the thought. "No. I am one hundred percent not grieving over a man who betrayed me. Who would be pathetic enough to do that?"

Kim sighed, and a melancholy look came over her face. "Me. I did it for years."

Damn it. She'd put her whole foot in her mouth. Still, there was a huge difference. "He was your husband."

"I would have mourned Beck no matter how long we'd been together," Kim admitted. "Sometimes we meet our soul mates and they aren't ready for us or we aren't ready for them. Sometimes an asshole decides to get in between the two of you and keeps you apart for years. All I'm saying is it's okay to still ache over what happened between the two of you."

Taylor took a long sip. The gin was slightly floral and nicely refreshing. Maybe she could drink all night.

Or she could walk into that dungeon and try to find what she needed.

"It doesn't matter. I won't be working with him for long." She'd thought about this all afternoon. "I know he's focused on this op, but I don't think it's going to go the way he thinks it will. I'm going to have to work my way up. It could be years before I find myself in a room with his sister."

Julia Ennis was all Drake and Kyle cared about. They would get her safely inside the organization and then they would get bored and find someone else's op to glom on to.

"I'm not sure about that," Kim said, glancing around the room as though checking to make sure no one could listen in. "You know I used to be a spy."

Kim's eyes had lit with mischief and her voice had gone low. Taylor couldn't help but grin. "I had heard rumors about that."

Out of the corner of her eyes she caught sight of Big Tag walking into the room. He'd changed into a white dress shirt but still wasn't wearing a tie. His sister-in-law was with him, smiling up at him as he said something to her.

Grace Taggart immediately flagged down the server carrying the tray of champagne around.

She looked so calm and serene that it was hard to believe she'd watched the woman yell at her adult son barely a few hours before.

"Well, I might have noticed earlier today that Big Tag cleared the conference room and I might have been super nosy and found a way to listen in," Kim admitted.

Taylor gasped and turned toward Kim. "Seriously? This is a classified mission."

"Oh, they were so not talking about the mission," Kim assured her. "Well, not the classified one."

"Nah, they were talking about Drake's delicate feelings, and my uncle was playing the dad role."

Taylor nearly jumped out of her shoes. When had Kyle joined them? "Hey, we were having a…" What had he said? "Drake's delicate feelings?"

Kyle had a glass in his hand. "Oh, so delicate. He is a fainting romance heroine, and my uncle is the elderly grandma who inspires him to go after the dangerous lover of his dreams. At least that's how I read it. Yeah, I caught Kim listening in. She's not so great at the spy thing anymore."

Kim frowned. "I am, too. And you might have caught me, but you didn't turn me in."

Kyle shrugged. "Those can be amusing conversations. I wouldn't keep them from anyone. I've often thought about trying to find a way to record them and turn them into a podcast. 'Granny Ian's Love Advice.'"

"I think he would be upset with that." Ian Taggart wasn't a man she would cross.

One side of Kyle's lips curled up in a hint of a smile. "Only if I didn't share the profits with him. But Solo's right. They weren't talking about the op. Drake is way more concerned with getting you to like him again."

Of course he was. She wouldn't be easy to work with if she didn't like him. "I suppose he was surprised to find out his one-night stand was coming back to haunt him."

"He was surprised to see you here since he'd been planning on breaking you out of prison after he offed his sister." The smile was off Kyle's face now.

She'd heard this before. "Yes, that's a ridiculous story."

"I don't know. I thought it was kind of romantic." Kim's nose wrinkled. "I know. I know. Still totally on your side, but he managed to sound so wistful even when Big Tag was talking about his dick brain."

Kyle snorted. "Nah. It was Drake's dick brain. Yeah, for some reason dicks always come in somewhere in these conversations. Big Tag is a philosopher. But seriously, Taylor. He was talking to me about finding you and breaking you out and life on the run before he knew you were here."

"Of course, his friend would say that."

"In this I am honest," Kyle replied. "Drake and I were friends, still are, though there are reasons we're not comfortable with each other anymore."

Taylor didn't want the well of sympathy that hit her. Friendship was hard for Drake. She remembered how easily they'd clicked when they were kids and how that had seemed like such a miraculous thing. And then she hadn't seen him for years and they'd clicked again.

Was Kim right? Was she mourning the loss of potential she'd seen in Drake? The loss of the life she could have had? She didn't want to think she was so shallow, but she couldn't fix the problem if she wasn't willing to face it.

"How was he this afternoon?" Kim asked. "Is he still trying to get you kicked off? Or did he listen to his dick brain?"

Such a weird world she found herself in. She kind of liked it. The last eighteen months of her life she'd been isolated, and when she did have interactions with other people they were serious. "No. He treated me professionally this afternoon."

She'd missed those moments when they'd watched Kyle's parents arrive and had fun with the drama. She'd enjoyed being so close to him, being able to lean back and feel him against her. There had been a deep sweetness to those moments that scared the hell out of her.

"And he made moon eyes at her." Kyle's eyes went wide and he fluttered his lashes. "He acted like a twelve-year-old girl with a crush."

"When I was a twelve-year-old girl with a crush I would punch people," Kim countered.

"Okay, he acted like a simpering girl and not a badass girl. Can we please acknowledge that prepubescent girls with crushes run a whole spectrum of behavior and Drake's was the girliest girl of them all?" Kyle corrected. "Hey, Mom, Uncle Ian. I was just telling Taylor that Drake likes her and if he passes her a note during the classified meeting she should check yes, she likes him, too."

"I think the afternoon conference went well," Ian said. "Way better than the morning one. Well, everyone except Tucker's kids, but I can't blame them. They have Tucker's DNA and are being raised as free-range kids. Now I see why Charlie thought that was a bad idea. I'm pretty sure I saw the boy trying to ride a goat, and Violet thought the St. Andrew's Cross needed glitter. Not sure Sandra's seen that yet."

Grace's head shook. "Those children were perfectly well behaved." Her gorgeous face frowned. "Which is more than I can say for mine."

Kyle's hands came up. "Hey, I don't know what David did, but I had nothing to do with it."

"Yes, David is the problem," Grace replied.

"Oh, are they about to go at it again?" Drake was suddenly behind her, his voice a warm caress at her ear.

Kim tilted her head slightly, acknowledging the man behind Taylor. "I think so. They got interrupted by the conference thing. I heard Kyle ran the minute Brad gave him the slightest work excuse. And by heard, I mean saw because I'm using this whole thing as a way to practice my spy skills."

"David? Seriously? You think your sweet, never-done-anything-wrong-in-his-life professor brother is the problem here?" Grace asked, rounding on her son and managing to not spill a drop of her champagne.

"In his life?" Kyle's eyes had gone wide. "Oh, how you forget our childhood."

"Excellent." Drake's reply came with a sexy chuckle, and she felt a hand on her arm. "I would love to listen to any good gossip you hear."

Kyle and his mom were arguing about something Kyle called the Great Root Beer Flood Incident, but Taylor turned to Drake. He was excellent at keeping her on her toes. It was time to start jarring him, too.

"I heard some gossip about you and Big Tag's dick brain," she announced under her breath.

She expected Drake to get upset. Most men did when she called them on their shit. Instead Drake's lips curled up in what seemed like a genuinely joyful expression, and he winked at Kim. "Your spy skills are still excellent, Solo."

Kim tipped her glass his way. "I'm glad you approve."

"And I hope she explained that Big Tag uses his dick as a metaphor," Drake explained. "He's kind of the Yoda of relationship stuff for our group, but instead of making me levitate and use a light saber, I have to survive him talking about his junk in incredibly explicit ways. But his advice almost always works."

Kim nodded. "He strangely is excellent at the romance advice. He's even stopped gagging when he uses the word *love*. I think the old guy is softening up."

"Well, parts of him at least," Drake agreed.

"Mom, I'm sorry I didn't call. I was busy trying to save Deke and Maddie," Kyle said, a deeply righteous tone to his voice. "I was working. I couldn't stop the op to call my mom. And don't tell me I should have texted. You never respect the text. I text, you call, and then the bad guy gets to listen in on me explaining I'm working."

Grace's finger pointed her son's way. It was a mom finger—both judgmental and fully authoritative. "You did not save Deke and Maddie. Boomer did that."

"From a tree." Big Tag was standing back. He nodded as one of the waitstaff offered him an hors d'oeuvre. It looked like a large shrimp. Big Tag took three. "I don't think Kyle was even in the same room."

Drake grinned. "You really want to keep yelling at me, but it's good drama, right? I was there that night, by the way. Well, I was busy blowing up a satellite."

He'd been the one who blew up Nolan Byrnes's manufacturing plant? "I always knew that man was evil. No CEO smiles that much. So what did Kyle do?"

"You were too busy trying to blow yourself up to help your friends," Grace accused.

Drake simply gestured Grace's way. "I think all will be revealed."

"I was not trying to blow myself up," Kyle insisted.

"If he was, he was real bad at it." Big Tag downed a shrimp. "Grace, you were going to send that kid to graduate school. I'm not sure that would have been a good use of funds."

Kyle's eyes rolled. "I obviously didn't intend to blow myself up. I was merely trying to make a statement."

"So you can make a statement but you can't call your own mother and give her a heads-up that you're playing spy games again and this time you're going to fake your own death?" Grace asked. "I have to hear that from Ian? You know your uncle is not great with tact."

"I am excellent at everything," Ian replied quickly. "Wait. Is that the part where you make up shit so the truth doesn't hit so hard? Yeah, I'm not good at that."

Grace's hazel eyes narrowed. "Obviously since you told me my son had faked his own death via the delivery of a box of cookies."

Ian shrugged. "I thought the cookies would soften the blow."

"*You* ate the cookies, Ian." Every word was ground out of Grace's mouth.

"I was very upset," Ian admitted. "And they were lemon. They soothed me. Hey, I helped pay for the fake funeral."

These people were crazy. She kind of loved them. She leaned back, whispering Drake's way. "Did you go to the fake funeral?"

He didn't give up an inch of space, merely let his hand find her hip so he could lean in. It brought their bodies together and sent a thrill of arousal up her spine. "They were mean. I didn't even get an invite, but I have heard rumors that it was weird as hell and the original headstone said *Here Lies a Real Dumbass.*"

Grace seemed to calm down, and she patted her brother-in-law's arm. "Yes, you did, and it was a good thing. It was nice to have Kai lead it."

"Kai led my funeral?" That appeared to be fresh news to Kyle.

Before she could ask the question, Drake was whispering in her ear again. "He's Sanctum's therapist. Also a total sadist, but very chill on the therapy side."

"What happened to getting like a pastor to preside?" Kyle asked.

"Well, son, when I'm burying something other than your Xbox, I'll see about getting religious counseling," Grace returned.

Drake gasped.

And then Kyle gasped, too. "My Xbox?"

"Shit. He loves his Xbox," Drake whispered. "Like more than a human being should love an inanimate object."

Kyle's mother nodded. "Actions have consequences, son. And I threw the controllers in, too. And all the games. At least you know where they are, which is more than I can say about you."

Grace turned on her heels and strode away.

Ian chuckled. "These shrimp are good, but nothing is saltier than a mad momma. And it wasn't just the Xbox we buried. We let everyone bring their own item to dump into the…should we call it a casket? It was more like a large cardboard box the girls decorated. It was a whole craft project."

"Ooo, what did you put in, Ian?" Kim asked.

She knew she should feel for Kyle, but she kind of wanted to know, too.

"I lined the coffin with beautiful confetti," Ian said with a wistful expression on his face. "I brought a big bowl of it. Like sometimes they let you lay a flower on the casket. I let everyone grab a handful of confetti and spread it on the blowup doll his brother laid out. Now that I think about it, she was holding one of the controllers."

Kyle's lips had drawn in tight. "Were they dicks? Were they glittery mini-confetti dicks, Ian?"

"Ah, he knows me so well," Ian said with a satisfied sigh. "If it helps, Kai led us all in a session where we talked about what a dumbass you are."

Kyle's frown deepened. "No, that does not help."

"I found it very healing," Ian admitted.

"Has anyone thought about the fact that this whole funeral wouldn't help MaeBe deal with the fact that I'm dead?" Kyle asked. "She was supposed to think I'm gone. I know I agreed to tell my parents, but everyone else was supposed to think I'm dead."

Ian flagged down the dude with the mini meatballs and simply took the whole tray off his hands. "Yeah, that wasn't going to happen. You see, your parents aren't that great with the acting thing. I told them they could support you by going into mourning for a couple of months and shutting down their whole lives and their other children's lives, but for some reason they decided to keep Carys and Luke in school. Also, MaeBe refused to go to the funeral. She said she wasn't playing out your dramatic bits."

Kyle groaned and growled. "I'm not trying to ruin their lives. I'm trying to save them. I've pointed out several times that I think Julia has already fucked my family over in several ways."

That was the moment she felt Drake pull away from her. As Kyle started to go over the numerous ways Julia could harm the people he loved, Drake moved to the bar.

"Damn, for a moment he looked almost happy," Kim said.

And then his sister's name had been brought up.

Was he pretending? She got the real feeling that Kyle wasn't pretending at all. Kyle hated and feared the woman named Julia Ennis.

She'd never had a sibling. Barely had any family at all. What would it have felt like if one of the only people in the world who'd known his secret had turned on him? He'd lost his sister and his friend in a single day. If he wasn't lying to her, he'd lost a lot.

Maybe even enough to push him over the edge when confronted with another possible betrayal.

She did not want to look at their situation from his point of view. She didn't owe the man anything.

So why did she walk over to him, abandoning the amusing Taggart family argument?

She got there as Brad strode in. He'd changed to a dark blue jacket and tie, and his head shook as he looked around the dining room.

"What the actual hell?" Brad had his hands on his hips. "Drake, when you told me they were serving dinner I didn't think we were holding a swanky dinner party complete with an open bar and roaming waitstaff. Waitstaff that absolutely have not been vetted."

Drake sighed and looked to the bartender. "Are you here to spy for a foreign country?"

The lanky bartender seemed slightly confused by the question. He was maybe twenty-five, with dark hair and cornflower blue eyes that should have every woman in the room panting after him. Maybe some of the guys, too. "I'm from Wyoming, Sir."

She stifled a giggle because that had been a Sir with a capital *S*, and not merely a polite one. He was a cute sub, and some top here at The Cowgirl's Choice likely had a lot of fun with him.

"See, he's homegrown, Brad," Drake drawled. "Nothing to worry about except his version of a double and mine are not the same."

"Sorry, Sir." The sub poured a generous extra portion of whiskey into Drake's glass.

Brad moved into Drake's space. "That is not what I mean and you know it. There are people with absolutely no clearance working this…is this a party?"

"I think it's the Taggart family way of dealing with issues," Drake explained. "Sean cooks, Grace organizes things beautifully, and Ian make sarcastic remarks. Brad, it's fine. I assure you no one who works for Sandra is a Consortium employee. She runs deep background checks on all her club members, especially those who serve as employees. Calm down and enjoy the fact that we're not eating cheeseburgers for dinner again."

"Hey, guys. I'm going to head home for the night." Tucker had his laptop packed in his messenger bag. Jax stood beside him.

She'd rapidly come to like both men. They were different from the Agency types she'd grown up around. They were happy and funny and asked interesting questions. "You're not staying for dinner? I've heard it's going to be lovely."

She wasn't sure what to expect. Gourmet food wasn't exactly a subject she knew much about.

Now that she thought about it, she might be the only one who didn't understand it. The Taggarts had made a good portion of their wealth off Sean's empire. Drake and Kim had grown up very wealthy. Brad as well.

Tucker and Jax might have been the only ones who would make her feel comfortable in a formal dining setting.

Tucker's head shook. "I'm taking ours to go. If I had some fancy meal without my wife, there would be trouble. She's happy out here but only because I'm careful about not mentioning things like five-star dining. Then there's the fact that I'm pretty sure the kids are asleep now. Transport will be so much easier if they're sleeping. Where are you guys sleeping, by the way? It didn't look like you were set up at the house. Did my mother-in-law actually put you up in the privacy rooms?"

Brad sighed. "I thought it was weird there was so much lube in there. Should I be worried about tonight?"

Taylor turned and shook her head. At least she felt comfortable talking about this. "She's closed off the floor for the night. The dungeon has a couple of aftercare rooms the Mistress will use as privacy rooms for the evening."

"Mistress?" Brad's brows rose.

"Yes, it's what Sandra should be called when she's in the club." Drake set his drink down on one of the high-top tables set throughout the room.

He'd been quiet most of the night. After lunch, he'd called them all back into the conference room and there had been no arguments about who was going into the field. It seemed whatever talk he'd had with Taggart had turned him around.

Or he was still plotting and didn't want to give away his next move.

Or he'd done exactly what Kim told her and he'd bared his soul to Tag and wanted to find a way to get close to her.

She thought briefly about getting super drunk and falling into bed with him. Then there wouldn't be a reason to stay away. The damage would be done, and she could spend the rest of their time together screwing him out of her system.

"So I should call her Mistress Sandra?" Brad still seemed generally confused.

"Only if you're planning on playing." Drake sent his friend a pointed look. "Which I assume you are not."

Brad's head shook. "Nope. No playing. I'm afraid of everything that could happen in that dungeon place. I mean should any of us be playing? We're here to work."

Jax glanced down at his watch. "Well, my worktime is over so I'm heading out with Tucker. I'm staying in his guest room, which is actually the bottom bunk in Gavin's room. No playing without the wife around. 'Night."

Tucker nodded her way. "We'll be back in the morning. You

175

guys have fun."

Brad pointed toward the door as Jax and Tucker left. "See, that's the point. We're not here to have fun."

"So we should ruthlessly cut out anything amusing that comes up?" Drake asked. "You know what, Brad, stay for dinner or go. I don't care."

"Well, I didn't mean to upset you." Brad was frowning. "I don't understand what's going on in your head. You've never been difficult to work with. We've always been on the same page when it comes to this kind of thing."

"Canapé?" A server held up her platter. "It's roasted garlic with goat cheese and sundried tomato."

It was pretty, but she wasn't sure she liked goat cheese.

Brad picked one up. "I suppose since it's here I shouldn't let it go to waste."

Drake took one, too, and then turned her way. "Try it. You might like it. It's not your norm, but new things can be good."

She picked one up, following his lead. "I'm not exactly a gourmand. I think that's the term."

"The goat cheese is creamy and has a bite to it. The cracker is buttery and garlicky, and then you get the brightness of the tomato," Drake said.

"Yes, that's excellent," Brad agreed.

She gave it a try and was surprised at the different but harmonious flavors. They seemed to work together, building layers of taste. "It's good."

"And we could have eaten it around the conference table," Brad complained. "I don't understand the need for a formal dinner."

"Do you honestly expect us to not do anything but work for weeks at a time?" Drake asked Brad.

Brad had been all business all day. Brad had only wanted to talk about the op, going over and over logistics and planning, asking them to question the mission from every angle. "I guess we'll have down time, but I would think we should spend that time reading a book or watching some TV. I don't think it's productive to…what? Have weird sex with strangers?"

"It's not necessarily about sex." She wanted to go into that dungeon, but it was probably a bad idea at this point. Brad was right about the fact that they were here to work. She wouldn't be able to trust anyone she didn't know, and D/s was all about trust. But she so needed a session. "I find a good flogging relaxing. I certainly don't have sex with every top who offers me a session."

"Some people find light pain can release endorphins," Drake explained. "For some it's heavy pain, but I've always dealt with the lighter side. Sex is not always on the menu. But you should think about the fact that we're going from here to London, where we'll be staying at The Garden. Do you really think those of us who are in the lifestyle aren't going to any play nights? The Garden is one of the most beautiful clubs I've ever been in. It would be a shame to be there and not experience it fully."

She'd never been to The Garden. When her father would meet with Nick it was always in neutral spots—places where it would be natural for the two former SVR operatives to meet up. No one had wanted her father too closely associated with McKay-Taggart and Knight.

But, oh, she'd heard rumors.

Was she going to go to her room on play nights and not step out into that dungeon for fear of what? That Drake would see her in a thong? There was a reason she'd packed a corset, and it wasn't because she enjoyed sitting around in one.

Because before she'd realized Drake would be here, she hadn't thought she wouldn't play. Not for a second. Why was she letting him dictate how she spent her nights?

And if Kim was right about his talk with Tag, he was probably thinking about playing, too.

"Well, I'm not in the lifestyle, so I will be reading my books," Brad said in an oddly prim tone. "Try not to wake me up if you... You're not going to bring someone back to our room, are you?"

Ah, there it was. She didn't want to watch Drake play. She didn't want to watch him give what he'd promised her to some other woman. It was irrational, but deep down she knew she'd be jealous.

So play with him. This is your chance. Get him out of your system and maybe get a little revenge on him, too.

Drake's eyes rolled. "No. If I do something to desecrate my

177

body, I'll do it far from our room."

"See that you do," Brad replied and then turned to Taylor. "I suppose one nice dinner isn't going to kill us, but after tonight I want to focus. I'll be available twenty-four seven."

"That sounds like a threat," Drake said with a snort.

Brad ignored him. "I think we should get the big call sometime soon. Jax has everything set up, and he's heard some talk on the Dark Web that something big is coming. I'm certain they're going to move on Dr. Walsh's research soon. I think I'll find a glass of wine. A riesling should pair well with that goat cheese."

He strode toward the bar, turning more positive in an instant.

"He must really like goat cheese."

"I swear I did not know he had so many pearls he could clutch." Drake sighed and sat back, his eyes going soft as he looked at her. "Did I apologize for being an ass earlier?"

She shouldn't engage him but found herself talking before she could make the right call. "No, you didn't."

"I'm sorry. I know you won't believe me, but it was mostly about your safety."

"And now you don't care about my safety?" It was perverse, but she felt like pushing him.

"It was pointed out to me that you're not a safe woman, and to try to make you one wouldn't be fair. I don't think a lot of life has been fair to you, Taylor. I get that, and I'm going to be as supportive as I can be. Now, let's talk about that dungeon."

"I don't think I'll go." She wasn't going to make a fool of herself, and honestly, she probably hadn't thought it through before. All she'd thought about was how nice it would be to have a few hours a week where she didn't have to think about the op, where she could try to find some comfort. It looked like comfort would have to wait. Again. "Brad's right. I wouldn't be able to relax because I can't really play with anyone. I guess I'll go use the gym and get my endorphins the old-fashioned way."

His gaze seemed to pierce through her. Like he could see what she needed. "Or you could let me help you."

There it was—the real danger. He was using that deep, rich voice of his to offer her the one thing she could never accept from

No Time to Lie

him again.

"I think the last time you helped me didn't go so well for me."

"Didn't it?" A brow rose over Drake's eyes. "I think the sex part went fine. It was the whole 'I was an asshole and didn't try to fight to keep you with me' part that didn't go well."

Were they doing this here and now? She wasn't sure she wanted a debrief concerning their one-night stand. "Why would you fight to keep me? The whole play was to get information."

Which was a good reason for her to stay close to him. She could figure out if he was working with his sister. She could take him down if he was.

"It wasn't a play, Taylor. Whatever else you believe, know that I wasn't pretending. When I first got to the safe house, I was told about the fact that your father was under investigation and that I should be careful around you."

That didn't surprise her in any way. "You were careful enough to wear a condom. I should be happy about that."

His lips turned down. "I always wear a condom. Trust me. That was drummed into my head. I never asked you a single question that would have led you to tell me what your dad was doing. Not one."

"I suspect those were going to happen after you got me into bed."

"I can certainly understand why you would feel that way, but it's not true," he replied. "I understand I've lost my chance with you, but I wasn't joking about what I said to Brad. Are we going to our rooms at night? Are we not taking advantage of these spectacular clubs?"

It didn't matter that she'd thought the same thing. "You seriously think I want to play with you?"

"I think I'm an experienced top and you enjoy a good scene." He sounded so reasonable.

"Is this what you talked to Taggart about when he kicked everyone out?" She was still surprised he'd asked for advice.

He seemed to consider how to answer her. "Yes. I thought I should try to protect you from what's going to be a dangerous op, and he thinks we should celebrate how deadly our women are or something like that. I guess I was still seeing you as that soft woman

179

who wanted nothing more than to go to college."

A bittersweet memory of being in his arms swept across her. They'd talked about the future that day. Had he gotten stuck in the past? "I thought the whole reason you let them take me away was the fact that you decided I was using you. That doesn't sound very soft to me."

His fingers traced the edge of his glass as though he was seriously considering whether he should take another drink. "The minute I heard what you were being taken for, I was right back in that place where my sister betrayed me. I was stuck in that moment, and I was mad, Taylor. That was my real sin. I couldn't see that you weren't her. In that moment I pulled back into myself and erected a wall between us that had no place there. I did that. I should have followed you. I should have used every connection I had to get to you, but instead I let the pain I felt lead me. I am so sorry."

Damn him. And herself. She should be able to hold a grudge for longer. She should be suspicious for longer.

It was Kyle who sold it. Kyle was obviously in pain, and he trusted Drake. If he didn't that man would be walking around telling every person who would listen how sus Drake Radcliffe was.

Still. She couldn't simply give over. They still had problems. They still would never work long term. "I suppose I can understand that. But it's probably for the best."

"It wasn't best for me," he replied, his eyes steady on her.

"I'm only saying, it wouldn't have worked, and I don't know that we should put ourselves in that position again," she explained.

"Do you want to play tonight, Taylor? Don't think about anything but tonight and tomorrow." His voice was soft but deep, comforting. "Don't think about the future. Think about what you need tonight."

She sighed. "I could use a session."

He nodded. "So could I. We're stuck together for a while, and I'm kind of your only option. I'm sure when we get to London, Master Damon could find someone he trusts and pair you up with him, but for the next two weeks it's me or an excellent vibrator. I happen to know Sandra has many."

That was an interesting way to put it. "How would you know

that?"

"Because I had an affair with her about eight years ago. She taught me most of what I know about D/s."

She felt her eyes go wide. He'd talked about the woman he'd bottomed for years ago. It had been Sandra? "But she's…"

"Old enough to be my grandmother? Yes. And she was still hot as hell. We're friends now. She found the love of her life, and I'm happy for her. If you think less of me because I had an affair with an older woman, well, then you're not the woman I thought you were."

"I don't think less of you." She kind of thought it was cool. She'd had it in her head that Drake was all style and no substance.

Also, Sandra had taught him incredibly well.

"I was in my early twenties, and all my sex up to that point had been quick and not entirely satisfying. I thought that was how it was supposed to be. I was taught how to spy not how to seduce women." He settled in as though they were old friends talking. "Sandra thought I could do better. We were working an op on this island, and I learned a lot. See, we knew we weren't some love match but still managed to give each other what we needed. And I'm pretty sure I'm a better operative when I'm relaxed. She actually did a lot of odd jobs for the Agency when she was working for Big Tag. When we worked together, we played together. We got to be pretty good friends. It was weird to go to her wedding, but then I realized I was not the only one of her mentees there. I wasn't even the youngest."

She felt a smile cross her face. "Okay, I kind of want to be Sandra when I grow up."

"It's not a bad thing to be. She had relationships with all of us. The sex was casual. The friendship was not," Drake explained. "She's one of the reasons I'm comfortable with my sexuality. Big Tag is another because he helped me get into my club."

She'd heard about the club in DC. "The Court?"

"Yes. It is a fun place to be," he affirmed. "And it's nice to be able to be a me I'm not most of the time. Which is why I wouldn't hate playing with you, Taylor. I'll be honest. I'd also try to seduce you because I want to prove to myself that the sex we had wasn't…it couldn't be as good as I remember."

Wasn't as… "You can't be serious. Are you actually telling me

I should fuck you to prove the sex we had was good?"

"It wasn't merely good," Drake argued. "It was earth shaking, life changing."

She rolled her eyes. "Sure it was."

"I haven't had sex since, so…" He gave her a shrug.

"You haven't had sex since we were together? That was a year and a half ago."

He simply stared at her.

Could she believe him? Or was this one more way to get back into her life so he could fuck her over again.

Or he made a mistake and he knows it now. Maybe he felt everything you did and he wants to try again.

Her vagina had terrible instincts when it came to men. Or rather man. She was pretty good at figuring out who wasn't worth her time. Drake had been the exception.

Not that she'd had a lot of experience before. And none after, and didn't she want to prove it hadn't been that good, too?

She was going into something so dangerous, and why shouldn't she take what pleasure she could? She could be the one to walk away this time. This time she would be in control. This time she would come out on top.

But who would she be if she gave in? She didn't want to be that sad-sack girl who went back to the man who hurt her, to the man who might have had a hand in her father's death.

So find out. He's offering you the keys to his kingdom. This isn't about pleasure. It's about investigating him. What's the best way to get close to a man? He wants you. He'll screw up, and you'll be there to use it against him.

It sucked when her brain and her vagina teamed up on her. Her brain made a little bit of sense, and her vagina offered her everything she wanted. It was perfect. And terrible.

"Why the hell would I trust you again?" She needed to ask even though she wouldn't believe him.

"That's the great thing about D/s. We can have a contract. We can keep that part of our relationship in one specific place, and we'll have two people who have control over it. Sandra here and Damon when we get to London. I assure you I won't piss either of them off.

I'll respect every limit you put on me, and I hope you'll respect mine. This won't be a boyfriend/girlfriend thing. It's about mutual need. I know I'm stressed. It's my sister out there. I have to take out a person I loved…love. I love my sister. I love the person I thought she was. D/s is my refuge when my emotions get too hard to handle."

She didn't want to believe him. She wanted him to be some asshole because if he was, she didn't have to consider that he'd made a mistake and wanted another chance. She didn't have to think about the fact that she might want another chance, too.

It was so much easier to live in the now, to only think about today and tomorrow because she was going into something she probably wouldn't come out of.

"I have to think about it." She turned away from him, noticing that night had fallen outside. It got so dark out here. The stars sparkled like diamonds, and a single car could light up the night like a firefly floating her way.

"Dinner is served," one of the waitstaff announced.

"Thank god." Kyle downed the rest of his drink and checked his watch. "I've got a raid in a couple of hours, and I'd like to check out the dungeon ahead of time."

Big Tag had finished that whole plate of meatballs on his own. "You're going to the dungeon?"

"Online dungeon," Kyle corrected, starting for the dining room. "I certainly won't have any fun at all because my mom is planning on playing tonight, so I will avoid the actual dungeon at all costs. I'm going to be online all night, so unless the world is on fire, don't call me."

So he would be doing that thing where he talked to his girlfriend without letting his girlfriend know who she was talking to. She kind of wanted to be there when this Mae person found out. She'd overheard Kyle and his uncle arguing about training. Kyle didn't think his beloved needed to know how to deball a man, but she was with Tag on this one.

"Thank god I had my laptop with me or my mom would have buried it," Kyle groused.

Drake offered to let her go first. "I'll be in that dungeon tonight.

If you want a session, we can start there. No sex if you are uninterested. You know how this goes. I'm the Dom but you have all the control. It's how it should be. Now come and sit with me. I'll tell you what everything is and which fork to use. See, I can be helpful."

She followed him in. That was Drake. Helpful and oh so dangerous.

* * * *

"What the fuck does that mean?" Kyle was in the locker room, which he claimed had the best Internet connection, but he wasn't playing his game.

His stepfather looked back from the locker he'd been assigned for the night. "I think it means she's not going to be going on that raid with you."

Drake wished Taylor was here. She liked the Kyle drama, and he was playing it hard right now. They'd watched Sean try to mediate between his wife and stepson at dinner this evening, with Ian taking on the role of the imp who poked at everyone. It had been very amusing. "Well, she might get raided, just not online."

MaeBe had sent "Kraven" a DM explaining that she'd gotten an invite to this club she enjoyed going to and was taking the night off from virtual life to have a real one.

Tag snorted but then stared Drake's way. "Don't wind him up."

But it was fun to wind Kyle up. And he kind of deserved this. "Come on. We all know what club she's talking about."

"She doesn't go to Sanctum anymore," Kyle insisted.

"No, she didn't go to Sanctum for a while. She certainly didn't give up her membership," Tag corrected. He glanced down at his phone. "And according to Charlie, she's absolutely at Sanctum."

"What the hell is Charlotte doing at Sanctum without you?" Kyle shook his head like the world suddenly made no sense to him. "Speaking of, why are you getting into leathers?"

"First, Charlie is hiding from the kids. Boomer and Daphne are hosting a slumber party at our house where she's teaching all the kids how to make cake or something. I don't know. All I know is

Charlie was left with all five of our kiddos, and Carys and Luke. Which means at some point Tristan and Aidan will show up."

Sean's head dropped. "I don't want to hear that."

From what he'd been able to put together, Carys Taggart had two boyfriends, and Sean Taggart was having to deal with the fact that his teenaged daughter was dating two guys who didn't mind sharing her.

In what he'd been promised was a wholesome way. Wholesome sharing.

The evening had been fun.

"All I'm saying is there's a lot of drama surrounding those kids, and she deserves a night off," Tag argued. "Also, how am I going to keep up with Sanctum drama if my baby is dealing with kid drama? And I'm here because I'm keeping Charlie in the loop on the local drama. She wants to know if the new girl is going to take Drake's ball sac."

"Could we stop talking about ball sacs? Like you do that a lot. You're obsessed with ball sacs." Damn, but he'd missed locker room talk. He'd spent the last several months working and working and…yep…working. He'd neglected this side of himself, and he was starting to understand it was because he'd been a dumbass about Taylor. He'd missed her and punished himself for not going after her.

"Well, my ball sac is empty now," Tag pointed out. "So I have to find my fun elsewhere."

"Because you used to have fun with your ball sac?" Sean asked, settling his vest over his chest.

"So much fun. It was my best friend," Tag replied. "And according to my Charlie, MaeBe is totally at Sanctum and she's ready to play. I think it's good she's getting back out there. She's gone through her mourning period and is ready to get in the saddle again."

Tag hadn't wanted Kyle wound up? "I don't think she was ever in the saddle. Not with Kyle. He never got that far. That's probably why she didn't need long to mourn him."

"Who the fuck is she playing with?" Kyle ran a hand through his hair, shoving it back.

Tag looked down to his phone. "She's apparently hanging out in the lounge right now, but the night is young. She's been spending some time with West Rycroft, from what I understand."

Sean put up a hand as though trying to ward off the tiger Kyle could become. "It's not the way it sounds. West has been her bodyguard for the last couple of weeks."

"West? West is barely out of training. What are you trying to do? Get her killed?" Kyle practically shouted the question.

Sean groaned and slammed the locker door shut, glaring his brother's way. "I'm not doing this. You wound him up. You deal with him. Kyle, if you don't want to see your mom doing things you can't unsee, hide in here. She's stressed and it's your fault, and I do not care about your eyes."

Sean strode out.

And Drake followed him because it was time to figure out if he had any chance with Taylor tonight. Still, he had questions. "Who is West? Is he related to Wade?"

Wade Rycroft was manager of Sanctum in addition to his duties as a bodyguard. He was married to Tag's longtime administrative assistant. He'd never met a West.

"Yes, West is Wade's brother, and he's good at his job and he gives Mae some of the space she needs right now," Sean replied. "She's been having to hang out with Erin and her family for weeks, and while they're lovely, MaeBe is a single young woman who needs to have her own life. She's staying with West for the time being. I don't think she's going to fall in love with him, but Kyle made that choice."

"If it's any consolation, I think he'll go back eventually." After they'd taken care of Julia. "I know he's insisting that he won't, but he already misses his family."

Sean stopped just outside the locker room. "I hope that's the case, but I fear he's going to have lost his chance with her. I don't know how he handles that."

He couldn't think that way. Kyle had done what he'd done to protect MaeBe. If she couldn't forgive Kyle, there was no way Taylor ever forgave him. "I think those two will figure it out. I think they're meant to be. I know when I watch them together, they fit.

Like Ian and Charlotte fit."

"Like you and me," a soft voice said.

Drake looked over, and Grace had walked out of the women's locker room.

Damn. Yeah, Kyle might have a problem with seeing his mom like that, but Drake did not. Grace looked stunning in a white corset and thong and killer heels.

Sean reached out a hand, and she moved to him. "Like you and me." He brought her hand to his lips. "Always."

That was the moment he realized Taylor had walked out behind Grace.

And he was pretty sure his jaw hit the floor.

She was stunning. He'd thought she was gorgeous with long blonde hair, but she was every bit as lovely with her chic bob of auburn. She wore a purple corset and matching thong, and over-the-knee boots that made her legs look a mile long.

She looked like every Bond-girl fantasy he'd ever had, and he'd had a couple.

The door to the men's locker room slammed open and Kyle walked out, his finger pointed Sean's way.

"You need to talk to..." Kyle stopped, turned, and walked right back into the locker room. "Nope."

Taylor's eyes lit with mirth, and she clapped a hand over her mouth.

Grace blushed. "We should go into the dungeon. I think he's learned his lesson now."

Sean led her away. "Oh, I doubt it, but we're going to forget everything for the rest of the night. For tonight it's just you and me. You are still the most beautiful sub in the world. Have I told you that lately?"

"She does not look old enough to be Kyle's mom." Taylor's lips had curled up, and there was a wistful expression on her face as she watched the other couple disappear into the main dungeon.

"She's a lovely woman, but Sean is wrong."

She stared at him, the soft expression fleeing. "I suppose I'm the most beautiful sub in the world."

It was good she understood. "You said it. I would never correct you. Have you thought about what we talked about earlier?"

"I don't think it's a good idea."

And yet she was here, and she'd made sure she looked like sin on two long legs. "Okay. Well, I guess I'll watch some scenes for a while. I hope you have a good night."

She frowned as though she hadn't expected he would move on so quickly. When he walked past her, she fell in beside him. "Seriously? I'm supposed to believe you're just going to watch?"

He held open the door to the main dungeon for her. From here he could see there was already a couple on the main stage, and it looked like they were doing a suspension scene. "I don't know what else I would do. I told you I don't intend to risk playing with someone I don't know while we're working this mission. I can't force you to do the same, but I can ask you to be cautious. I think it would be best to wait until we get to The Garden if you need a play partner. Sandra doesn't have the same physical security Damon has. The Garden is locked down tight. Sandra has a whole other business going on in another part of this building. She's careful, but not the way Damon is. If you need a session, I could ask Kyle if he would help out in one of the privacy rooms. He's serious about not seeing his mom."

Her eyes rolled like the brat she was. "I think I'll forgo getting in the middle of Kyle's drama."

"Oh, but he could probably use a little stress relief because MaeBe called off their raiding date for what could be a real date."

Taylor gasped. "Really?"

He had her full attention now. "She told him she was going to a club she'd been invited to."

"She's going to a club? Like a dance…oh, shit. Is she going to Sanctum?"

"She is indeed, and Big Tag is going to sneak his phone into the dungeon so he can trade gossip with his wife, who is also at Sanctum this evening." He wondered if that was what Big Tag used his ball sac for now. It might make a nice pouch for his cell. "Kyle is reaching *Housewife* levels of drama. I wouldn't be surprised if he sneaks away in the middle of the night and drives back to Dallas to yell at the dude who MaeBe's staying with."

"He wouldn't really do that. Would he?"

"No. I kind of wish he would. I understand why he did what he did, but I wish he'd taken Mae and gone into hiding and let us deal with this. He's had enough pain from my sister." He could be amused all day by what Kyle was going through, but there was guilt mingled with it.

"You know you aren't responsible for what your sister did," she said quietly.

"Doesn't feel like it."

She started to say something and then shook her head. "I wasn't going to do this."

"You weren't even going to talk to me?"

"No. This. Talking about anything that doesn't have to do with the mission or anything personal. If this is going to work, I need you to understand there's no you and me at the end of this."

"This? What is this?" He needed her to work through this in her head.

"You know what I'm saying. If I let you top me for the purposes of relaxation and stress relief, I need you to understand that's all this is."

His hope surged, and so did his damn cock. That part felt good. He'd been utterly unaroused by anything for months and months. It felt good to want something again. To want someone. He felt himself shift into that place he found on a dungeon floor, his shoulders going straighter, his voice deeper. Most of the time he needed to be unthreatening, easy to look over. It was the mark of an excellent spy that not many people noticed him.

He wanted her to notice him.

"I think I can handle what you need." He was lying, of course. He fully intended to be with her at the end of this op, but he wasn't about to tell her. "Should we negotiate a contract?"

"I think a standard will do fine, and we can go over it tomorrow. Tonight, I want to forget I'm here for anything but to decompress. I want to watch some scenes, and then I'd like for you to make me cry. It's hard for me to cry, and I feel it building up. I might need some dominance play to get me into the right headspace if I decide I'd like to try sex."

He hated the fact that they were talking about this like she was ordering takeout, but it was where he'd put himself, and he wouldn't argue with her. But he needed to make sure he understood. "Dominance play? Are you asking me to force you?"

"I'm asking you to pretend to force me, and not exactly," she tried to explain. "I'm asking you to be dominant with me when it comes to sex. I know how to use a safe word, and I won't hesitate if the scene gets to be too much."

She wanted him to play the bad guy. He hated that, too. She wanted to take all the tenderness out of any sexual encounter they might have.

Well, Tag had told him she might have to compartmentalize in the beginning. He wanted to argue with her, wanted to have the discussion they needed to have, but he would lose if he did that. Instead, he moved into her space, looming over her. "Are we starting?"

He wouldn't touch her without permission, but once she'd given it, as long as they were in this dungeon he would have all kinds of rights. He intended to use them.

She stared for a moment and he worried she might change her mind, but then her chin dipped slightly, a nod of agreement.

He let his hand find the back of her neck, cupping it and tightening slightly so she could feel his strength. Sure enough, her eyes started to dilate.

Maybe she wanted the dominance for more than mere compartmentalization. Maybe she needed it to enjoy sex.

He could give it to her.

"Then let's begin."

Chapter Ten

W hat the hell was she doing?

Taylor took a long breath—not an easy thing to do in a corset—and tried not to think about the man who stood behind her. Yeah, that was going to be impossible because his body brushed against hers and his hand had settled on her hip as they stood watching that god of a chef start to make a meal of his wife.

Sean had worked his wife over with a flogger, her hands over her head attached to a hook that came down from the ceiling. Grace had started out in the lovely corset she'd been wearing, but it hadn't taken her husband long to get her naked, putting her body on display.

Dom. Not husband. They were a Dom and a submissive in this place, not husband and wife. They weren't Sean and Grace Taggart. They were Master Sean and his sub, Grace.

Except she was pretty sure they would argue against that. She rather thought they would tell her they were always husband and wife.

Which was fine for them. That was the whole point of this lifestyle—finding something that worked for a person and their partner so they could enjoy their sexual sides.

The only way she could enjoy Drake was if she wasn't enjoying Drake. She could enjoy the Master without ever trusting the man he was underneath.

At least that was what she told herself.

They'd watched three scenes so far and had little talk in between. She felt awkward as fuck, and she was pretty sure that was all about her.

She needed to get close to him, needed for him to trust her enough that she could find the information she needed.

Yep, she was still telling herself that lie.

"Hey, let's hit the bar and talk for a while," he whispered in her ear.

They weren't even close to a scene. He wasn't any more comfortable with her than she was with him.

So different from the first time. The first time had been the easiest thing in the world. It had been like sinking into a soft bed and relaxing.

She turned, well aware they were surrounded by other members. The dungeon was small, and she suspected there were at least twenty other couples hanging around. And a surprising number of multiples. The threesome energy was strong out here in the West.

"Why don't we go to a privacy room instead?"

He frowned, looking down at her. "You want to go to a privacy room with me?"

She gave him what she hoped was a saucy smile. "I thought that's what we were here to do."

She took his hand and started walking toward the aftercare rooms.

He stopped, forcing her to do the same.

She turned and he was staring a damn hole through her, his gaze predatory and every line of his body straight and hard.

"So that's a no?" She hoped he could hear her over the thud of music that filled the room.

He dropped her hand but before she could move away from him, he gripped the nape of her neck and drew her in close. "That's a *who the hell is in charge of this*?"

Every submissive bone in her body responded to him. She

would have said she didn't have any of those bones until she'd met him and that part of herself felt like it had fallen into place. "You are, Sir."

He was stunning in his leathers, every bit the dominant dream man she'd known he could be.

If he was anyone else, she would be a puddle of submissive goo at his feet.

Sure. That's why you just drop to your knees for every hot Dom you meet. Face it. He's the only one who has ever made you feel this way.

She ignored her inner voice.

His jaw tightened. "I've been playing this wrong. I thought I would give you some time to ease into it, but all time did was let you think. You don't need to think. You need to feel. What's your safe word?"

"Red." It was the easiest thing for her to remember. "Yellow, if I'm getting nervous."

"And how do you feel about public punishment?"

She nodded. "I'm okay with it, but I would rather any real physical intimacy happens in private. I think I could work up to a more intimate scene, but I'm not there yet. Are you okay with it?"

"I would fuck you in the Oval Office in the middle of a meeting with the president if you let me."

She should have known the man wouldn't have a problem putting himself on display. "I need more time to work up to that particular scenario."

His eyes ate her up. She'd been nervous that she looked so different than the first time around, but he hadn't seemed to have a problem being attracted to her. She was far more muscular than she'd been before, and she'd dyed and cut her hair. Sometimes she didn't recognize herself. She'd done a lot to become Constance.

Maybe that's who she was right now. Maybe she was Constance Tyne and this op had begun.

He was the target, and she didn't have to open her heart to him in any way. It was all part of the op. He was the bad guy, and she was going to take him down.

He lowered his mouth to her ear, whispering softly. "Have I told

193

you how gorgeous you look tonight? I thought you were lovely with blonde hair. You're just as lovely now. I think you'll always be lovely to me. And being alone with you is everything I dream about at night."

She pulled away and for a second thought seriously about screaming out the word *yellow*, but that's not what Constance would do. Constance wouldn't care. Constance would see his whispered words of devotion as proof that what she was doing was working.

Taylor wanted to scream at him, but that would give him power. And he didn't have any power she didn't give him.

"You look good, too, Sir. Where would you like me?" If he wanted control of the scene, she would allow that.

He looked almost disappointed, but he reached for her hand again. "Come on. I saw a small space in the back when I checked this place out yesterday."

They moved away from the stage, and she could speak a bit louder.

"I thought Sandra had it locked down." If she hadn't thought so, she likely would have done the same thing.

Drake's smirk was arrogant and oh so sexy. "I broke in. She gave me a hearty lecture this morning, but I told her if she didn't want me to break into her dungeon, she shouldn't have made me sleep in a sex room with Brad, who is not in any way sexy. And he talks in his sleep about baseball stats. Nothing else. He recites baseball stats all night long."

When he was being charming, it was hard to remember how much she hated this man. He amused her so much.

He led her over to one of the corner sections. This one was small and a bit on the utilitarian side, but they didn't need much. There was a St. Andrews Cross and a spanking bench, along with a waist-high table that Drake set his kit on.

Most of the club members were involved in the scenes on the big stage, so they were relatively alone. However, the mood and feel of the place couldn't be denied. This was a place of decadence, where people could play out their fantasies in a safe way.

Except for her. There was nothing safe about this, about him.

Drake turned away for a moment, opening his kit. "You should find your position."

Her position? She'd forgotten about that part. Was she ready to drop to her knees in front of him? She'd only done this a couple of times, and absolutely never for a Dom she was probably going to see more than once. She'd barely played. She'd read and studied and watched other people but...

"Taylor, I need you on your knees, knees spread and head down. I'm not a stickler for a certain position, but I would prefer a straight spine."

Constance wouldn't hesitate. She would do the job.

Taylor took a deep breath and got to her knees. It wasn't as easy as she'd hoped it would be. Grace Taggart made that shit look graceful. Like super graceful. She kind of started out that way and then slipped.

Drake was right there, catching her before she fell too far. His arms went around her, and he easily lifted her and got her into the right position. "These floors can be slippery."

They weren't. They were hand-scraped hardwoods. Sandra's sub, Angie, had delighted in describing all the ways they'd refurbished the place so it somewhat resembled its former glory. "It used to be a brothel."

He stepped back, but his gaze remained on her. "I've heard the rumors. Tell me what you liked about the scenes we watched."

She wasn't about to tell him how much she'd appreciated the beauty and intimacy of the scenes, how open the participants were and how she wished she had someone she could be so vulnerable with. "Chef Taggart has a nice chest. Honestly, so does his sub. Those two have the beautiful torso thing down."

"Brat. Spread your knees." He took a step back, his arms crossing over the best chest in the room—though she wasn't about to tell him that. "And drop your head down. This is how we'll start our scenes when we're in a public space. In a private space they can start any way we like. If we're alone, I'll walk up to you, put a hand around the back of your neck, and you'll know I'm in control. All you have to do to stop that play is to tell me *red* and I'll stop."

"I thought we were keeping it to the club."

"I think we should consider our D/s relationship to have time constraints rather than place. I don't want to not be able to take care of you if we're stuck in a hotel room in London when we're on the actual op. Also, I don't want to have to go run here any time we need to throw down."

He was so arrogant. "I didn't say we were going to throw down at all."

"But you didn't take sex off the table," he pointed out. "As long as it's on the table, I'll try to seduce you. I'll try to get you in my bed every single night."

"I think you promised Brad that wouldn't happen."

"I'll find a bed that doesn't include Brad. I promise you. If you agree to sleep with me, I'll find us a place to do it. And once we get to The Garden, we'll have the privacy we need."

She really should have taken sex off the table because now that she was sitting here with her knees wide and the low thrum of music playing across her skin, with his deep voice promising her all kinds of pleasure, it didn't sound like a bad idea.

Because it isn't. It's exactly what you need. Get close. See if what you had that first time was real, and maybe he's telling you the truth. Maybe he really was planning on coming for you.

"Stop thinking. I can see how tense you're getting, and I'm pretty sure it's because you're overthinking this. Eyes down."

She did as he commanded, dropping her head forward into the submissive pose she'd learned. She watched as his boots came into view.

"What are you supposed to do in this place?" he asked.

"Whatever you tell me to do until such time I find something I don't want to do."

"Well, that takes the fantasy out of it, but it's true enough." The words came out in a slightly grumpy tone.

She wished that made him any less attractive. "Do you want the fantasy, Sir?"

"Do I want the fantasy that you could ever truly be here with me? Yes. Do I want the fantasy that you would choose me even if I wasn't the only Dom available to you? Yeah, I would like that, but I'll take what I can get when it comes to you. Yes. I want the fantasy that I'm in charge, and I think you want the fantasy that there's nothing you can do, that this is inevitable and I'm not Drake Radcliffe, the man who fucked you over. I'm someone else, someone who will give you what you need and not try to take more than you would like to give."

But he was right about that. It was a fantasy. He would try to take more from her, try to seduce her and trap her again.

It was a game, and if she played this right, she could win.

"Yes. I want that fantasy now that we've put the truth out there." It wasn't a lie. She did want what this man could give her physically.

His hand curled around the back of her neck, sending a thrill through her. It meant they were about to truly start. It tightened, and he gently forced her head up so she could see the look in his eyes.

He wanted her. He was going to have her.

She was going to have to take what he gave her. All the pain. All the pleasure. Everything.

She let go of the warring dialogue in her head. For the next couple of hours nothing mattered but what happened in this dungeon. She was going to allow herself to float on sensation, to exist in the moment.

"Are you ready to serve your Master tonight?" Drake asked.

She felt the moment her brain gave over to her body's needs. "Yes. I am, Sir."

The hand went soft and he moved, stroking it over her hair. "Then I'd like you on the cross."

She took the hand he held out and allowed him to help her up. She would practice more, wanting to be as graceful as the other subs around her.

Time seemed to slow as she moved to the cross. She felt languid as he carefully bound her wrists. Taylor allowed herself to feel the way his hands moved over her skin. The calluses she remembered were still there, scraping over her in the most delicious way. She would have expected those hands of his to be soft. He was from a spectacularly wealthy family, had all the best of everything the world could offer. But his hands were working hands, and they did something for her.

She'd only been flogged a few times, and mostly by Dommes.

The women who'd helped her learn what she did and didn't like hadn't brought the same feeling of sex that she felt this time. She'd found comfort from them, enjoyed how her body had hummed at the experience but her pussy hadn't been involved.

It was now.

There was a heat taking over her body and it came from her pussy. She could already feel herself getting soft and wet and ready for him. Like it knew who her real Master was.

She let the thoughts flow as he finished, let them pulse through her brain like they rode the wave of the music that surrounded them.

Somewhere in the back of her mind she was aware that they weren't alone, but she let go of that thought, too. His fingertips brushed down her spine to the place where her corset sat under her shoulder blades. "This has to go."

She'd known it would. She wasn't as panicked at the thought as she should have been. She'd been naked in a club before, but not with anyone she was probably going to have sex with. Maybe.

Not with anyone she'd had sex with before.

She nodded her assent and then felt him move in behind her.

The fact that he'd bound her hands before taking off the corset fed into the fantasy.

She couldn't see him as he started to work the ties of her corset, but she could feel as he tugged on the strings, loosening them.

"It's like unwrapping the best present ever. You're a pretty plaything, Taylor. Did you know that? Did you know that I'm going to play with you? I'm going to unwrap this gift and admire it, and then I'll touch it and play with it. I'll stroke my hands across your skin to feel how soft it is. I'll run my nose between your legs to smell how hot you are. I'll suck your nipples and nip them ever so slightly to see if I can make my toy squirm."

He was already making her squirm. She remembered how it had felt to have those talented hands on her body.

She'd never been able to forget how well he'd used his mouth and tongue on her. Never. She would likely go to her grave remembering how that had felt.

The ties on her corset came loose quickly, proving how often he'd done this service for the women of his club. That was a good thing to remember, too.

In quick time he eased the corset down her hips and held it open for her to step out of.

She was left alone for a moment as he moved away from her.

She didn't like him being away. She wanted his hands on her. When they were on her, she didn't think. When his hands were on her, she was warm and back in that place she'd found with him once before.

In that moment, it didn't matter that the place she'd found had been temporary and false. She wanted to be there again even if only for a night.

Then she felt something at the nape of her neck, something slightly cool but soft.

Not a flogger. That was a crop. She would bet it was a soft, leather-tipped crop that would have some flexibility so the top using it could control the pain level of the strike.

"What do you need, sub? Do you need something soft and sweet, a little snap to get your motor running?"

The crop moved like lightning, flicking over her left cheek and making her gasp.

He'd been right. It was a slight pain, barely enough to sting, but it warmed her skin, made her aware of her body in a way nothing else could.

But it wasn't enough.

"Or do you need something more? Do you need a bite to get you going? Because, baby, I can be the big bad wolf when it comes to you."

Before she could answer, he brought the crop down on her other cheek, and he wasn't playing. It wasn't a hard strike, like the ones she would want later in the session, but it got her attention. The pain exploded and then quickly turned to heat that sizzled and seemed to go straight to her core.

"More." She managed to get the word out. "I like more, Sir."

"Prove it."

The words flustered her. "Prove it?"

"Prove this is what makes you hot."

He was a bastard. He knew it made her hot, but he wanted

more. He could probably smell her arousal, but he needed more.

Like she needed more.

"You can touch me. You'll find the proof you need."

"Touch you where, Taylor?"

She wanted to curse him, but that wouldn't get them anywhere. "My pussy."

"And what will I find?"

There was nothing but honesty from her now. She'd moved past pretense. All that was left was need. "You'll find I'm wet. So fucking wet."

"Wet for what?" He kept pushing her.

"Wet for you."

His free hand gripped her hip, and then there was no space between them. She could feel his leather against her backside and the hard line of his erection. She fought to breathe as that hand made its way around her hips and slipped under the edge of the thong she wore.

She was glad her hands were tied down because she wasn't sure she wouldn't have reached down to hurry him up. The impulse to drag his fingers where she wanted them was almost overwhelming, but those bonds held tight. She was forced to wait as his fingers made slow progress.

"I hope you're right. I hope that pussy is getting wet. Otherwise I'll have to try something else, and I so wanted to flog you. What do you like, baby? A thud? A sting? Would you like me to warm you up with this crop, to make you squirm and cry, and then take out a flogger with soft falls and make everything better? I'll have to touch you often to make sure the therapy is working."

Therapy. She would need a lot of therapy after all this because it was working so well on her. Her whole body was primed, and he'd barely touched her. Her nipples were tight, breasts ready to be cupped.

"I want that. I want everything you said."

"Well, you have to give me what I want, and I want this pussy wet," he demanded. "I want it soaking wet. I want it begging for me to touch it."

There was zero chance she was holding out on him. Not when

his hand was so damn close to her pussy.

"Please touch me."

The pad of his finger slipped over her clitoris, and she forgot to breathe. She wanted that finger to stay there, to rub her and make her come, but it didn't. His hand slipped lower and dipped inside her.

Easily, because she was so damn wet.

"Oh, that's exactly what I wanted." His breath was hot against her ear, and he slowly pressed his finger inside.

It wasn't nearly enough, but she pressed against him.

And then he dragged his hand away. "Not yet."

She growled and then felt a nip to her ear that sent a shudder through her.

"Be a good girl," he commanded.

He wasn't making it easy on her. She wanted the orgasm, but the point was to heighten it, to make her wait for it so when it came it took her breath away.

Like this man always did.

She let that thought float away, too, as he stepped back.

"You still taste sweeter than any honey," he whispered.

She didn't have to see him to know what he'd done. He'd taken those soaked fingers into his mouth and sucked them dry.

That shouldn't be so sexy, but it was.

The first crack of the crop hit her, sounding before she felt the sweet sting.

And then again. And again. He peppered his strikes all over her ass and thighs, stopping where her boots began.

What would it be like if he had access to every inch of her skin? If they were alone and she was tied to a bed and he could do anything he wanted to her?

Her head fell forward with the next strike, pain flashing through her and making her groan.

His hand cupped her ass. She would feel that tomorrow, a pleasant ache that would remind her of the night before.

"Where are you, Taylor? On the stoplight?"

He was asking her to tell him how she felt, where her anxiety was. Many D/s couples used a stoplight system to communicate.

Red meant stop. Yellow would tell Drake she was entering a territory she wasn't entirely comfortable with, and he should be careful. But she only had one answer. "I'm green, Sir. I liked the crop."

"I'm glad." He was behind her again, and she felt the leather tip of the crop run along her inner thigh. "A little wider."

She changed her stance, giving him the access he'd requested, and the crop moved up her core, the tip brushing her pussy.

Her body went tight. This was what she loved. She couldn't be sure what he would do. He could press that tip and rub her with it. He could slap her pussy and make her cry out. He could keep moving.

The anticipation heightened the pleasure that was sure to come.

He eased the crop over her mound and up to caress her clit. "I think we can move to your flogging after we settle a little business."

She hoped he was talking about the same kind of "business" she needed. "Whatever Sir wants."

"That's what I like to hear, baby. Anything I want. What I want right now is for you to come against my fingers. I want to feel you come all over my fingers. Can you do that for me? Can you squeeze that pussy and soak my hand?"

She nodded as she spoke. "Yes. Yes, Sir."

"Then show me."

One hand worked its way inside her thong while the other kept the crop close, caressing her and reminding her that punishment could start again at any time. He could take that crop back to her ass and she wouldn't get the orgasm he was promising.

His fingers slid over her clit, index and middle fingers splitting her labia and sluicing through the juice they found there. He pressed her open, leaving her deliciously vulnerable. His thumb settled over her clit while those two big fingers dipped inside her.

She bit back a groan. It felt so good. She pressed her backside against his cock, wanting to feel him there.

"Do you like that, Taylor?" His teeth grazed the shell of her ear. "Will you like it more when it's my cock fucking into this sweet pussy of yours? I've never once forgotten how good it feels to be inside you. I dream about it every night."

She knew if she wasn't so damn aroused that those words would start alarm bells in her head. But in the heat of this moment, they simply sent her higher.

"That's right. Work for it. I love how tight you feel. I can't wait to feel this sweetness around my dick." His dark words encouraged her to move against him. He held his hand still and let her work against it as he nipped her ear and kissed his way down her neck.

All the while she could feel his erection against her ass. It was hard and thick and long, and she was thinking seriously about begging him to use it on her. Nothing but his cock would do, but that was her brain. Her pussy was perfectly fine with his fingers since she managed to send herself over the edge, and blissful relief claimed her.

She felt her whole body relax back against his, let her head drift to his shoulder.

"Yes, that's what I wanted, baby. Tell me we can keep playing. Let me take you to a privacy room and give you the rest of what I promised."

She should say no. She should walk away right now.

"Yes." She couldn't do it. She wanted to stay in this place she'd found if only for a little while more.

He worked the ties on her wrists and then he lifted her up, cradling her to his chest.

And she knew she was in so much trouble.

* * * *

Drake laid her out on the massage table and thanked the universe that Sandra knew how to build a privacy room. She'd called them aftercare rooms, but the ones he'd experienced were much smaller. He'd worried he would have to change his plans, but nope, he had plenty of room to move here.

Plenty of room to get her hot all over again, to get her so hot she wouldn't even think about turning him away.

He knew he could have had her but they'd had an audience, and he didn't want their first time back together to be in public. It would give her another way to separate herself from the real emotions he hoped she was feeling.

Sex was the key. He'd decided it as they'd watched the scenes and she'd been uncomfortable. Not with the scenes themselves but with him, with their connection. He'd frayed that connection when he'd let so much time pass, and now he had to rebuild it.

They'd found that connection before. It was still there. He could feel it. He wasn't sure it could be destroyed on his end, but he had to make her feel safe enough to want to acknowledge the connection from hers.

"That was nice." Her eyes drifted open. She was lying face up on the table, her body relaxed and lush against the blanket that covered it.

It had been beyond nice. It had been everything he'd hoped for. He needed to keep her in that moment. He laid a hand against her boots. "I think these are sexy as hell, but they're coming off now, baby."

He liked that he could call her *baby* here and she wouldn't argue with him. She simply bit that sexy bottom lip of hers and held her leg up. He eased the zipper down and dragged the boot off before doing the same thing to her other boot.

"I don't know if I should have sex with you," she said quietly, her eyes drifting closed.

Fuck. He knew giving her the slightest bit of time to think would let all those questions roar back into her head.

"All you have to do is say no." He turned and grabbed the flogger he'd brought in his kit. "I assure you I won't slip in without you knowing about it."

Her eyes opened and lips curved up. "I think I would notice."

"That was my point." He stared down at her. "You either trust me this far or you don't. If the answer is no, then I'll find a robe for you and we can end this session."

Her eyes closed again, and a long breath caused her breasts to move, nipples tightening in the cool air. "Don't be so dramatic. I'm thinking out loud. Are you going to use that on me?"

He would slap her hard with it for that bratty reply, but the falls were buttery soft and wouldn't sting at all. Instead he started at her toes and brushed the falls against her skin. "Only if you're a good girl."

"I feel good right now. I've played around with D/s and bondage, but not like this."

He was curious. "You hadn't tried D/s before we met."

Her muscles relaxed as he continued his slow motion up her body. He dragged the falls over her thighs and onto her belly. "I hadn't, so yes, I was curious after what you told me about it, but it doesn't mean that I was thinking of you when I did it."

"Not at all." He wasn't going to push her on this front. Not yet. He pulled the flogger over her breasts and watched how her heels dug into the bed. Her skin was exquisitely sensitive now, and he could use that to his advantage. "You went through a part of your life where you were out of control. D/s can help you feel like you're in control. It's precisely why I got into the lifestyle."

"I thought you got into it for the sex." Even with her eyes closed she had a wry expression.

"I got exposed to it for the sex. I stayed in it for the control," he corrected as he moved around her body to start down the other side. "I like the discipline and the seriousness, and I love how fun it can be."

"You know discipline and seriousness don't usually go with the word fun."

But this involved all three because he took her pleasure seriously. It took serious discipline to not fall on his knees and beg her to fuck him. And this next part was definitely going to be fun. "That's why D/s works for me. It's way too easy for me to get lost in my head and not think about my body. For the longest time my body was merely an instrument to be used for the good of my job. My father made me take karate and krav maga. I was on a strict physical fitness regime from the time I was seven."

He dragged the falls down her other leg.

"I knew where to stab someone when I was thirteen," she admitted on a sigh. "I didn't go to school. I did this online school thing. It was a good education, but Dad wasn't big on all the other things you're supposed to do when you distance learn. Things like social groups and outside classes. My outside classes were taught by blackhat hackers and a nice assassin who also liked Disney movies.

I learned some Italian from him. Super great guy, if you weren't on his list."

"Flip over." He wasn't playing who had the crappier childhood with her. Comparatively, he'd had it easy because his mother had given him some normalcy. Well, as much as a politician could. "I went to a world-class prep school and mostly spied on my classmates for my spymaster father."

"Oooo, spymaster is kind of sexy," she replied.

"Only because you've never met my dad." He brushed his fingers over the barely there pink lines his crop had left. "He was the original blend-into-the-background kind of spy. They don't all look like Big Tag, you know. He's not the norm."

"Or you," she murmured.

He was sure she wouldn't have said that if he hadn't gotten her all nice and soft and relaxed. And that had just been his fingers. He was going to make her remember what he could do with his lips and tongue. "I can blend when I want to. I look like every douchebag, overly privileged politician's son."

"You do not."

"You say that because you haven't seen me work." He needed her to remember that. She'd never seen him work because he hadn't been working her. He'd watched her, but he'd been himself. He hadn't manipulated her even once.

He brought the flogger down on her ass with a flick of his hand. There was a nice thud and she sighed. This particular flogger was what he thought of as a light flogger. It would be a nice massage. It didn't even pink up her skin the way the crop had. Her shoulders relaxed and her arms came down around the massage table.

So fucking submissive.

"When I'm out in the field, I'm quite the blender." He started to work her over, watching her every sigh and shudder. He could put her to sleep like this if he wanted to, but that wasn't his plan tonight. "Usually I'm the guy no one notices. My father taught me how to blend in, so no one questions the quiet boy in the back of the room. Although it's a fine line. You have to be likable enough to get on the inside, but not so shiny people think about you a lot."

"My dad mostly taught me how to hack into things and shoot

guns. I don't think our dads were the same kinds of spies. Mine was mostly black ops work. He extracted a lot of captured operatives and stole shit. Mostly intel. He got shot at a lot. Ooo, I know how to extract a bullet."

"Yes, for which I'm eternally grateful." He moved around her body, feeling incredibly comfortable being intimate with her. It felt right to be here with her, to take care of her.

Her head came up, eyes opening and a sly look coming onto her face. "Yours was a through and through, buddy. I didn't have to do anything more than stitch you up. And park your car."

Brat. He brought his hand down on her ass and was rewarded with a squeal. "It felt like a terrible accident at the time. I'm now fairly sure the bullets had poison in them. Or at least a hallucinogen."

He went back to flogging her, and a sweet smile crossed her face. "I'm sure that was it."

He didn't want to leave this place. This place was safe and warm and happy. He didn't want to go back to the outside world where he had to face the fact that she was going into a dangerous place, and he would have to use her to find his traitorous sister.

Honestly, he wanted to go back to that week they'd spent in the cabin together and simply never leave.

He worked her over, something settling deep in his soul. At least in this she trusted him. She'd trusted him to bring her pleasure and to give her comfort. Now it was time to see if she trusted him more.

Drake finished and put a hand between her shoulder blades, running it down along her spine and stopping at the curve of her gorgeous ass. "Taylor, I'd like for you to turn over again."

He wasn't going to ask. He didn't need to. In D/s, every command was a choice for the submissive.

She hesitated but only for a moment. When she turned, her eyes were sleepy.

How much rest had she gotten? He was being selfish. "Let me get you a robe and I'll carry you up to your room." He touched her hair, smoothing it back with a tenderness he'd only ever felt for her. "You're sleepy, baby. You should rest. We can play again tomorrow night if you want."

She stared up at him for a moment and then raised a hand, letting her fingers brush over his jaw. "Or you can give me what you promised. I know I'll sleep better with another orgasm. Or two. You said we didn't have to be ourselves in this place."

The sad thing was he felt more like himself here with her than he ever had before. "We can be whoever we want to be."

"I want to be your sub in this place. Show me how you would take care of a sub who's been a good girl and followed your every order," she said, not at all sounding submissive.

He could handle that. His cock tightened. He'd been perfectly willing to do what was best for her, and now she'd told him what she wanted. His cock could totally take over now since his dick wouldn't be selfish either. His dick wanted to get inside her, but only after she'd come a couple of times.

Patience was always rewarded during sex.

He slipped the leather vest off his shoulders, his brain already shut off to anything but the instinct to please her, to fuck her so long and so well she wouldn't even consider walking away from him.

He started at her mouth, lowering his and taking her lips in a hungry kiss. Her arms stayed at her sides, but when he stroked his tongue over her lips, she opened her mouth and allowed him inside. Their tongues played for a long moment, warmth spreading through him that was more than mere arousal.

He kissed his way down, brushing his lips over her chin, stroking his lips across her throat and down to her breasts. He licked and nipped at her nipples, giving her the barest edge of his teeth and loving the gasp that came from her throat.

Her body had tightened beautifully, every line a testament to her need.

He kept up his long, slow exploration of her body, moving down to her belly. "What part of that promise do you want first?"

"You know what I want."

Not what he'd asked. He moved back up to her breast, giving her nipple a nice hard twist and watching her squirm. "What part of my promise do you want?"

He wanted to hear her say it, wanted dirty words out of that sweet mouth of hers.

"I want your mouth on me."

Another twist. He would give her everything she wanted but only after she'd given him what he needed, too.

"I want your mouth on my pussy."

He leaned over and sucked a nipple into his mouth, laving it with affection. "Your wish…"

He resumed his path down her body, kissing and licking and enjoying her soft skin. Her legs had fallen open, and she looked lovely and wanton and ready for pleasure.

This was everything they needed—to shut out the world and concentrate on each other.

He leaned over the table, pressing her legs wide. He breathed in her scent, heightening his arousal. Her pussy was soft and wet from the first orgasm. She moaned as he put his mouth on her. He fucked her with long strokes of his tongue, diving deep before moving up to suck on her clit. He pressed his fingers inside as his tongue worked that pearl of hers, his fingers getting coated once again.

She tightened and gasped, and he felt the moment she came. He let her ride the pleasure out before sliding off the table.

His hands went to the ties at his waist, freeing his cock. "Touch me, Taylor."

She rolled to her side, a sleepy look in her eyes, and he knew he had her. She was in a sweetly submissive state and showed absolutely no signs of wanting to come out of it. Her hand came out, circling his cock, and he bit back the need to lose it right then and there.

She let go for a moment, pushing herself up and sliding down to the floor. She was on her knees in front of him, and damn, if that didn't do something for him. It wasn't that he'd never had a woman give him a blowjob before. He had, but it was different with her. Taylor being on her knees, willing to take him in her mouth and give him pleasure, made him feel stronger than he'd been before, more worthy.

Her hand reached out again, cupping his balls and then brushing her fingertips up his cock. "I didn't get to touch you the first time. I didn't get to do this."

His breath caught in his chest as she leaned forward and placed a soft kiss on the tip of his cock. Her tongue darted out to catch the drop of arousal that pulsed from his body. He watched as she licked at his cock, giving him soft strokes of her tongue.

She was definitely going to kill him. He was forgetting about everything except the feel of her mouth on him, the sight of her pleasuring him. She was starting to fill his whole world again, but this time he wouldn't shy away from it. This time he meant to let it happen, to let her become the most important thing in the world.

"You're going to let me fuck you, aren't you, baby?" He wanted to use more tender words, but she wasn't ready for that yet. He would play this game with her because he knew their intimacy would thaw the ice she'd built up. She'd felt for him once. He could make her feel again.

Her gaze came up. "If Sir tells me to. Sir has been so kind to me all evening. It would be wrong to deny him."

She was distancing, but he would allow it. He would take what she gave him tonight and then retreat briefly to plot and plan his next move.

But first, he would have her. He would revel in her body and let the world fall away. He would fuck her so long and hard that she would fall asleep in his arms. They could stay right here. They could cuddle up and sleep. Sure it wasn't an actual bed, but he could make it work.

She stroked him, letting her mouth find his cockhead and sucking at him lightly.

He was never going to last. He had to make this last.

It was all whirling out of control, and he didn't care when a loud bang and someone shouting his name made Taylor start. She sat back on her heels, reaching for the sheet.

"What is that?" Taylor asked, her eyes wide, and not with wonder this time. All of her seductive playfulness was gone.

There was another knock. "Drake. Drake, we need to talk."

Kyle. Fucking Kyle.

Anger flooding his system, he tied his leathers and crossed to the door. "Taylor, cover up, baby, but don't go anywhere. I'm getting rid of him."

He would have to get her back in the mood, have to coax her back to intimacy. He opened the door and lowered his voice. "What the fuck do you want?"

Kyle's expression was far from apologetic. His eyes were an icy blue and his jaw tight. "I want a world where your sister stayed dead. Get dressed. She called your mother. We have problems."

His gut dropped.

His night was far from over.

Chapter Eleven

Drake felt his hands shaking, and he wasn't sure what he was more angry about—getting interrupted or where the interruption had come from.

He'd been so close to getting inside her again. So fucking close to taking the first step that would bring them back together. The need still pulsed through his system.

He pushed through the conference room door. He couldn't do this on a cell phone. He needed the computer Jax had specially rigged so it was as safe as it could possibly be, the same one Taylor used when she talked to her Consortium contact, though it would show a different number.

Big Tag was sitting at the conference room table. "She's already called Adam. She wants his company back on the case. She yelled a lot, but she still thinks he's the best, and we can use that to control the situation."

"I'm going to talk to her." He glanced at the clock. It was long past midnight on the East Coast, but his mother often stayed up late working. "Tell Adam I understand the position this puts him in, and I appreciate his discretion. How much does he know?"

"Not enough, but he's got security clearance," Tag pointed out.

"He's smart enough to know Julia likely wasn't who she said she was, but he's been discrete to this point. He knows about Kyle and that Kyle had a relationship with Julia. He's a smart man. He can put two and two together and come up with rogue agent."

"Fill him in." He needed Adam to keep what he found private. Adam and the company he'd started with former McKay-Taggart employees had worked for the Agency several times. They specialized in missing persons, and Julia Ennis had been one of very few failures for the company. A necessary failure.

"Why would Julia call your mother? I thought she was trying to stay under the radar." Big Tag sat back, a deep furrow between his brows. "Does she want the whole world looking for her?"

Well, they might be looking for Julia, but that particular woman no longer existed. She'd had extensive plastic surgery, and she'd killed anyone who could ID her. She was living as a woman named Jane Adams. She'd stolen her identity, and it would likely be hard to prove she wasn't who she said she was. Julia would be careful, making sure everything was in place.

"She wants chaos," Kyle replied. "She knows damn well Drake isn't going to let this go anywhere, but she wants him scrambling to try to deal with the situation. At some point she'll call him."

He had no doubt about that. "This is a distraction, but a smart one. I can't ignore it, and I'll have to spend resources on it. Apparently my mother's already been in contact with my longtime tech. After Kyle came down to tell me what's happening, I realized Lydia had been trying to contact me. I didn't take my phone into the dungeon. I thought the world would be stable for a few hours."

"Well, you forgot Julia's still in the world, so that's your fault." Kyle turned his uncle's way. "Do we have eyes on MaeBe? This could be a distraction to kidnap MaeBe."

"She's still at the club," Tag said. "Charlie's already talked to West, and he's going to hang with her at Sanctum tonight. A couple of the guards will take turns watching until we're sure it's okay to leave. She's safe, but she's not going to be happy about it. I think she was planning on going to some festival this weekend. Running Man or Burning Twat. I don't know. I can't keep up."

Kyle's eyes went wide. "She's doing what?"

"Well, probably nothing now, and that's why she's going to be pissed," Tag replied with a shrug. "She's been wearing boho shit around the office for weeks trying to figure out her festival chic look. It's cool because West is going with her. Though I'm worried because he's lived on a ranch all his life. I don't think he knows what drugs are. If someone gives him candy, do you think he'll wake up two weeks later married to a goat?"

Kyle seemed to grow two inches. "I think someone's going to get their ass married to my foot if they don't take this seriously."

"I feel for that person," Tag said with not an ounce of irony as he turned Drake's way. "Just so you know, I had Chelsea check Jax's work. He rigged it so all of our cells get pinged through the system as long as you're within a hundred feet of the building. Your cell will show that you're in LA. You can call her. I know you would rather keep this private…"

He would, but sadly this was now part of the op, and at least Brad wasn't around. He trusted Tag and Kyle to keep anything privately said to themselves.

The door came open again, and Taylor slipped inside.

Fuck. He did not want to do this in front of her. Kyle knew about his family. Tag wouldn't care. Not exactly. Tag wouldn't hold it against him.

What he was about to do to his mother would make him look worse to Taylor, would remind her of all of his lies.

He hated what he was about to do, but there was no way around it.

He didn't have another choice.

His cell rang, and he slipped it out of his pocket. Lydia. He slid his finger across the screen to accept the call. Anything to put off the inevitable. "Hey. What am I looking at?"

"Your mom is freaked out." Lydia sounded a little freaked out herself. "I tried to explain to her that this had to be some kind of scam."

That would be the way the Agency would handle the situation. Lydia didn't know about the fact that his sister had come back from the dead, but she knew how to handle a freaked-out parent of an agent. "Of course it is. Tell me again exactly what happened and when."

He was well aware he wasn't alone in the room. Everyone was looking at him, and he wished he could tell them all to leave, but that wouldn't foster the trust he needed for this op to work. Unfortunately, his family was the op this time.

Anger at his father threatened to boil over. His father had put him in this position and now refused to have anything to do with it. He didn't even want to talk about Julia. In his father's mind Julia was already dead, and he'd put his feelings aside like a real man should. He probably wasn't even awake for this freak out. They'd had separate bedrooms for the last decade, and his mom wouldn't want to bother him.

"About an hour ago I got a call from your mother," Lydia explained, tension in her tone. "She was practically hysterical. Like I've never heard her so upset. She's always calm."

His mother had been a woman in politics for forty years. She'd learned to be calm in even the most emotional of circumstances. His mom had stared down protestors screaming in her face and calling for her head and never raised her tone. "I'm sure having her dead daughter call her in the middle of the night was disconcerting."

"She was trying to call you, but you weren't picking up your cell."

Because he'd left it in the locker room, and once he'd realized there was a problem, he couldn't simply call her back without coming up with a plan. "I was indisposed. But I think I would have probably handled this poorly. I'm glad I'm going into the situation knowing what's going on. I could have screwed it up."

"That's not true." Lydia's voice went soothing. "No one would have handled this better than you, Drake. It's a hard thing to deal with. I know you wanted a vacation, but it might be time to come home. We have the job in London coming up, and I think we should talk about sending someone else. I'll stay here in DC with you, and we can figure out how to deal with your mother. I can't imagine this is the only time someone is going to try to scam her."

He was absolutely sure Lydia was right about Julia not stopping, but he couldn't cancel the London trip. The London trip was about more than his cover. He hated that he needed cover from his own tech. She thought he was going to England to gather intel at the conference that would bring Rebecca Walsh to London and allow Taylor to begin her dangerous mission. As far as Lydia knew, though, this was a routine intelligence-gathering op. "I'm fine. I'm not the one going into the field. So what exactly did the caller tell my mother?"

"I'm not entirely certain," Lydia said. "I didn't hear the conversation. Honestly, I'm surprised this took so long. Everyone in DC knows about the senator's missing daughter. You know she's gotten letters where the writer claims to have seen Julia and tried to demand a reward. This is just another person looking to exploit your mom's grief."

"What did she say?" He knew this wasn't a scam. This was Julia's next move, and he should have been ready for it. Her first had been to show herself to Kyle and go after MaeBe. She'd surely known where they all were since they hadn't exactly been hiding. They'd thought she was dead, and she had the power of surprise on her side.

It had only been the fact that Boomer had managed to follow her that they'd been able to save MaeBe and Deke Murphy's fiancée, Maddie Hill. Otherwise, Julia would have gotten what she needed out of Maddie and killed her and used MaeBe to force Kyle to her side. What she would do with him once she got him there was anyone's guess.

He wondered if she'd known he was involved in that op or if her own brother hadn't mattered at all.

He got the feeling she would shoot him and walk over his dead body to get to Kyle.

"The woman who called told her she'd escaped from her captors and then pretty much pretended she was being taken again," Lydia explained. "How do you want me to handle it? I can be at her place in half an hour."

"Has she called in the police?" Kyle was right. Julia wanted chaos.

"No, because the kidnapper—and I'm using air quotes—came on the line and said he would kill Julia if she called the police. Which is why she called me. I hope it was okay for me to send her to Adam Miles," Lydia said. "I know he and Chelsea Weston have some clearance, and they were brought in on the original investigation."

"That's exactly the right thing to do," he replied. He looked to Big Tag, muting the phone for a moment. "Is my mom talking to Adam right now?"

Tag nodded. "He was at Sanctum. Charlie got him, and your mother had already called him when he got to his cell. He called her right back, and he's reassuring her now, but you're going to have to talk to her."

"I know." He took a deep breath and touched the screen to unmute the phone. "All right, Lydia. I'm going to call her. I'll handle everything from my end. Don't even worry about this. Did she ask for money?"

He noticed Taylor sank down to a chair beside Kyle. She was buttoned up again, wearing the clothes she'd worn earlier in the day.

She was supposed to still be naked. He could have convinced her to sleep with him, to stay with him. They should be cuddled up and resting together.

Instead, her shoulders were back up and every line of her body was tight again.

"Yes, but I don't know the exact amount," Lydia said. "It would probably be best if you come back to DC for a couple of days. She's going to need to see you."

"I don't think that is possible right now."

"You can't cut a vacation short for your mom?" Suspicion had crept into Lydia's tone. There was a shuffling sound. "That doesn't sound like you. I expected to have to figure a way to get you on a private jet tonight."

"I'm about to call her. I'll deal with travel if I need to come home. It's nothing you need to worry about."

She sighed over the line. "Okay. But if you have any trouble, call me and I'll help. It feels like you're keeping something from me, but I suppose if it was important enough you would let me know."

"Thank you. I'll call you tomorrow."

"Okay. I hope you're safe, Drake. Be careful," she said, and the line went dead.

"The tech is curious?" Taggart asked.

"She's been a friend for a long time." He wouldn't exactly call Lydia a close friend, but she was as much a friend as he could have at the Agency. She was like Brad. He trusted her to a point. He would be happy to work with her when they were in London. She would be good cover for him to be there, but he wouldn't let her know he was staying at The Garden. He wouldn't tell her about his real mission.

"What are you going to tell your mother?" Taylor asked, her tone entirely professional.

Like he hadn't recently had his mouth on her. Like twenty minutes ago they hadn't been on the edge of making love.

"I'm going to calm her down and tell her the truth—that I'm going to handle the situation."

"You're not going to tell her that her daughter is alive and she should be careful?" Again, she used a polite tone, but he could sense the bite underneath. "Everything I've read about Julia Ennis tells me she's dangerous. Especially to the people she was close to before she disappeared."

"I can't tell her."

"Why not?"

Was she going to make him say it? "Because that's classified information."

Taylor nodded like she'd known that would be his answer. "So you lie to her and she's potentially in danger?"

"Legally he can't tell his mother anything." At least Big Tag was on his side. "Not only could Drake lose his job, he could go to jail. Not that it stopped Kyle."

"I didn't tell anyone," Kyle argued. "My whole freaking family is made up of busybodies who can't keep their noses out of anything. They figured it out. And MaeBe didn't know at all. I didn't talk to her about Julia. I mean I did, but in a 'she's out of my life' way. You can't imagine how much I regret not protecting her better than I did. She only knows now because she's actually met my psychotic ex. Julia recently broke her arm and shot her. I'm also starting to wonder if the stabbing that happened a couple of months ago wasn't Julia, too. One of her men, at least."

"I thought that guy was after Michael's wife." Drake had heard some of the trouble MaeBe had gone through when she'd been injured on the job. Mostly because Kyle liked to complain.

"I wonder now. It was a miracle he didn't hit an organ, and he managed to not get caught even though there were a ton of people and police around. He was either terrible at stabbing and ridiculously lucky or he was quite good at stabbing and knew how to get away. I think it was one more way to fuck with me before she was ready to spring her trap." Kyle turned to Taylor. "Didn't you say you thought The Consortium operatives often work with males who serve as muscle?"

She nodded. "Yes. We believe they often work with mercenaries, but also there are some men who support the women in positions of power. And yes, they often do the dirty work, especially when it comes to violence. We have every reason to believe they also hire assassins if they can't get the job done themselves or they believe it could harm them politically to do it in a way that could be tied back to them. Are you wondering if the male voice who spoke to your mother was Julia's partner? That would likely mean he works for The Consortium as well. I would be surprised if she used a contractor for something like that."

"Is there any way you could look into him, Taylor?" Kyle stood and started to pace. "His name is John Smith, and according to the records he's from Colorado. I know it's a bullshit name, but it's all we have."

His gut felt tight. He didn't want to drag Taylor in further than she already was. "She's not involved in this."

"Not involved?"

"Not in this part of the op. You are going to meet a Consortium contact and gain intel from working as a double agent in the organization." Even saying the words made him sick to his stomach. "That operative is not Julia."

"We can't be sure of that," Kyle said.

"The likelihood is low," Taggart pointed out. "But I'm interested to see how Drake tries to wiggle out of this. You know it's her op, right? You're the interloper. Either she's aware of Julia and working on your project or there's really no need for you to work on hers."

He was back to thinking Tag was the world's biggest ass. "I'm just saying she doesn't need to be involved in researching a person she's not likely to encounter."

Taylor sighed and pushed her chair back, standing. "Mr. Taggart, do you have the files?"

"I do indeed," Big Tag said. "I can have them in your inbox shortly, and I'll have Adam send you everything he found out about Julia's disappearance the first time he investigated. Spoiler alert—it's not much."

"I appreciate this, Taylor." Kyle nodded her way.

Drake didn't appreciate any of this. When Taylor walked out the door he hurried after her. "Hey, we weren't finished."

She didn't stop. "You don't get to order me around. We're not playing. Now, I have some research to do, and I suspect you're going to need someone to put together a lively fiction to fool your poor mother that the police are actually looking into this. I assume you don't want the Capitol Police involved."

That was his worst nightmare. "Of course not. My mother knows I have connections. She believes I work for Department of Defense in an advisory role in their intelligence department. She thinks my connections to the CIA, Homeland Security, and the FBI come from there. She's calling me because she'll want me to take over."

"Then she knows how this works," Taylor said, walking toward the stairs.

No. She didn't. His mother had no idea how his world worked. And that was why it would likely be all right. Someone would craft a fiction that would include an arrest and proof of the plot that would have bilked his mother out of a ton of money.

He just didn't want that someone to be her.

But did he have the time to do it? Bringing Lydia in would mean telling her Julia was alive. Brad wasn't good at this, and Kyle's computer skills were more about cyber stalking his girlfriend than anything else.

His cell phone trilled, and he looked down at it.

His mom.

Taylor's expression softened slightly. "Talk to her. You should honestly go see her. I'll be fine here until we're ready to go to London. I'm safe here. You don't have to worry."

Oh, he was worried. So fucking worried. "This doesn't change anything, Taylor. We made a deal tonight."

"One I can change my mind about at any moment," she returned. "I'll see you when you get back."

"I didn't say I was..." he began. But the phone was still ringing, and he was trapped.

He couldn't go after her. Likely couldn't stay here with her. He would have to go back to DC and make a show of going through the motions.

He hated his sister. He picked up the line. "Hey, Mom."

She began to cry, and Drake moved back to the conference room.

It was going to be a long night.

* * * *

Taylor took the stairs as quickly as she could. She could hear Drake talking to his mother in the background, but the sound was definitely getting fainter. He was moving one way and she in the opposite direction.

Wasn't that a good metaphor for their lives?

They'd come together for one brief moment, and now they were spiraling outside each other's spheres again. Although he wanted to actively control hers even when he wasn't involved.

He might have been able to do that at one point in time. The first time around, she'd been happy to leave the Agency and likely would have found herself in a relationship where Drake controlled much of how they spent their time. She would have moved where he'd wanted her to move and spent her time waiting for him because the relationship would have been the whole of her world. Not his. She would have been the sweet thing that waited for him at the end of each mission, but he'd missed his chance. If he wanted her in a neat box at this point, he would have to shoot her and stuff her in it.

She was already thinking of how she could tie this John Smith—very creative there—to Julia Ennis, and from there she could start drawing some lines to corporations behaving badly and maybe start making headway taking them all down.

She's not involved.

She could still hear him saying the words, still feel the need to stand up and tell him to fuck himself, but she'd held off. To show him so much emotion would be giving herself away. That was what stupid-girl Taylor would do. She would be hurt by the man who'd brought her such pleasure and then acted like she wasn't worth working with. Smart operative Taylor was willing to keep up the rules of their game. There was work and there was play, and the two should never meet.

He'd looked so genuinely shocked at what his sister had done. Could that all be acting? She didn't think so. She was starting to believe him when he said he hadn't been a part of his sister's betrayal, but he'd still shoved her away. He was right back to taking over her op, and she wasn't about to accept that from him.

For the moment, she would concentrate on what she needed to do. Find out who John Smith really was and who'd gone to such pains to hide his true identity.

"Hey. Is something going on?" Brad came out of the room he'd been assigned to. The one with all the lube she was almost sure he'd been farting around with since strawberry-scented lube had a distinct smell. Brad was in a white T-shirt and flannel PJ pants. He pushed his glasses up his nose and looked like someone's confused dad. "My phone is blowing up, but I can't get anyone to call me back. There's this tech who works with Drake…"

"Lydia," she supplied. "He's already talked to her. His mom got a call she wasn't expecting, and now he's got to deal with the consequences."

"A call she wasn't… Damn it. Tell me she didn't." Brad's jaw tightened. "Was it Julia?"

She wished she could tell him no. "Apparently Julia is now demanding money for her own kidnapping. As money grabs go, it's a creative one. Anyway, I've got work to do, and I think you should probably talk to Drake."

He nodded but then moved farther into the hall, close enough that she could see the worry in his eyes. "I will but I think I should talk to you first. I'm going to assume you and Drake…found that place you seemed to find before."

The man needed someone to remove the stick from up his backside. It was lodged in there pretty tight when it came to sex. He also wasn't great with the metaphor. "The place where we had sex?"

Brad turned a slight pinkish color. "Yes. That is what I am referring to."

"It depends on your definition." She did not have a stick in any of her orifices. Although she'd had a tongue there recently, and it had been magnificent. She did not care who knew she was probably going to screw Drake Radcliffe in several ways. "If you're one of those guys who thinks only dick in vagina equals real sex, then no. If you run the opposite way and touching of any kind between two adults is intimacy, then absolutely yes."

Brad stared at her for a moment. "I'm not sure how to respond to that."

She shrugged, unwilling to make this easier on him. "And I'm not sure what you're looking for here, Brad. You want a list of sexual acts? I'm a middle-of-the-road kind of girl. I do not think kissing has to be purely sexual, but when a man's mouth is on my pussy, I tend to think we've had sex of some kind."

He'd gone a bright pink. "I don't understand how you can talk like that."

Brad was a delicate flower, and she needed to remember not everyone had grown up with a father who left books about human sexuality sitting around as his birds and bees talk. "All right. I'll be more discrete. Drake and I spent a bit of time tonight enjoying the physical side of a relationship that two consenting adults can have without their coworkers having any say in it. So if you're done…"

He stopped her. "I'm not. I'm also not trying to butt into your relationship, but the truth is any relationship between the two of you is going to be a problem for my mission."

She put a hand on her hip, eyeing him. "Don't you mean my mission?"

"Look, you set this up and it was brilliant." In this he seemed far more confident. He didn't give up a bit of his space. "I have no doubt you'll do well. I'm more than willing to work with you, but at the end of the day it's not your job on the line. It's mine."

No, it was her life, but she hadn't cared about that in a long time. "I won't be around to get fired if things go wrong."

"And I'll have to live with that for the rest of my life. I already see the faces of people I sent out into the field who didn't come back. I see them every night before I try to sleep. I don't take this lightly. You are my operative no matter what Drake says. No matter what Taggart says. You were given to me and I intend to see you alive at the end of this, but you have to help me. Drake is my friend, but he can't see straight when it comes to his sister."

"Then you should help me get him removed because his sister isn't my contact," Taylor explained. "I'm almost certain of it. I've read the files he sent me, and I was talking to my contact the night she was in California with Drake and Hawthorne. The timing doesn't work for Julia Ennis to be the woman we've been talking to."

"It doesn't matter. The truth is if you are successful, at some point you will meet Julia, and that's what Drake's counting on," Brad insisted. "He's using you to find her."

Which made her think that he wasn't involved.

Deep down she knew he wasn't, but she wasn't willing to allow herself to be sure just yet.

Because if you're sure, then you have to give him up, and that was an amazing orgasm. You haven't had that kind of orgasm since the last time he was in your life. The world seemed so much nicer after an orgasm, and he would have given you another one if Kyle hadn't knocked on the door. Don't be reasonable now. Be reasonable later. After you've had all the orgasms. Like a couple of years from now. If you leave him then it will really hurt. Maybe marry him and have a couple of kids and then tell him it was all about revenge. Good luck with our five children. Thanks for the sex.

Yep. She was faltering and being ridiculous, and she couldn't quite make herself walk away.

"I can contact him when I get in touch with her. He doesn't need to take over running the op," she argued. If she could have a couple of months without him around, she might be able to talk herself into staying away from him. Or she was fooling herself once again. "He's got a lot on his plate, and have we thought about the fact that he and Kyle hanging around with me might get me killed? I'm not sure I'll be able to explain why I'm chilling with the very people who my contact has to know have been looking into them."

"Right now no one truly knows what you look like, so I'm not worried about that," Brad yawned again. "But it's definitely something we need to address once we begin the op. As to whether or not they know Drake and Kyle were investigating The Consortium, that depends on what Julia's told them. She could have kept that under wraps since it might make her look bad."

"Or she told them she shut it all down since that makes her look good," she countered.

"Either way, if this works and you're undercover long term, you won't be able to have any contact with either of them. They will have to stand back."

She would have to go away, and it could be years. Surely she would get over him.

She could be with him as much as she wanted right now because they only had a few weeks left, and then this job would save her from being an idiot. She would have to give him up to avenge her father. "He has to stay away. No calls. No contact. Any contact has to run through you once this job truly starts."

"I think I can make that work." Brad nodded slowly. "I'll talk to the higher-ups about it. Not even a request from the president would make my boss put an operative in unnecessary danger. Once you're in, I'll convince them to completely separate the ops. Drake and Kyle can run theirs, and we'll do the heavy lifting when it comes to bringing down The Consortium. I worry they'll ruin the entire op just to get to Julia."

She wanted Julia Ennis's head on a silver platter, but beyond that she wanted to finish the job her father had started. Ending The Consortium was what he'd set out to do. Even when he'd been so sick and fighting for his life, he'd worked toward that goal.

"Excellent. Then we're on the same page." She wasn't sure how close she and Brad would ever be, but so far he'd been professional, and he seemed dedicated to the mission. He would be her contact with the Agency, would be responsible for getting her any help she needed.

Drake would likely try to pull her the minute things got dangerous.

But why? If you accept that he's not working with his sister, then you would have to ask yourself why he would pull you out. It would be because he thinks you're incompetent and you're going to screw everything up or...

She didn't want to think about the other reason. The other reason was precisely why it was a good thing they wouldn't see each other again.

Once she was in, he would be gone, and she wouldn't look for him again. It might be years before she had enough intel to bring it all down.

Or she could die and none of it would matter.

Brad stared at her for a moment as though trying to figure out if she was telling him the truth. "Good. I was worried if you and Drake started a relationship, you would choose him over me."

Now she wanted to figure out if he was willing to tell her the truth. "You were there that night, weren't you? The night they took me into custody. You came in with the investigators."

His jaw tightened but he nodded slowly. "I was. Drake had a hard time on that op in Kraków, and I wanted to check in on him."

"You told him to investigate me."

"Like I said, he'd had a problem, and I suspected the leak came from within."

Well, of course they thought it was her. "I didn't know anything about the op in Kraków."

"No," he agreed. "But your father did. The asset who died had worked with your father several times."

No one had told her that. She'd merely known that Drake had problems and had lost the agent he'd been meeting. Now things made a bit more sense. She could be reasonable about this. "So you thought because I was in the area, I might have been involved. I can understand that. I hope you don't still think I was involved."

"I don't, but I still think someone talked." Brad slid his cell phone into his pocket. "However, I did ask Drake to watch you while he was there. I told him to find out what he could. I knew your father wasn't where he was supposed to be, and you covered it up for him. If you're asking if I feel bad about it, no, I don't. He was lying to his handlers. I know the reasons now, but you should also know I would have fired him. He knew the rules. I take a slightly softer position on you."

"Why?"

"He was your father, and he would have died without those drugs," Brad said, his tone softening. "I would have done the same thing in your position. But if I'd been in his, I would have followed the law and not put my daughter in harm's way. The least he could have done was quit before he broke our laws. We had every right to try to figure out what was going on. Were you mistreated?"

She'd been scared out of her mind. She'd been left alone for hours and hours. They'd used a bunch of tactics to get her to talk, but nothing that was illegal. "No. Once I realized my father was gone, I answered their questions fairly quickly. After they corroborated all of the information I gave them, that was when I was brought back to the States and met with the director and went over all the work my father left behind. He'd started to flesh out how The Consortium worked. I helped them make sense of all of his notes and they formed the beginning of this operation. But you know at least part of that. I'd like to know if Drake gave you information about me. If it's classified, I understand…"

"He wouldn't say a word about you." Brad sniffled and seemed to try to wake himself up again. "Not to me. I only knew you'd been intimate because of how we'd found you. Drake wouldn't talk about you to anyone. I know his boss asked him and he said he hadn't gotten any information from you."

"He never asked me," she admitted. "We talked about things, but he never asked me what my father was doing. Our conversations about my father were more of a historical and personal nature. I talked about how I was raised. He did the same. I have to wonder if he was waiting until he had me in a more trusting position before he asked more direct questions."

"Are you asking me if he slept with you to get information?"

Brad asked.

"Is he capable of it?"

Brad nodded. "Absolutely. He's done it many times. Did he do it with you? I don't know."

At least he was honest. They could go from there. "All right. Well, I've got work to do, and you should figure out what your friend is doing. Maybe the two of you should talk about whether or not he should stay at The Garden when we get to London. It might be better for him to distance now."

She was being a coward, looking for any way out. Or she was being an excellent agent and putting her mission above all.

She wasn't entirely sure which.

"I'll talk to him." Brad sighed. "I hope this garden place isn't as weird as this one. There are hooks in the bed here. I should have stayed at a motel. Also, I'm pretty sure this place is haunted."

"It used to be a brothel, so I'm sure even the ghosts are horny." She was getting used to the idea of working with Brad. The fact that he'd been willing to talk to her about his friend made her think he might be able to put her needs as an operative first.

His head shook. "Yep. Next time we're moteling it. Good night, Taylor. Get some rest because you're going to be evaluated tomorrow. I sent you a copy of the testing I need to do. I was going to let you spar with Drake when it came to the self-defense portion of the evaluation, but I'm afraid Jax and Tucker are going to have to do." His eyes lit up, and a smile lifted the corner of his mouth. "Unless you think we can get Solo to do it."

So he did have some horniness of his own. "I think I'd rather beat on the men. 'Night, Brad."

She turned and started to her own room.

"Taylor." A masculine voice called out her name.

She turned and Drake was standing there.

"Hey, Drake. We should probably talk." Brad didn't seem to notice that Drake wasn't looking at him.

His gaze was trained solely on her.

"It's late, Drake. I should get some rest." She didn't trust herself not to go to bed with him. He was obviously her kryptonite. She knew he was bad for her, but she couldn't resist.

He strode down the hall, ignoring Brad completely. She had the slight instinct to run since he looked predatory, like he was hunting for a meal and she was definitely on the menu. Instead, she found herself holding her ground, bracing herself for impact.

And what an impact it was. Drake strode right up to her and got into her space. She didn't have a second to think before he had an arm around her, pulling her close, and his mouth came down on hers.

The kiss was hot, sending sparks through her body, reminding her of everything this man could do for her. Every cell of her body responded to him, and it didn't matter that she knew he was wrong for her. She simply wanted him in that moment.

He pulled back, and his gorgeous face stared down at her. "I have to go. I'm leaving tonight, but you should understand that I'm not done with you. Don't try to convince Brad to get rid of me. Don't think I'll change my mind and stay at some hotel while we're in England. If I can, I'll be on the plane with you. If I can't, I'll be there as fast as I can, and I'm going to take you in the dungeon every night I can. You will sleep with me, and you'll do it because you want to, because you can't stop yourself. Take the next couple of weeks to wrap your head around that truth. I'll call you tomorrow, and it won't be about work. The fact that I'm not physically with you doesn't mean I can't play with you. Answer the phone, Taylor."

She could barely breathe after that kiss. "Maybe I will. Maybe I won't."

It was up to her, after all. It would be smarter to not pick up that call. She could only imagine the things he would want from her.

. "You will." He leaned over and kissed her forehead and then stepped back. "Get me what I need. I know you think I should tell my mother, but I'm not going to. It would ruin her life, and I'm unwilling to put the mission in danger for something my mother doesn't need to know. I need proof that this was a scam, and she'll check into it. So make it good."

All she could do was nod. He was bending. He was trusting her with something deeply important to him.

He brushed his lips over hers once more and then turned away.

"Be good, baby. I know I will be." He walked down to the room he'd shared with Brad and disappeared behind the door. Likely to pack so he could make his way to an airport.

"Well, that doesn't make me feel better." Brad had a frown on his face.

It didn't help her out either. She forced herself to walk to her room and get to work. After all, it wasn't like she was going to be able to sleep.

Chapter Twelve

Taylor rolled over as her cell phone rang. It was barely eight a.m. Who the hell would be...

Dom of My Dreams read the caller ID.

"When did you steal my cell and put your number in?"

Drake's low chuckle came over the line. "Hey, I'm a good spy. I swiped it when you went to the bathroom at dinner."

"Dom of my Dreams?" She took a long breath and stretched, feeling looser than she'd been in forever.

Thanks to the man on the other end of the line.

"Well, you might know other Drakes. I wanted to be clear."

Yes, because Drake was such a common name. The good news was she could change it, and she would. Later. Probably. It was kind of cute. She rolled on her back and stretched. "It's early. Did you make it to DC?"

"Yes." There was a deep weariness to his voice. "I found a charter pilot who could take me, but I just got to my apartment. I'm supposed to go see my parents after I take a nap. I hope my mom doesn't insist I stay with them." She could hear him yawning. "Did you sleep okay?"

"Yes." She wasn't about to tell him she'd slept better than she had in a long time. Again, thanks to the long, slow care he'd given her.

"I'm glad because I barely slept at all," he groused. "I want to say I didn't sleep because I couldn't stop thinking about how hot you were last night, but the honest truth is I'm worried you think I'm a monster for lying to my mom. I can't stand the thought. We were doing so well and…"

"I do understand." There was something about his weary words that reached across the distance between them.

He was quiet for a moment. "When I was a kid he told me I had to keep it from her because I was protecting her. Because everything we did was for Mom. She was kind of a superhero. She was a good mom. In a modern way, of course. I'm sorry. I'm rambling. I didn't want to go to sleep until I talked to you."

"So talk to me." If he wanted to talk about his parents, it could help her do her job. Anything he could tell her would be information she could use to make proper decisions. "When was the first time you remember your dad asking you to spy for him?"

"The first mission he sent us on was more Julia's than mine. I was supposed to back her up. I was ten and Julia and I were going to a friend's birthday party," he said with another obvious yawn. "Sally Girard. Sally's dad was an ambassador from a European country. We were supposed to get into the dad's office and take some pictures. If he caught us, we were supposed to pretend we were being goofy. Julia managed to convince the party to make a little movie and the ambassador opened the doors for us himself. Everyone trusts a kid."

She sighed because Drake's father had obviously been ruthless. "Never once did my dad ask me to do anything but monitor situations or help him clean up a wound."

"I'm starting to wonder if your dad didn't love you more than mine did me," he admitted.

"Maybe just differently." She hated how defeated he sounded. "Tell me something happy, Drake."

She knew she shouldn't care, but she couldn't help it. She had to reach out to him.

His voice went low. "Well, I topped this pretty sub last night."
This she could do. "Tell me all about it…"

He started to talk, and for the first time since he stormed back
into her life, she truly listened.

* * * *

Dom of my Dreams
I'm in hell.

Taylor
It's just DC. You can handle it. You've lived there all your life.

Dom of my Dreams
My mom wants me to stay at her place. In my old room. She
hasn't changed it since I left home. I used to care about Topanga
from *Boy Meets World* more than I should have.

Taylor
Well, at least you have a childhood room to go back to, mister. I
have motel rooms across the world. Suck it up, buttercup. I have to
prove to Big Tag I know where a ball sac is and how to deflate one.

Dom of my Dreams
See, that sounds like fun. Send me video. Also nudes.

Taylor
Not happening. You want to see these babies,
you got to view them in person.

* * * *

"Hey, I liked the ultimate fighting video you sent." Drake's voice
was warm over the line.
It had only been a couple of days, but she already enjoyed these

calls way too much.

She'd thought Drake having to leave would be her salvation, thought his absence would be an easy way to put distance between them, but instead they'd talked more over the last week than they would have if he'd been here. If he'd been here, she would have retreated to her room and found ways to distract herself. She wouldn't have spent most of the day looking at her phone to see what new weird fact Drake had sent her or what picture he'd taken as he was out and about. It was stupid. He sent her pictures of his favorite bagel place and the park behind his parents' house. He sent her pictures of the dog who tried to hump his leg while he was jogging, and he'd detailed his old room for her. Yes, he had definitely been too invested in Topanga.

She'd sent him the things he requested. He wanted some footage of the training she was doing, so she'd had Kim tape her while sparring with Tucker and Jax.

She'd had to stop herself from taking pictures around the bar the night before. She and Kim had gone down and done some dancing and had eaten fried candy bars and had a good time.

She'd wanted to share that with him, but she'd forced herself to stop.

"I'm glad you approve because Brad was still not convinced." She sat down on the bed that seemed bigger than it had been before. It wasn't like he'd slept with her in this bed, but she'd dreamed enough about it that the bed felt too big. Damn man had taken over her subconscious life.

"Was? That sounds like the past tense. What did you do, little predator?"

She wished she didn't love the sound of his voice so much. "Well, Brad decided what my training lacked is the element of surprise."

"Oh, shit. Is he alive?"

It was good to know one person in the world was confident she could take care of herself. She was surprised it was Drake. "He snuck up on me. Well, he tried. He thought he was being so quiet, but I picked up on him two flights down. I think I managed to not break his nose. His will to live is another thing altogether. He took it pretty bad. I don't think he liked getting his ass kicked by a girl."

"Well then he shouldn't be trying to supervise such badass chicks," he murmured. "You still have time to watch with me?"

He'd asked if they could do a group watch of some anime he'd loved when they were kids. Of course by group, he meant the two of them.

She hadn't watched anime in years. It might be nice to spend some sweet hours with a hobby that meant so much to her childhood.

"Hey, it's okay if you can't. I know you're working and you're two hours behind me. I already ate. My mom scolded me about not eating broccoli. You would think I was still ten," he complained. "Anyway, I don't want to push you."

"I would love to watch, and I'm eating dinner right now." She had brought up her turkey sandwich and cup of veggie soup. "I'm ready for a show. I've never watched this one. Tell me why you love it."

"Well, it's about a haunted toilet." There was pure sunshine in his voice.

She clicked the button on her computer to start the show and settled in.

* * * *

Dom of my Dreams
These are perfect. I hate why you had to do them, but I can't deny that your fake records are impeccable.

Taylor
I try. I'm going to admit that Jax and I had fun with the deep-fake video. Though I'm sorry you have to take it to your mom.

Dom of my Dreams
It's going to make things easier in the long run. I wish I could tell her, but my father is insistent. I've tried to talk to him but he's so distant. Anyway, how are you, baby? Tell me what kind of trouble you've gotten into.

> **Taylor**
> No. Talk to me. Call me. Tell me about your dad.
> Just call me, Drake.

Taylor's phone rang and she put it to her ear. "Hey."

"It's so hard to be here, baby," he said quietly.

"Taylor? Do you need a moment?" Brad's brow was raised. He sat across from her at the conference table, his eyes on her phone.

He was being sarcastic, but she did not care. Drake needed her. Over the last few days, he'd been more and more open, and her heart was threatening to soften and she couldn't manage to stop it. She could tell herself later on that he was only doing it to keep his hold on her, but in the moment, all she wanted to do was help him through this. She nodded Brad's way. "Yeah. Probably more like a couple of hours. I'll be back later." She walked out of the conference room. "I'm sorry. Your dad's being a butthole."

Drake laughed. "He is. He is indeed. And it's weird. I like realized my mom had changed her security detail a couple of years ago, but there are so many women here. So many, and they all have guns."

She chuckled. "You should be careful then. So tell me how your mom is doing. Is she ready for the report?"

As he began to talk, she slipped inside her bedroom. This was far more important than anything else she was doing this afternoon.

* * * *

> **Brad**
> Stop distracting Taylor. She has work to do.

> **Drake**
> Nah.

* * * *

Drake put the phone on speaker and closed the door. She'd called him. Up until now, he'd always been the one to call her. A little panic had gone through him when he'd seen her name on the screen. Was she calling to tell him to fuck off? Or that the op was moving forward and he wouldn't see her again?

He was shockingly scared of taking this damn call.

"Hey. What's going on?" He was only slightly out of breath since he'd been downstairs when she'd called. He'd been sitting in the front lounge with his mom and dad, who were hosting a few colleagues of his mom's for dinner this evening. He hadn't minded running away from that scene at all.

"Nothing. Just wondering what you were doing."

He took a long breath. "Well, panicking for one thing. I thought you were about to tell me they called and you were going in and I wouldn't get to see you again."

There was a pause on the line. "No. We still haven't heard from her. She's gone quiet on the Dark Web, too. Jax has been tracking her. He's pretty sure he's going to be able to ID her eventually. She's a bit reckless, according to him."

He didn't like the idea of some reckless criminal asshole meeting with Taylor, but he also knew what his role was. To support her, not drag her down. She was smart and resourceful, and she absolutely wasn't reckless. "I'm hoping to get back to Wyoming before you have to leave. I'd like to be on that plane with you."

She was quiet for a moment and then her voice came over the line, all breathy and sweet. "What will you do to distract yourself? It's a long trip to London."

His dick tightened. "I can think of a few things."

"You better prepare me. I think I need to hear those things, Drake. Sir."

The dinner party could definitely wait.

Chapter Thirteen

It had been nine days since he'd last seen Taylor, and Drake sat across from his parents feeling the miles between them. Both from Taylor and his parents. If there was one thing he'd learned from staying at his parents' place this time around, it was that his childhood was done. So was his youthful phase. He was ready for his good boyfriend phase, but that would have to wait another few days.

They were in the club they belonged to that catered to the DC powerful, a place he'd been in a thousand times before, but this time felt different. This time he was keeping secrets from both of them, and he was surprised at how alone that made him feel.

Donald Radcliffe had been quiet and somber the entire time Drake had been home. They'd had no more than three conversations that didn't involve his mother, and none about what was important. They'd talked baseball and how his dad's golf game was going. His father had barely mentioned Julia, and only once to tell Drake he knew he would handle it.

If his father cared about Julia in any way, it didn't show. There was no guilt or remorse. No longing for the girl she'd been. She was simply a problem to be dealt with and any nuance to the situation was ruthlessly squashed down.

His mother was another story. She closed the file he'd given her and passed it to his father, who quietly studied the information laid out there. Taylor had done an excellent job, and there was nothing in that folder that didn't make perfect sense.

Drake took in the pain in her eyes. "I'm sorry. I know you were hoping for better news."

Samantha Radcliffe looked older than normal. She was a lovely sixty-four-year-old who was always immaculately dressed. Her upbringing was obvious in the way she gracefully held herself. Even in grief. She was always aware that people were watching. "I talked to the lead detective this morning. He confirmed everything you brought to me."

"Yes, he seemed knowledgeable," his father murmured.

They'd spoken to a carefully selected Agency employee who had known how to answer her every question. His father had none, though his mom kept trying to prompt him. His father had sat there in his perfectly pressed slacks and expensive button-down and nodded and asked not a question about the woman he'd called daughter.

The records Taylor had forged were beyond perfect. They were so well done, he'd wished they were true. She'd been careful in her every detail, from the way the report would have been written to a spectacularly well-done deep-fake video of the lead detective "interviewing" the woman who'd been cast as the scam artist. Taylor had taken on that role, managing to alter her own features so she looked a bit closer to Julia and not at all like herself. She was a master with a computer, though she'd given some of the credit to her new bestie.

She was getting along well with Jax Lee.

He was fucking jealous, and he knew damn well Jax was in love with his wife and wouldn't ever think about cheating on her. Drake was jealous because Taylor trusted the man.

He was starting to hope she could trust him.

She'd answered his calls. For the time he'd been gone, she'd only missed one and had texted him explaining she'd been busy proving to Brad that she could take a man down with a hairbrush and a tube of lube.

He'd loved listening to that story.

"I'm sorry, Mom." He reached over the white linen of the table and put a hand on hers. "I know you're still holding out hope."

"But you think she's dead," his mom said quietly.

"My darling, if she wasn't, she would be here with us," his father replied, closing the folder. "I think it's time to face facts."

His mother took a long breath. "I never thought I would be here. You know I've talked to many mothers who had to face the fact that their children were gone. I thought I knew what that would feel like, but it's an ache I can't express in words."

She'd always been close to Julia. Julia had been the only good thing to come out of her first marriage, the reason she'd hung on for so long.

His mother had never honestly known Julia. That was one of the reasons he wanted to keep her from ever finding out the truth. There was nothing but misery in that particular truth for his mother.

If she found out about Julia, she would also learn that her beloved second husband—the one she called her truest love—had lied to her all their marriage. Drake didn't doubt that his father loved his mother, but he was a practical man. His mother had been a good cover for his true vocation. No one questioned the spouse of a senator. The moment his father had married her, doors had opened for him. His place in the CIA had been settled, and his path meteoric.

"I know. I sometimes think finding her body would be a relief." He knew he would be relieved. "Do you want me to go back to Hong Kong? I can try again."

Julia's Agency cover had been that she was a consultant who worked for several multinational corporations, and her work took her around the world. The last place she'd been seen was Hong Kong at a conference.

Her hand flipped over and squeezed his. "Absolutely not."

"We do not want you to put yourself at risk," his father insisted. "Even if there was some proof that she was alive, I would want you to be safe. I think the proper authorities should handle that situation if it were to arise."

Stay away. Let the Agency handle it. He knew what his father was saying, but he was already in too deep. Even if he was willing to hand it over to someone else, there was the problem of Kyle. He wouldn't be able to sleep at night if he left Kyle all by himself.

His mother nodded in agreement. "I don't want you to put yourself in a bad position. The State Department assure me they've exhausted every avenue in looking for her. That awful woman and her partner…they unsettled me. I had started to normalize. As much as any parent can wrap their minds around the fact that their child is gone. I was ready to admit that she was dead and then that call came and I… Thank you for coming home and helping me through this. It's been hard."

"I knew it was some scam artist," his father said with a huff. "Knew it the minute your mother woke me up. Always trying to take advantage of us. I'm going to get the car. Drake, it was good to see you, son. Thank you for handling this for your mother, but the next time we'll call the authorities and not bother you."

His father pushed back from the table and walked away.

His mother sighed. "He's still struggling. He doesn't like to talk about it. I think it's his way of distancing. He's perfectly fine unless I want to talk about Julia, and then he shuts down."

"We all handle grief in different ways." Or in his father's case it was probably more guilt than real grief. He needed to remember that just because he couldn't see his father's guilt, that didn't mean it wasn't there. He'd never been an openly emotional man. Years of working for the Agency, of hiding who he was, had hardened his outer shell.

Sometimes he could feel that shell forming around himself. If he wasn't careful, he would end up like his father—unable to even feel for the daughter he'd lost.

Was that why he was so painfully crazy about Taylor? Because she made him feel something that had nothing to do with job or duty?

His mother nodded and then sat back. "That's what I tell myself. He seems distant since she went missing. I think he blames himself. You know he helped her get that job."

Oh, he knew that quite well. "Yes, but Julia would have found a way. She always wanted to travel, and she could be fearless."

Mostly because she was deadly. She didn't fear because she didn't truly have feelings. With the exception of rage and selfishness. He often wondered if she would have made it past the evaluations had she not been the daughter of Donald Radcliffe. Malignant narcissists didn't make the best operatives. The Agency always looked for a certain moral flexibility in their field agents, but the capacity for true loyalty tended to be a need as well. Julia was loyal to no one but herself.

"I simply want to know what happened." His mother stared at the floral arrangement on the table, though he was sure she was seeing something else. "I know she went hiking on one of the outer islands and was never seen again. I sit up at night and think about what could have happened to her. Did she fall? Was she taken by someone? The not knowing eats at me every day."

He needed to fix that.

Would it be wrong to ask Taylor to help him fake his sister's death? To build a fiction that would give his mom some peace? Of course this time he should make sure she was actually dead first.

"I'm sorry I ruined your vacation." His mother took a sip of her iced tea and nodded to someone a couple of tables from theirs.

Drake glanced over. Congressman Andres. He didn't have enough fingers and toes to count all the wealthy, powerful political figures in the room.

Such fertile spy ground. There would be a couple in this room, too. At least two or three who reported back to countries who wanted to know what was happening in the States.

And then there would be the spies who worked for corporations. Lobbyists liked intel, too.

Were any of them watching him right now?

Sometimes he wished he didn't know what he did about that dark part of the world.

"Well, I should be going. I have a meeting with some people who are bringing me up to speed on the forum." She grabbed her Chanel bag, setting it on her lap. "Did I mention your father and I will be there? Aren't you going? It's in London. What exactly are you doing there? I'm not sure why the DoD is sending people."

"There are several panels on protecting business interests in dangerous political climates. Specifically when it comes to mega corporations, in this case medical tech and pharma. There are some new technologies coming out that my bosses are worried could be used for more than medical advances. I'm pretty sure Defense and Homeland Security are sending people." He sat up and wished he'd been able to drink. His mom had been sober for thirty years, and while she didn't mind people drinking around her, he preferred to honor her sobriety. But sometimes he really needed a drink. "You're going to be in London?"

"Yes. It's the funniest thing," she said. "We were sending Senator Phan, but he was in a car accident. Luckily he wasn't seriously hurt, but he broke his leg. The majority leader thinks we need a presence there given how many new therapies they're talking about at this conference, so I was the next in line."

His mother was a long-term member of the Health, Education, Labor and Pensions Committee.

"You can fly over with your father and me and perhaps we can have lunch while we're there," she continued. "I know you'll be busy, but I would love to see you more often. I don't want the only times we see each other to be about you having to calm me down and use your connections to solve some terrible crime."

"Of course," he promised, his brain already working. He didn't like coincidences. Not at all.

He would be in London. Taylor would be in London. Now his mother would be there, too.

It felt like someone was moving pieces into place.

She gave him a smile that didn't quite meet her eyes. "Good. You can bring along your friend. I feel like it's been ages since I saw Lydia. I'm afraid I scared her the other night."

"She doesn't scare easily." Lydia had probably told his mother he would be in London soon. She played the eager assistant well. "She was worried about you. I'm sorry I didn't pick up that night."

"Were you with a woman? I know you said you were visiting some friends, but I got the feeling from Lydia that you were."

He frowned. "How would she know who I was with? I assure

you she doesn't schedule that part of my life. And no. I was with some old friends, although one of them is a woman. She's someone I worked with a few years back. It was good to see her again, but she's married now. Why would Lydia think I was with a woman?"

He hadn't told Lydia much about what he'd be doing while he was gone.

"Oh, she didn't say anything, but I know that tone."

"Tone?"

She seemed to think for a moment and then leaned forward, a soft look on her face. "You need to put that poor girl out of her misery. You have to know she's been in love with you for a long time, Drake. She sounded jealous."

His mother was reading way too much into this situation. "We're friends. Nothing more. I assure you Lydia isn't in love with me. She's been my assistant for seven years, and she's dated plenty of men. She's mostly annoyed with me."

His mother didn't look convinced, but she stood anyway. "I've watched her, you know. Just think about it. You're not getting any younger, and I would like grandchildren before I'm too old to enjoy them. She's a pretty girl, and you two seem to get along. Sometimes friendship can turn into something more if you let it. Your father should have the car pulled around by now. I'll send you our flight information. I know the department will put you on a plane, but I promise mine is nicer. You can bring Lydia along and I'll see if I'm right."

He shook his head, a little horrified that his mother was thinking of him having kids. He was too young to have kids. Also, now he wouldn't get to fly in with Taylor and would have to bring Lydia. He couldn't exactly explain that the DoD knew nothing about his trip.

"I thank you for the ride, and you'll see you're wrong about Lydia."

She gave him a real smile and strode away.

He missed Taylor. He slid his cell phone out and looked to see if she'd texted him. Nothing. She was probably working on the many evaluations Brad seemed determined to put her through.

She'd apparently managed to take down Kyle, though she'd

refused to spar with his stepfather or uncle. She'd told him Big Tag had recently had his balls kicked in by Kyle's girl, and she really liked Chef Taggart's food, so she wasn't risking pissing him off.

Kyle had sent a text detailing all the ways Taylor was mean and would be fine on the op because she did not respect his masculinity at all.

He wished he'd been there for that session.

He wished he was there right now.

Drake glanced down at his watch. Could he hop on a plane and see her before he needed to be back here? Maybe he could come up with a reasonable excuse to get out of going into London with his parents. If he could make it out to Wyoming tonight, he could maybe fit in one more session at Sandra's, and then they could play on Taggart's private plane and he wouldn't care who knew about it. The truth was no one but Brad would care. Tucker and Jax had been around the D/s lifestyle for years. Jax was around actual crazy threesomes most of the time. Kyle would gag and ignore them.

Brad would point out all the reasons having sex on an airplane wasn't sanitary or some shit. Sex wasn't supposed to be sanitary. It was supposed to be dirty and glorious, and if he didn't get his dick inside her soon, he was going to die.

Was his mom right about Lydia? Lydia did sometimes seem to take too much of an interest in his life. He'd kind of thought she was just nosy and bored, and it was hard for people who worked for the Agency to find friends, so she hung on to him because he was safe to talk to.

He glanced down at his phone again. He wanted to call Taylor and order her to go to one of the dungeon's privacy rooms and touch herself, to pretend it was his hand sliding under her panties and stroking her clit.

She was probably working, but didn't she deserve a break? He could imagine what she would say to Brad. She did not have a lot of fucks to give, and he kind of loved that about her. She would tell Brad her top had called and she needed to go masturbate so he didn't get spanky on her when he finally came home.

Home? He was home—at least in the academic sense of the word, but he was starting to think home was wherever that woman was.

Suddenly it was important to get to her. He'd spent days without her, and every second of it he'd felt his aloneness with the exception of the times he'd been able to talk to her. He'd gone over thirty years without being so aware of his singularity in the universe.

Except that one day in the park with the girl who was growing up the way he had. It had been the first time he'd actually longed for a friend.

"You look like you could use a drink."

He stopped as a feminine hand slid a drink in front of him.

Whiskey sour with a single maraschino cherry because they deserved some sweet to go with the sour.

It was what she'd made for him after most missions. After a while she'd made them for Kyle, too. It was one way she'd made them feel like they were a family.

Fuck.

"Hello, Julia."

His heart threatened to seize as she moved around him, her own drink in hand. She settled into the seat his mother had been sitting in. She wore a chic sheath dress, killer heels, and another woman's face.

"Hey, baby brother. How is Mom doing?" Julia's long blonde hair was in a neat bun on her head, and her green eyes were now covered by blue contacts. She looked like Jane Adams—the woman whose life she'd taken over as cover.

"Well, Mom is freaked out because someone called her. I thought you were looking for money, but you couldn't find me, could you? That stunt was all about getting me right here so we could have this conversation." And he'd fallen for it. "You know you could have called."

"So you could ping me around the world and I would have no idea where you are? Besides, maybe I missed my little brother." She took a sip of her drink. "It was a good bet that Mom would call her precious baby boy and you would trot right back home because you're the good son. She always comes to her club, so I knew you'd show up here eventually. Tell me, did Lydia do the work on the cover-up? She's not as good as she thinks, you know. She's one of those mediocre loyalists the Agency loves so much."

"I'll let her know you like her work." He wasn't about to tell his sister someone else had done that work. It was far better to let her underestimate his team.

Julia frowned his way. "You can drink it. It's not poisoned, you know."

He glanced down at his drink. "Well, you've been known to lie, so I think I'll pass."

She groaned, a frustrated sound he remembered from his childhood. "I'm not trying to kill you, Drake. You're my brother. I felt bad about calling Mom but Dad changed his number, and I got the feeling you wouldn't meet with me."

"Oh, I would have met with you."

"Yes, with a lot of guns, I suspect." She sat back, considering him. "You were in LA, weren't you? You worked with Kayla Summers and blew up that asshole's satellite, didn't you? I didn't see you. You're very good, brother."

It had been a way to distract the bad guy so the rest of the group could find where Julia had taken MaeBe and Maddie. He'd enjoyed his work that night. "I have no idea what you're talking about. Did you have something to do with Nolan Byrne and his company tanking? Which member of your group wanted him gone?"

Her eyes rolled. "Sure you weren't involved. You've never even heard of that op. The Agency doesn't work on American soil. I've heard that one before. Fine. I do understand you not being willing to give me any information."

He had some questions of his own. "Was Dr. Blumenthall the last of the doctors who knew who you were? I assume that you got close to Byrne so you could gain access to the doctor."

"He was the only one who saw me before my transformation," she admitted. "The rest of the doctors were trustworthy, but he couldn't be bought, and I couldn't take the chance that he would put it together. I was lucky that he wasn't a big follower of politics, but we're coming up on the second anniversary of my disappearance, and I happen to know there are a couple of true crime assholes who are doing a documentary. Don't people have better things to do with their time?"

What was the point of being involved with evil corporations if they couldn't handle problems for her? "Why don't you have your group shut it all down?"

"The funny thing is when you start telling annoying documentarians they can't tell a story, they dig their heels in. Which would be fine because we could kill them. The trouble is there's always another nosy documentarian looking for a conspiracy theory they can make money over," she explained. "And if too many of them die, someone important starts asking questions, so it's better to let that sucker flounder on some half-ass streaming site. But I did have to clean up loose ends."

"So you found an op that brought it all together." She had always been good at multitasking.

"A lot of things came together on that particular mission," Julia admitted. "Did I request the job? Of course. I knew a couple of things would happen. Byrne actually reached out to us, you know. It was precisely why he had to go. He thought he could come into the organization and take over. Well, I was working for a group who wanted his tech—the same tech Maddie Hill was working on. I knew about her relationship with Deke Murphy and Murphy's job at McKay-Taggart."

"Of course. This was about Kyle. You knew your ex would likely be put on the team that supported Murphy." For his sister the world revolved around Kyle Hawthorne and had from the moment they'd met. Kyle had been reluctant at first, but he'd sort of fallen into a relationship with her. It had made sense to Drake, and he'd liked the idea of having Kyle as a brother.

Her mouth formed a mulish line. "Kyle is my fiancé."

"Are you insane?"

A slim shoulder shrugged. "Technically? I don't know and I don't care. It all makes sense to me. Kyle asked me to marry him. Kyle knows I'm the only woman in the world for him. He's being stubborn."

"Kyle died." He was going to hold that line.

A low chuckle came from her throat. "Sure he did."

"He died when Byrne's house exploded." It was a story he didn't intend to deviate from, though it was obvious she knew the

248

truth. "There was a funeral. His family is still in mourning."

"Well if anyone knows how to put on a good show, it's the Taggarts. Do you ever think about the moment in time that would change your life for the better?" She was acting like they were having a pleasant chat. "Like if you had one shot to change the past, what would you change?"

"I would shoot you as soon as I could hold a gun?"

Her lips curved up. "You wouldn't, you know. Anyway, mine would be to stop Kyle's mom from meeting Sean Taggart. Granted, I would need everything else to go the way it did, but having no Taggarts in my life would be so much simpler. They screw everything up. I would go back and cockblock that motherfucker so hard." She laughed. "See, that's funny because he was actually fucking Kyle's mom."

"Julia, I'm not here to chitchat. Kyle is dead, and that's all I'm ever going to say."

She looked at him like he was a terrible party pooper. "He's not dead. Kyle simply understands the rules of engagement. He knows that if he wants me to stay away from that pathetic hacker, he'll keep this game of ours to me and him. He's mad. I get that. I should have told him what I was doing and brought him in at the start. I should have done the same with you. We were a family, the three of us."

"We were two guys and a psychopath. Not a family."

"Because you're so normal." She took another sip. "You know you've killed as many people as I have, maybe more. You do it to protect your country. I do it to protect a system that has worked for hundreds of years. It's worked far better than our government does and protects more people. I work for a group that employs people, makes things. You work for people who can't get anything done."

"You work for billionaires who don't care about anything but money," he countered.

"And you don't?"

He wasn't playing this game with her. He knew the system wasn't perfect, but it was better than putting a bunch of companies who only thought about profits in charge. The world would be so much safer if it was completely run by ten to fifteen CEOs. Sure.

But arguing with her wouldn't help. He couldn't kill her here.

He wasn't sure he could kill her at all. Even knowing what she'd done, he could still see the child she'd been.

"What happened, Jules?" The question came out on a wistful tone, and he realized if he could see the child she'd been, the boy who'd loved his sister was still in there, too.

Her expression softened. "Life, I suppose. It wasn't one thing, really. It was a gradual opening of my eyes to the fact that the world isn't salvageable. It isn't. It's always been run this way, and it always will be. It is better to be one of them than one of the sheep they lead to slaughter. You know there is good work to be done here, too. When you're high up in the organization you get to choose."

He understood what she meant. "You get to play God."

"Isn't that what you do every day? Isn't that what the Agency does when they send you out to do what you do? How many times have you made the call in the field to save someone or blow them away? You're not that different from me, Drake. You simply are less honest about what you do."

He could at least be honest with her. "I'm going to have to bring you in."

She sat back, a smirk hitting lips he didn't recognize. "I'd love to see you try. I'm not alone. You think you're safe because you think you're in your world. In Mom's world. But the truth of the matter is, you're in mine. Don't worry. I have no need to take you out. You are my brother, and I love you."

"I doubt that."

A brow rose over her eyes. "You think I'm incapable of love?"

"I know what you did to our mother was cruel."

Her eyes flared. "What you did to her was cruel. What Kyle did to her was cruel." She took a long breath and seemed to come to some decision as she relaxed. "But I also understand that the day Kyle tried to kill me was a confusing one. My fiancé has a naïve soul, but we're going to work it out because we were meant to be together."

He felt a momentary sympathy for her. "Julia, he hates you."

She seemed to consider the notion for a moment. "What is hate?

No Time to Lie

It's the strongest emotion on earth besides love. He's confused and I lied to him, so he's punishing me but playing around with sad little girls who have daddy issues. Now that Mae Beatrice Vaughn is out of the picture, we can have this out. I accept the wrongs I did to him. I even accept that he might have thought I was going to kill him. He should have had more faith in us, but we were young. We're going to be stronger this time."

There was a piece of his soul that felt sorry for her because she really did need help. He leaned over, his voice going quiet. "You need to leave Kyle alone. Nothing good is going to come of going after him. Let me take you in. I have contacts. I can get you the help you need."

For a moment, she paled and stared as though that had been the last thing she'd expected from him. Then she flushed, anger obviously replacing her shock. Her eyes narrowed. "The only help I needed was loyalty from you, but I can see I'm not going to get it." She stood, clutching her designer bag. "It's time for you to ask some questions. My organization has a lot of pull with politicians. Perhaps it's time you figure out I'm not the only one in our family who can be swayed by practicality. Tell Kyle I'm coming for him and if he wants to keep this between the two of us, he'll stay far away from that little bitch of his. If he brings her back into this, I'll consider everyone in his life fair game. I'll take them out one by one until he decides to honor the vows he made to me. Do you understand?"

He stood, ready to finish this. "I…"

He felt something hard at the back of his spine. "Mr. Radcliffe, I think you should sit down now. We wouldn't want to cause a scene, would we?"

"No, of course not." He held his hands at his sides and realized there were several sets of eyes on him. All male. All brawny and likely armed. She'd brought her own army. "I was going to give my sister a hug."

"Somehow I doubt that, Drake, and I know you won't believe it, but it makes me sad." She didn't move an inch toward him. "I don't know what you're working on but make sure you stay far away from me and mine. Don't think for a second I'm the only person who worked for both the Agency and The Consortium. I assure you I wasn't and I'm not. My group has eyes everywhere, and we'll figure out what's going on with you sooner or later. Tell Kyle he should answer when I call. I get impatient. He knows I can lash out when I'm impatient, and if I can't lash out at him…"

She turned and walked away.

Drake knew the real battle had just begun.

* * * *

Taylor looked down at her phone and then hated herself for doing it because she was disappointed Drake hadn't called. The conference room was achingly quiet. Normally she craved quiet and solitude. It was how she lived. But now she wished she was surrounded by the team because then she might not be thinking about phone calls from a man who'd ripped her life apart once upon a time.

She shouldn't be disappointed. It wasn't like this was anything more than a game to pass the time until she had to go deep undercover.

For over a week he'd called her at least twice a day, and texted more often than that. Mostly he'd talked dirty and told her all the things he wanted to do to her the next time he got her in a dungeon.

A few times, though, he'd talked about his mom and how hurt she was. He'd talked about his father and how distant they were now when they'd always been so close.

She didn't know why she hadn't hung up on him. He was breaking their agreement. It was supposed to be about sex, about D/s, and yet she'd found herself sitting there and feeling for him. She didn't share her own aches. That would make her too vulnerable, but now she had to wonder if listening to him was making her vulnerable, too.

"Hey. I was told you might have found something out," Kim said. She walked into the conference room, a tray in her hand.

Kyle's parents had left a few days before after a big argument. Still, she'd watched them each hug Kyle, and he'd hugged them back. He was being stubborn. Big Tag had escorted his brother home and told her to call if she needed anything at all.

So now it was Taylor, Jax, Tucker—who was only around about

half the time because his kids had activities—Kyle and Kim. They spent a lot of time on the phone or on their computers talking to their families.

She and Brad just worked. They didn't have families. They had jobs, and that had seemed okay a few months ago. Now she'd started to wonder if it wasn't kind of sad.

Kim sat down the tray, and Taylor noticed there were three glasses. Margarita glasses. And some chips and salsa.

It reminded her that it was almost five o'clock, and she hadn't stopped for lunch.

"I did." She thought about the conversation she'd had with Adam Miles earlier in the day. "Should I think it's weird that apparently everyone knows I'm playing with Drake? Why would Adam know about that?"

Kim's lips curled up. "Because Big Tag lives to gossip."

"Oh, yes, he does." Sandra walked in with the pitcher that paired beautifully with those big salt-rimmed glasses. "Who's he talking about now?"

"Who do you think? The rest of us are boring married people," Kim pointed out.

"Ah." Sandra grinned as she slid into the seat beside Kim. "Yes, I was asked to keep the old guy up to date. It's okay. He's sending me info about MaeBe. I'm going to drop hints that she's doing extremely well around Kyle, if you know what I mean."

She wasn't sure she understood. "Are you trying to make him explode?"

"I'm trying to make him see he should go home and take care of the woman he loves," Sandra corrected. "And the family he loves. He's trying to sacrifice himself, and he needs to understand that's not the way things work in a family. He should know that. He's letting his fear lead him."

"He's right to be afraid." She'd learned a lot in the last couple of days. "I've talked to him quite a bit while we've been working, and I think he's right about Julia fucking with his family. Before his parents went back home, I detailed everything odd that's happened to them in the last year or so, and it's either an enormous amount of bad luck or Julia Ennis has been quietly screwing with them. She's a predator."

"And a predator pounces at some point in time no matter what," Kim said with a solemnity she wasn't used to seeing on the ex-agent's face. "I should know. I lost years of my life to a man who decided he owned me. He wanted me. It didn't matter that I couldn't love him back. He decided he could make me love him, and he did everything he could to ruin my life and my husband's."

"You went into hiding. Would you do it differently now?" She was interested in the answer to that question. It was one she'd been asking herself for a while. Would she take back the week she'd spent with Drake? She might have spared herself the heartache, but the end result would have been the same.

She would be right here and Drake would be here, and there wouldn't be the pain of that betrayal between them.

Had it truly been a betrayal?

Kim sat back with a long sigh. "I don't know. In some ways we needed that time. Beck changed a lot in those years. He got help with his anger issues. I'm not sure he would have gotten that therapy had I been there. But my son missed years with his father, so I don't know."

"The question is meaningless," Sandra said. "If there's one thing I have learned in my many years of life, it's that you can't go back. There is only one way and that is forward. I lost a daughter to people very much like the ones you're hunting now. I still feel that loss every minute of the day. It's a hole that will not be filled until the time comes when I can see her again. Her father was an abusive shithole of a human being. I can't go back and fix those things. I can only try to make something of what I was given. I can try to help other women who were in that same situation. I can spread the love I have around."

Kim's lips quirked up. "You did that. A lot. In so many places."

Sandra's laughter filled the room, a light, joyful sound. "I sure did, and I had a good time doing it. And I got something beautiful this time. I got a wife and amazing daughter and grandkids. I got friends and yes, I got Tucker, but I wouldn't give him back, either. All I'm saying is don't spend your time looking to the past. The answers aren't there. The truth is there are no answers. There's only how we feel and who we love."

Sandra was getting to her. "What if who we love isn't worthy of our love?"

"Are we pretending to talk about general life things? Or are you going to be brave and name your problem," Sandra challenged.

"Drake." She hadn't grown up with a group of women who advised her. It was weird to be talking to her lover's ex, but she was going with it. "I don't know that Drake is worth the pain that will inevitably come."

"Why is the pain inevitable?" Sandra asked.

"Because it can't work out. Even if I decide to forgive him for taking me to bed under false pretenses, even if everything goes well with us, I'm going undercover and I won't be able to see him for a long time," Taylor replied.

"First, you have no idea how long this job will take or if it will work out at all," Kim countered. "When was the last time you heard from your Consortium contact?"

This was the thing that kept her up at night. Not the only thing, but it was certainly there. "She was supposed to contact me three days ago."

Kim nodded. "Which means she's either late or she got what she wanted from you and she's walking away. So there might not be a mission at all. If there isn't, what will you do?"

She had zero idea how to answer that question. Her whole life had revolved around this op for so long she had no idea what to do if it didn't happen. If it never happened. "I guess I would try again. I would start from scratch and try to find another way in."

"Well, Drake could help you this time." Sandra poured a margarita and slid it Taylor's way. "You might be working with him closely in that case. Or you could take it as a sign and find a life outside the Agency. I could use a good waitress."

Kim's eyes rolled. "She is not waitressing, but Sandra does bring up a point. What do you want to do with your life when this op is over?"

Again, not something she'd thought about. "I'll figure it out when I get to it."

Sandra sent Kim a knowing look. "You were right."

"Right?" She wasn't sure what they were talking about. They seemed to have a silent conversation between them through raised brows and knowing looks. "What was she right about? Also, I'm not sure we should be drinking. I've still got work to do."

Kim picked up hers. "You did all your work, and you're getting on a plane in a couple of days. Best to take a break. As to what I was right about, well, I was right about you."

"You see, I thought you were one of those agents who takes herself way too seriously." Sandra took a sip of her drink. "Like Brad."

"I am not like Brad." Though she was starting to appreciate the man's serious work ethic. When she needed something, Brad worked hard to get it for her. He was a little stuffy for her taste, though.

"No, that's the point," Kim agreed. "Brad lives for this job. He's what I like to call a true believer, and the Agency is sort of his religion. He doesn't have anything but this job, and if he's not careful he never will. You, on the other hand, don't care about the job."

"Excuse me? I've done nothing but prep for this job for almost two years. I would definitely say I care about it."

"You don't care about the job. You care about what you're going to get out of the job," Sandra argued. "There's a difference. Brad has a goal. He wants to get this job done and look good to his bosses so he can move up in the organization. I'm sure there's a part of him that wants to bring down The Consortium, but that's his primary motivation. It's why he's been testing you so hard this week. Also, way to punch a tit, Taylor. Solo here was massaging that sucker like it was her life's work."

Kim frowned, and sure enough her hand came up to cover her left breast. "Hey, that was painful and yes, to Sandra's point, I do believe that's exactly why Brad is so serious about this op. He's ambitious, and he thinks he sees a mission and an agent who can aid him in those ambitions."

She did not understand what point they were trying to make. "I don't see why that's a problem."

"Because you do not want the same thing," Kim replied. "You

don't care about the outcome of his op for the same reasons. He wants it to work for professional reasons. You want revenge, and you don't care about how you get it. You don't think about your life after the op because you don't think it'll be a problem."

"You're walking into this op thinking you're not walking back out," Sandra added. "And that, my girl, is going to get you killed. Normally I wouldn't care, but I've come to like you, Taylor. So I'm going to give you advice I normally would never give another woman. Pick the boy."

"Pick the boy," Kim said with a half smile. "I would tell you something different if I thought you were passionate about this job, but you're not. You think this is what your father would want for you. I'm a mom. I wouldn't want my son to avenge me. I would want him to have an amazing life. I would want him to love all the good things we had and find his happiness. There is no happiness with revenge. You're not going to finish the job and sit back and find the peace you're looking for. You're going to die or grow old looking for something that doesn't exist."

"I assure you the person who killed my father exists," Taylor argued. "The person who set him up exists."

"And the person who signed off on killing him exists," Sandra said. "There was probably someone else. When does it end? When are you satisfied? And what do you do after? Like I said, I know it seems like a route I would never advise another young woman to take, but this isn't your career. You haven't found that yet. This isn't your passion. You haven't found that either. You're running on rage and fear, and it's going to get you killed."

Taylor sat up straighter. "Did you have this conversation with Drake?"

"No, I did not because it's different for him," Kim replied.

"Because he's a man?" She didn't like how they were making her feel. The truth of the matter was she'd only ever worked for the Agency because of her father. If he'd been alive a few more months, she would have been out of the game altogether. She would have been halfway through her first semester at whatever community college would take her. She would have been Drake's girlfriend and looked forward to the time they spent together. She would have made some friends and put down roots for the first time in her life.

She shook her head at the thought. She wouldn't have been Drake's freaking girlfriend because he'd been playing her. He hadn't meant to follow through on any of his promises. He was playing her now because he wanted in on the op.

They'd had good talks, but there was still doubt in her mind. He was excellent at his job, and right now his job was managing her.

"Because his family is at stake." Kim set the big glass down. "Because his sister is alive, and she's coming for one of the only people he's ever called a friend. I'm sure if Julia has her way, she'll burn down everything and everyone she has to in order to get Kyle. I know because that's what Levi would have done to get to me. He would have killed Beck. He would have killed our son. He would have burned the world down to satisfy his belief that all he needed was to get me alone and I would love him. He didn't understand the meaning of the word. You know Drake had a hand in taking him down. He could have lost his job for what he did, but he did it anyway. His favorite cousin had fallen under Levi's spell. When Levi couldn't find me, he decided to marry someone who could help further his career. He made a mistake. He thought Drake was like him. Drake does understand what the word *love* means."

"He was willing to put his career on the line to help his cousin, and now she's married to a nice man who isn't trying to use her," Sandra explained.

"That's great for her, but I don't think it's the same for me. I am willing to accept that maybe he didn't betray me before. I can see things from his point of view, but I still worry that what he truly cares about this time around is the mission." It was the doubt that crept into her head at night after she hung up the phone—that Drake would do anything to take his sister down. That Drake might genuinely have feelings for her, but they would pale in comparison to how much he hated his sister. They were too close to Drake to see what he was capable of.

You're too close to see anything at all, and you won't ask the right questions because you don't think you can trust the answers.

She wished her inner voice would shut the fuck up.

"He's trying very hard to get you out of this," Sandra argued.

"Although I'm pretty sure Big Tag told him to fuck you until your eyes crossed and you can't fight him anymore. It's sound advice and definitely the advice likely to not get you killed."

"I would have hoped that the last several days' worth of evaluations would have proven to you that I'm capable of holding my own," Taylor said with a huff.

"You're physically capable, but when an agent goes into a mission with nothing to lose, they usually lose the only thing they think they have. Life," Kim said quietly. "I think you have decided that life took everything from you. Your mom. Your dad. It feels like you're next, doesn't it? It feels like nothing good could possibly happen to you because it never has before."

"My father was a good thing." She could still remember standing there looking up at this big scarred man who promised he would protect her.

"I know, but he should have shown you that you came first," Sandra pronounced. "He shouldn't have risked himself the way he did, and he should never have had you out in the field. It was selfish of him. He wanted to have his kid and his job."

A thread of anger flared in her. "He didn't know anything else. He didn't know any other life."

"And he hated his former agency, and continuing to work was his revenge," Kim explained. "I know. I talked to him. I worked with him. He adored you, and at the time I thought it was kind of cool that he had his kid with him, but I'm a mom now. You needed stability. Drake needed stability. You both grew up in a world that trained you to distrust. Your fathers, for one reason or another, demanded loyalty to them and not much else."

"That's not true." Why were they attacking her father?

"I didn't say he meant to," Kim corrected. "But the very nature of taking you with him made you loyal to him above all. Drake's father actively demanded loyalty from his kids to the point of keeping secrets from his wife and making sure his children did the same. And you can see how that turned out. One of them betrayed everything she once professed to believe in. And Drake couldn't believe you were real because nothing has been real to him. Your dad merely let you be his tech in the field and took you into dicey places with him. Drake's dad made him a spy when he was a child. Drake doesn't remember a time when he didn't know how dangerous the world could be. He doesn't know how to trust."

"He does, but it's not his first position." Sandra refilled her glass. "It's hard for him to trust. How did you meet him? He's been quiet about it."

"We met at a safe house. He was trying to get valuable intel to base, and the house I was at was the closest place. We got snowed in and had to stay together for almost a week," she explained. "It would have been longer but my father was killed and the Agency came to get me. I didn't know the Agency had been watching me for a while because my dad had been sneaking into Cuba to treat his lung cancer, and yes, I know that was a breach of trust and I helped him hide it. They thought he was a double. When I proved he wasn't, that was when we decided to send me undercover."

"So Drake could have believed you were helping your father do something wrong," Sandra mused.

"He did." It was good to finally put it out there. "He went to bed with me because he wanted to figure out what was going on. Brad's told me he asked him to do it."

"I doubt that. I mean I'm sure Brad would have told him what was happening, but Drake isn't going to sleep with someone because Brad told him to. He might have flirted with you, but he wouldn't sleep with you unless he was attracted to you," Sandra said.

"So he's never fucked for information?"

"I didn't say that. He was a horny kid when he started going undercover. I happen to know he liked the James Bond stuff in the beginning," Sandra replied.

"It gets old fast," Kim said. "Not that I ever really got into that. I got married before I went out into the field, so I didn't play around with that. I agree with Sandra. If he slept with you, he wanted to. Did you like him? Or were you bored?"

"I was stupid over him," she admitted. She could still feel that rush she'd gotten in those days with him. It had been a magical feeling, something she'd never felt before. "I was about to get out, and he was the first man I got close to. I'd had some guys I dated before, but it wasn't like Drake. We got deep fast. At least I did."

Kim leaned over, getting closer to her. "Be honest. Did he get deep with you?"

She'd never been able to forget their long talks and how comfortable she'd felt with him. "We seemed to click right away. It felt like we understood each other. That's why it hurt that he thought I could betray my country and everything my dad worked for."

"He'd known you for a week," Sandra pointed out.

She didn't get to have it both ways. "So he'd known me long enough to want to get serious with me but not long enough to trust..." Fuck. She was caught neatly in that woman's trap. "He'd known his sister all his life. He loved her but he couldn't trust her."

"She shoots, she scores." Kim held up her glass in a toast. "He can fall for a woman quickly, but trusting is a problem. Welcome to the world of most of us. Our men are complex and usually need therapy. Oh, I know Charlotte Taggart will tell you her vagina healed Ian, but he did his time on a couch. You probably need some, too."

She felt a frown come over her face. "You know I thought that when I went to college I would try finding someone to talk to, to sort through my messy upbringing. And then my dad died and I shut down. I think I need that drink."

"It's good," Sandra said. "Kim has a heavy hand with the tequila, and I promise you're safe here. When was the last time you sat around and talked to your girlfriends and drank and ate a ton of cheesy nachos?"

Never. Not even once. She felt the weirdest thing. Her eyes had gone watery. She'd kind of thought she was all cried out after her dad died and the world seemed to go dark.

Was she just passing time until she could find that fight that would take her out?

Wasn't there more the world had to offer her than revenge for a father who would probably tell her to walk away?

You will find what you want to be in the world and my life will be complete, dushka. *That's what I learned. I am not a smart man, but I did one thing right. You are my brave girl, going out into the world. I will be so proud when you discover who you want to be.*

He'd kissed her on the forehead, and that had been the last time she'd seen him.

Would he be proud now? What was braver? Moving on in the face of her grief? Or giving over to it and letting it hold sway for the rest of her life?

How had she avoided asking these stupid, necessary questions?

The answer was simple. She'd made her whole life about work—every minute focused on the op ahead of her so she didn't have to grieve, didn't have to be angry or sad.

She took a deep breath and picked up the glass.

The last person she'd shared a drink with had been Drake during those long cozy days they'd spent in a cabin where the world had been shut out and yet there had seemed like there was more potential for life than she'd ever felt before.

"I don't see the nachos, Sandra." If she said anything else she might lose it, and she would at least like to be drunk off her ass before she made a fool of herself in front of her new friends.

Before she let herself feel. Maybe there was nothing at all foolish about that.

A brilliant smile crossed her face. "Oh, they're coming."

The door flew open and Kyle stood there, a fierce frown on his face and a big platter in his hands. "Am I the errand boy now? I thought we were keeping this to me washing your dishes. Now I'm your personal waiter? Are those margaritas?"

Kim stood and crossed the space between them, taking the platter out of Kyle's hands. "Margaritas are for people who need to talk about their feelings. Do you have feelings, Kyle?"

"I feel like I want a margarita. I feel like not going back downstairs where Angie will throw another bucket of dishes at me and tell me to clean. You know for someone who does as much yoga as she does, she's mean," Kyle announced.

"You'd get more places with her if you would work without a shirt," Sandra quipped.

Those nachos looked delicious.

Kyle's hands went to his hips. He honestly wasn't wearing much of a shirt to begin with. It was a thin white tank that molded to his every muscle. "She's supposed to be a lesbian."

"Yes, and lesbians enjoy a nice work of art as well as the

straights," Sandra shot back.

"The sexual fluidity of the older generation screws with my head every time. I'm only working here for another couple of days, and this shirt stays on," he announced. "And I'll go find another drinking partner. I bet Tucker and Jax could use some margaritas, too."

He marched out.

"That boy is in for some major suffering," Sandra said with a shake of her head. "Dumbass. Let's eat and we can talk about how sometimes it's way better to pick joy over duty. And I'm a former nurse. I've seen where joy can lead a person. Usually to the ER. The things I've seen that managed to fall in a person's anus. You can't unsee that."

She nearly choked on her drink. She barely managed to swallow and then a laugh took over her body. It made her shake and feel light at the same time.

Joy. Amusement. A little peace.

Yes, she had a job to do, but maybe there was a place in her life for some joy, too.

She sat back as Sandra started telling stories, and for the first time in forever, let herself be.

Chapter Fourteen

"Do you know how happy I am to see you? I can't believe... I swear you were this high the last time I saw you." Nikolai Markovic had a massive smile on his face. He looked almost exactly the same with the singular exception of a light dusting of gray hair at his temples. He was still tall and broad, with jet black hair and blue eyes that would have made her heart thump had she been an adult when she'd met him. Instead she'd been a girl and he'd been a family figure, so when she hugged him now all she felt was a deep sense of comfort.

Uncle Nick remembered her father, had known him for longer than anyone else.

"It's good to see you." She stepped back and nodded to Nick's wife. "Hi, Aunt Hayley."

The pretty American with deep brown hair stepped up and gave her a hug, too. "It's so good to see you, sweetie. I wish we'd been able to have a gathering for your dad."

There had been no funeral for Lev Sokolov, though she'd identified his body and they'd given her a lovely urn full of his ashes. It was sitting in her drab apartment since she'd never figured out what to do with them.

Now she wondered if Drake wouldn't mind taking her on a trip. Her dad had been happiest in Greece. He'd kept a tiny apartment in a seaside town. It had been where they spent all their downtime. He'd told her he'd wished he been born a fisherman, but she would tell him it was good he wasn't because they would have starved.

She missed her father. Since that day with Sandra and Kim, the waves kept hitting her but it felt different now. Before her grief had felt entirely bitter, and now there was an amazing amount of sweet that came with it.

"You know how the Agency works," she said with a sad smile. "I'm afraid the mission is more important than societal rituals."

"His entire existence was classified." Brad had come in with her. He'd spent the entire plane trip going over and over the mission. Since she'd gotten the call from her Consortium contact, he'd gone into overdrive, and it made him way less relaxed than he'd been before.

And he hadn't been particularly relaxed before.

"He was still a person," Nick said with a frown. "He deserves respect. Especially since he gave his life for a country he wasn't born in. He chose to work for the Agency. He chose to believe in America."

That seemed to rattle Brad a bit. "Well, I wasn't in charge of that decision. I'm sure we can work something out."

"What do you mean my old room has been taken over by someone else?" Tucker was complaining as he strode into the lobby, rolling his suitcase behind him.

An attractive man with red and blond hair was walking beside him. Owen Shaw had met them at the airport, and he'd been excited to see Tucker and Jax. They'd spent the whole trip to the club catching each other up on how their wives and kids were doing. They'd talked endlessly about carpools and schools and how hard it was to coach Little League. That had seemed particularly rough on Jax, since the town he lived in had never had a Little League before and one of the townspeople was worried it might be overrun by aliens. Brad had looked at her like he did not understand that world, but she'd thought it was nice.

It would be nice to have something to talk about besides her job.

She'd started to wonder if Sandra's "choose the boy" advice wasn't actually about choosing herself.

"What did you expect, brother?" Owen asked. "You've been gone damn near a decade. Damon brought in new people, and they needed a place to stay. Were they supposed to keep it pristine in case you ever bothered to show up again?"

The red-haired hottie had a Scottish accent and was married to her "target." Well, The Consortium's target.

"I was told he would never show up again. Tag promised me." A tall, dark-haired man with an upper-crust British accent stood at the door that likely led inside the inner parts of the building.

Jax gave Damon Knight a sunny smile as he followed Tucker. "Hey, Damon. Man, it's good to see you. Where's Pen and the rest of the crew?"

"My wife is at our country home." Damon strode forward. "The boys are out of school for the week so she's taken them up north to visit. Her brother and his husband live up there. Robert and Ariel moved into a flat in Westminster after their second child was born. Brody and Steph recently moved back to Australia to take care of his mum. I'm afraid the days of us all living together over a large sex club are over. Does that make anyone else feel old?"

"I am perfectly happy with our flat. No one ever raids it," Hayley admitted. "And we're still here in Chelsea, so a trip to The Garden is a ten-minute walk and an expensive babysitter away. And so many things make me feel old."

Nick pulled his wife close. "You are timeless, *dushka*."

"I will say I've come full circle and I enjoy a few days in my old apartments," Damon admitted. "It's nice for about forty-eight hours, and then I miss my family. We should make this quick."

Kyle was the last to walk in. He had a duffel over his shoulder and looked around the old-world style lobby. "I was told this place was cool. It looks a lot like where I just was. Was this place a brothel, too? I'm telling you, man, my dishwashing days are over."

"Ah, he might not have the Taggart DNA, but I know he's related to Ian because of the words that come out of his mouth," Damon said with a sigh. "I assure you I have plenty of dishwashers when the kitchen is open on play nights. Otherwise, you're on your own, and I expect you all to clean up after yourselves. I'm the father of two boys. Don't make me dad you. I can do it. I've been told my overbearing-father game is strong. As to Tucker's room, I think you'll find we've got one of our bodyguards living in there. He's a six-foot-seven-inch former SAS officer. If you want to evict him, you should feel free to try."

"Hey, I used to sleep on spanking benches," Tucker replied with a nod, his decision made. "I'm good wherever."

Jax was staring down at his tablet. "Yeah, we can stay wherever, but I probably need to set up my system. Is the big office space still open?"

"Do you have something?" She'd talked to her contact two days before, explaining she would be in England when the conference started.

"I've been tracking her on the Dark Web," Jax said, never looking up. "I have some contacts I want to check with, too."

Owen stepped over to look down at the tablet. "Is this the woman who wants Rebecca's research?"

"It's not merely a woman. You can't think of it like that." She needed to manage Owen's expectations. The Scot had once worked for McKay-Taggart and Knight, but he'd been out of the business for years now. "She's a representative of a group that wants to either steal your wife's research or put an end to it."

"Why would they want that? She's on the cusp of changing the way we deal with degenerative brain diseases," Owen said, still looking at the tablet.

"You know why, babe." Dr. Rebecca Walsh let the door close behind her. She wore a blue cardigan over a white dress with bright yellow polka dots. She looked sunny and happy. Not at all like a woman who spent her time staring into microscopes should.

Or maybe exactly the way she should. She'd been thinking a lot about the talk she'd had with Sandra and Kim, and she'd come to some conclusions. Her father had known one life, and deep down he hadn't thought he could be anything but a spy, so he hadn't changed his lifestyle even when he'd had a kid. He'd thought that was the only life he had to offer her.

She didn't have to make the same choice. Her father had

actively advised her to leave the Agency. He'd wanted her to have a life, to explore the world.

She could make her own choices. The past didn't have to affect her future, and that might mean trying to come to an understanding with the only man she'd ever... She wasn't ready to say *loved* yet. Cared about. Wanted. Longed for.

"Because there's money to be made," Owen said with a sigh.

"When there's more money to be made curing the disease than there is treating it, they'll make it available," Rebecca said. "But they want the choice." Rebecca moved toward Taylor, holding out a hand. "I suspect you're our Agency friend. I only know you as Constance. It can stay that way if you like."

"Constance will work," Brad agreed.

Taylor took the doctor's hand in hers. "It's Taylor. I don't know why he thinks I should hide it. My uncle isn't going to call me Constance. There are a lot of people here who knew my father. You have to forgive my handler. He's got the whole Agency employees' guide shoved up his ass."

"I do not." Brad frowned and seemed to realize nothing had changed. "Also, it's online now, so even if I did it wouldn't be a big deal."

At least he'd found something of a sense of humor. Although he might be serious. Sometimes she couldn't tell.

"Hayley, dear, would you mind showing the lads what's new with the building?" Damon asked. "I'd like a moment to talk to Taylor, and I think Owen and Rebecca should be involved. I also doubt your husband will leave."

"I will not." Nick leaned over and kissed his wife's forehead before looking back to Damon. "I consider her my family, and I will watch out for her."

Damon nodded. "You've made your thoughts on the operation clear."

Nick had thoughts? She hadn't heard them, but then it wasn't like she'd reached out since her dad had died. She'd avoided him and anyone who might have made her feel something other than rage.

She watched as Hayley led Jax and Tucker out. Rebecca and

Owen settled onto one of the plush sofas that lined the lobby, while Brad took one of the big chairs and Damon stood by the reception desk.

Nick looked to Brad. "I was rather hoping we could have a moment alone with Taylor. She's family."

"She's my asset, so no." Brad sat back.

"The fact that you call her an asset makes me uncomfortable," Nick said with a frown. "I don't like the idea of her being used by the Agency, and neither would her father. He's not here to watch out for her. You should understand that makes it my job. I owe Lev Sokolov. I will not fail his daughter. No matter what I have to do or who I have to do it to."

A weird, warm feeling swept through her at Nick's words. His Russian accent had thickened with his emotion, like her father's used to.

"This is an important operation, Mr. Markovic." Brad's jaw had tightened, a sure sign he was going stubborn. "It has far-reaching repercussions to not only American interests, but the whole world. If your organization isn't interested in helping us, I assure you we can find somewhere to stay. Personally, I would welcome the change."

"Taylor, if you don't want to do this, we'll find another way." Rebecca had a hand on her husband's thigh, his arm around her. They were connected, giving each other comfort. "I'm ready to announce that I'm pulling out of the conference for health reasons. It's a good cover, and it should buy us some time to lock down."

"Are you okay?" Taylor asked. She hadn't heard anything about Rebecca being sick.

"I'm perfectly fine, but we can put a rumor out that I'm pregnant and cutting back on work for a while," Rebecca explained.

"She's not. Nope. I just got our youngest in preschool." Owen shook his head and had visibly paled. "We're done."

Rebecca grinned. "He's been a stay-at-home dad for the last couple of years. He's ready to get back to work. But seriously, if you want out we can make it happen."

"She doesn't want out. She's worked hard on this op, and she's not about to walk away now," Brad replied, not waiting on her to speak for herself. "And again, if you have a problem, I can have

Agency support here by tomorrow. I would actually rather do that."

"Brad," Taylor began.

Nick proved he could be an overbearing parental figure by cutting her off and moving so he could loom over Brad. "You need to understand that I will not allow this to move forward if I suspect that you won't take care of her. I will not allow her to go into the field on such a dangerous mission without someone who truly cares about her backing her up, so don't think you can walk out of here with her."

She was about to point out that not only was she a full-ass grown adult but also an employee of the Agency, and she would make those decisions.

But then the door slammed open, and Drake was walking through. He looked like he'd run from wherever he'd been. He was in sweatpants and a T-shirt and athletic shoes, with a set of earbuds dangling around his neck.

He strode in, and his eyes went straight to her.

"Hey," she began and then stopped because the look in his eyes made her freeze in place.

Longing. Want. Need. He ignored everyone else in the room and walked right up to her. He got into her space and his hands went to her neck, sliding around and sinking into her hair. "I'm going to kiss you now, Taylor."

The Dom was in the house. He wouldn't ask, but he would accept a refusal. She could tell him no or back away.

She didn't want to. Not even her pride was speaking up now because she didn't think he could fake that look.

Desire and something more. He was happy to see her. He'd felt every moment they'd been apart.

She went on her toes and then his mouth was on hers and her hands found his waist. The kiss wasn't sweet. It wasn't a hello that promised more later because they were in front of others.

That kiss told her he would back her up against the wall and take her right then and there, and he didn't care who was watching because she was his and he was hers and they were together again. The long days of nothing but talk had left him hungry to be close.

As hungry as she was.

He kissed her for what felt like forever and still not long enough.

Not a voice in her head spoke up and told her to step back. There was no voice, just the warmest feeling of belonging.

He finally broke off the kiss but let his forehead rest on hers. "They didn't tell me when you were coming in. I saw Jax and Tucker and I got here as soon as I could. I missed you, Taylor. I fucking missed you, and I'm not going to pretend that I didn't."

If he was playing her, she was going to get her heart ripped out.

And she would pick it up, dust it off, and move forward with her life. Grief had done funny things to her, but the cloud had started to lift, and life suddenly wasn't as dark as it had been before. "I missed you, too, Sir. Drake. I missed you, Drake."

He pulled her close and hugged her before shifting to the side and looking around until he found Damon. "Mr. Knight, I know Brad is technically her handler, but you should understand that I have control of this mission and she gets to decide what she wants to do, what she thinks is the best course of action, and if she wants to go through with it at all."

Nick pointed his way. "This one, I like." He frowned at Brad. "You, I am watching."

Damon smiled. "Yes, I like him more now that I know his attitude comes from being horny. The good news is we're going to play tonight. Let's get you settled into your rooms."

"Room," Drake said stubbornly. "Taylor's staying with me."

She didn't even roll her eyes. "Taylor is choosing to stay with you."

"Isn't that what he said?" Owen asked, holding a hand out to his wife.

Lifestylers.

"I will never understand places like this." Brad stood and looked her way. "I hope you know what you're doing."

For the first time in over a year and a half, she didn't. She had no fucking idea what she was doing, and that felt pretty good. She found her arm winding around Drake's waist.

"Now, young man, we should have a drink." Nick had an assessing look in his eyes as he took in Drake. "I would like to know more about how you and Taylor got to know one another. I was not aware Taylor was in a relationship."

To be honest with herself, she hadn't been totally aware of it either, but she was overwhelmed by how he'd greeted her. She could take it one of two ways. She could be wary and attribute his enthusiasm to the fact that they were close to the op now and he would want a firm hold on her.

Or she could accept that he wanted her and she wanted him. She could accept the risk that came with embracing life and everything it had to offer.

"We met a long time ago," she said. "But we only took it to a romantic level recently."

"She's simplifying things." Drake's arm tightened around her as though he was afraid she might break away from him. "We were involved a while back, and I hurt her. She's giving me a second chance, and I'm not going to waste it. I'm more than happy to talk to you, but I'm going to settle her in first."

"Good." Nick had a smile on his face, but it was the kind her father used to have when he was going to kill someone. A shark smile. "I'll meet you in the bar in thirty minutes. I'll bring the vodka."

Hayley shook her head. "Nope. We're going to leave the young ones to settle in, and we'll meet them for dinner or lunch sometime this week. You have work to do, and Taylor needs to get some rest."

She could have sworn a low growl came from Nick's throat.

And then Hayley's eyes narrowed.

Nick sighed, obviously giving up the fight. "Yes, we would love to have you out to our place while you're here. And I'll be in the office all week. Hayley has a class to teach this afternoon, but I'll be here."

The last was said with a hint of threat.

"We'll all be here." Damon pushed off the reception desk, straightening his big body. "Let's plan for a conference room meeting first thing tomorrow morning so everyone can get some rest. The club is open tonight for anyone who wants to play, and the lounge opens early."

Everyone left in the lobby got up and started to make plans for the day.

She was tired, but also not tired. She had that wired feeling she got when she knew she was close to something major.

Or it could be jet lag.

"I will drop by your office before this evening," Drake promised, holding a hand out to Nick, who shook it. "You know, I've been here for two days and you haven't spoken to me once."

"I didn't care about you until I found out you're sleeping with my niece. Now I care," Nick announced.

"He's going to behave." Hayley threaded her arm through her husband's. "Come on, babe. Let's grab some lunch with Owen and Rebecca."

Drake took her hand. "If your uncle is going to kill me, at least let me watch while you get your first look at The Garden."

"He's not going to kill you." She was fairly certain. Mostly. She followed behind him.

"You're going to play in my club, Drake?" Damon asked, one elegant brow arched over his eyes.

"Hell, yes, Mr. Knight. It's the most spectacular club I've ever seen, and she's the only sub I would want to see it with," Drake replied.

Nick growled again.

"And she's more than a sub. Far more." Drake squeezed her hand.

And she walked into paradise.

* * * *

Drake walked Taylor into The Garden and stopped, allowing her to take in the dramatic dungeon.

Taylor's eyes lit up as she made her way inside, turning so she could take in all sides. "I can't believe how beautiful this is. Is this really a club?"

It was kind of hard to call it a dungeon. There were no stark walls or gloomy atmosphere. Where Sanctum was an ultra-modern pleasure palace and The Cowgirl's Choice was all about the Western brothel chic, The Garden was almost primeval, in a lush way.

During the day it was a vibrant green jungle. At night, when the moon came out, the flowers bloomed and the scent of jasmine filled the air.

"Look around and you'll see the scene spaces." He gestured toward the alcoves that contained spanking benches and St. Andrew's Crosses. There were spaces for suspension play where the sub would look like they were part of the trees and vines around them.

Taylor's lips had curled up. "It's beautiful."

"Will you play here with me?"

A brow arched. "You're asking?"

"Don't get used to it." He moved into her space again, looming over her. He gently brushed back a lock of her hair. "You know I like to be bossy about sex. But this time, I'm asking because I need to hear you say yes. I missed you, Taylor. Not in a 'hey, I wish my friend was here' way. I missed you in a 'my life isn't whole' way. I need to hear the word."

Her expression softened, and she went up on her toes. "Yes. I will play with you."

Her lips brushed his, and he felt like something fundamental had changed between them, something had eased inside her, and it made her open to him in a way she hadn't been since those days they'd spent together closed in and warm.

He let his hands find her hips. "How is it coming on the ID? Have you figured out who our mysterious John is?"

She kissed him again. "Still not much. It's frustrating and has the feel of an almost government-like cover up to it. I think someone did a spectacular job erasing his history, but I suspect there are a few social media companies involved in The Consortium. Are you worried you can't be professional when we talk about business?"

He knew he couldn't, but it didn't look like she could either. "I don't want to talk business at all, but I saw Tucker and Jax heading for the offices instead of their rooms, so it feels like something happened."

Her hand ran down his side. "I'm supposed to meet with my contact in the next couple of days."

Fuck. He'd known it would happen at the conference. It was

precisely why they were all here. But now it was moving far too fast, and the uncertainty of what would happen was going to kill him.

"Don't borrow trouble, Drake." Her lips brushed his jaw.

His whole body went on red alert. "I was going to let you settle in and play with you tonight, but I won't be able to if you keep doing that, baby."

Her cheek rubbed against his, and her hands moved inside his shirt, finding skin and connecting them. "I think this is a very professional way to talk about things. I think doing our own personal meetings this way might help to keep you calm."

He wasn't fucking calm at all, but if this was how she wanted to update him, he would take it. He leaned over and shoved one arm under her knees and the other balancing her back as he hauled her against his chest. "I was going to shower before you got in, but now you have to deal with the sweat. Now tell me what you know and talk fast because you won't be able to talk once I get my mouth on your pussy."

"Hello. You should understand that the club is not open yet." Damon Knight shook his head like he'd found a couple of dumb kids playing where they shouldn't.

"Then we'll have to come back, won't we?" Drake turned and strode toward the elevator that would take them up to the apartments.

He heard Knight chuckle behind him and murmur something about how much he missed the good old days, but Drake only had eyes for her.

He managed to hit the button for the elevator, and it opened immediately. He carried her inside. "Talk to me, Taylor."

She seemed perfectly comfortable in his arms. "She told me she would contact me sometime in the next forty-eight hours. Dr. Walsh is supposed to give her speech the day after tomorrow, so I think things will move quickly once she calls."

He pressed the button for four and the doors closed, the elevator starting to move. "Brad has plans?"

"There's not a lot we can do until she calls and we figure out what she wants from me," Taylor replied. "I think she's likely to have me break into Rebecca's hotel room and download the contents of her laptop. They weren't able to get to her personal laptop before. The data I gave them came from the institute Dr. Walsh works for. You know she hasn't actually mentioned Dr. Walsh's name yet. It could be one of the other doctors."

He didn't think so. "Rebecca is the one they want. Everything points in that direction. It should be a fairly easy job. Especially since I've already made a dupe of her system. She redacted the important stuff but faked some reports that should lead The Consortium to the wrong conclusions. It buys her a whole bunch of time because they should ignore her after this."

That was the plan, at least. Rebecca had faked information on her research that should lead The Consortium to believe she wasn't as far along as they'd previously understood.

It should be an easy job. They would leave the laptop in the hotel room for Taylor to find. They would do all the things normal people did—lock the room, leave the laptop in the safe, password protect it. Taylor would do her thing and get through all of that security on her own in case anyone was watching.

He wouldn't be there to protect her. He would be somewhere in the hotel playing the part he was supposed to play when all he would be able to think about was her.

The elevator doors opened and he strode out, making his way to the apartment he intended to share with her.

"You're worrying again." Her hand cupped his jaw. "You have to have a little faith."

He would worry every second she was involved in this mission. "I'll try not to let it show, but I can't not worry about you, Taylor. I'll never not worry about you. I know you think I callously tossed you aside, that I was investigating you, but after that first day, I didn't care about anything but getting closer to you."

"You didn't fight for me because Julia had recently turned on you," she said quietly.

He didn't stop, though he wanted to. This was a conversation they needed to have alone, without anything between them. He managed to make it down the hall, managed to get inside the apartment that had seemed so damn lonely without her there. He kicked the door closed and set her on her feet.

"What changed?" She hadn't been this open when he'd left Wyoming.

She was quiet for a moment, her eyes studying him. She moved in closer, as though she couldn't stand the distance between them. "I think I'm coming out of a dark time. I think the gloom is lifting a bit and I'm able to see things more clearly."

"Gloom?"

"I didn't really understand I've been mourning," she said quietly. "The world has seemed incredibly heavy, and I've felt so alone. I numbed out my pain with work, but seeing you again was the jolt I needed. I still don't know if you're playing me or not, but I'm not playing you, and that's all I can control right now."

He dragged her into his arms. "I am not playing you. I'm crazy about you. I would use the word *love* if I thought it wasn't going to scare you off, but I'm going to someday. I'm not going to change my mind, and you're not going to find out this was part of a job. You are all that matters to me right now. I meant what I said. I'm going to support you. If you need to work this job for a couple of years, I'm still going to be waiting for you. I'll figure it out. I'll sneak in and out, or I'll just fucking wait. Nothing matters as long as we're together at the end. I'm going to do everything I can to make sure that happens. Even if I have to fight the scary dude who is not your blood uncle but who looks like he's willing to fight me like he's your dad."

He knew he sounded like an idiot, but he meant every single word. He was putting it all out there, and he wasn't even sure he had the right to.

Julia would try to hurt anyone he cared about if she decided that was a way to make him do what she wanted.

"But you should know my sister…" he began.

She put a finger to his lips. "Your sister doesn't matter. If you're worried she's going to try to screw with me the way she did with Kyle and his family, you should know I'll kill her. I will take her out so she can't hurt you anymore."

It was stupid. He should explain to her that he would protect her. It was his job, what his father had charged him with from the time he was very young—protecting the country. Protecting his mother from the truth. Protecting his secrets.

Taylor was the first person he could remember who offered to protect him. It made him feel weird. Warm and taken care of.

"You will run the other way if you see her," he said, his voice going thick with emotion. "You will protect yourself because you have to know that nothing is more important to me than you. Nothing. Not the op. Not the Agency. You. But I'm not going to push you away like Kyle did with his girl. I'm going to trust that you know what you want, that you know what you can risk."

"This is a risk I want to take. You need to remember that even if things get bad," she said. "Even if she's coming at us, you have to remember that I wanted to be here. I wanted to be with you no matter what happens. We can get through it together."

He gave in to the overwhelming desire to kiss her, wrapping his arms around her and losing himself in the way she tasted and felt and smelled. He wanted to surround himself with her. She was rapidly becoming the center of his world, crowding out what had been there before. His job. Always his job. But now he had to wonder why he'd been doing the damn job at all. He'd done it because he'd been trained to, because it had become the only home he had. He'd been set on a path and he hadn't veered from it, hadn't even thought to until he'd met her.

She broke the kiss, moving back. For a second he thought she was going to walk away entirely, and he realized it would break him if this had all been a bit of revenge on her part. It would be a good revenge—letting him bare his soul to her and then walking out to let him know she could never forgive him.

"Taylor," he began.

Her lips curled up. "No. If I let you, you'll have me on my back before I can take another breath, and I have something I want to do. We're not on the dungeon floor. Tonight I'll let you take me into The Garden and I'll be your sweet sub, but now I'm going to do what I've been dreaming of."

She slowly dropped to her knees, and his whole body went tense with anticipation as she tugged at the waistband of his sweats.

She'd been dreaming of blowjobs? Fuck. "I don't know what

brought you out of your cloud, baby, but I am so glad it did."

Taylor dragged his sweats and boxer briefs down, his cock coming free. "I had some time to think and to be around people who have actual lives. I've spent too much time by myself. Being at Sandra's and around the Taggarts and Kim and Jax and Tucker reminded me of what I wanted before my father died."

"A life." He remembered every word she'd spoken about her dreams of the future. "You wanted to go to school and find yourself."

"I did. I don't know if that's still in the cards, but I want to have a life that isn't tied to this job." Her hand came up, and he was surrounded by the soft skin of her palm, and she stroked him.

His eyes nearly rolled to the back of his head. "You can have anything you want. I'll help you, baby. You want out of this job, we'll walk away today. I can have us on a plane tonight, and I promise we won't look back."

"I think you mean that." She leaned forward and licked the head of his cock.

He damn near forgot how to breathe. "I mean every word. You're more important than the job."

"I'm going to do this job," she vowed. "At least the part in London. I'm going to identify The Consortium agent I've been working with, but I need to think about the rest."

It wasn't everything he wanted to hear. He wanted her to walk away and be safe, but he would take it. And if he didn't get the answer he wanted, he would still support her. He let his hands find the silk of her hair. "Take all the time you need. I'm not going anywhere. We get the job done here and then reassess when we get back to DC. But you should understand that you're going to be spending a lot of time with me."

"Will I?" That soft, lush tongue dragged over his sensitive flesh, lighting up his whole body.

Thinking was starting to get hard. Thinking about anything except her was almost impossible. He watched as the head of his dick slowly disappeared behind those gorgeous lips of hers. "You will. I don't know how closely you'll be watched, but I'll make it work. You should understand I want to live with you as soon as possible."

"You move fast." She seemed to be determined to explore every inch of his cock. Her tongue licked long lines across the underside, her hair moving like a wave as she shifted.

"I moved way too slow." They could have had all these months. A year and a half. They could have moved past all the bad parts.

She settled in and started to work his cock, running her tongue over and around.

Her free hand came up to cup his balls, rolling them and sending sparks through his system. Her tongue moved over and over him, and he couldn't handle another second.

"If you don't stop, baby, you're going to get a mouthful." He was so emotional about this woman, but his inner Dom was starting to make an appearance. He twisted a hand in her hair, the softer feelings being pushed aside in the quickly rising tide of lust.

She hummed around his cock, teasing him and threatening to push him right over the edge. She wanted to play? He could play.

He tightened his hand and felt her gasp, the sound moving across his cock.

"Take more."

She was playing with him, and he was ready to move on. He was ready to give her what she wanted, but she was going to stop teasing him with shallow passes. He used his hold on her hair to force his cock a little deeper.

"More." It was a gentle fight to get further into her mouth.

Her teeth scraped lightly against him, making him hiss and sending sparks up his spine. He liked the tiny bite of pain.

"More." He pressed in another inch as she sucked at him and rolled his balls.

"More." It was a word he always thought when he was around her. *More. More. More.*

He would never get enough of her.

She settled in, sucking his cock in long passes as she played with his balls, taking him in until he could feel the soft skin at the back of her throat.

She sucked him hard, and he couldn't hold back another second. He fucked her mouth with pure abandon and filled her, every second a searing pleasure.

She sat back, licking her lips and looking every bit the satisfied little brat she was.

He was so fucking in love with her, and she wasn't even close to being naked enough for him.

He kicked off his shoes and got out of his sweats before dragging his shirt over his head and reaching for her.

"Pay back is going to be fun, baby." He picked her up and started for the bed.

Chapter Fifteen

Taylor could still taste him, the salty essence of his sex on her tongue and coating her lips. She'd wanted to get her mouth on him. He'd brought her so much pleasure with that talented tongue of his. No one could accuse Drake of being a selfish lover, and she'd wanted to pay him back.

He crossed the small living room, moving to what looked like the bedroom.

Was she really going to stay here with him? Was she diving in?

Yes. You are diving in, and the water is going to be deep and you're going to be okay no matter what happens because nothing at all can happen if you never take a chance.

No life. No love. Only more numbness and darkness.

There was no joy without risk.

Her father would want her to live, to find love, to build a family. He would want her to look to the future and not the past. He would want her to try and fail and get back up and try again. She'd fallen into darkness for a bit, but now it was time to find the light.

"Baby, are you okay?" He set her on her feet, close to the bed.

She had to ask, had to put the question to him, look him in the eyes and decide if she was going to believe the man she was rapidly falling for.

He was going to press her back against the bed and make love to her, and no one would stop them this time. She couldn't fool herself and say she was using him or that this was casual.

So she had to ask, and if it ruined everything, then at least she would know.

"Drake, I have to ask you a question. I promise you I'll only ask it once."

He seemed to understand that this was serious for her. His hand cupped the nape of her neck. "Ask me anything. I promise I won't lie to you. I know you don't believe me, but I didn't lie then and I won't now. I'll tell you the truth no matter how much it hurts me."

He was so beautiful to her, standing there wearing nothing but his own glorious skin. "Did you have anything to do with my father's death?"

He sighed as though relieved, and she knew they'd needed to get this out in the open, to drag it into the light. "No. Baby, no. I promise you that I didn't know what Julia was doing. If I'd had even a hint... I'm so..."

She shook her head and went up on her toes, stopping the apology with a kiss. "No. It's over and we move on now. It's over and we don't look back."

If she was going to be in, she would be all in. She wasn't sure what would happen tomorrow, but she would face it.

Drake's mouth came down on hers and she felt the moment he totally took control. Like he had when she was sucking his cock. He'd let her play for a moment, and then his hands had tightened and he'd led her. It shouldn't have been so hot, but it was. This was the man she'd fallen for. Drake was a partner who knew what she needed in the bedroom and trusted her out of it. He was a man she could build a life with.

He stepped back, his naked body such a work of art to her. "Take off your clothes."

"Why don't you take them off me?" she replied in a saucy tone.

His lips thinned to a flat line. "That's not what I told you to do, Taylor. Are you going to play with me tonight? More importantly, are you going to do the job that scares the fuck out of me? I'm going to support you, but I feel out of control, and when I do and it concerns the safety of the person who means the most to me in the world, I'm going to need something to soothe me."

She could handle that. Everyone needed something comforting. Drake's comfort simply came from filthy, glorious sex he got to control. She would get something she needed, too. An orgasm. Connection to him. She kicked off her shoes. "Do you want me to go slow, Sir?"

"Drake. Call me by my name. I need to hear it so I know you're with me."

Because he had to give up his name so often. He had to become Mr. Black or Mr. Brown. Some spectrum of Agency-approved names to obscure who he really was. He'd probably used it so often it would be hard to remember who he was.

He needed a place where he could simply be.

"Drake, you want me to go slow? Do you want me to show you everything I'm offering you?"

His cock was starting to stir to life again.

It was funny how much control there was in submission.

"Do it slow, Taylor. Show me."

He stepped back and allowed her some space. She undid the top buttons of her blouse. She'd dressed comfortably given how long the flight had been from Wyoming to London. She probably needed a shower, too, but it could wait. She had a feeling Drake would dirty her up nicely.

There was something deeply empowering about undressing for her lover. She moved slowly, giving him a show she felt one hundred percent certain he was enjoying. She knew because at some point between when she shed her shirt and tossed away her jeans, he'd started to stroke his own cock as he watched her. His thick dick lengthened and swelled as she stood in front of him wearing nothing but her bra and undies. They were plain cotton and comfortable, but he made her feel like she was wearing expensive lingerie.

He made her feel beautiful. When she was with Drake she felt sexy, aware of her body in a way she wasn't when he wasn't around.

Now she could feel the cool air on her skin and the way her nipples hardened under his gaze. They stood out against the cotton of her bra. Her pussy was wet from the arousal she'd gotten when taking his cock in her mouth. She was deeply aware of how she'd flooded those cotton undies with her arousal, and they were white so they were probably see-through now. Drake's eyes went straight there.

How far could she push him before he was on her, giving her what she'd needed every day for the months and months they'd been apart? She let her hand slide down her torso, delving below the waistband on the undies. Her fingers brushed over her clit and between her labia, gathering the cream she found there. She brought it back up and held her glistening fingers out to him. "I'm definitely offering you this."

He moved in and gripped her wrist. "You're being a brat who didn't do what I told her to. I wonder how I should deal with that."

"I told you I would show you what I was offering you." She wasn't afraid of him. If he was going to punish her, it would likely lead to a whole lot of pleasure.

"And I told you to get naked." He brought her fingers to his lips and slowly sucked them inside, his tongue whirling around them, taking in her taste. He scraped his teeth as he pulled her hand out, lighting up her senses. "You don't seem to want to listen to me, Taylor."

"Well, I just thought…"

He pivoted, somehow managing to get an arm around her waist as he sat down on the bed. She found herself over his lap in a heartbeat. "Brats who think get spanked, baby. And they don't get to wear panties at all."

His hand came down on her ass, and she gasped at the sensation. Pain flared and then seemed to shoot straight to her pussy. He gave her three hard smacks and then his hand eased under her panties and brushed over the spot he'd spanked.

"Do you know how good you taste to me?" He seemed intent on exploring her backside. He rubbed and squeezed and stroked across her cheeks. "I love eating your pussy, baby. I think about it all the time. I want you to know something. I didn't lie when I told you I haven't slept with anyone since that night with you. No one. I haven't thought about anyone but you."

"I haven't either. I played a little, and yes, I did that because I wanted to understand you better. I told myself it was so I could separate myself from you and prove I didn't need you to find pleasure, but I never took another Dom." She hadn't been able to. Even then when she'd hated him, she'd seen his face everywhere, felt his touch.

Wanted him.

It was easier to accept that now that she'd figured out what had been wrong.

"I didn't want anyone else, Taylor," he said. "It has been you since the day we met. That car crash might not have changed my life, but crashing into you absolutely did."

She had to smile. That first crash had been nothing but the second...oh, the second had changed everything.

"When we get back home, I'm taking you to The Court and I'm showing you off, and I'm going to get the worst ribbing of my life because I've always said I would never take a submissive."

She was still feeling saucy. "Don't tell them you took a sub. Tell them your wife won't let you play without her."

He stopped, and for a second she worried she'd said something wrong. And then his hand slipped out of her undies and came down again. "That's exactly what I'll tell them. And when they want to tell me I got tamed, I'll tell them fuck yeah I did, and I'm so happy about it. But we're going to talk about you minding me better. I said naked."

She gasped as he ripped the panties off her. They slid out from under her, rubbing against her clit as he pulled them along.

"What do I mean when I say naked, Taylor?" His voice was deep and dark and promised her so many dirty pleasures.

"You mean naked, Drake. When you want me naked, I'll take off my clothes and you can have me any way you want me."

His hand came down again, and she felt that slap all the way up her spine. "That is what I mean. Any way I want you. Any time I want you. Anywhere I want you."

They would have to talk about that because she still had to work and she would have classes and stuff in her future, but she rather thought this was more play. He could be perfectly reasonable outside of the bedroom, but he was a little cavemany in it. "Yes, Drake."

She felt him twist the clasp of her bra and then dragged it off.

"That's what I want to hear. Yes, Drake." He flipped her over with an ease that took her breath away. He stood, cradling her to his chest. "You keep saying that, baby."

He laid her out on the bed and immediately covered her with his big body. She let her legs spread open so he could make a place for himself there. He devoured her mouth, his tongue sliding along hers while his hand palmed her breast, and she could feel the hard length of his cock against her thigh. She gave as good as she got, wrapping her arms around him and letting her tongue play with his.

He dragged her hands high, and she felt something slip around them. Rope. She hadn't noticed the rope ties at the top of the bed, but then this was an apartment over a sex club, so the fact that it was built for play shouldn't surprise her. Her breath caught as she felt him tighten the rope.

"It's built into the bed," he said as he checked to make sure the rope wasn't too tight. "All I have to do is slip your hands in and tighten and then you can't get away from me."

"I don't want to get away from you," she admitted. "Though I think it might be fun to pretend like you have to chase me down."

His lips kicked up in a heart-stopping grin. "I can make that happen, baby."

He started to kiss his way down her body, nipping at her neck and making her hold on to those ties at her wrist. Her body felt tight, bowing in pure arousal as he made his way to her breasts. He sucked on her nipples, giving her the barest hint of his teeth and making her squirm.

She gave over to him, letting him control her body. His hands moved over her in time with his lips and teeth and tongue. There didn't seem to be any place Drake didn't touch or stroke or lick.

He spread her legs and feasted on her pussy, quickly pushing her over the edge and making her call out his name. She held on to the ties as he fucked her with his fingers while he sucked her clit. Waves of pleasure rolled across her system.

It felt like forever as she rode those waves, but before long he was reaching for a box on the nightstand.

He rolled the condom on his cock. "I'm not letting you go, Taylor. This is it for me. This is the rest of my life."

She couldn't forget how she'd asked him if he was serious about her.

He wasn't finished. He reached over her head and showed how well designed those bindings were because with a flick of his wrist her hands were free.

"Even if you change your mind," he said as he moved between her legs. "Loving you is the rest of my life. I'll wait for you."

Tears blurred her eyes as she reached for him. He was giving her every out, but she wasn't going to take it. "I won't make you wait long. We're going to work it out. We're going to be together."

"I did lie to you. I said I wouldn't say it." He pressed his cock against her pussy, starting to stretch her.

She had to smile because she wasn't going to hold back a second longer. "I love you, too, Drake."

He pushed inside and brought them together, filling her up in the sweetest way. "I love you. I've never said it before. I love you, baby."

She wrapped herself around him, and he kissed her as he began to thrust and pull out, finding a rhythm that she could match. He kissed her over and over as his hips moved, cock going deep and finding the perfect spot that sent her to that place she'd only ever found with him.

Then he was going over the edge with her, his big body stiff and rhythm failing as he let go.

He fell on top of her, pressing her into the bed as her blood pounded pleasantly through her veins.

He nuzzled her neck. "Did that just happen?"

She nodded. "It did."

His head came up and he stared at her for a moment. "You won't regret it, Taylor. You'll see. I'm putting you first this time. No matter what happens, you come first in my life."

She wanted to believe him and so she brushed his hair back and let resolve settle over her. This was a choice. A choice to protect herself or risk her heart and maybe get it broken. There were no guarantees in life. There was only the choice to be brave.

"You come first in mine." A pleasant lethargy rolled over her. She hadn't slept much on the plane. "But I do have to figure a few things out."

He rolled to the side, gathering her close. "And I have to figure out how to survive having a drink with your uncle. I'm not dumb. He's going to try to get me so drunk I can't play with you tonight. It's an old Russian technique."

"I don't think Uncle Nick drinks much anymore," she said with a yawn. It felt so perfect to be close to him, like she was finally where she was supposed to be. "Just hold out as long as you can because I want to play tonight. But, babe, I think I'm going to need a nap."

He chuckled, holding her close to his chest. "Go to sleep. I'll handle your uncle and everything else. You rest and know I'll be here when you wake up. I promise."

She let the world go fuzzy and fell asleep to the sound of his heartbeat.

* * * *

"There's so many plants, man." Kyle looked around the dungeon. He wasn't dressed for play like the rest of the people here. He'd come down to the bar and complained bitterly about the time difference and the fact that he would have to stay up all night if he wanted to go on the planned online adventure with PnkHr123.

Apparently MaeBe was handling her lockdown by going online and complaining to her friend Kraven, and Kyle was eating it up.

Kyle was definitely going to be staying up.

Drake intended to be in bed early. Very early. Wrapped around Taylor because he'd not only been a good modern man who let her make the decisions concerning her safety, he had managed to get through an afternoon with Nick Markovic and stay perfectly sober because his sleight of hand was spectacular.

Nick had called him down while Taylor was still sleeping. He'd known exactly what the man was doing, pouring shot after shot of vodka. He was trying to get him so drunk he couldn't play with

Taylor. Well, the joke was on him since the Russian was passed out and his wife thought it was all hysterical. It had taken two bodyguards to get him in the cab and send him home.

Damon would probably be upset when that plant died of alcohol poisoning though.

"That's why they call it The Garden." It was a truly magical place, and he didn't even feel weird thinking a sex club was magical.

He wanted to play with Taylor here, wanted to have the place all to themselves so he could chase her around and they could pretend to be the only man and woman on earth.

He'd spent most of the day watching Taylor sleep. She'd laid her head on his chest and slept so peacefully. He'd felt like something was settled between them.

I have to ask you a question. I promise you I'll only ask it once. Did you have anything to do with my father's death?

His heart had threatened to break, and then it had been put back together again because she'd accepted his answer. It was the truth. He knew nothing about her father's death that she didn't know. He hadn't been part of Julia's plan.

Julia. There was a reason he'd asked Kyle to meet him down here.

Kyle had slept the afternoon away, too, so this was his first chance to speak to his friend.

"We need to talk. Julia came to see me."

Kyle's jaw tightened and looked to the bartender, a pretty sub with glossy black hair. "I'm going to need whiskey. Neat and a lot of it."

He definitely would need that drink. "She's not hiding anymore. She came to the club our parents have belonged to for thirty years."

Kyle glanced around. "Should we go somewhere to talk about this?"

Drake had thought a lot about this and come to some conclusions. "Only if we don't trust Damon. He's promised me every single person in The Garden has been vetted. Unlike Tag, he doesn't invite the local elite into his club."

"Because he didn't need their money to keep the place going

like Tag did in the beginning."

It was good to know Kyle was quick to defend his uncle.

"I'm only saying that almost all of the club members either work for or are close to people who work for Damon." He'd decided he felt comfortable talking in the space after Damon had shown him his protocols. "If we can't talk here, we shouldn't use it as our base."

The bartender passed Kyle a couple of fingers of whiskey and looked Drake's way. He shook his head and started for one of the tables overlooking the dungeon.

Kyle settled in. "Is there a reason you didn't kill her on sight?"

Drake's gut tightened. There were a lot of reasons. He wanted to hate her, and there was a part of him that did. But she was still his sister, still his childhood playmate. "She brought along muscle. I'm fairly certain it was John, though I didn't get a great look at him because he had a gun to my spine."

"In the middle of a DC country club frequented by politicians?" Kyle asked, a bit of horror creeping into his tone.

"We have to assume they've infiltrated that particular club. Julia inferred they've infiltrated a lot of places." He'd gotten on a plane for London the day after his meeting with Julia. His mother had offered to give him and Lydia a ride, and it would have looked odd if he'd turned down a private plane in favor of flying back to Wyoming. His mother would have questioned the move, and so would Lydia.

Lydia was already asking why he wasn't staying at the hotel with her. As far as Lydia knew, they were there to meet with a couple of assets who had information they needed to pass on. They were meeting tomorrow, and Lydia had already explained that she'd set up a cover for them. He wasn't sure why they needed a cover, but there it was. It was all nice and normal, an easy job and one she could help facilitate.

Lydia had been all over his mother during the trip, asking her about Drake's childhood and her career.

His mother might be right, and that was going to be a problem.

"I told you if Julia got recruited, there were probably others." Kyle picked up on his line of thought quickly. "It would explain a lot. Including how your asset got identified in Kraków. I know at first you thought it might be Taylor's father, but The Consortium would be the better bet. By then Julia was out of the loop on a personal level. She wasn't working for the Agency at the time. It had to be someone else."

"Or it could have been bad luck." He didn't like to think about how many Julias there were looking at classified information every single day.

Kyle took a long drink, obviously fortifying himself. "So what did my nightmare woman have to say?"

Drake glanced over to the path that led to the women's locker room hoping for the sight of Taylor coming toward him. Nothing. "You were right to leave MaeBe. She told me flat out she would have kept coming after her if you hadn't. She definitely doesn't think you're dead. I didn't tell her anything, but she knows."

Kyle sighed. "Well, I didn't expect it to work entirely, but I did buy Mae some time. I wish my uncle would listen to me about getting her into hiding."

"I don't think that's going to happen. He seems determined to help her get ready for the fight." He didn't have to worry about that with Taylor. According to Brad, she was well trained and in excellent physical shape. Drake had spent an hour going over Brad's evaluations, looking for any way to talk Taylor out of the op. Despite his earlier announcement, he didn't want her to go through with this.

There had been nothing but praise for her ability to defend herself with or without weapons. According to those evaluations, Taylor could likely take him down.

"Has she tried to call you?" Julia had specifically told him to warn Kyle.

"She can try but I'm supposed to be dead. I left my phone behind. The number isn't mine anymore," Kyle said. "I'm running on burners."

"She said you better pick up if she calls you." Drake didn't want to say the words, but he couldn't keep the warning from Kyle. "She suggested if you don't talk to her soon, she'll go after Mae."

There was the sound of glass crushing, and Drake looked down to see blood on Kyle's fist.

Drake had to keep him calm or he would be on a plane back to the States. "I've already talked to Tag. MaeBe's got a shadow detail she doesn't know about. For now she's got West with her, and someone else is watching them twenty-four seven. If anything changes, Tag promised he'll shove her in a safe house."

If Kyle felt the fact that he had glass buried in his palm, he didn't show it. He merely set what was left of the glass down and stared at Drake with dark eyes. "You didn't call me first?"

He'd known he was taking a risk. "I wanted to sit down and talk to you in person. I made sure Mae was safe, but I thought this was the best way to tell you. I would have talked to you earlier, but you took a nap."

"Well the next time your psychotic sister decides to threaten my girlfriend, wake me the fuck up." He stood, ignoring the glass around him. "I think I'll talk to my uncle myself."

"Go see Tucker first." Drake stood and started to go after him. "You need to get that hand looked at."

"Fuck you, Drake." Kyle strode off.

Damn it.

The last thing he'd wanted to do was fight with Kyle.

"You're not going to win with him." Brad moved from behind him as the bartender scurried over and quickly had the glass up and off the table and floor.

"I'm not trying to win." He was surprised to see Brad down here. He'd expected him to hide in his room the way he had in Wyoming.

"No, you're trying to get that friendship back, and you can't. It was a moment in time, and what happened in Singapore marked the end of that time. You were friends because you had similar interests and were stuck together in some ways. Your interests have now diverged, and the friendship won't last." Brad had a beer in his hand and sat down across from Drake, avoiding the chair Kyle had used. "Do you think I don't understand how that feels? It's hard to maintain relationships in our business."

"Relationships are the nature of our business," Drake heard himself saying. It was what his father had told him time and time again. He'd been taught how to manipulate people into trusting him, into believing he was who he said he was.

"Yes, and that's why it's hard," Brad replied with a sad sigh. "Because our job is to trick people, to make them do what we want. It can be hard to shed that coat and be ourselves because our everyday work requires us to not ever truly be ourselves. Kyle Hawthorne would never be able to completely suppress himself. He's incapable of it."

He felt the need to defend his friend. "He was good at his job."

"And what was his job?" Brad asked pointedly. "Don't tell me he was the lead because I've read the mission reports."

"He wasn't muscle." Kyle had a strong background in weapons and hand to hand, but he wasn't merely there as backup.

"He was support," Brad insisted. "He was quite deadly and excellent in a fight, but he rarely worked assets. He was the guy you sent into a dangerous situation to pick up a package."

It wasn't exactly true. Kyle had been in on all aspects of the operations the team had been involved in. He wouldn't have left him out, but Drake had been the one to handle much of the undercover work. Kyle had often gone in with Julia, posing as her husband or boyfriend, but Julia was always in charge of those. Julia wouldn't allow anyone else to be. He'd thought she was merely a control freak, but now he knew she'd used that control to get away with her crimes.

"I'm trying to explain that Kyle can't truly understand what it means to do the job you do. He can't understand the function you serve, and it's an important one," Brad said. "I've looked into him, you know."

"What do you mean looked into him?" He didn't like the idea of Brad doing research on Kyle.

"When I understood that you were going to let him come back, I made a study of him." Brad set his beer down. He was as casual as Brad ever got, wearing khakis and a collared shirt. "I delved into his past. He was in grad school when he quit and joined the Navy."

"He was going to business school. He was in an MBA program. You are not telling me anything I don't know." He'd recruited Kyle. He knew his history backward and forward, and yes, he'd definitely known about his relationship with the Taggarts. It was precisely why he'd been sent to recruit him when Kyle had shown aptitude in the Navy.

"I know you understand him on paper, but I don't think you've analyzed him the way you should have," Brad explained. "You liked him and he seemed to like you, and you hadn't had a friend in a long time. You did figure out he's not capable of the true manipulation the rest of us are. Have you thought about the fact that you were attracted to him for the same reasons Julia was? Obviously not sexually, but friendship is a type of attraction."

"What the fuck is that supposed to mean?" He definitely didn't like the fact that Brad seemed to be psychoanalyzing him.

"It means that you were both drawn to something, to someone unlike the people around you. You grew up in a household with a political figure. I know you love your mother, and by all accounts she's a good person, but she's a politician. She chooses her words carefully, and I would bet she did even around you. She was always two different people—the senator and the mom. I would bet she was more senator than mom most of the time. And then your father actively taught you how to trick people into giving you information they shouldn't."

"Yes, I know my own history." But hearing it put that way along with the idea that Julia had been through it as well was making him think, and not about anything good. "We're fucked up, my sister and I."

"I didn't say that," Brad chided. "I was simply pointing out that you and Julia were both drawn to Kyle for the same reasons. He's honest about who he is. Oh, he might lie about it with words, but his actions never lie. He doesn't plot and plan. He goes on his gut even when his gut is dumb and should be ignored. You don't understand that but what you figured out was that if Kyle liked you, if he was your friend, you could trust that. You can trust him in a way you don't and won't ever trust me."

He hated to admit it, but Brad was right, and that led him to the inevitable conclusion. "But Kyle figured out who I really am and now he'll never trust me again. He'll see me the same way he sees Julia."

Brad seemed to consider that for a moment. "I wouldn't say the same, but I would say you represent a lifestyle he wants out of."

There was something Brad was forgetting. "He says he wants back in."

"Again, his gut is dumb," Brad said with a sigh. "Getting back into the Agency will kill something inside him, and you know it."

"Like it will with Taylor."

Brad's head shook. "Taylor is a different case altogether. I would hesitate to take Kyle in the field. I'm happy to do it with Taylor. I think she'll be excellent if you let her."

He didn't like the sound of that. "She's not like me."

"She's exactly like you, which is why it didn't work the first time." Brad leaned over, his elbows on the table. "You didn't trust her because she's like you. She was raised by an operative. It's why it can't work between the two of you. Your backgrounds are similar."

He thought Brad was wrong about that. Taylor's father hadn't intended for her to follow in his footsteps. He'd brought his daughter into the only world he'd ever known, but he'd wanted her to go to college and have a life. Drake's father had passed on his job like it was a crown and then wouldn't even advise him on how to move forward. She'd been trained to protect herself and to help her dad out. It was a completely different situation. Taylor was open and willing to be vulnerable.

She'd made him willing to be vulnerable, too. He would have said that wasn't possible, that the ability to open himself had been cut out of him during childhood. The only person he'd been taught to trust was his sister, and she'd proven so unworthy of it.

But Taylor was different. "She's not like me. She's not like I was."

Brad stared at him like he'd grown two heads. "Like you were?"

"The last year and a half have changed me. I'm done with undercover. I still believe in the work the Agency does, but we often go about it the wrong way. I think I'm going to move into an analyst role." He'd been thinking about it for days, and they both couldn't be in the field. If she needed someone to pose as her husband or boyfriend or she simply needed someone she could trust to back her up, he would be there.

But he would hold down the home front if this was something she wanted to pursue.

"Are you fucking kidding me?" Brad sat up. "You want to go into management?"

"I want to be able to stay in DC or wherever Taylor wants to be." He also had been thinking a lot about how he could affect a new generation of operatives. They didn't have to sell their souls to make it easy to get the information they needed. It would take him a while to move into the proper position, but he could do it.

"She won't be anywhere she can tell you about," Brad pointed out.

He wasn't sure it had to end up that way. "Taylor is posing as a CIA operative. Julia didn't join The Consortium full time until Kyle figured out what was going on. She was worth more to the group being an active CIA agent. If Taylor is still working for the Agency, then she can still have some normalcy. This is something we can work out."

"No, it's not. It will compromise the operation, and I won't have it. You have to understand that this isn't about your love life. This is important, and I'm not going to let it fail." Brad stood up, a fierce frown on his face.

"This is more than a mission to me. I love her."

"You have no idea what love is," Brad countered. "You're still a selfish asshole, and you've decided she's the new thing you want. You're a rich boy at heart, and you can't handle the idea that you won't be able to indulge every single whim you have."

The sound of a cell trilled, and Brad huffed and pulled out his phone while Drake sat back, shocked at the anger he'd seen from a man who'd always been so calm. Despite what Brad thought, he had considered the other agent a friend. Perhaps not in the way he had Kyle, but he would certainly have said they liked one another.

He'd apparently been wrong.

Brad frowned down at his phone. "It's Lydia. Why is she calling me and not you?"

Drake winced because Brad was going to hate his answer.

"There are no cell phones allowed on the dungeon floor."

Brad's eyes narrowed, and he brushed his finger across the screen to accept the call. "This is Perry. What do you need, Lydia?"

Drake stood, every instinct in his body telling him this was about to go bad.

And then she was walking out of the locker room, across the stone path, and his breath caught.

She wore a white corset and matching boy shorts, her legs miles long in white stilettos. She looked like a wet dream angel come to raise him up.

She was his fucking dream.

She gave him a big smile as she crossed the distance between them. "Hey."

He put his hands on her hips and drew her in close. "Hey."

This was everything he wanted. Being here with her. He was going to change his whole life for her.

He was going to make his whole life about her.

"Drake, we have a problem." Brad's voice was an unwelcome intrusion. "Lydia got a call. You have to meet your contact tonight."

He turned. He wasn't supposed to meet his contacts until tomorrow. "Tonight?"

"She says it's important. The contact needs to do the drop off tonight," Brad said with a frown. "If you need to... What do you call it? Play? If you need to play more than work, I'll go and meet Lydia and try to handle it."

He felt his jaw clench, and he didn't look back at the man he'd thought was his friend. He stared down into Taylor's gorgeous eyes. "I'm sorry, baby. I have to go."

She went up on her toes. "Stay safe. I'll be here when you get back."

He kissed her and then steeled himself to go to work.

Chapter Sixteen

Taylor sighed as she watched Drake jog off.

From what she understood this wasn't a dangerous assignment. It was mostly there as cover for what he was really doing in London. She shouldn't be worried. It was something he'd done a million times before, and yet there was a bit of dread tickling up her spine.

She didn't like it when things changed. Things had changed for her father, and he'd wound up dead.

"So he's meeting with his tech?" She'd known Drake had a job he was using as his technical reason to be in London, but they hadn't talked about it much. He'd wanted to concentrate on the future and not the present. They were kind of avoiding that. "She's been with him a long time, right?"

Brad was still here, still frowning like a disappointed dad. "Yes. It's a bit surprising since when she started I know she wanted to be in the field. She's turned down work that would get her promoted. I don't understand it, but if you're worried, I can tell you she's perfectly competent and she'll have his back."

She was worried about a lot of things. "I've never met her. I think my father worked with her a couple of times. She used to work logistics for a larger group, right?"

"She still does from time to time," Brad agreed. "You've almost surely dealt with her in some capacity. She's one of those unsung workers the Agency runs on. She pretty much knows everything because everyone depends on her. Not just Drake, though she primarily works for him. His father found her for him. Recruited her right out of college."

Drake's father was still a problem. He'd told her he still wouldn't talk about Julia. They had a lot of decisions to make, and she intended to help him through it all. "I thought he was a field operative."

"Don Radcliffe? Oh, he was so much more than an operative," Brad explained. "He worked at the highest levels of the CIA, and recruitment was his specialty."

So much he'd even recruited his own children. "Did he recruit you?"

She wasn't sure why she wanted to know, but she suddenly had an interest in finding out how far Don Radcliffe's influence went.

"No." Brad's head shook. "To be recruited by Mr. Radcliffe meant you were one of the elite. I wasn't recruited at all. In military terms, I was a grunt. I hired on after I graduated and worked my way up from there. You should probably go and get dressed."

She arched her brow at the change of subject. "Why would I do that? It's fet wear only in the club. You're the one who should change."

Brad sighed. "You're still planning on attending the orgy then? Wow. Drake is going to be upset. You know he thinks he's in love with you. This is going to hurt him. Is that what you're trying to do?"

He was a confusing man. She hadn't realized it until now. Up until the last few days she'd known little about the man who was her handler beyond the fact that he was competent and got her everything she needed. He hadn't asked about her personal life, and she hadn't asked about his. He'd seemed a bit like a machine who simply did his job, and at the time she appreciated that. Now that the ice around her had thawed, she wanted to figure out this man she was supposed to work with. He seemed like he was a friend of Drake's.

"I was going to hang out," she offered. "No playing involved because my partner isn't here, but that doesn't mean I have to go up to our room and hide away waiting for him. I'd like to watch some scenes, maybe have a drink, make some friends. I'm feeling confident, and I kind of want to show off this body because I think there is weight gain in my future."

Because she was going to turn down the long-term assignment. She was going to ID The Consortium operative and then set it all up for someone else. Someone who wanted to spend her every minute undercover. She wasn't sure if she would be kicked out of the Agency or if they would let her do what she was good at—building covers, making sure operatives were safe.

Kind of like what Brad did except she could handle the background and logistics, too.

It was what her father had taught her.

She would still go to college, but if she could stay where Drake was comfortable, that would suit them both. They could figure out if they could work.

Drake seemed to think that they could. That they would.

"I don't understand any of this stuff. My mom and dad would never have done this. The woman I've been seeing would be horrified by the entire idea of a sex club."

"It's okay if it doesn't interest you. It's a lifestyle. It's not for everyone." It wasn't her job to put him at ease, but they were stuck together for a couple of days, and he didn't seem like a bad guy. Just a little misinformed. "But I don't judge you for the stick up your ass, so how about you not judge me for being comfortable with my body."

She wouldn't make it too easy on him, though.

He stared at her for a moment as though he wasn't exactly sure what to say and then he sat down in the chair at the table Drake had been sitting at. Drake's half-drank glass was sitting there. Brad picked it up and drained it. "I never thought of myself as a prude, but you're right. This isn't hurting anyone, so why does it make me uncomfortable? I've had more than enough training to know it makes me uncomfortable because I am not comfortable with myself. I think it's weird to be so secure in one's sexuality that you put it on display."

"In a safe place," she pointed out. "Well, it was before you came here."

"I'm not…"

She wasn't having his excuses. "You are judging everyone here, and that's not supposed to happen. It's why Master Damon only allows fet wear on the dungeon floor. It's fine to walk through when the club isn't open, but it's a private space otherwise, and you should leave."

He sighed. "I'm not judging. At least I'm trying not to. I don't understand, but I'm not supposed to. I don't know. It's not like my sex life is some raging success. I guess I'll head up to my place, although I do have a question for you. Are you going to quit on me?"

Damn. She hadn't wanted to get into this. "I think I'm changing my mind about the longer-term job. I will absolutely meet with the contact. I can do it for the next couple of months even, but anything that sends me undercover in The Consortium for an extended period of time, I don't think I can do. I know that makes me seem flaky, but I haven't been thinking straight for months."

"You've been in mourning," Brad said with a nod. "If I had been brought in on this project in the beginning, I would never have allowed you to work on it. Not because you're not competent. Because you'd just lost your father and whatever had happened with Drake would be weighing on you. You were vulnerable, and the Agency took advantage. Had I been the one making the call at the time, I wouldn't have done that to you. To tell you the truth, I wouldn't have done it to Drake either. He didn't talk about what happened between the two of you, but I knew it had a profound effect on him. I didn't know he was trying to find you until much later. There were far too many emotions involved, and both of you should have gone on leave."

"He tried to find me?"

"Yes. He had no idea I was your handler by then, and I couldn't talk to him about it," Brad admitted. "I didn't realize he had feelings for you. According to him, he didn't."

Drake was good at hiding his feelings, at not recognizing his feelings at all. He'd said he'd been planning on breaking her out. It appeared he hadn't been lying. The idea of Drake busting her free brought a smile to her lips. "I wonder why he couldn't find me. His security level is higher than yours, right?"

"It's the same," Brad replied. "But you know this op is delicate. It's on a need-to-know basis, which is why I'm still pissed that he knows at all. His sister not being dead and where we think she is in The Consortium hierarchy made the director give him access. I personally think it's a mistake to let him in. His objectives aren't the same as ours."

"He wants to take down The Consortium."

"No. He wants to take down his sister, and you should understand that he'll do anything he has to do to make that happen," Brad said. "He'll burn down the whole op so he can take her out."

"She's dangerous." If there was one thing she'd learned it was that Julia Ennis would hurt her family if she had to. "I think he's worried about what she'll do to Kyle."

"Yeah, I think he's holding on to something that won't work out in the end, but that's not my call." He stared at her for a moment. "Are you going to give all of this up for him?"

She wasn't sure what she was giving up beyond an unforgiving job that would likely grind her to dust the way it had her father. She rather wanted to know what Brad's play was going to be. "Are you going to tell me what a bad bet he is?"

"I think you know what a bad bet any of us are," he replied. "Unless we get out and find some other work, it's hard to have relationships, and then there's the problem of his family. Have you thought about that? His mother has no idea who he really is. Who his father is. His dad, well, I knew his father before he retired. I worked a few ops trying to learn some of his techniques. Quite frankly, I considered them barbaric. He didn't give a damn about anything but looking good on paper, and that included his children. Drake's mother is too involved in her career to really figure out what was going on in her home. His father was polite and didn't cheat on her, so he was acceptable as a partner. It's all screwed up, and it's affected Drake. It's precisely why he stood there and let them take you the first time. Even though he'd been to bed with you."

"Why did you let them take me, Brad? You were there, too."

"I let them take you because you'd lied to your handlers, and your father looked damn guilty," he said matter of factly. "I don't feel bad about that either. Your father had been killed, and no one knew what was going on. You cleared that up."

"Yeah, but not before I enjoyed some of the Agency's hospitality." There was some bitterness to her tone.

"And yet when they offered to let you take lead on this op, you jumped at the chance."

"They offered me revenge, and at the time it was all I wanted. Lately I've been reminded that when you seek vengeance, dig two graves." Her father had often repeated the words of Confucius when he was working like they were his mantra. He'd sought to right wrongs, not vengeance.

She would do the same thing.

Was Drake seeking vengeance on his sister? Or was he trying to make up for what she'd done? It was obvious he felt the guilt for not having seen what she was capable of.

No. Even if that was how it had started, he'd promised her he would put her first.

"One for your target and one for yourself," Brad said, proving he knew a bit about philosophy. "Drake told me he was getting out of the field for you."

A warmth spread through her. "I'm glad. I think he could be great at overseeing projects, at helping agents in the field. He knows what it feels like to be manipulated. What if we could change the way the Agency treats its assets? The ones like my dad. What if my dad had been comfortable talking to his handler about what he needed? He might be alive today."

He would have been able to take time off to deal with his

cancer. He wouldn't have been working and a target for Julia.

"I don't know about that," Brad said. "I think there are forces inside the Agency that would have made sure your dad went down. I think there are still moles on the inside. Julia couldn't have been the only one. That's why this op was so important. Taylor, I know you think you're in love with Drake, but we need you. I need you to think about your obligations to this organization."

She did understand she was putting him in a bad position. "I do not owe this organization years of my life. This organization eats up agents and spits them out. I owe those human beings, not some institution. I think maybe we owe it to ourselves to fix the problems on the inside instead of continuing to throw bodies at the problems on the outside. I've been thinking a lot lately about the fact that we need real teams. Not an agent who uses the military like they're chess pieces. Real teams who have each other's backs."

Brad's hands fisted. "That's naïve bullshit and you know it."

She didn't. What she did know was that too many agents died when they didn't have to. Too many agents got left behind with no one watching out for their interests, and that led to people like her father dying because the rot sometimes came from within. "I'm sorry you feel that way. Like I said, I'm going to meet with the contact and try to get everything we need to ID her. If that takes more than one meeting, we'll deal with it. I'm not walking out."

"But you're no longer committed to the long-term assignment." Brad's jaw tightened.

"Taylor?" a deep voice said.

. She turned and Damon Knight stood there. He was still wearing the clothes he'd been in earlier in the day. He did not look like a man who was about to oversee the dungeon floor. "Yes?"

"I'm so sorry, but we're going to have to delay play night. Jax is asking that I bring you to the conference room," Damon said. "You've had a call from the contact, and Jax and Tucker are seeing some movement at the hotel they're concerned about. Whatever's happening is going down tonight."

Brad stood, his expression going perfectly professional. "But I thought tonight was nothing more than the welcome party? Why would they want Taylor to go in now? They can't be sure of Dr. Walsh's location throughout the evening. She could go back to her room at any time. It makes far more sense to take her laptop when she's in one of her sessions or when they can confirm she'll be gone for a while."

Damon's head shook. "I don't know what's happening. I know it feels off. Perhaps she'll make contact and they're only trying to confirm Taylor is in the city, but that's not what Jax thinks. He believes whatever is happening is going down tonight, and I trust his instincts."

"Well, his instincts are years old." Brad pointed out. "He hasn't been in the business in over a decade, which is precisely why we should have Agency backup, but here we are. I'd like to see what he's found." Brad turned her way. "Get properly dressed, please. Whether you're committed or not, I expect you to do the job tonight."

Her gut tightened, some instinct flaring as Brad walked away.

The big Brit looked around. "Where is Drake?"

"He got called away." And wasn't that spectacular timing?

Damon sighed. "Bloody hell."

Bloody hell indeed.

* * * *

Drake sat down at the outdoor table overlooking the Thames. He supposed it was a nice enough view, but he wished he was back with Taylor instead of sitting here waiting for a dude to drop off a thumb drive. The drive was filled with intel an asset had gotten from a recent visit by a dictator who'd taken his mistress to Harrod's and met with a bunch of terrorist groups while she charged up his credit card.

It was valuable information. It was important information, and letting the asset know he was here and appreciated the information he'd risked his life to get was part of his job.

But his mind was on Taylor and how pretty she'd looked in her corset, how good it had felt to lay there and let her sleep on him. Even dealing with Nick Markovic had been kind of fun. For once he was in a relationship important enough that a father figure wanted to intimidate him. He would prove to Markovic that he was good enough for Taylor. He would make himself good enough for her.

"Are you okay?"

He forced himself to focus. Lydia sat across from him, a glass of wine near her hand, though she hadn't touched it. She'd dressed for the occasion and looked far more like she was on a date than he did. She'd worn a sundress and heels and jewelry he didn't remember seeing her wear before, but then he never exactly paid attention to what she was wearing. "I'm fine. You said he was supposed to be here at eight?"

"Eight thirty," she assured him. "And I've already checked to make sure no one can hear us talking. Between the outside noise and the blocking equipment I have on, we should be able to speak frankly. I've also assured that there are no CCTV cameras pointed this way. I'm not going to have a repeat of Kraków."

He glanced back toward the hotel where his mother was staying. A mere two blocks away, he probably needed to go by and do a walk-through before Taylor went in. He had all the schematics, but there was nothing like actually seeing a place. The fact that his parents were there would be good cover.

He fully intended to be in that luxury hotel when her op was on. He had several good reasons to be there, and he would use any one of them to ensure Taylor wasn't alone.

"I wish we'd been able to figure that out. I would feel far safer." Lydia had dark hair that she normally kept in a neat bun. Tonight it was down, one side held back by a flower clip. "I always worry that I'm working with someone who tried to kill you."

He frowned. "I don't think they were trying to kill me in Kraków. They simply didn't want the intel that was passed to me to get to HQ. I don't think it was personal in any way, though I was lucky to get out alive. I still wish I knew how they found us. I've gone over the CCTV around the site, and my asset was good. He kept his head down. If I hadn't known it was him, I wouldn't have suspected a thing. He managed to hide his identity well, and I didn't ID anyone who was following him. So they didn't tag him at the train station. They knew where he would be. They knew where the safe house was."

She bit her bottom lip as though wondering if she should say something. "Have you ever thought about the fact that Brad knew?"

"Of course he knew. He was helping me. A lot of people know where the safe house is, you included."

"The location isn't well known for obvious reasons," she pointed out. "The only reason I know about it is the fact that you've used that safe house in Kraków three times over the years and the first time I had to figure out how to get you there without using public transportation. There were very few people who knew where the safe house was and that you would be meeting an asset close to there, and Brad was one of them. I only say this because I'm worried about you. I know you weren't meeting friends earlier last week. That wasn't a vacation, and you weren't on the West Coast with friends."

"And how would you know that?"

"Because I know you. You don't have friends outside of the Agency. I can put things together. I'm not stupid, and I wish you would trust me after all these years. What happened with Kyle? I read the reports, but it feels like something is off. Did you leave because you're in mourning? I know he was your friend. He was my friend, too. I enjoyed working with him. I understood why he left after Julia died. He was heartbroken."

He didn't want to have this conversation with her. He'd made the decision to leave her out of any knowledge of what was going on with Kyle, the same way he'd left her out of the loop when it came to Julia. He would have left Brad out of it, but that had been decided by people higher up than him. Brad had taken on the operation to map The Consortium and its companies and hierarchy because Drake had been too close to the subject.

He often wondered how many eyes he'd had on him in those first days, how many people wondered if he'd been in on it with his sister. He thought if it hadn't been for his close working relationship with McKay-Taggart, he might have been left out of anything to do with The Consortium altogether given his relationship with Julia. He'd been brought in to work the Maddie Hill case because they'd decided he could handle it if her old boyfriend got involved since that would mean Taggart would be involved. Sometimes being the only one the big guy didn't necessarily want to murder was a good thing. Of course it had gotten him punched by Deke Murphy, but Tag had let the op continue, and he rather thought that was because of him.

"Kyle died," he stated plainly. He would never say anything else. "He got caught in Byrne's house when it went up."

"That's what I don't understand. Why would Nolan Byrne blow up his own house?"

Kyle hadn't considered that in his ill-thought, hasty plan. He'd only been thinking about putting on a show for Julia. "The authorities said it was due to faulty wiring. The gun fight we had in there caused the wiring to blow, and Kyle was left behind."

"But then shouldn't everyone have died?" Lydia pointed out the flaw in his reasoning.

Drake merely shrugged. "The rest of us were out. Kyle stayed behind. He was still fighting when the house went up."

She stared at him for a moment, but then her eyes drifted away. "I miss him, you know."

He wasn't sure why. They hadn't been close, but then sometimes different people viewed relationships from places others didn't understand. Their versions of close could be totally off. "I do, too. I miss him and I miss my sister."

He wasn't lying. He missed the sister he remembered from his childhood. Sometimes he missed her so much it was an ache in his soul. He missed the family he'd thought he'd had, the one that felt like it loved him, like he'd been safe there.

Safety was always a lie.

He took a deep breath. That was a reflex position. He had to be okay with the idea that he was truly safe with Taylor, and she was safe with him. Otherwise nothing mattered. He was going to exchange vows with her.

It struck him forcibly that vows hadn't meant anything to his father. He'd married his mom and then lied to her their whole relationship. Drake had been raised in a lie, and it scared him that he would perpetuate that lie.

He didn't want to ever lie to Taylor. Love wasn't a lie. It wasn't supposed to be a lie.

His marriage wasn't going to be a lie. He would tell Taylor everything. If he couldn't tell his wife, he wouldn't take on the job. He would leave the Agency. He needed her to know who he was—needed the right person in the world to know who he was.

"I miss Julia. I was their tech, too."

He wasn't sure what Lydia wanted from him. It seemed like he was supposed to validate her suffering. "I can imagine that you do."

"It hasn't been the same."

"No. Missing two of our former teammates means things are definitely different." He knew he wasn't dealing with this properly, but he wasn't sure what else to do. It wasn't the time to try to figure out if his mother was right and she was more involved with their relationship than business would dictate. He looked down at his watch. "He's late."

Lydia frowned. "I'm sure he's fine. You know these things aren't precise."

Now it was his turn to stare. "They're supposed to be. He called in and moved up the time. He should be here."

Lydia sat back, her eyes on him. "If you have something else to do, feel free. I'm sure I can handle it."

She was touchy tonight. She definitely wasn't used to him being anxious, and he could understand how that would upset her. "I'm sorry. I don't mean to make you uncomfortable. I just have some other things I was planning on doing this evening."

"Are you working with another tech?"

He sighed. He should listen to his mother more often. He still wasn't sold on the idea that Lydia had a thing for him. Taylor was kind of a miracle. He was an info geek, and not the hot hacker kind. The fact that he'd found a woman willing to deal with his damage was amazing. But he could understand the territoriality of an Agency tech. Lydia's job was somewhat tied to his, and he'd pushed her out lately because he wasn't willing to bring her into his hell. It was weird. He didn't need to. Despite what Brad had said, he still had hope for his relationship with Kyle.

It was stupid. It shouldn't work, but he liked Kyle. He cared about Kyle. Kyle felt like family.

He wasn't willing to give up on Kyle, and that was something different for him. Like he wasn't willing to ever give up on Taylor.

He was changing, and it felt good.

If he stayed at the CIA, maybe he could change the culture. Maybe he and Taylor could have an impact, could make sure other kids who'd come up in the system could have a safer place than they'd had.

"I've never worked with any tech but you." It was true. She'd been involved in everything he'd been assigned to. She'd known almost everything he did with a few exceptions.

He'd kept some truths from Lydia. He'd done it because it was simpler, because she didn't have his clearance. But sometimes clearance didn't mean much when your whole life was the Agency.

"What exactly are you asking me, Lydia?" It was time to cut to the chase.

She frowned again. "I'm not asking anything."

"It feels like you're looking for something," he pointed out.

"I look into everything about you," Lydia said quietly. "It's my job. You and your safety are literally my job, and sometimes you lie to me about both."

"Sometimes you don't have clearance," he replied.

Her shoulders came up. "That's not my fault. You don't give me the recs to get a better clearance."

"That's not true." The entire argument was giving him a bad feeling, a restless feeling. It was time to start preparing her for the eventual move. "I promise I'm going to give you the best references I possibly can in the next few months."

"Good, because I know you're working on something," she said. "I know more went on in California than you told me about. You cut me out of the end of that mission."

"I didn't cut you out. That night went wonky. The tech went out, and I didn't have time to fix it. And this is starting to feel like some weird, uncalled-for resentment." He was starting to resent the way she was talking to him. "I'm not the only operative you work

311

for."

"You could be. All you have to do is ask and you know they'll take me off my other clients and let me do what I should do which is concentrate on the most important one. You."

How had he not seen how much she had invested in this job—in him? Drake checked the impulse to point out to her that she was not in charge. He needed to be kinder. He'd never led her on, never been more than friendly with her, but it was obvious she'd seen things differently. "I think that would be a bad idea given my plans for the future."

"Plans?"

"I'm thinking about moving to the analyst side of things."

"What?" She nearly shrieked the question and then glanced around, and her voice came down. "What are you thinking? You're a field agent. You are the best field operative we have working today."

He doubted that. "I think it's time to move to a desk job. I have some goals I would like to accomplish, and I can't do it out in the field. There's also the fact that I'm serious about a woman, and you know no relationship works if one of us is constantly pretending to be someone else."

She'd gone slightly pale in the glow from the overhead lamps. "You have a girlfriend? Have I been wrong about everything? I thought you were lying when you said you were seeing friends. I thought you needed time to deal with what happened to Kyle, but then Brad said…"

He stopped, a chill going up his spine. This was one of those times when his instinct poked at him and told him something was wrong. "Brad said what, Lydia?"

Her mouth closed. Tears pooled in her eyes. "I know you were with him and not in California."

He felt himself laser focus in. Something was going on. Something he'd been negligently unaware of. "Why would he tell you that?"

She straightened up, her shoulders going back. "He trusts me."

That fact truly surprised him. "He never mentioned the two of you were close."

"We work together, too, you know. He needs someone to talk to. It's not going to be you. You kind of dumped him when you found your bestie, Kyle Hawthorne," she complained. "Like you dumped a lot of your friends, including me."

She was not putting this back on him. "Do you know how dangerous it is that he's talking to you about not merely classified assignments, but critical operations?"

"Operations I should know about. Operations I should be working," Lydia insisted. "I don't understand why you cut me out. He said it was your choice."

"My choice to do what?"

"To not work with me. To bring in your own tech."

"This is nothing I can talk to you about," he replied, his voice tight. "But you should understand I'm definitely talking to Brad. If he's been leaking information to coworkers who don't have clearance, then we're going to have a problem."

Her jaw tensed. "I don't think that's a good idea, and not because it could get me in trouble."

"Why then?"

"Brad hates you. He's always been jealous of you," Lydia said in a whisper. "I think he's involved in something bad. I think he's trying to either get you involved, too, or take you out."

Lydia knew far too much and way too little. "Why do you think that?"

"It's more than the way he talks about you," Lydia explained. "I've caught him using secure lines. I think he might be contacting foreign agents."

He started to stand. It was time to go and have this out with Brad. He would figure out quickly what the hell was going on. "I think we should call this whole thing off. It's obvious the asset isn't going to show."

She put a hand on his arm to stop him. "Please, Drake. I think Brad could be dangerous to you."

He doubted that, but he'd been wrong before.

So very wrong.

"Why? What makes you think that he's dangerous to me? I've been around him for days with no problems at all." Except for

Brad's complaining about having to sleep near butt plugs, he'd been pretty easy to work with. Taylor didn't seem to mind him, but Lydia could know something he didn't.

She seemed to be making a decision, her hands clutched together on her lap. "I overheard him talking to someone one night. Why would Brad be talking about Julia?"

Now nothing was going to keep him from moving. He wasn't going to waste another moment of time. "I'm going back to the...hotel. I need to talk to Brad."

She was on her feet, moving after him. "I think you need backup. I'm not joking, Drake. I think he could be dangerous to you."

He glanced down at his phone and noticed he'd gotten a text. From Kyle, though that wasn't how he was stored in the cell.

Something's going down and I don't like the timing. You need to get back here.

Drake felt his gut lurch.

Where was the asset? He wasn't the type to take forever. He was always on time, one of Drake's more responsible informants. "When did the asset call you?"

"He didn't." Lydia frowned and then she brushed away a tear that fell on her cheek. "Damn it, Drake. He didn't call. Brad asked me to call you. He said he needed some time without you looking over his shoulder. I'm so sorry. I thought it would be okay because I needed to talk to you, too. I'm so sorry."

Drake took off running because now he saw tonight for what it really was.

A trap.

Chapter Seventeen

Something was wrong but she couldn't put her finger on it. The car turned down the long road that would take them to the conference hotel in central London. It was getting late, but the streets were still crowded with tourists in this part of the city.

Brad frowned as he looked her over. "I can't send you in with a comm device."

She nodded. "I know. I'm sure the first thing she'll do is make sure I'm not wired."

"The good news is we've already got a room and Jax will be able to cut into the CCTV around the hotel." Kyle Hawthorne was driving, and to his credit he didn't have a single problem with driving on a different side of the street.

Tucker and Jax had gone on ahead. She would be dropped off a few blocks from the hotel and walk in to avoid showing up with Brad and Kyle, who would be using a worker's entrance. Damon Knight had set everything up so they could slip inside without causing a scene.

Everything felt rushed, like time had suddenly sped up and she was in light speed mode.

She hoped this was all over before Drake found out what was

going on. She knew she should have called him, but he was on his own op, and they were both professionals. A good spy didn't call her boyfriend when she got scared.

There was nothing at all to be scared of. This was a simple break-in and a bit of thievery, and then she would have an in. She would be able to ID The Consortium operative and give the Agency a bunch of important information, and then she could be out if she wanted to. She could even kill off Constance Tyne and help the Agency create a new construct another operative could work with. Taylor Cline could have a life again.

So why was her gut twisting in knots?

"I'm going to have eyes on you everywhere. Owen made sure the suite he and Dr. Walsh are using has some high-tech cameras in it. They're brand new. Undetectable right now. If anything seems to be going wrong, I'll be there, Taylor," Brad promised her.

"And I'll be in a room of my own, monitoring the situation from another part of the hotel," Kyle explained. "We took out a couple of rooms to make sure we have good coverage."

Brad huffed. "I don't think we needed to do that. The suite Jax and Tucker are in is down the hall from where Taylor will be working. We can get to her quickly if something goes wrong. Which it will not. She's going to be fine. This is a simple job. An audition, if you will. They have zero reason to hurt her. If things go poorly, I expect The Consortium operative will simply never call back. It doesn't make sense to harm her because the Agency would have questions."

"Logic doesn't always work in an op like this. Something you would know if you had ever been in the field," Kyle argued.

"I've certainly been in the field." Brad managed to sound both prim and annoyed at the same time.

"No, you've monitored safe houses and picked up dead drops." Kyle moved through the light traffic with ease. "I'm not insulting you, Brad. You do a good job taking care of logistics and watching out for the men and women you support in the field. Your analysis can be spot on, but you don't know what it means to have to make choices without any backup. You don't have to make the hard calls."

"Like you did when you killed Julia Ennis?"

The car seemed to go cold, a silence lengthening between the two men before Kyle pulled the car over to the side of the road. "Yes. Like I had to make the choice to kill Julia. You haven't had to choose between someone you care about and your job, your morals. You've never had to make that choice."

"You don't know that," Brad said quietly. "You have no real idea what I've done, what I've had to sacrifice for this job. You're a showy guy. You're the main character in every play, the alpha male who roars his pain. I'm not. I'm a guy who doesn't take center stage, who keeps his pain inside. So you believe what you want, Kyle. I'm done with operatives like you. You think the whole fucking world revolves around your pain, your needs. You're a child and you behave like a child. You create drama and chaos where patience would serve you better."

Damn. She might need to stay behind to make sure Kyle didn't kill Brad. The tension was so thick between these two men. But she had a job to do, and she had to trust that these were professionals.

Hopefully.

She checked her Glock, ensuring it was ready. She had everything she needed, including the small device she would use to get past the hotel's key card system on the rooms.

It was go time, and she couldn't hang out here and watch the drama unfold. "I'm going in."

Brad seemed to calm. "Okay. Be careful. Do what you need to do and if things get too hot... Taylor, if things get too hot, I want you to think about the op. I want you to genuinely consider what we're trying to do. Identifying The Consortium is the most important op of the last ten years. If we identify the members, we can figure out where our leaks are and we can save lives."

"So her life is less important?" Kyle seemed ready to argue.

"You don't go into this job if you're worried about your own damn life," Brad argued.

Oh, she was so done with them. She deeply wished she'd been able to have an all-women team. Far less drama. She would bet if she'd been here with Sandra and Kim, she wouldn't be listening to endless arguments. She opened the door and slipped out into the night, shutting it behind her before she could get another lecture.

Drake would be giving her one. She was absolutely sure of that. She started toward the hotel, noting that Kyle had driven away. She was on her own.

Like her father had been. Like her Uncle Nicky had been before he'd joined McKay-Taggart and Knight.

She walked toward the Tube station, pulling her hoodie up over her head. The plan was to let the CCTV cameras catch her on the Tube, taking the line toward the hotel. It was only three stops from here, but she'd been instructed to approach the hotel this way. They should only know she'd walked in from the east. Kyle would have been careful about where he dropped her off, avoiding the CCTV cams.

She forced herself to stop and breathe for a moment.

Don't ever walk into a mission worried. Turn that part of your brain off. The only thing you should be concerned about is acting and reacting to whatever happens. You'll do that best if you're calm, dushka.

It was so good to be able to hear her father's voice in her head again. After he'd died, she'd shoved her feelings down, and being able to acknowledge them in a way that didn't include anger was a revelation.

Her dad was still here with her. Would always be. No one could take his love away. Not even a bullet. She was the only one who could make the choice to ignore her father's love. It had been given fully and wouldn't fail her as long as she opened her heart to it.

Her father had always been alone in the field with the exception of the few jobs he'd had partners he worked with. They were never regular partners. His job had been solitary. He'd always talked about how he'd loved the camaraderie of the military teams he'd been on, how there had been a good mix of working the op and watching out for each other.

Once many years before, she'd heard rumors that Tennessee Smith had tried to build a team he could use, the same men every time. Men who would get to know each other, watch out for each other. A true team for spies.

It had fallen apart because Smith had been disavowed. The team he'd carefully organized had been pulled apart and only brought back together outside of the Agency. They'd gone to McKay-Taggart where the teams operated so differently.

Her brain was working overtime as she swiped her Oyster card and found the proper platform.

A team wouldn't work for all missions, but it could help to have a couple of groups that worked together, learned everything they could about the operatives around them so there wasn't this crushing sense of vulnerability.

She felt it. It pressed on her chest. Why should she trust Brad—a man she'd barely spent any time with?

Of course Drake had tried that with his sister and Kyle Hawthorne and it hadn't worked out for him either.

The Agency would have to be careful. Each team member would have to be thoughtfully selected.

Wind gushed through the Tube station, and she heard the whirring sound that let her know a train was coming in.

Almost time.

Get in. Do the job. Get home.

Home was anywhere Drake was. Drake would be waiting for her. He wouldn't be gone this time, and he wouldn't allow the job to sweep her away. He wouldn't let her get drowned by this, her personality and wants ignored in favor of the mission. Drake wouldn't let it happen. He would come for her and fight to have a place in her life, to give her a space outside the job.

No matter what happens to you in life, do not forget who you are, dushka. *You, my darling girl, you have been my salvation. You are the reason I am still me. I got to be your father or I would have only ever been a weapon. You made me human.*

Tears pierced her eyes at the thought of her father's words. He said them a few weeks before she'd gone to Romania to wait for him. They'd been in Havana for the doctor's appointment. He'd been staring out over the ocean, and they'd had that comfortable silence they always seemed to find together. Then he'd said those words and kissed her forehead and they'd gotten breakfast.

She'd built Constance Tyne as armor she could place around her body and soul. She'd created Constance so she didn't have to be Taylor, and if Drake hadn't come along, she would have stitched

Constance into place and allowed Taylor to recede into the background, the bare foundation of the weapon she would have become.

"Hey, are you all right?"

She turned and there was a woman standing next to her as the train whooshed in and the doors opened, letting out the passengers that were still traveling past ten in the evening. There were only a few people waiting on the train, and it unnerved her that she hadn't realized this woman was standing so close to her. She gave the blonde a smile. "Oh, I'm good. Thank you."

She turned and entered the train, hoping she could shake off the woman with the long blonde hair. She was wearing a pair of sunglasses despite the fact that it had been dark for hours, and her accent was pure American.

Yet when she sat down, the blonde sat beside her. The train pulled away and the blonde sat back, flipping her sunglasses up and showing off vivid blue eyes. She crossed one leg over the other. "Are you nervous, Constance?"

Fuck. She felt a chill go up her spine and realized that she wasn't ready for this. Not in any way. Maybe Constance was, but falling in love with Drake again had softened her up enough that she wasn't sure she could play the Constance role.

But she had to. Starting right now.

She banished all softer thoughts and forced herself to go cold. No one else was sitting in the car they occupied. "I thought we were meeting in the lobby."

"Why do you think I told you to get on the train? The lobby of that hotel is busy even at this time of night. There are too many eyes and ears, and I suspect someone is onto me," the woman said. "I've got connections I don't like to think about. Now let's talk."

"We haven't been talking all along?" Something was off with the woman.

"We've been dancing around, and it wasn't always me. That's what you need to understand. When you talk to one of us, you talk to all of us. There aren't many of us, and you should understand that if you can't get the job done, the severance package from the group is rather permanent. Which is exactly what happened to the last woman you spent time talking to. Hence, I'm here to do cleanup."

She didn't like the word *cleanup*. "If you aren't the woman I've been talking to, I think I'll get off at the next stop. I've decided I don't need a side job."

Blue eyes rolled. "Don't be so dramatic. I'm not here to off you, but I thought I should be open. Would you be happier if I said our group is one big family and we're all happy sisters and it's going to be fun? Or would you rather know that if this job goes well, you'll receive fifty grand and the option of another job in the near future? Feel free to walk right off this train and never look back, but you're walking away from cash and the opportunity to stick it to the man. The man being the Agency. Come on. Who doesn't want to fuck over the Agency?"

She wasn't sure what this woman was angling for, but she wasn't giving her anything. She was giving off a vibe that made her think the other woman was trying to figure her out, to get under her skin, and she might not like it if the woman decided she wasn't up to snuff.

"I don't care about the Agency. I care about money and power. If you're going to tell me this group of yours is some kind of therapy session for wounded operatives, then I definitely should get off because I don't want to join your cult, lady." Taylor stood up.

A husky laugh filled the car. "Oh, now I like you. Excellent. This could work out. I read through Cleo's reports on you and you sounded like such a drab bitch. I wasn't looking forward to this. Cleo's the dead one, by the way. We all pick a couple of different identities. One for the regular world and one for the board. They like to use call names. I think it makes them feel...smart or more manly or something. Even the female CEOs have annoyingly large balls and like to swing them around. It's a lot of testosterone. Anyway. If one passes the audition, so to speak, they select a name the board will call them by. Typically it's a historical female. Cleo was short for Cleopatra. But it was totally a bullet that took her out, not an asp. I thought that was the way we should go but I got voted down by Joan and Helen. Yeah, Arc and Troy. I hate those bitches. Stuck up. Full of themselves."

"And I should call you?"

Her lips curled up. "Lizzie."

"For Queen Elizabeth?"

The blonde snorted. "No, darling. For Borden. I'm honest about who I am. I'm a straight up psychopath you don't want to cross. Brace yourself. We're coming into the station. You getting off?"

She should. She should run, but she was suddenly intrigued. And Brad and Kyle, Jax and Tucker would be watching for her when she got to the hotel. She needed to figure out as much about this organization as possible, and she now had a few key tidbits of information. "I think I can handle another stop. Do you want to outline what this audition is about?"

The train stopped and the door opened again, the announcements of the station and to mind the gap coming on the overheads.

"You like to get straight to business, don't you?" The blonde looked her over. "You're shorter than I thought you would be. You know I think we might have worked an op together once."

So she was former Agency. Or current Agency. "I've been with the Agency for almost a decade. I've worked many ops. I don't remember you."

"Well, we're supposed to be forgettable, aren't we?" The doors closed again and the train started to pull away. "That's what they want from all of us. They want us to be pretty but not spectacular. Just pretty enough to catch a dick. That's what one of the board members told me. Of course I think he's overestimating how hard it is to catch a dick. It's not like they're an endangered species, and most of them aren't too picky."

"The man actually said you were pretty enough to catch a dick?" Taylor was surprised.

The blonde's shoulder shrugged. She was dressed in all black and looked chic. Like she'd spent the evening wandering an art gallery. But what she wore seemed carefully chosen. The pants were flexible and likely comfortable, and the shirt covered her fully. All she would need was a hat to hide the hair and she could be invisible in the darkness. "I think he used the word seduce, but come on. Most men don't require seduction. You know it's precisely why they use women as operatives. Female operatives don't tend to lose their heads over a pretty man. Only the idiot ones do, and if they're lucky they get a second chance to correct their mistakes."

It felt like she was talking about something very specific. "I wouldn't know. I haven't had many relationships, and I don't intend to get into anything beyond a base sexual relationship with a man."

She had to think of this as an odd sort of job interview. She would gather knowledge and then the next operative to take on the job would know exactly what to do.

"Good for you, girl," the blonde said. "Keep the fuckers at arm's length. Do you have any family you're close to?"

"Shouldn't you already know that?"

"I like to ask."

"I don't have any biological family left." In this Taylor could be honest. "At least none that I know of. My parents are dead, and I didn't have any siblings. It's precisely why the Agency recruited me. I don't have any ties."

"And you don't mind selling your country out," the blonde replied.

"That's rich coming from you."

"No hypocrisy here," the blonde assured her. "It was merely a statement of fact. Honestly, when you think about it, America is capitalism. It's our real religion, so chasing after money makes you the most American of all. At least that's how I think of it. I grew up in a very rah-rah, America rocks home, but one of my parents got it. He understood that personal power is worth far more than any patriotism." She stood and straightened her clothes. "We're going to my room first. I need to grab something before we get started."

Taylor didn't like it when plans changed. "I thought I was doing this on my own. I prefer to work alone."

The train pulled into the station close to the hotel and the blonde moved to the door. "I assure you that you'll be acting alone tonight, but I do need to be able to watch you. You're going to wear an earpiece so I can direct you."

"I thought I was simply going to download Dr. Rebecca Walsh's laptop."

"The parameters have changed slightly." The blonde looked her up and down, one brow rising. "I need to know you can think on your feet. If this goes well, I'll get you in touch with the board. Like I said before, we're down an operative and we need someone competent in place. There are some big things happening on the horizon, and I don't have time to train some newbie who would probably faint at the sight of blood on her hands. So let's go or you can run away and I'll handle it myself."

The doors opened and the blonde stepped out, starting for the ramp that would lead up and out of the station.

She could stay here on the train and let it all go. Drake would cheer her on.

And The Consortium would kill more men like her father. Drake would continue to worry about his sister, and Kyle wouldn't be able to rejoin his family, and that girl he kept chasing online would end up with a dude named West.

One night. It was all she had to give this mission and she could feel satisfied that she could build another. Taylor stood and followed the blonde out.

A man was standing up ahead, his eyes on the blonde. He was silent as everyone moved around them. The train filled and the station went quiet.

"Good. You're coming." She went right up to the man and patted his lapel before looking Taylor's way. "This is our muscle for the night. He'll help us out if we need it. You can call him John."

John.

Fuck. She was staring right at the man she'd been trying to ID for weeks. The man who worked so often with Julia Ennis.

The dark-haired man who killed at Julia's command nodded her way. "Let's get going. Everything looks to be in place. I'm expecting the op to begin right on time."

They turned and started up the ramp.

Taylor followed. Her night had gotten way more dangerous.

* * * *

Drake raced into the lobby of The Garden, still holding his cell. He'd lost Lydia back at the restaurant, though he was certain Damon would have his ass for not calling in before he came back.

He couldn't tip off Brad. Taylor had been in the dungeon. She wouldn't have her cell on her so calling her would have been useless. Brad might be listening in on her cell. He hadn't thought to check, hadn't thought to protect her from a person who should be watching over her.

Damn it, he'd trusted the wrong person again.

He was the worst fucking spy in the world, and this time Taylor would pay the price.

"I need you to find Kyle Hawthorne." He approached the woman at the front desk.

She was a tall brunette wearing a corset and miniskirt. "I'm sorry, Sir. I can't disrupt the evening's play. If you would like to find someone, I can check your membership and you can enter the dungeon after you change."

He didn't have time. Luckily The Garden had protocols. He pulled the keycard he'd been given when he'd gotten here. "My name is Drake Radcliffe. This is about Mr. Knight's other business."

Her shoulders straightened immediately, and she ran his card without another word. She picked up the receiver to the hardline telephone and stated the proper code before hanging up. "He'll meet you at the door, Mr. Radcliffe. Should I put the club in lockdown?"

Oh, he would bet she was either military or law enforcement of some kind since the words were said without a hint of panic. "I want to keep things quiet for now. Do you have a record of who's left the building in the last two hours?"

She opened the laptop that was sitting on the front desk and started typing. "I'm showing a group left here forty minutes ago. I would need to get on the garage security system to find the names and the security cameras. Sorry. We keep that on a closed system in case we need to quickly get rid of files."

Because The Garden had been raided before, and Knight would do what it took to prevent bad actors from harming his people. "I can run down there after I find Kyle."

The door from the dungeon came open and Damon Knight walked through. He was in leather pants but the white T-shirt he had on let everyone familiar with the man know he wasn't playing that evening. "Drake, I'm glad you're here. We didn't want to tell you too much over text because you weren't on a secure line. The op is going down tonight."

His gut tightened. "Where is Taylor? Tell me she isn't with Brad."

Knight's brows came together. "Of course she is. He's her handler. I overheard them briefly talking about how they were going to run logistics. Jax and Tucker went separately, but Taylor left in a car with Kyle and Brad."

"I need a car. I need to get to that hotel as soon as possible, and I need to know the route they took." Adrenaline was starting to pump through his body. He needed to get to her.

Knight pulled his cell and touched a number. "Yes, Nick. I need you to get to the hotel. You are? Excellent. I'll be in contact soon." He hung up. "Nick is already on his way, and Owen and Rebecca have been informed that this is going down tonight. They'll stay out of their room."

"Taylor called Nick and Owen?"

Knight's head shook. "Nick told me Brad contacted him to let him know they were on the move and by the time Nick got in contact with Owen, Brad had called him as well."

Why would Brad call them? Yes, they'd talked about bringing them all in, but why go to the trouble of sidelining Drake if he was going to turn around and tell a man who acted like Taylor's uncle where they were going? Nick would protect Taylor. For that matter so would Kyle.

"What's going through your head?" Knight asked, starting for the door again. He led Drake through and made a beeline for the exit that took them out to the garage. "It's obvious something's got you rattled. We were all surprised but we knew we wouldn't be given much of a heads-up when it came time to go. It's in The Consortium's best interest to keep things quiet until they're ready."

Yes, he understood that rationale, but it was obvious to him that Brad had ensured he wouldn't be around when the op went down. "I was meeting with my longtime tech. We had a side job to do while we were here. I needed a plausible reason to be in London in case anyone asked. That timeline got moved up this evening, and after a while I managed to get Lydia to confess that Brad was the one who asked her to distract me."

Knight fished his key card out and got them through the door to the garage. "Please bring around the Benz, and I need to be equipped."

The two guards who'd been standing at the desk moved to do Knight's bidding.

"You think Brad is up to something?" Knight asked.

There was another scenario to consider. "Or Lydia is lying."

Knight nodded as one of his guards handed him a shoulder holster. "Yes. She could be lying. Are you suspicious of Brad?"

Drake pulled his cell and quickly sent a text to Kyle.

Keep eyes on Brad.

"I haven't been. He and I joined around the same time, though we came from two different places. I have to wonder if he doesn't resent me for moving up easily because of my father."

Knight secured the holster and checked his weapon before sliding it in and taking the jacket the guard offered. "I would assume he would want to make you look bad or himself to look good. That could be why he would cut you out. He could want a good op without you being able to claim any credit."

That seemed petty. "I don't know. Now I'm worried I've fallen into some kind of trap. If Lydia is lying, what game is she playing?"

The Benz pulled up, driven by the other guard. It reminded him of all the security around his mother. He'd grown up in a wealthy household, and with his mother's career in politics, there was always security around. During his childhood it had been big burly men. Lately his mom was concerned about diversity and inclusion. She'd hired an all-female team, so now there were always badass women around.

"I don't know. I rather wish you'd talked to her more instead of deciding she was telling you the truth." Knight gracefully slid into the driver's side.

Drake looked down at his phone as Kyle texted back.

I'm trying to keep eyes on Taylor, but she hasn't shown up yet. I'm covering a different part of the hotel. What's wrong with Brad?

Damn it. He got in the car and slammed the door, then Knight took off. "I'm sorry I didn't handle it as well as I should have. All I cared about in that moment was Taylor. She's still all I care about. The op can go to hell."

Knight eased the car onto the road. "I can understand that, but you need to calm down and think. Have you reached out to Brad?"

It hadn't been his first instinct. His first instinct was to quietly creep up on the fucker and kill him before he had a chance to fight back. But Knight was right to consider other options. "If he's dirty, he could try to take her out."

"Or he could realize you're onto him and stop whatever he's doing," Knight pointed out. "Would he give up his career to fuck with you?"

"Brad's whole life is his career." That fact was what didn't make sense to him. "He's always been the most by-the-book guy I've ever known."

"Well, that would be excellent cover for a man who wanted to hide his true ambitions." Knight turned onto the main road that would take them to the hotel. "What does he get if he hurts Taylor? From the way he's been talking, this operation is the largest he's had a hand in. Why would he want that op in danger?"

"It's already in danger because Taylor's changed her mind about sacrificing her entire life for an undercover op." He was texting Kyle as he spoke.

Something is wrong with Brad. He sent me on a wild-goose chase to keep me from being on the team when Taylor was called in. That means he knew when Taylor would be called in.

It didn't matter who was fucking with the op. He meant to get Taylor out of there. Nothing mattered beyond ensuring she was safe.

"He can't force her, and killing her wouldn't make him look better to the Agency. No matter how callous they can be, they don't tend to reward handlers who get their operatives killed." Knight was far more capable of being logical than he was. "So I'm still not understanding why he would want to hurt Taylor."

"It doesn't make sense because he couldn't possibly have known they would call her in tonight. Unless he's working with The Consortium. We've known for a while that Julia wasn't the only one working for them. We've been fairly certain they were behind the killing of an asset of mine a year and a half ago. Brad was the one who pointed it out. That could be a smoke screen."

"What kind of contact did Brad have with your sister?" Knight asked.

"None that I know of. I mean he knew her and he'd worked with us a few times, but they never paid attention to each other. Which, of course, is what they would do if they wanted to keep things quiet." Something Brad had said before tickled across his brain. "He mentioned he's been seeing a woman, but he's been secretive about it. I can't see him with my sister. She's got a very specific type."

"Yes, his name is Kyle Hawthorne, who happens to be here."

Fuck. If Brad was working with The Consortium, then this could all be one long play by his sister to get what she truly wanted—Kyle.

Lies on lies. That's what he was dealing with. Everyone was lying or hiding something, and he couldn't see through the lies to get to the truth.

He quickly texted Kyle.

Watch your back. I think Julia is here. She could find a way to take Taylor hoping I'll trade her for you. Get out of the hotel now.

If that was true, then Brad had betrayed him on every level. Brad was the only one who knew how much he loved Taylor.

"If Brad is working for The Consortium, then Julia knows about the op and Taylor."

"And if he's not?" Knight seemed determined to force him to look at this situation from all angles. The trouble was there were so damn many angles, and all of them were dependent on information he didn't have.

"Then he's innocent and Lydia is the one working for The Consortium, but if she's the one lying to me, I don't understand why because she doesn't know about Taylor. She doesn't know about the op at all."

"So you've got two different people in two different boxes and you can't figure out how they could be connected."

Drake's phone buzzed, announcing a text had come in.

I'm not going anywhere, but when Taylor walks in, I'll find a way to shadow her. If Julia shows up, I'll handle it.

That was Kyle. Stubborn to a *T*.

He was going to get himself killed. "Can you go faster?"

"We're almost there. Keep thinking, Drake. I know it's hard because the woman you love is in danger. If this was Penelope, I would be as panicked as you are, but you have to calm down and think this through. You know the answer. You simply haven't put the pieces together yet. So take a deep breath and let your mind work."

What had his father taught him?

Nothing is more important than the work. Not your life or your family. At the end not even your country. The intelligence we receive is what we serve. We take that information and create or destroy as it guides us.

Where was the information guiding him?

And how had he not realized how deeply fucked up his childhood had been?

He shoved that thought aside. He had the feeling he was going to need more therapy before he settled in and thought about having his own kids.

"Breathe, Drake. You've never been in this position before. You've never loved someone. It's hard. But you can do this." Knight's voice was deep and soothing, as if he genuinely knew exactly where Drake was in this moment.

Because he probably did. He worked with his wife, and they'd worked together when they'd both been in British intelligence. They still worked together, though now they oversaw the younger operatives, helping them and keeping them safe.

He and Taylor could do that.

Was there a connection between Lydia and Brad that went beyond their working relationship?

"What if Lydia is the mystery woman Brad talks about?" Drake mused. "Lydia only said they were friends, but she could be lying. He's mentioned he has a girlfriend but won't tell me her name. I would absolutely have been concerned if he was sleeping with Lydia."

"Excellent." Knight made a turn, and Drake could see the lights of the conference hotel up ahead. "What you're telling me is that Lydia worked with both your sister and Brad."

Fuck. "She's the connection between them. But why would she want me to turn against Brad?" His brain was whirling, answering his own questions. "She wants me to get rid of Brad because they're done with him. But if she's working with Brad, then she likely knows about Taylor. If she's lying, then she'll tell my sister and Brad that I'm on my way. I need to have Kyle grab Taylor the minute he sees her." He was moving past texts now. He dialed Kyle's number.

"Hey, I can't talk right now," Kyle said as he picked up.

"You have to listen to me. This is a setup. Julia is behind it," he said as quickly as he could. "But Lydia and Brad are in on it, too."

"Yeah, I'm starting to get that." Kyle sounded slightly out of breath. "Taylor just walked into the lobby with Julia and her asshole enforcer. I was about to call Brad when Jax told me he was in the room Brad was supposed to be in and Brad's gone. Left everything but his gun behind."

Drake's stomach churned. "Knight and I are almost there. Start moving toward Owen and Rebecca's suite. If you have any way to get Taylor away from them…"

"They're not going where they should be. From what I can tell, they're in the opposite wing. They got on an elevator using a key card," Kyle said. "I think they're going up to the larger suites, the ones they reserve for celebrities."

Or for government employees who required a ton of security.

There was one other target Julia could go after.

"She's going after my parents."

Knight sped up, and Drake prayed they made it in time.

Chapter Eighteen

Taylor followed Julia Ennis through the lobby, a low level of anxiety coursing through her mixing with the adrenaline she hoped she wouldn't need.

The truth was she should have been prepared for this outcome. Julia was the only ex-Agency operative they knew of. Likely not the only, but it made sense to send her in to deal with the recruitment of a new Agency contact. She knew the language, so to speak.

So far they'd done nothing at all that made her feel like they were trapping her. They were walking ahead of her, giving her every chance to leave if she wanted to. In some ways, she felt silly even wanting to run since they were being so deeply unthreatening.

Which could be the point.

She glanced up at the security camera and then pulled the hat over her forehead in case Julia or John looked back. They were both excellent at avoiding the cameras, but now she thought Julia's sunglasses had some kind of tech in them since she'd briefly taken them off outside and then made sure they were securely on again before they entered the hotel.

What kind of tech did a Consortium operative get? Likely way better than government agents.

The good news was she had four guys on her side, and they would all be watching those CCTVs, and they now knew where she was and who she was with.

She wanted Drake to be one of those men, but she trusted Kyle and Brad and Jax and Tucker. It was going to be okay. She would get in, steal something that didn't matter, and get out. Drake and Kyle would have good intel on Julia, and she could be done with the op.

One hour tops and this would all be over and it would be fine. Drake would be pissed but the anger would truly be fear, and she would let him top her until that fear subsided.

The lobby was still filled with people milling around.

"The conference is having a big party in the ballroom," Julia said as she walked around the elegantly appointed lobby, sticking to the outer edges. "It's two floors up from here so we'll avoid that entirely. We're going to take a service elevator to where we need to go. John, my darling boy, please take out the CCTV there and on the fortieth floor."

They turned down a quiet hallway, the lights dimmer than they'd been before.

John had his cell in hand and pressed a few buttons. "Cams are off now but they'll show the loop I locked in earlier today, so we've got an hour."

Jax would likely figure out something was going wrong. He wasn't planning on taking control of the cameras, but he would notice someone else had.

"Oh, I won't need an hour," Taylor promised. "It shouldn't take more than ten minutes to download Dr. Walsh's laptop."

John frowned as they made it to the service elevator. "Uhm…"

"Of course," Julia assured her. She slipped the glasses up on top of her head, pushing her hair back. "I'm glad Cleo went over that with you. And we'll get to that but first I need to take you up to meet my boss."

A cold tendril of fear crept up her spine. "Your boss?"

She shrugged. "We all have one. Mine's just been around longer than most."

Her gut tightened. "I don't like surprises."

Julia chuckled. "Well, then you should probably get out of the spy game because let me tell you, sister, it's one surprise after another. Like we're a whole industry that runs on shocking the fuck out of people."

"I get shocked all the time," John agreed as the elevator doors opened and he hopped inside.

Out of the corner of her eyes she saw something moving in the background.

"You get shocked because you lack imagination," Julia shot back as she entered the elevator.

"I do not," John argued.

They were distracted enough that Taylor felt comfortable glancing over to her left. She saw Brad with his back against the wall. His whole body was tight, as though he wanted nothing more than to join them on that elevator.

She wasn't alone. Brad understood the plan was going awry, and he would watch to make sure he knew exactly where she was going. He would work with the other guys to keep an eye on her.

She could do this.

She put on a breezy smile and got on the elevator.

"I have a great imagination," John was insisting.

"He doesn't but he's attractive and excellent at what he does, which is anything I tell him to do." Julia reached over and hit the button for the fortieth floor. "If you work hard and prove yourself to the group, you'll get one of him, too. Think of him like a coworker and a party favor all at the same time."

John snorted. "Party favor. I do like to party."

Julia leaned over. "They're pretty and flexible morally, but loyal enough to trust. I like to think of the men of the group as golden retrievers who've been taught to kill."

"I tend to work alone," Taylor replied because it seemed like Julia wanted to make this a whole discussion. She could do that. Any information Julia wanted to give would be helpful.

"That's such an Agency thing to say," Julia replied with a sigh. "Come on. You're failing the 'would be fun to kill people with' part of this test, and for me that's really a thing."

"Somehow I doubt you have a lot of girlfriends."

"Well, other women don't like me. I can't imagine why. It's probably because I'm too honest with them. And I sleep with their husbands sometimes. Usually that's because they've either been mean to me or I like them and I need them to see that their husbands are cheating jerks," Julia said with a sigh. "You have to find the right partner. Too many women find the first man to pay attention to them and give it all up. You have to find your soul mate."

A groan came from John's throat.

"I didn't think spies got soul mates." Taylor was starting to understand that Julia Ennis was batshit crazy.

"Then you probably haven't met yours." Julia's boot tapped against the floor of the elevator.

"Don't get her started on soul mates." John shook his head. "Her ex tried to kill her but she thinks she can fix the relationship."

"I think that true love is worth a little work," Julia corrected. "I'm not some delicate flower who wilts the first time something goes wrong."

"He shot you." John seemed to be more of a realist.

"And he didn't do a good job of it. I'm alive and stuff. He was angry. He didn't truly want me dead." She waved off the whole Kyle-tried-to-kill-her thing. "And now he's punishing me, but we're working our way through it. He's gotten rid of the ridiculous doll he'd been playing with, and soon we'll meet up and have an actual adult discussion."

She talked like they'd had nothing more than a minor argument and it could be easily handled. She didn't understand how much Kyle loathed her.

Would Kyle try to kill her tonight? Suddenly she was happy Drake wasn't around because he should be able to avoid the scene that was going to happen.

God, this woman had killed her father and she was thinking about how to protect her boyfriend.

And that is how it should be, dushka. *Life is for the living. The best revenge is to live and love and have a happy life.*

Her father had never said those words to her, but she heard him in her heart. It was like he was standing there with her, giving her his strength.

She didn't have the advantage with John here or she might pull her Glock and deal with the Julia situation once and for all. It was odd that she didn't feel the rush of emotion she thought she would. If she killed Julia, it would be to help Drake and Kyle. It wouldn't be for her father. He didn't need that from her. He needed her to be happy, to have the life she wanted. To marry Drake and have children and tell them stories of the grandfather who would have loved them so well.

"Constance here doesn't have a boy toy," Julia said as the elevator was starting to slow down. "It's a good thing. The group I work for prefers single women. I think part of the reason we all get Johns is for stress relief. Sorry, buddy. I don't mean to call you a walking vibrator, but if the shoe fits…"

"Hey, I'm good at my job and I like sex. Sex and violence work for me," John admitted.

"Like I said, I prefer to work alone," Taylor lied. She would be doing a lot of that in the next few moments.

"Good, because we are looking for a self-starter," Julia announced. The doors opened and she strode through. "I think that should be part of our ad. *Evil organization looking for self-starter to terrorize the world for profits.*"

John followed her but Taylor stopped because they weren't alone. There were two women dressed in dark suits standing outside the big double doors to one of the suites on the floor.

She started to back up, to get in the elevator again because her every instinct was telling her something was wrong.

Julia stopped and glanced back, one brow arching. "Something wrong?" She seemed to understand. "Oh, the guards. It's cool. They're with us, though they are also a bit on the grumpy side. What is it with personal security details that they have to be so grumpy? Smile a little. Don't you know how pretty you could be if you would smile more?"

"Fuck you, Lizzy," the first of the guards said, revealing she wasn't merely with Julia. If she knew Julia's code name, she was with The Consortium.

The other one chuckled. "I don't know. I think she's got a point.

Who's the new girl?"

"Cleo was recruiting her," Julia said. "She's with the Agency. I'm giving her an audition tonight. Everything's in place?"

"As far as I can tell," the guard said and looked down at her watch. "I think I'm going on my planned break. Sheila will be here if you need anything. Your friend should be here soon."

"Excellent." Julia nodded Sheila's way as the other guard headed down the hallway and disappeared. "Keep an eye out. I'll be right back. I need to make sure everything is ready for Constance's first mission. We need to get her out of here before the party downstairs breaks up."

Good. They were getting this thing moving. Drake would get back from his meeting anytime now and then she had to hope Damon Knight could convince him to wait patiently for her.

"Okay, lock down that elevator to anyone who doesn't have the right code. I'll be back." Julia slid a key card over the lock and the door came open.

Taylor barely got a glimpse of a marbled foyer when the door closed again.

She felt awkward. This was not how she'd seen the evening going. Something was off, and she wasn't sure what.

Why would Julia be in such a high-profile room? The point of spying was to blend in.

John stepped back, pulling his cell out and putting it to his ear. "Yeah?"

He walked a little distance from her.

"Chill, new girl," the guard said. "We're alone on this floor. There are only four rooms, and three of them are controlled by our group. The fourth is being monitored, and if the ambassador and his wife decide to leave the party, we'll be informed. You can relax. This is going to go off without a hitch."

She wasn't so sure about that. "I don't suppose you want to tell me what 'this' is?"

The grim-looking guard shook her head. "Nope. She looks all sophisticated and civilized, but I've seen what she can do. Daddy raised a psycho, if you know what I mean. Follow her orders, get into the group, and once they trust you, they'll let you work alone.

This is all a test. You have to survive her first. I wouldn't be surprised if she's not the one who took out Cleo herself. That one lives for the kill. Me, I just like the paycheck."

The door came open again and Julia stood there. "Come in. We're ready. Your audition begins now."

"This isn't Dr. Walsh's room," Taylor said.

"And this isn't Cleo's mission anymore," Julia countered, her expression more serious than she'd seen all night. "Stay or go, Constance? If you walk through here, you're committed. I can't let you know the truth about my plans and walk away, so you've got like ten seconds to think about it."

"Hey, we might have a problem." John's voice had dropped to a whisper. Taylor had to lean in to hear. "And it's likely on its way here."

Julia's breath hitched as though she'd gotten news and she wasn't sure if it was good or bad. "Which problem?"

"Not the one you want," John returned. "One of the programs I'm running identified him on CCTV coming down the street about ten minutes ago."

Julia's eyes narrowed. "Then we should work fast, and you should make sure he doesn't get up here. Constance, it's time. Stay or go?"

She had to figure out what Julia was doing because she was almost certain they were talking about Drake. Brad knew where she was, and the whole building was being monitored, so if Drake did walk in, they would know it. He would have backup.

She stepped forward. "I'm in."

Julia nodded as John pushed the button for the elevator and gave the guard some instructions.

Taylor walked through the door and felt the whole world shift because the last thing she'd expected to see was Senator Samantha Radcliffe still in her cocktail dress from the party, asleep on the couch.

"For your audition, I'm going to need you to kill my mother."

* * * *

Drake hit the lobby with Knight behind him. He was well aware that he'd been caught on every single security camera.

"Hey," a familiar voice said. Kyle had a grim look on his face as he crossed the space between them. "I still can't find Brad, and I lost Julia and Taylor and whoever that fucker John is. Nick is already in the ballroom. He's going to escort Owen and Rebecca up to where Jax is trying to figure out what happened with the CCTV. He thinks someone took over the cameras around the elevator on the north side, the one that leads to the secure floors."

"The lift is working but the cameras aren't?" Knight asked.

"My parents are on the fortieth floor." Drake's gut tightened. "I think she's going to go after them."

"Why would she do that?" Knight asked.

"Because she's Julia," Kyle replied. "Because they didn't pay enough attention to her or she's trying to get my attention, or she thinks it will hurt Drake and then he'll give her attention. She's got it all worked out in her head, but the truth is it's nothing but one more pathetic and cruel attempt to put herself in the spotlight. If she can't have good attention, she'll take bad."

He wished he could argue, could find anything good to say about his sister, but he couldn't. The fact that she was here meant his parents were in trouble. He should have known she was planning something when she'd shown up at their country club in DC. "She's come here to fuck with our parents, and she's apparently going to use Taylor to do it. I have to think she knows who Taylor is and what she means to me."

"How would she know that?" Knight followed as Drake and Kyle began to walk through the lobby.

"I don't know." Kyle's long legs led the way. "We've been incredibly careful about protecting her true identity."

"Not careful enough since Brad knows and he's been working with Julia."

Kyle stopped in the middle of the hall and turned, his jaw tight. "He did what?"

"I need him alive, Kyle." He knew the man. Kyle would take Brad's head off if he had the chance. Anyone who helped Julia would be ruthlessly dealt with by Kyle. "He's probably with Julia right now. We need to get to my parents' suite."

The good news was Brad wasn't around to argue that the op was more important than his parents.

He was trying to wrap his head around the fact that Brad had betrayed the Agency, betrayed all of his coworkers and his country.

It didn't make sense, but then when did any of it make sense.

He wanted to sit and think about it, to reason this out the way Knight had suggested, but he didn't have time. Taylor's life was on the line and if she died…

He couldn't think that way. He couldn't do it. He jogged on.

"Drake, we need to think about how to move ahead." Knight seemed insistent on him not roaring into the situation blindly.

"Yes, because you have to know she'll be ready for us," Kyle agreed. He touched the comm unit in his ear. "Jax, I need you to take a look at the plans for the fortieth floor and how we can sneak up. I've got to think they'll have someone on the elevators."

Kyle fished another unit out of his pocket and handed it to Drake. Drake had it fixed to his ear in no time. "Is Brad on this line?"

Jax's voice came over the link. "Of course, but he's gone silent. I'm not sure where he is."

"Cut him off. Now." He wasn't about to let Brad listen in. "I need you to restore cameras on the fortieth floor, in particular the Royal Suite. That's the one my parents are in. I'm going up the service elevator, and Damon and Kyle will use the regular bank. Take that over so they can get to forty. You need a code to access that floor."

"I'm in the system," Jax confirmed. "I think I have a way for you to get up without using the service elevator. That dumps out close to the suite, and I'm certain there's security on the door. If you take the east bank of elevators and go to thirty-nine, you can use the stairs to get to forty. You still need a code, but the door and elevators are on two separate systems. They might not get the notice that someone opened the doors from the stairs and yes, I can open it from here. You should have a shot at surprising the guard if they're on the door."

"We need someone on this elevator," Drake said. "This is how they got up, so I have to think they'll come down this way."

"I'll stay and Nick will join me once he's secured Owen and Rebecca," Damon explained.

"I'll go with Drake." Kyle moved to his side. "Once we get to thirty-nine, I'll move to the opposite side so we can flank them."

"Tucker is on his way," Jax said, "and I'm here in Overwatch. Am I assuming Brad is no longer in charge?"

The idea of Brad being out there sent a flare of anger through him, but there was confusion in there, too. "He's very likely working with Julia. Stay in contact. We're going for the elevators."

Kyle jogged alongside him as they made their way across the lobby. "They never liked each other. Julia hated Brad. She thought he was a pain in the ass. How can they be working together?"

"I don't know. I always trusted him." Luckily there weren't a bunch of people milling around in this part of the hotel. Apparently most of the guests were either in the bar or the conference ballroom party. He and Kyle managed to get into the elevator alone.

"I'm going to kill her," Kyle said quietly, his eyes down.

"I know." He hated it, loathed the idea that Kyle would get more blood on his hands, but he couldn't argue with him. "Please be careful with Taylor. She doesn't know what's happening. I don't know if Taylor would actually recognize my sister. She could still think she's working with the same contact she's been with the whole time. Hell, as far as I know Julia's been playing us all along."

The elevator started up, and Drake's heart was pounding.

Why would Julia go after their parents? Why bring Taylor along? What was the point?

It hit him quickly now that he had seconds to think. "She wanted the kidnapping thing on the record. She wanted the threat on paper and the Agency to not be able to finagle their way out. She's going to kill them."

"What does she get out of it?" Kyle asked.

"She's never been declared dead."

"But she would have to account for the plastic surgery," Kyle countered. "And we've got proof she's been involved in criminal endeavors. You think she's trying to get her inheritance the old-fashioned way?"

"Mom had her will changed last year. Dad gets everything if she dies, and if they both go, it's all me. I assure you Julia's not in my will. So she can't get the money." His brain was going a hundred miles a minute.

"Or The Consortium wants your mother out of office and this is how they do it," Kyle mused.

That made sense. "I know she's been working on a bill that would punish polluters. She's worked on a lot of things. They could simply want the seat for someone they own. They're using Taylor to hurt me."

"For Julia, the cruelty is the point," Kyle replied. "I'm going to take the stairs from the left. You go right. Take out anyone you have to. She won't be alone. She's probably infiltrated the guards or she'll have taken them all out."

"Mom usually has three guards on her detail when she's traveling," Drake explained. "They switch off. I know she had three on the plane. At this time, there should be at least two on duty, and all three are women. I didn't even think about it because Mom changed them out last year. She said she liked the optics of having an all-female security team."

"Or more likely an all-Consortium team." The doors opened and Kyle moved out. "Be careful, Drake. If you can, get Taylor and run. Let me handle Julia. She's my mistake."

"She's my sister."

"Yes, and I have no idea how I would handle it if I found out David wasn't who I thought he was. I know I've given you shit, but I don't blame you. She was your family. That's hard to see through. And I don't think I would be able to kill my brothers or sister even if I found out they were evil," Kyle said. "So let me do this, Drake. No matter what it costs."

Kyle turned and jogged away.

Fuck. He was going to get himself killed. Drake strode the opposite way, quickly moving to the stairs. When he got there, he opened the door and took out the semiautomatic, flipping off the safety. There was no safety from here on out.

Jax opened the door that led him to the fortieth floor. "Kyle's already coming from the other side."

If he got through this, he was going to go to the gym way more often. Kyle was in better shape.

Or he would go to the gym with his wife because he was taking a desk job. He was moving into analysis, and he would work to make sure no more Julias got through. He would dedicate his life to making the Agency safer and better and to making sure Taylor got everything she needed.

"The suite is in the middle of the floor. You've got two turns, and I'm still blind, brother." Jax's voice was a soothing presence. "Be careful. Someone else is coming up. I've got a woman taking the service elevator. She's in a uniform, so she might be a civilian. I'm still working on the cams. Whoever took them over is good, and I'm worried they know I'm in here."

"It doesn't matter now. Get Damon and Nick up here as soon as possible. I'll try to get the civie out of the way." He made the first turn and could hear someone talking in the hallway ahead.

"This isn't Dr. Walsh's room," Taylor was saying.

She was close. Maybe a hundred feet away. So fucking close, and he couldn't reach out and pull her to safety. He couldn't see her, and the voices were coming in and out, but he knew he was close.

"And this isn't Cleo's mission anymore." His sister's voice hit him like a slap in the face. Damn it. There was a deep mourning rolling around with the rage and fear. How could she do this? "Stay or go, Constance? If you walk through here, you're committed. I can't let you know the truth about my plans and walk away, so you've got like ten seconds to think about it."

Constance? She was keeping up the illusion? Was that for Taylor's sake?

There was another explanation.

Julia was up to her own fuckery and didn't know who Taylor was. Didn't know what she meant to him.

He heard someone whispering but couldn't make out the words.

"I'm in," Taylor's voice came through loud and clear.

Drake eased around the corner, trying to figure out how vulnerable he was. Kyle would be coming up the other side. They could catch Julia in between them and there would be nowhere for her to go.

But Taylor could be caught in the crossfire.

Kyle was right. He had one job—to get Taylor out of there.

He turned and stopped because there was a body on the ground and Brad was standing over it. One of his mother's guards lay on the tastefully neutral carpet of the quiet hallway, and it was obvious she was never getting up again.

Brad's eyes flared and his hand came up, a clear command to stay silent.

Drake held up his gun, getting Brad in his sights.

"What are you doing?" Brad whispered the question. "You're going to get her killed. She's in trouble. I managed to follow her up. I saw her on the cams come in with… I think she's with Julia."

A woman in a dark suit rounded the corner, her eyes widening when she caught sight of the two of them standing in the hallway. "Hey."

He'd seen this woman before. She worked on his mom's security detail, but he realized with dawning horror that she might have been on his mom's team, but she wasn't working for her. She pulled a gun and began to fire. Drake realized he was about to die. That bullet would hit his chest, and there was nothing he could do about it.

But there was something Brad could do. Brad threw his body in front of Drake's and got off a shot of his own. The force of Brad's body hitting his dropped Drake to his knees, his own gun slipping from his fingers.

The woman went down, her eyes open even as she fell to the floor.

Drake scrambled from behind Brad, easing the man down. There was a hole in his chest, one he wouldn't survive unless they got him to a doctor now. Drake touched his earpiece. "Jax, I need you to send Tucker. Jax?"

"They dampened comms on this floor," Brad said with a wheezing cough. "Julia…Drake, Julia…"

He'd been wrong. "Julia's here. I know. Brad, we need to get you some help."

Brad's head shook. "Too…too late. Drake…Lydia…"

"Lydia is with them, isn't she?" He knew now. It had to be at least one of the two of them, and he'd guessed wrong.

"She knows...a lot... Drake, I thought she loved me," Brad whispered. "But Drake, I didn't tell her. She doesn't know about Taylor. Never would have told her. Never."

A ping sounded and Brad's body tensed and then the light in his eyes died.

Drake looked up and there was the woman he'd been talking about. The one who had betrayed them all. Lydia stood there wearing the black slacks and white shirt of one of the staff. Her hair was up, and she held a gun in her hands.

"Poor Brad. I was hoping I could keep him around a little while longer," she said with a frown. "But at least I got the real prize. Come on, Drake. It's time you started paying attention to me. I thought you would argue with me. What the hell was that? You just took off running. That's not the Drake I know. But Brad was exactly who I thought he was. He was more loyal to the Agency than he was to me. A good man is hard to find. Get up and come with me. Now we have to figure out what to do with you."

He thought about going for the gun, but then Lydia wasn't alone.

"Damn it." The man Taylor had been working on identifying stood beside Lydia, and he had a gun, too. "You were supposed to make sure he was distracted tonight. What the fuck happened? Julia's going to kill us both. Come on, Drake. I think it's time for a family meeting."

Drake stood, his heart racing.

It was time to see his sister.

Chapter Nineteen

Taylor fought to stem the rising tide of panic. She had to stay calm. They'd come in the main door, but this was a massive suite and there would be more than one way in, meaning there was also more than one way out. One of the things Brad had forced her to do was study all the plans for this hotel. The big suites had two to three doors. If she was right, the door close to the bedroom would be located next to the stairs. It might be her best escape.

But she had to figure out a way to save Samantha Radcliffe first. "What's wrong with her? She looks like she's already dead."

"We slipped her a sleeping pill. It's cool. They were prescribed for her." Julia sounded like she was talking about the weather rather than matricide. Although it wouldn't be matricide since she was passing the job off to Taylor. "It won't be a scandal when the toxicology report comes in."

"No, I think the murder of a US senator would take up the headlines," Taylor shot back. She had to play this as cool as Julia was. Drake's mom was lying there in the cocktail dress she'd likely worn to the conference party that was still going on. Had they slipped her pill in one of her drinks? Or waited until she was back up here to force her to sleep? It didn't matter. What did was the fact that she wasn't about to let the senator die. She wasn't going to stand here and kill Drake's mom for the op.

The problem was she suspected Julia wouldn't allow her to pull out now that she knew what it was.

"Yes, I'm counting on those headlines," Julia admitted.

"What is the play here?" She needed to buy some time. The boys would figure out something had gone wrong, and they would give the distraction she needed to get the jump on Julia.

"You don't need to know." Julia's lips turned down as she seemed to get serious. "You have a job to do, and I expect you to do it."

"Is this why you killed Cleo?"

One shoulder shrugged. "Maybe. I do tend to take advantage of opportunities when they present themselves. I can't do it myself, and I can't trust a full operative. When I realized Cleo was running an audition in London, I simply took over. I'll get you what you want after you give me what I need."

"To kill your mother?"

"She wasn't a particularly good one." Julia looked down at her sleeping mother with cold eyes. "Oh, she did and said all the right things, but in the end she was only truly devoted to her job. And my brother. She loved my brother. I think it's because my biological father was such a piece of shit she couldn't stand to look at me."

She couldn't exactly argue with the woman. She wasn't supposed to know who she was. "So this is a personal vendetta?"

"I told you it's not your business. I have a gun for you. I printed it this afternoon so it's completely unregistered, and it will be easy to dispose of," Julia said, getting down to business. "If you do this, I'll make sure you get one of the new 3D printers. One of the companies we work for has perfected printing small arms. They're single use, but that's rather the point. You use it and then easily destroy it. A couple of minutes in the microwave and it no longer looks like a gun. I would wear gloves though. The plastic heats up like a motherfucker when you fire it. They're still working some bugs out."

It was good to know the corporate world was busy looking to

make a buck off industrious criminals. She filed that away in the back of her head. She would be looking through the lists of possible Consortium connections to try to figure out who was working on perfecting guns that could get through metal detectors and were easy to dispose of. If they were working on guns, they were likely working on explosive devices, too.

Terrorism was big business.

But for now she needed to deal with Julia. "I'm not here to be your errand boy. I'm here to work for The Consortium, so if this is a personal job, I'm going to pass. Look I know what Cleo was planning and it wasn't killing a United States senator."

Julia froze. "How do you know who she is?"

Fuck. But no. There was a simple answer to this. "Lady, I work for the Agency. Do you honestly believe I don't know who our government officials are and where they are traveling, especially when I'm in the same country? That is Senator Samantha Radcliffe, and if she's your mother then…"

She let the sentence dangle because this way she didn't have to pretend.

Julia's face flushed, and for a moment Taylor was worried the other woman would shoot her then and there for embarrassing her. Then she seemed to calm. "All right. Those are excellent powers of deduction, and I should have known you would be up to date on your information."

"I wouldn't be of much use to the group if I wasn't."

"Fine," Julia replied. "And it's not personal. The truth is I wouldn't have chosen to do this, but my boss thinks it's time, and I don't argue with the boss. The Consortium wants to put its own person in my mother's place. Rigging an election is way harder than you would think. So eliminating the problem and allowing the governor to name her replacement is the way we're going."

"The governor will choose someone the group likes?" She wanted to know how deep this went. Did The Consortium own governors too?

"The governor will do what we tell him to. So let's get this done and get you out of here. I have things to do tonight, and I want the actual work done before there are people on this floor again."

Drake was right. His sister was a damn monster. Unfortunately, she was a monster with a big-ass gun, and she was still paying attention to Taylor. She was going to have to make a choice and take a chance, because there was zero way she shot a sleeping woman.

Especially Drake's mother.

The door came open and John walked through, a frown on his face. "We got problems. Your other project is here, and she brought along a friend."

"I didn't bring him here. He showed up on his own. How was I supposed to know he would react like that?" A young woman in a hotel uniform walked in, but Taylor barely noticed her because she wasn't alone. She had a gun trained at Drake's back as she forced him along.

Drake. Drake was here and he was in serious trouble.

Julia stopped and stared at her brother for a moment, her eyes wide in obvious surprise. "What the hell is he doing here? You told me he was working a job tonight."

That answered one question. She didn't know who Taylor was, and she hadn't planned on her brother walking in.

"He was," the woman in the service uniform said. "And then he figured out something was wrong and he took off running. I knew he was involved in another op here, an op he wasn't willing to talk to me about. Why would you come here, Drake? And why the hell was Brad here?"

Taylor thought quickly. She had to get ahead of this or things could go very wrong. "Who is Brad? And that dude right there is Agency. I've seen him before. Have you fucked this up so badly that I've been made? Are you fucking kidding me?"

She'd learned that it was easier to throw people off with accusations than explanations. If they knew about the Agency team here, she needed to distance or Julia would simply blow her head off.

"I don't know, Constance," Julia said with a frown, looking the new girl's way. "I'm not the one who literally works for the Agency and is supposed to know things like this. Lydia is. I asked you specifically what you knew about your boyfriend and why he was going to be in England. Maybe you're working with Constance."

Or Julia could try to turn it all around.

"I have no idea what the hell is going on here," Drake said. He knelt down beside his mother, his face ashen. He reached for her hand. "Is she okay? What the hell did you do to her?"

Julia stared for a moment, and then her head fell back and she laughed. "For fuck's sake. No one knows what's going on. I asked Lydia to distract you while I did a job. She fucked it up somehow, and now you're here. Does anyone want to explain why Brad's here?"

"He was working with me." Drake held his mother's hand and didn't pay a bit of attention to the guns trained on him. "We're trying to identify the leak, and I think we've done it. How long have you been working with her, Lydia?"

"Since I realized you would never give a damn about me," Lydia replied. "That no one gave a damn about me."

"Brad did," Drake shot back.

"Brad wasn't capable of loving anyone more than he did the Agency." Lydia's eyes held a sheen of tears. "The Consortium is giving me a chance to have power. Far more power than I could ever achieve working for the government. Governments are outdated and outmoded. The Consortium is the future. The sheep don't even see it coming and never will understand who their overlords are."

Taylor let her eyes roll. It would have been hard to stop them. "Look, if that's the level of fuckery you expect from your agents, I'm out. Did you take a class in overdramatic evil? I'm not going to stay here while you kill a senator and an Agency operative. Is he really your brother? This is completely messed up and you both need therapy."

She needed some chaos. It appeared Brad was down, but that left Kyle, Tucker, and Jax. She had to buy them some time.

Julia's head shook. "You're not going anywhere. I have to think. I have to figure out what Drake is doing here and if Lydia is working with him. She always had a thing for him."

"I'm not working with him," Lydia argued. "And we need to hurry. The helicopter is waiting, but it can't stay on the pad all night."

"I'm here trying to save our parents. I figured out what you're planning. Are you going to kill them both?" Drake ignored Taylor completely.

"Our parents?" Julia had two guns, one in each hand. "You still act like we're some happy family and I'm the only one who messed it all up. You act like I'm the outlier. I'm not. Do you honestly think she didn't know?"

"I know she didn't know," Drake replied.

Taylor's heart ached for him, but she was watching the woman who had a gun trained on him. She would have to get it away from her. They were so outnumbered, and Drake didn't seem to have a weapon on him.

But he did have blood. A lot of blood. Was he hit? Or was that Brad's blood?

"Of course she knew," a deep voice said. "She knew deep down, but your mother prefers to ignore problems. She likes to pretend we're a normal American family like the ones she purports to represent."

The sound had come from her right, from someone walking through the hallway that led to the bedrooms. An older man, his body slender and fit, walked through, and there was no way to deny the man wasn't related to Drake.

The world had turned again, and she wondered if this time the betrayal wouldn't kill the man she loved.

* * * *

Drake felt bile in the back of his throat as his father walked into the room and stood by Julia.

His mother's hand was warm in his, but it wouldn't be soon. They were going to kill her, and he couldn't understand why. He looked at the father who'd taught him everything, who'd taken his life and molded it one way only to shatter it in an instant.

He couldn't come up with anything more than a simple

question as he stared at the man who'd ruled his life for so very long. "Why?"

His father's hair was salt and pepper, his demeanor stately and cold as he looked down at his wife and only son. "There is no answer I can give you that will satisfy you. I loved the game, and the Agency couldn't keep up. I don't think I feel the way other people do. This chess game is what gives me life, and I don't care who I hurt as long as I win. Your mother has been an excellent cover all these years, and don't think I haven't screwed up and let the mask slip from time to time. She turned a blind eye because all she really cared about was the fact that I didn't cheat on her and I didn't embarrass her in public. I made her life easier, and she was unwilling to upset that relationship."

"So now you decide to kill her?" He couldn't believe this was happening. It couldn't be happening. Not again.

"It's the next move. She's being stubborn. She's the swing vote on a measure that could make the group billions of dollars and settle the power struggle that's going on in pharmaceuticals right now. She won't listen to reason."

Naturally this was all about money. "And you don't think there will be an investigation?"

"I think the Agency will do anything to cover up the cover-up." His father sighed as he looked down at his sleeping wife.

"The cover-up." Drake stood because now he could see how well he'd been played. "That's why Julia called her. You knew I would take over and cover it all up. You're going to use the documents my team forged to build a narrative where those people who don't actually exist are the ones who killed Mom."

"And the Agency will back me up because they can't admit they tricked a sitting US senator," his father pronounced. "And then I will take my wife's seat. I will promise to be tough on crime in her honor, and I'll quietly vote the way I need to. If it helps at all, I do care for her. More than I do anyone else. I won't take another wife."

"I'm supposed to be impressed with your fidelity to the wife you're about to kill, to the wife you lied to all of your life?" Drake felt rage start to build in his system. "You lied to our whole family, and you made Julia and I your accomplices."

"Don't talk that way about Dad," Julia said quietly. "You're the one who was willing to murder me, and for what? Your morals?"

"I told her it was a mistake to try to bring you and Hawthorne in," his father explained. "She wouldn't listen. She thought you would care more about her than you did some irrelevant moral code. She's more my daughter than you are my son, and that makes it far easier to do what I'm going to have to do."

"You're going to kill me, too?" It was the only possible solution. But Taylor might live. Taylor might be able to survive this, and that was all that mattered in the moment.

"I don't want to." Julia's voice had gone tight, as tight as the grip she had on those guns. "I know you think this is easy, but it's not. Kyle's going to be upset with me, but it's his fault. He should have kept you out of this."

Taylor sighed and those bratty eyes of hers rolled. She was playing the callous operative to the hilt. "This is boring me at this point. Give me the gun. I'll take care of both of them and you can get to your helo. I want double the money though."

"I still don't understand who this is." Lydia was looking her over with suspicious eyes. "I know everyone. I know all the operatives, and I've never seen her."

"She's Constance Tyne." Drake had to save this. If Taylor could get that gun in her hand, she had a real shot. "I've worked with her before. She's a deep ops agent, and the fact that she's obviously going to be working for The Consortium scares the shit out of me. She's got one of the highest clearances of any agent I've worked with."

"Precisely why I want to recruit her," Julia affirmed.

"I don't know." His father seemed to be studying Taylor.

He'd met her before. Oh, she'd been barely a teen, but his father's memory was excellent. The good news was she didn't look like her father, and she'd changed her hair color. She was leaner and more predatory than the sweet girl they'd met that day.

She was his whole world.

"She's been vetted, and this is my op," Julia said. "And our time is running out. If she's willing to do this particular dirty work, I say we go for it."

"We need to move because someone broke through my hold on the CCTV cams. I got it back, but whoever is on the other side of this is good." John was standing at the desk, looking down at an open laptop.

Jax was busy. It looked like years of Bliss living hadn't dulled his skills.

Julia turned her father's way. "Where do you want it?"

His father shook his head. "No. Something's wrong. I don't trust her. I know all the operatives, and she wasn't one of them. Kill her. Kill them all. We'll figure out a cover story later."

Drake couldn't wait another second. He kicked back and caught Lydia in the gut, shoving her against the wall. Her gun clattered to the floor.

He scrambled for it. Lydia picked up one of the heavy books on the coffee table and clocked him with it, making him spin and fall to his knees.

He had to get the gun. Lydia was going for it again, but he couldn't let her have it. He needed that gun. She'd killed Brad and who knew how many others. She was absolutely the one who'd gotten his asset in Kraków killed. She'd likely been behind many of the leaks that cost Agency operatives.

She'd also been someone he'd counted on. Someone he'd trusted with his life.

Drake got his hands on the gun first, and he didn't even think twice about firing.

There was the sound of a door flying open and the sweet sight of Kyle Hawthorne storming into the room.

Chaos was all around him, but one thing was clear. Lydia's hand touched her chest, blood starting to bloom. She fell to her knees, her eyes accusing him the whole time.

Julia was fighting with Taylor, both women trying to get one of the guns Julia had been holding. Drake tried to get a shot but the women were fighting, their bodies dancing around and eliminating any chance to take out Julia.

Kyle fired toward John, but the man was already moving. He

returned fire, and Kyle's left shoulder flew back as he spun around and started for the floor.

The suite was massive, and Drake had to maneuver around the big sofa where his mother was starting to stir.

"Stay down," he ordered.

"Drake?" His mom's eyes closed again.

He rolled her to the floor. At least it was some cover. He couldn't watch over her. He had to get to Taylor and save Kyle. He couldn't let either of them down.

Taylor had to come first.

Where the hell had his father gone? The suite had too many ways out, but he doubted his father would run without getting the job done. He caught sight of his father's leg from behind one of the marble columns that decorated the classically designed suite.

The sound of gunfire in the hallway distracted him briefly.

Kyle took another shot at John, but he'd found a good spot behind the big bar. They were facing off, John behind the bar and Kyle using one of the arches to protect himself.

"Who's in the hall?" He moved to Kyle's side in the foyer.

"It looked like two guards." If Kyle felt any pain, he didn't show it. He simply lifted his gun and took another shot. "Two women. One in uniform. One in pajamas. Tucker is dealing with them. The last I heard Damon and Nick were making their way up, but Jax still can't get the elevator working."

His mom's guards—though they wouldn't be saving her. He knew what had happened. His father had convinced his mom to change guards for the optics. Then he'd hired Consortium agents to guard her.

Now they would try to kill her and her son and his friends.

"Stop!" Julia yelled and the air seemed to still. "Or I'll kill her."

Drake's heart threatened to stop because Julia had her arm wrapped around Taylor's throat, and there was a gun to her head.

Kyle was a big presence in the room. He got to his feet, gripping the Glock he'd always preferred. "Julia, don't do this."

"Hey, baby." Julia's voice went soft even though she was still holding that gun against Taylor's head. "Are you okay? You're bleeding."

"Why don't you let her go and we'll talk." Kyle held his hands out, palming the gun to show his finger wasn't on the trigger. "We can go somewhere and be alone. I've had time to think, Julia."

"I want to believe you," she said, her voice tremulous.

"Don't be a fool." His father hissed the words. "You have one weakness. I didn't invest years in you to watch you blow it over a boy. Can't you see this is all your fault? You spend all your time thinking about this idiot. You couldn't see that the woman you were trying to recruit was bait, Julia. Your brother sent her out as bait, and you took it."

"Hey, let her go, Jules." Drake used his sister's name from childhood. "Let her go and you can walk away."

"I'll go with you," Kyle promised.

"Who is she?" Julia asked. "She's not who I thought she was."

"I think she's Lev's girl," his father said, still hiding behind the column. "I saw her a couple of times when I met with him. Lev showed me pictures of her. The idiot. Are you trying to get revenge... I don't remember your name."

"It's Taylor, and I don't care about revenge. I want justice." Taylor was still, and he knew she was going to try something any minute.

"You're a naïve moron then." His father's voice sounded over the fight that was going on in the hall. "Julia, we're going to the helo now. Take the girl with you. It's obvious Drake has feelings for her. We'll deal with the fallout later."

He couldn't let that happen. "I won't allow you to take her."

"I think Kyle should come with us." Julia ignored him completely, her eyes never leaving Kyle. It was so obvious his father was right. Kyle could make Julia forget everything, and the minute he had the chance, Kyle would take her out.

"I want to." Kyle's voice had gone soothing. "I told you. I've been thinking about us."

Taylor chose that moment to drop, putting her entire weight on the arm Julia had around her neck.

The gun went off, and Drake's whole soul threatened to crack as Taylor slid to the ground, but not before he saw blood.

His father stepped out and fired Kyle's way as Drake tried to get to Taylor. He pushed aside a chair and knew someone was coming in the door, but nothing mattered except getting to Taylor.

"No!" Julia screamed and she was shooting, but he didn't know if she was coming for him or someone else.

His heart was beating so loud he would have sworn he could hear it.

"Dad?" Julia's voice had gone gentle. "Daddy?"

She'd shot their father in the back. His dad had fallen forward, and his blood stained the marble all around him.

Drake got to Taylor, who was on the fine carpet, blood matting her hair. He dragged her into his arms as he caught sight of John running back to the bedroom. He'd thrown Julia over his shoulder and was running.

"Fuck." Kyle stumbled over, his hand at his side. "Fucker got me twice. I can't keep up with them." He touched his earpiece. "They're going to the roof. They've got a helicopter waiting. Try to catch them. And we're going to need a bus. We've got two gunshot wounds, and the senator was drugged."

"I'm fine." Taylor's eyes came open and she sat straight up, her hand going to her ear. She was yelling. "I can't hear. I think my eardrum burst."

He had her wrapped in his arms in a second, no thought to going after his sister. She didn't matter. With any luck Nick and Damon would catch her. "Baby, are you okay?"

Taylor's vivid eyes stared up at him, her head nodding. "I think so. She killed your dad. I can't believe she killed your dad. He shot Kyle and Julia lost it. She looked completely crazy, like utterly disconnected from reality."

"Yeah, all the girls adore me." Kyle sat back against the big leather love seat. "I hate getting shot, and I have two fucking bullets in me. My mom is going to be pissed."

"Is your mom okay?" Taylor looked over to where his mom was starting to stir again.

"Don?" She called out for a dead man.

Taylor managed to get to her feet. "Go check on your mom."

He followed, standing. His heart threatened to seize.

"Drake, I know he betrayed you, but you have to know I…"
Taylor began.

He didn't need her to say a thing. He dragged her close. "You
would never betray me. You're mine and I'm yours, and we're out
of this, Taylor. We're out of the lying part at least."

There would be no made-up stories. No more covering.

He had to tell his mom everything this time.

He kissed Taylor and then got to his knees beside his mom.
She looked weary and confused.

"Drake? What are you doing here? What happened?" She
frowned. "I thought I saw Julia, but she had a different face. What
happened to my baby? Your father won't tell me, but I know he
knows. I think he had a hand in it."

She was just drugged enough to be honest. Tears pierced his
eyes, and he held her hand. "I'll tell you everything."

Taylor put a hand on his shoulder.

It would be okay. No more lies. He didn't need them because
she was here, standing beside him.

Chapter Twenty

"Well, we are fairly certain that Julia is still alive," Damon said with a sigh. "We have some evidence to support the idea that she took her partner to a hospital to treat his gunshot wound, but she left him there. From what we can tell, the helicopter made it to the countryside, and she had an ambulance pick up John and then she flew away again. Kyle put a bullet in his side."

. "That fucker still outran me." Nick had been fuming since that night.

"The Consortium obviously has stricter physical training than I do." Damon seemed much more relaxed now that his wife was back in town. She'd brought their boys to London the day after the debacle, and Damon had handled everything with calm and competency.

Drake had not. He'd pretty much taken Taylor into the bedroom and not let her out unless they had something they needed to handle.

It had been a full week since that day in the hotel when he'd realized he could survive pretty much anything as long as Taylor Cline was by his side. Getting through those first few days with his mom, having to walk her through what must be done, had been some of the hardest days of his life.

One last lie, but one she was in on. Technically his father had died in a robbery gone wrong, and now there was an Interpol red notice on his sister with her new face out there for all to see.

Julia was injured. Maybe not her body, but her whole life was damaged, and that was often when a predator was at their most dangerous.

Taylor turned to her uncle, giving him a sympathetic look. "Well, you had to run up a bunch of stairs first."

His mother knew the truth now, and it had devastated her. She'd lost her husband, her daughter, and all of her memories were now tainted. She'd told Drake she'd known something was wrong, but didn't want to know, didn't want to admit to the possibilities. She'd never thought he was working for anyone but the government. The idea that he'd been working against the country she'd served all her life had taken the spark from her eyes.

But she'd vowed to not stop, to fight as hard as she could. She'd flown back to DC days ago because mourning wouldn't stop her from voting. The bill had passed, and The Consortium could suck it.

"I'm surprised Julia didn't push him out of the helicopter and move on." He was a little bitter about his sister getting away. It meant there was still danger out there. "I don't think she considered that we would be looking for him. He's in custody, but he's not talking yet."

The man named John would be transported back to the States in a few hours. His wounds had started to heal, and Drake intended a bit of light torture to get the fucker talking. Oh, he wouldn't be able to do what he wanted, but he could see if the guy scared easily.

"I'm due back in DC to begin his interrogation," Drake explained. "And we've got some paperwork to deal with. You would think covering stuff up would require less paperwork."

"I think it's called covering the Agency's ass," Taylor quipped, but then sobered. "We're going to escort Drake's father's body home for burial. From there we'll start to work on finding Julia. Hopefully John knows something, but he seems incredibly loyal to her. Does anyone have an update on Kyle?"

Damon groaned. "The update is he's a stubborn arse. We know he survived the surgery to remove the bullets and when they finally moved him to a private room, he located his clothes, got dressed, and disappeared."

"I would bet he'll find his way back to Dallas." Drake hadn't had a chance to talk to Kyle. There had been far too much to do. He'd been planning to pick Kyle up and bring him back to The Garden to recover, but Kyle had other plans. "He'll watch over MaeBe now that Julia's in the wind. Have we asked Taggart if he's seen him?"

Damon shook his head. "Big Tag wouldn't tell us if he had. Make no mistake. Ian might think his nephew is handling this wrong, but he will back him up if he can't change his mind, and that will include keeping Kyle's secrets. Our job is to look for Julia here in Europe. Ian and his group will do the same in the States. Ian's already talked to some contacts in Asia and India, and they'll look for her as well. I called Brody this morning, and he's going to be our eyes in Australia. We'll find her now that we've been able to out her."

"The question is how much damage can she do before we bring her in," Taylor said softly.

Yes, that was the big question.

His sister was obsessed with Kyle. So obsessed she'd killed the only real father she'd ever known. Of course he was also the father who'd seen the darkness in his stepdaughter and used it ruthlessly. He'd had a foot in both worlds—Drake at the Agency and Julia at The Consortium. He'd offered up both of his children as sacrifices to get ahead.

Taylor's hand squeezed his own, and he was able to breathe again.

He was trapped between hating and mourning his father, but it would be all right because she would be the light on this dark road he had to walk.

"I'm sure she'll try to burn the world down around her," he said. "But I'll help in any way I can. Taylor and I are going to spend some time with my mom. We have to rebuild her security detail, and I'm going over every inch of the house and her office to ensure nothing was left behind."

"She's also agreed to let us go through Don's office," Taylor said. "We're going to analyze everything he's done for the last forty years. Maybe we can piece together something that helps to bring down The Consortium. We've got the house and all the properties they owned in lockdown and under guard. If Drake's father had something hidden, we worry Julia might try to find it."

"Hidden?" Nick asked. "Do you think he had an insurance policy?"

Drake nodded. "I'm sure of it. My father always kept back information he could use to put pressure on those around him. He would have kept copious notes, and I intend to find them before Julia does."

"Would he have told her where this insurance of his was kept?" Damon was in a suit this morning, every inch the smooth businessowner he was today.

"I don't think so." He'd been over this in his head a hundred times since that terrible night. "I don't think he would have trusted her enough. I would bet he had insurance on her, too. And likely me. It's how my father worked."

But it wasn't going to be how he worked. He'd already talked to his bosses and explained that he was leaving the field. He would do this last job to find out what he could about his father, but then he was coming home. Taylor was going to college, and then she wanted to come back and work with him.

They were going to build something new. It might take years, but he would put together a team that would work differently. A team for the new age of intelligence opening up right before his eyes.

A team that watched out for each other. A team that could help keep the worst of the Agency in check so the best could thrive.

He was going to shake things up so what happened to him didn't happen again.

Damon pushed back from the table, getting to his feet and holding out a hand. "Well, I'm sorry about Brad and your father. No matter what he did, you'll still feel his loss."

Drake stood and shook his hand. "And we're grateful for everything you've done to help us."

"We'll help in any way we can." Nick had gotten up and moved around to envelop Taylor in a bear hug. "You tell us if you need anything at all. And don't be a stranger. I've missed you, and we would love to see you more often."

"I promise." Taylor hugged her uncle tight. "And I'll let you know when we're going to Greece for Dad's memorial."

It was something they'd planned the night before. They'd come down to The Garden, though the club was closed. Damon had given them permission for private play. They'd made love and laid back, looking up at the starry sky, and she'd talked about her dad. He'd promised to take her to their little place in Greece and help her spread her father's ashes.

Somehow he thought in honoring her father, he might find a way to deal with his own, to process his death and find any good he could in the man.

He wasn't his father, and the things his father had done didn't have to define his life.

"I would love to be there and honor my friend," Nick said before hugging her one last time. He stepped back. "All right then, you have a good flight and stay safe." He turned Drake's way, his eyes narrowing. "And you take care of her."

"It's all I want to do in life," Drake admitted.

Nick's mouth turned up in a smile, and he shook Drake's hand. "Welcome to the family."

Nick and Damon left, and he was alone with the woman who would be his wife someday. He had no doubt.

"Are you packed?" They were leaving for DC in a couple of hours.

"Do you mean did I shove everything I own in a single bag?" She moved into his arms, tilting her head up. "Yes."

He kissed her forehead and held her close. "That's not going to last long. Mom was talking about taking you shopping when I called her earlier. She already adores you. I think she's about to be way more nosy."

His mom. He ached for her, but she was throwing herself into trying to make things better.

"I adore her, too." She wrapped her arms around him. "We still have to deal with Julia."

"I know, but not today."

Today was for loving her, for going home.

Tomorrow... Well, tomorrow was for loving her, too. And fighting for their future.

* * * *

Later that day
Dallas, TX

MaeBe Vaughn opened the door to her apartment and sighed in relief.

It was so good to be in her own place. It was late so she hadn't seen any of her neighbors in the lobby, but she would find her footing again.

She'd been gone for what felt like forever, first moving from friend's house to friend's house and ending with two weeks of lockdown at Sanctum. It was one of her favorite places in the world, but she was staying away for a while.

She stopped for a moment, letting the peace of her own home roll over her. This had been her sanctuary, her pride, proof that she was living a bigger life than her stepmother thought possible.

You need to get married, Mae. It's the only way to honor your womanhood.

You can be anything you want to be, my darling girl. Don't let anyone hold you back.

The second had been her mother's advice. Sometimes she wondered what had happened to her father to have gone from the loving woman her mother had been to the judgmental, cold bitch her stepmom was.

"You okay?" A deep voice reminded her that while she might be home, she wasn't alone. She never got to be alone anymore.

West Rycroft was with her. Always, these days. The bodyguard had become her constant shadow and sometimes playmate.

Oh, not in a sexual way. West was fun. West was younger than her other bodyguards, and he was enjoying living in a city for the first time in his life. They'd been to movies and concerts and had game nights. He was looser than the first guards her boss had put on her, and she kind of thought that had been Ian's point.

As she got more capable of taking care of herself, the rules relaxed. As she proved to Ian and Erin that she took her training seriously, they gave her more and more freedom.

Freedom was a sweet word.

How sad was it that being able to be in her own condo felt like the peak of joy she might be able to achieve?

Once she'd thought there might be more. Once she'd thought Kyle Hawthorne was the secret to her happiness.

Turns out he was one more cliff she'd walked off of willingly. She'd hit the ground hard after Kyle. So hard she'd thought she might never get up again.

"You hungry?" West moved into her kitchen, opening the fridge door. The light illuminated his handsome face. "Looks like Hutch did not lie. He fully stocked this sucker. And there's only a little candy. Actual food. I didn't think he was capable."

MaeBe sighed and put her bag on the counter. "I'm sure that was Noelle. I'm not hungry. I'm going to take a shower and go to bed. We've got an early meeting in the morning."

"Yeah, Big Tag said he had some news." West pulled out what looked like turkey or chicken. "I'm going to make myself a sandwich and then I'll sleep out here."

"There's a perfectly good daybed in the office," she pointed out.

"Yeah, that daybed is too short." West reached for the mustard. "I think I'll take my chances with the couch. Besides, you know you'll end up in there. I can sleep anywhere, but that office is your safe space."

She didn't sleep anymore. Not well. Sometimes Big Tag managed to push her hard enough with physical training that she fell into a dreamless stupor, but mostly when she drifted off she saw Julia Ennis looking down at her with pity. Right before she broke her arm.

While she'd been thinking Kyle Hawthorne was the love of her life, his violent, obsessive fiancée saw her as a mouse to toss around and play with. She was the toy two predators fought over to see which one could do more damage.

"I do have some work to do. You could take my bedroom. I'll be good in the office." One of them should be comfortable.

"Nope." West's head shook. "Not going to happen. I was joking about the comfort thing. I've studied the floor plan for this place. The couch is optimal. We're high up. There's no way someone's scaling the side of the building and getting in through a window. The only way in is that door, and I'm sleeping in front of it."

She knew better than to argue with him. Something had happened. Big Tag had been in his office all day, and he'd had that blank look on his face that she associated with him being worried. Tag could express a range of emotions. Anger? He was excellent at anger. Amused. He could do that one, too. He was amused most of the time.

Worry shut the big boss down.

She hoped he wasn't worried about her.

"I'll go grab some sheets and pillows for you." It was Big Tag's worry that had made her agree to these overbearing protective protocols of his.

"Can you set the alarm first?" West asked, prompting her to remember that she'd only locked the door. She had a brand spanking new security system—another of Tag's edicts.

She pulled her cell out and quickly checked the system. It was smart, and she could control the thing from several places. Her phone, laptop, and tablet all had the software she needed.

"Huh." One of the reports caught her eye. "I guess Hutch had to make two trips. He was here at noon and then about an hour ago."

"It was probably because I complained about almond milk. Milk should not be made from almonds," West pointed out. "It looks like he got you Sriracha, too."

There was a big bottle of Sriracha on the bar, a little bow around it. Her favorite. She put it on pretty much everything.

Spicy girl. One day I'll show you how hot you can be.

She shook her head because everything Kyle Hawthorne had told her was a lie. Every word. She'd been a comforting presence after the storm of his real love.

Julia fucking Ennis.

She knew it wasn't fair to think that way. Julia had hurt Kyle. Kyle had tried to take care of her by putting a couple of bullets in her, but evil found a way.

She knew Kyle didn't love Julia, but she wasn't feeling fair tonight.

Kyle hadn't loved her either.

She set the alarm and grabbed a bottle of water. "'Night, West. Thanks for taking me out. That movie was exactly what I needed. I hope your brother enjoyed it, too."

West's lips kicked up in what she would have once thought was a heart-stopping grin. "Caught that, did you?"

She didn't have a heart to stop anymore. "Yes. He shadowed us all day. We've had a shadow for at least a week now. Something happened, and hopefully Big Tag will tell us tomorrow."

West turned and looked at her, the bar between them. "You're getting so damn good at this, girl. Pretty soon you'll be the one protecting me."

He was such a gorgeous guy. With sandy hair and smoldering eyes, he had the sexy cowboy thing down.

How much easier would her life be if she could feel something beyond friendship for him? If she could even consider falling into bed with this man and letting it happen between them. West made sense. It could be fun. He wouldn't have to sleep on the couch if he was in her bed.

"Somehow I doubt that. I'll be right back." She couldn't. Her stupid broken heart still ached, and she couldn't even think about another man.

She walked down the short hallway to her bedroom and moved inside, starting to reach for the light.

That was when she saw the shadow at her window.

There was another explanation for the two entries on her security files.

She really should be better at passwords.

"Hello, MaeBe."

Kyle Hawthorne moved out of the shadows, the moonlight illuminating him, and for a moment he looked like the ghost he'd wanted her to think he was.

Anger thrummed through her, and she realized her fight was far from over.

* * * *

Kyle, MaeBe, and the whole McKay-Taggart crew will return in *The Dom Who Came in from the Cold.*

As for Drake and Taylor's plans for a new kind of Agency team—keep reading for a little glimpse of the future...

Epilogue: Sometime in the future

"Give me one good reason I don't kill you."

Ian Taggart stared straight into Drake's eyes and hoped the kid felt his will. His will to murder him in any number of ways. To be honest, he didn't need one good reason. He had two.

Kenzie and Kala. His twins. The lights of his life and the bane of his very existence.

He'd wanted to be a dad why?

"Ian, babe, come on. We talked about this." His Charlie was sitting, not pacing like a caged tiger the way he'd been. His Charlie was composed and reasonable.

When he thought about it, this was all Charlie's fault. *Let's have a kid, she'd said. It'll be fun.*

One had turned into five, and every one of them came with their own troubles.

"Dad, you can't kill him. I told you I do not do cleanup. I tried it once and my stomach can't handle it. Blood is gross."

It made sense that the child he didn't share actual DNA with was the most reasonable of all of his kids. Tasha sat next to her mother, insisting on being a part of this "let's save the twins from themselves" session.

Tash was ever the dutiful daughter. She'd gotten excellent grades in high school, gone to college and earned her degree in management, and come home to help run the family company. Tasha Taggart was the office manager for McKay-Taggart, and one day she would likely run the place when he retired. Many, many years from now.

Because his sons didn't give a damn about security and business, and his twins would be dead because they couldn't stay away from the spy game.

"I'll do the cleanup on this one myself," he vowed. "It'll be fun."

If Drake was worried, he didn't show it. He sat back in his big comfy chair that went with the oak desk covered in paperwork and pictures of his family. Drake had a wife and two kids who looked really sweet but would one day likely break their father's heart by refusing to listen to him. It's what kids seemed to do. "Ian, I know you won't believe this, but I was going to call and set up a meeting in Dallas. You didn't have to come all this way to threaten to disembowel me. I would have come to you. I always meant to talk to you about this."

"About the fact that you're forcing my baby girls to work for you?"

The two women behind him snorted at exactly the same time and proved that sometimes nurture was stronger than nature.

Drake sighed, though it was an oddly patient sound. "Ian, you know that's not true. I did not recruit Kala and Kenzie. Have they talked to you about how they came to the Agency?"

He didn't want to listen to Drake. He wanted to pummel his face and get him to promise that his twins would never be put in danger again.

Except he knew damn well they would find it.

Ian growled and started to pace again. "They don't tell me anything."

"Probably because you lose your shit, babe," Charlie pointed out.

She was so fucking pretty sitting there in slacks and a silk shirt and those heels that made her legs look a mile long. And she was

370

right. He had been known to perhaps overreact slightly to news that his girls had placed themselves in danger.

It was easier with Seth. Seth just wanted to play his guitar and write sappy-ass love songs. The worst danger Seth was in was from the obvious diseases he would catch from the bars he played in. And Travis had really rebelled. It made Ian a little sick to his stomach. His youngest son was…a bit of bile rose up…in law school.

Damn it. They were all supposed to go to college and then come back to McKay-Taggart and work under him where he could watch over all of them and make sure they were safe and…

Fuck all. They'd successfully raised five kids who wanted their own damn lives and would fight for it. Even him.

Again. Charlie's fault.

"All right. Tell me."

Drake sat up, a smile on his face. "We were working with MI6, tracking a potential threat in London."

Ian snapped his fingers and pointed his wife's way. "I told you we shouldn't let them leave the country. We should have hidden their passports. We should have never allowed them to have passports."

Charlie's eyes rolled. "And my point is made. You know they would have just forged them. Lou learned how to do that a long time ago."

"Boomer's daughter is a bad influence." She wasn't. He was fairly certain Lou's friendship had saved Kala from time to time, but the kid had a genius-level IQ, and there wasn't anything she couldn't learn to do and quickly. Lou could build anything, including a false persona.

"Lou is wonderful and you know it," Tash corrected. "Kala's the bad influence."

"Anyway, we were having trouble catching this guy." Drake proceeded, obviously understanding that a Taggart family discussion could derail the world. "It was a time-sensitive case because we had intelligence stating he was planning something for the following week, and he potentially had gotten his hands on bioweapons."

Ian's stomach took a deep dive. "They were supposed to be spending a year abroad."

"Well, what they did was find our terrorist and bring him in. Kala showed up at Scotland Yard dragging in the suspect. She got arrested herself because the police weren't sure what was going on. She knew the section head of MI6's name and his phone number."

Ian groaned. "Fuck me. She's lucky they didn't interrogate her in some foreign country that doesn't follow the Geneva Convention."

"Oh, it's worse. Or better." Drake's lips quirked up. "At some point during her time with the police she managed to switch places with her sister. We still don't know how they did it. The detective left her alone in the interrogation room for less than twenty minutes, and it's a damn secure location. But somehow she did it. When they walked back in she was wearing different clothes, explained that she was Kenzie Taggart and demanded to talk to…me."

"They were auditioning." Charlie sounded proud.

"And I told you we should have had them tattooed as infants," Ian announced. His heart was going to explode, and not from love. Nope. Sheer fucking panic. They were going to kill him. He'd known it from the moment they'd been born.

Charlie stood and crossed the space between them, putting her hands on his chest. "Babe, they are so good at this. They were kind of born for intelligence work, and you fighting it is going to do nothing but put a strain on your relationship with them. Can we talk about this? Ask Drake some questions?"

She was altogether too reasonable, but she was right. He'd kind of exploded when the twins had told him they'd been CIA employees for the last year and not happy grad school students in New York.

He should have known they hadn't gotten scholarships.

He'd kind of lost his shit and vowed bloody vengeance, and then Seth had offered to sing a song to bring them back together. Travis had pointed out a bunch of legal theories on how killing CIA directors could be a bad thing. Tash had baked cupcakes and the dog had peed.

Then Charlie showed him her boobs and he'd calmed down a bit. Enough to realize he was taking it out on the wrong people.

That was when he'd decided to sneak into DC and face Drake.

He had a private plane. If he couldn't use his private jet to attack his enemies, what was it good for?

He'd explained to Charlie he had some business to do and would be gone for a few days, and when he'd boarded the jet, she and Tash had been sitting there waiting for him.

No one ever let him have fun anymore.

"Come on, babe. I want you to really think. Could anyone have talked you out of joining the Army when you were a kid?" Charlie asked.

"Yes. If someone had walked into my life and said 'Hey, kid. You don't have to get your ass shot off. Here's a bunch of money. Go to college.'" It wasn't like he'd wanted to go into the military. He'd had zero cash and a mom and brother to take care of. He honestly hadn't thought about what he wanted to do for a profession because he hadn't had the luxury.

His daughters did.

"And when the Agency came calling?" Charlie continued to press her point.

He growled, but she merely stared up at him with those kick-him-in-the-gut blue eyes of hers.

Because she knew. He might not have loved military life, but oh, he'd loved intelligence work. He still liked solving a mystery. He felt vibrant and alive when he was working intelligence.

Did he want to take that away from his girls because he couldn't handle the fear that went with it?

Charlie went on her toes and pressed her lips to his. "There's my husband."

She knew him so well.

He turned to Drake. It was time to listen to his wife. The twins wouldn't be swayed, and it looked like they'd worked to get the jobs they wanted.

"I want them on a team. I do not want them out in the field alone. They need to work together." He hated this, but he hated the thought of them being alone more. "And they need a tech they can depend on."

Drake chuckled. "I agree. Kenzie and Kala are going to be in a program Taylor and I have been working on for the last couple of years. We recently got funding. Years ago Tennessee Smith recruited a team to support him, a team he continually worked with and could depend on. This team will be smaller and have more ground support. The twins are the technical field agents. They've identified who they want for support, and I've gotten clearance to use them. Cooper McKay will handle logistics and transportation."

"I bet he will," Tash said under her breath.

Kala had a thing for Alex and Eve McKay's oldest son. A big thing. A practically from birth thing. "Does Cooper know?"

He had to ask because sometimes he wasn't sure Kala understood the word *consent*. She could be a hurricane.

"He's already accepted the offer. He was ready to leave the Navy," Drake explained. "He's interested in intelligence work, and I got the feeling he didn't like the idea of someone else taking the job."

"That's interesting." Charlie sat back down.

Sometimes he got the feeling he was left out of the loop when it came to the next generation's connections. Mostly he was cool with that. Seth put all of his relationship angst to music, so the other kids being silent made up for it. "And you have someone for commun...fuck. Does Adam know?"

There was only one person the girls would go to. Tristan Dean-Miles.

"More importantly, do Carys and Aidan know?" Tash asked, a frown on her face. "He promised he would come home."

"I think coming home would be hard for him." Charlie's voice had gone tight. "I think he's avoiding the wedding, and if you know the reason why, you should talk because god knows no one else is."

Something had happened between those three. They'd been a happy if odd threesome for a long time, and then Carys and Aidan had announced they were getting married and Tristan was running away to join the Agency.

And no one was talking.

"Tristan is eager to start. The technical role will be taken by Ms. Ward. If she says yes. Kala wants to ask her in person, but she's sure she'll agree," Drake explained. "We're being flexible with this team. Lou is going to be both analyst and our version of Q. If she says yes, she'll be given a big wad of cash and her own lab to make innovations where she can. However, that means we need someone to handle some of the more organizational jobs. Someone who can liaise between the group and the Agency. And of course they'll need an experienced operative to oversee the team, though I see that as more of a part-time role."

"You're not doing it yourself?" He was surprised. He'd at least thought Drake would handle it himself. He would never admit it, but he might be okay if Drake was watching over them. Might. Probably not.

"I was kind of thinking you would want the job. Like I said, it would be part time. Mostly the team would handle things themselves, but you would oversee their work and step in when they need help," Drake explained. "You would be like the mom and dad of the group, since I know damn well if I give you clearance, Charlotte will know everything five minutes later. I'm okay with that, Ian. This whole project is about not stifling our talent. You and Charlotte could oversee the team, and you don't even have to be in DC. The team can split their time between DC and Dallas if they like. You'll know where they are, Ian. I won't keep anything from you."

Sometimes being a nice guy paid off. Years before he'd taken a chance on this guy when he'd been a barely out of the womb asshole operative. And now he could watch over his girls. "We can work that out."

"I'm the manager." Tasha stood up. "I'll be the liaison, and I'll make sure everything runs properly."

"You have a job," Charlotte pointed out. "Are you sure you want this?"

Tash nodded. "I've been organizing my sisters' schemes for years. It's only right that I do it when everything is on the line. I want to. I want in."

All of his girls in one place. All of them in danger.

Sounded like an ordinary Saturday night at the Taggart house.

Ian sighed. "Well, then we should let them in and let them know what we've decided."

Drake got up and opened the door. His daughters strode in, Kala in her normal goth-girl uniform and Kenzie looking so much like her mom it hurt.

"You know we're adults. You don't get to decide what we're going to do." Kala was a pretty pit bull. She could growl and snarl, and in the end she was loyal and loving to those who deserved it. "I don't even know why we're here."

"Because they're our parents and we love them and want them to feel comfortable with this new job we're doing." Kenz was always the reasonable one. "Dad, Mom, you know one of the reasons we want to do this is because you taught us so well. We want to make you proud."

She also knew how to bullshit with the best. "I wish you luck with your new boss."

Kenzie stopped, her eyes going wide. "Seriously? That's it? And I think Drake is our boss. We get along very well with him. It's going to be okay. You'll see."

Charlie snorted as she helped herself to the Scotch Drake kept on an elegant bar in the corner of his big-ass office. The kid had done well for himself.

"Guys, I never said I would be in charge," Drake admitted. "I oversee most of the analysis for the Agency. I don't have time to directly oversee you. Which is why I hired someone."

Kenzie smiled, but Kala's eyes had narrowed in suspicion.

"Dad." Tasha seemed to like knowing something her sisters didn't. "They hired Dad."

"That's not fair." Kala sounded like she was fourteen again.

Kenzie looked panicked.

And Charlie just laughed and passed him a Scotch.

Yeah. This was going to be fun.

Author's Note

I'm often asked by generous readers how they can help get the word out about a book they enjoyed. There are so many ways to help an author you like. Leave a review. If your e-reader allows you to lend a book to a friend, please share it. Go to Goodreads and connect with others. Recommend the books you love because stories are meant to be shared. Thank you so much for reading this book and for supporting all the authors you love!

The Dom Who Came in from the Cold

Masters and Mercenaries: Reloaded, Book 5
By Lexi Blake
Coming February 21, 2023

Kyle Hawthorne once believed his future would be a job in the private sector—a simple, normal life. Fate had other plans and he wound up in the military. Some newly discovered talents caught the eye of the CIA, and in no time he was working with a covert team. He found himself in a relationship with fellow operative, Julia—until she turned out to be the enemy. When her betrayal was uncovered, things got bloody and Kyle returned home broken, searching for a chance to walk the road not taken.

MaeBe Vaughan has never been interested in normal. Her happy place is a dark corner of the Internet, where she disrupts all the bad guys. She has a great circle of friends and a full life. She doesn't need a man. Until Kyle Hawthorne walked into her life. He's all wrong for her. Surly. Damaged. His uncle is her boss. But she couldn't help getting close to him. When his past threatened her safety, Kyle walked out without saying good-bye.

Kyle will do anything to keep MaeBe safe. He faked his death, hid in the middle of nowhere, and watched over her from afar. But when Julia resurfaces, he knows that to protect MaeBe, he'll have to get close. So close that if they manage to survive, he will never let her go.

Sapphire Sunset

A Sapphire Cove Novel
By Christopher Rice writing as C. Travis Rice
Now available

For the first time New York Times bestselling author Christopher Rice writes as C. Travis Rice. Under his new pen name, Rice offers tales of passion, intrigue, and steamy romance between men. The first novel, SAPPHIRE SUNSET, transports you to a beautiful luxury resort on the sparkling Southern California coast where strong-willed heroes release the shame that blocks their heart's desires.

Logan Murdoch is a fighter, a survivor, and a provider. When he leaves a distinguished career in the Marine Corps to work security at a luxury beachfront resort, he's got one objective: pay his father's mounting medical bills. That means Connor Harcourt, the irresistibly handsome scion of the wealthy family that owns Sapphire Cove, is strictly off limits, despite his sassy swagger and beautiful blue eyes. Logan's life is all about sacrifices; Connor is privilege personified. But temptation is a beast that demands to be fed, and a furtive kiss ignites instant passion, forcing Logan to slam the brakes. Hard.

Haunted by their frustrated attraction, the two men find themselves hurled back together when a headline-making scandal threatens to ruin the resort they both love. This time, there's no easy escape from the magnetic pull of their white hot desire. Will saving Sapphire Cove help forge the union they crave, or will it drive them apart once more?

About Lexi Blake

New York Times bestselling author Lexi Blake lives in North Texas with her husband and three kids. Since starting her publishing journey in 2010, she's sold over three million copies of her books. She began writing at a young age, concentrating on plays and journalism. It wasn't until she started writing romance that she found success. She likes to find humor in the strangest places and believes in happy endings.

Connect with Lexi online:

Facebook: Lexi Blake
Twitter: authorlexiblake
Website: www.LexiBlake.net
Instagram: authorlexiblake/

Made in the USA
Columbia, SC
28 July 2024

39422101R00228